Magic of Moonlight

TRACY BROGAN

OLIVER-HEBER BOOKS

All rights reserved.

No part of this publication may be sold, copied, distributed, reproduced or transmitted in any form or by any means, mechanical or digital, including photocopying and recording or by any information storage and retrieval system without the prior written permission of both the publisher, Oliver Heber Books and the author, Tracy Brogan, except in the case of brief quotations embodied in critical articles and reviews.

PUBLISHER'S NOTE: This is a work of fiction. Names, characters, places, and incidents either are the product of the author's imagination or are used fictitiously. Any resemblance to actual persons, living or dead, business establishments, events, or locales is entirely coincidental.

Magic of Moonlight Copyright 2024 © Tracy Brogan

Cover art by Dar Albert at Wicked Smart Designs

Published by Oliver-Heber Books

0 9 8 7 6 5 4 3 2 1

one

"You know I'm not one to engage in puffery," Breezy VonMeisterburger whispered dramatically, "but as you can plainly see, the Imperial Hotel is a most magnificent oasis arising from the panoramic majesty of Trillium Bay, just as I promised."

Standing with her siblings on the red-carpeted steps of the palatial resort, Trudy Hart smiled while knowing full well her Aunt Breezy was *absolutely* one to engage in puffery, sometimes to the point of pure fabrication. In this instance, however, the blustery declaration was accurate.

Four stories tall and gleaming white against the vibrant greenery of the island, the hotel *was* magnificent, and Trudy *was* dazzled by its scope and splendor. The freshly painted front porch ran some six hundred feet from end to end and was (*according to her aunt*) the largest porch in the *entire* world. A dozen cozy seating areas dotted its length with floral-cushioned rocking chairs, wicker footstools, and lace-covered accent tables upon which to set one's teacup—or perhaps a spirited libation if the mood was right. A string quartet played a lively tune as finely dressed guests strolled past the profusion of colorful blossoms bursting forth from ceramic pots as large as whisky barrels. Even the late afternoon sun played a part, adding a shimmer of gold to every surface, as if the atmosphere wasn't already sufficiently opulent.

"How fortunate you are that I invited you all here," Aunt Breezy reminded them, speaking in a slightly louder whisper this time so eavesdroppers might be privy to her altruism. She ran a silk-gloved hand over her expansive, satin-clad bosom adding, "But as my guests, I must remind you to exercise the utmost decorum at all times. Fine manners are the order of the day, and I will not condone any coarse behavior that might besmirch the fine VonMeisterburger name. So, behave yourselves."

Breezy swished her parasol shut with a vigorous snap, and while Trudy very much wanted to defend herself and her siblings against their aunt's presumptuous insult, she'd learned the value of maintaining a discreet silence when the situation warranted, as this one did.

Throughout medical school and during the past few years working as a physician in her father's medical practice, Trudy had dealt with virtually every manner of humanity, from bloviating physicians to judgmental classmates, to frightened, irritable patients. With hard-earned patience and far too much practice, she'd learned to navigate other people's tirades and tantrums without giving in to her own frustration.

However, a single week in Aunt Breezy's company while traveling from Illinois to Michigan's Trillium Bay had pushed Trudy's exasperation to the edge of eruption. Her aunt had all the charm of a boil in need of lancing, and Trudy longed to say so, but she swallowed down the mean-spirited words like bitter medicine and smiled politely. Because the truth of it was, she and her family *were* fortunate to be here.

The invitation to spend an entire summer on this idyllic island as guests of their wealthy VonMeisterburger relatives had been as unexpected an offer as it was an uncharacteristically generous one. Although Breezy and Trudy's mother were sisters, never had two such diverse entities existed. Other than their lineage, the shape of their noses, and a shared childhood full of comfortable privilege, Ada and Breezy had virtually nothing in common. While Breezy had married Albert VonMeisterburger for prestige and position, Ada had *(according to society)* squandered her pedigree by marrying Dr. Samuel Hart, a country physician.

For *love*, of all things! *How very tawdry.*

Ada always assured her children they were rich in all the ways that mattered, and they believed her. They didn't miss the frivolous material things the rich seemed to cherish. Instead, they had each other. They had the pursuit of education and parents who encouraged them to be whatever they wanted to be. While Trudy and her older brother, Calvin, pursued medicine like their father, Lucy planned to study astronomy, and Coco *(when she wasn't too busy admiring her own reflection)* wrote clever stories. Asher, at fifteen, still straddled the line between boyish games and adult responsibilities, and Poppy was, for better or worse, a clever, precocious child whom they all indulged.

They were content and wanted for little, but Breezy's sudden and inexplicable invitation was a welcomed one, even if it did require spending the next three months under the oppressive cloud of the VonMeisterburger's pretentious philanthropism.

"Well?" Breezy prompted when no one spoke. "Have you nothing to say about the hotel's magnificence?"

Coco smiled wide. "Oh, my, yes, Aunt Breezy," she exclaimed effusively. "We're all just speechless. I don't imagine the gates of heaven could be more awe-inspiring! You have certainly blessed us with your thoughtfulness."

Trudy turned her face away to hide another smile at her sister's facetiousness. Though only seventeen, a full eleven years younger than Trudy, Coco had the charisma to shift virtually any situation to her advantage. She played people like violins and left them moved by the music. While some might consider her disingenuous *(along with being vain)*, Trudy appreciated her willingness to stroke Breezy's grandiose sense of self-importance.

"Yeah, it's neat," Asher added loudly. "But I'm starving. Can we go inside now and get some food, or do we have to stand out here all day gawking?"

Breezy's head swiveled in his direction with such rapidity the spray of peacock feathers on her hat quivered, as if the plumes themselves were agitated by his lack of decorum. Trudy lightly pinched his arm, causing Asher to blush and mumble sheepishly, "Sorry, Aunt Breezy. What I meant was if I don't get something to eat soon, I might keel over dead and find myself outside the real gates of heaven."

Lucy chuckled and pulled some wrapped taffies from the pocket of her traveling dress, offering them to her brother. "Here. I was saving these for later, but you may have them if you promise to be nice to me for the rest of the day."

He eyed the treat for a moment as if weighing the cost, then snatched them from her palm with a grin. "Until midnight, then," he said. "Tomorrow, you're fair game."

"Pah! Such impudence!" Breezy groused before turning back to face the hotel's entrance. Squaring her shoulders and lifting her chins, she ascended the staircase with the artfully measured gait of a society matriarch about to greet her public—whether they wanted her to or not.

"Please, mind your manners," Trudy murmured quietly to Asher as they followed. "Mother told me to make sure you all behave until she and Father arrive. Don't make me give her a bad report."

Asher's unabashed grin was lopsided, his cheek bulging with taffy as if it were a wad of the very best tobacco. "I promise to be at least as good here as I am at home," he said.

"Oh, good heavens, please be better than that," Trudy responded.

Ada and Samuel Hart were on their way to Boston to visit Trudy's brother but would join the rest of the family on the island next month. While Aunt Breezy was ostensibly in charge until they arrived, Trudy knew the true weight of guardianship fell squarely upon her own shoulders, and it worried her. Matters of a medical nature she could face with confidence, yet issues beyond the realm of illness or injury might prove altogether too perplexing, and in this unfamiliar world of rules and refinement, hurdles were inevitable.

Especially when it came to Asher...
And Coco...
And Poppy...

At least Lucy would be no trouble, thank goodness. At nineteen, she was Trudy's closest companion and confidante, as much a dear friend as a beloved sister, but little Poppy could be willful, Asher was a scamp, and Coco? Trudy tamped down a sigh of concern, for the only thing Coco enjoyed more than gazing at her own reflection was gazing at strapping young gentleman in well-cut suits, and as Trudy quickly surveyed the surroundings, she noted an abundance of dashing lads who would undoubtedly be all too eager to make her sister's acquaintance. Trudy would have to be vigilant lest Coco's naïve and impetuous nature lead to disastrous consequences.

Following their Aunt Breezy, the Hart siblings traversed the hotel steps and walked through open French doors, entering a palatial lobby even more elegant than the exterior of the hotel. Plush, jewel-toned rugs adorned the smooth pine floor, and sparkling, crystal chandeliers cascaded down from a pink-painted ceiling. To the right was a wide staircase leading to the upper floors, and to the left was a long mahogany registration desk gleaming in the sunlight. All around, hotel employees in blue serge jackets moved with rapid but smooth efficiency, carrying luggage and guiding well-heeled guests in one direction or another.

Everywhere she looked, Trudy saw luxury. Velvet sofas, striped damask covered chairs, ornate clocks, vases full of roses and peonies, and a curio cabinet bursting with curiosities. While she preferred the ambience of their uncluttered home and modest furnishings, she was not immune to sumptuous extravagance.

"Opulence does have its appeal, I guess," she murmured to her sisters, trying not to stare at the abundance of fripperies.

"I've never seen anything like it," whispered Lucy.

"It's even more amazing than Hudson's department store," Coco agreed reverently, which, from her, was high praise indeed.

"Jumpin' Jehosaphat! It's the Mona Lisa!" Trudy heard Asher exclaim. She looked back over her shoulder, hoping to glare him into silence, only to realize he was indeed staring at a replica of the Mona Lisa.

At least... she assumed it was a replica...

"Mrs. VonMeisterburger!" cried out a balding, jowly-faced man from behind the desk. "How delighted we are to welcome you back to the Imperial Hotel."

"Thank you, Beeks," Breezy responded imperiously. "This my niece, Miss Gertrude Hart, and her siblings. I trust our rooms are prepared?"

Trudy grimaced, both from being called *Gertrude*, and from being called *Miss*. She was *Doctor* Hart but there was no point in reminding Breezy of that, again. Especially knowing her aunt considered Trudy's dedication to medicine more fetish than vocation.

"Indeed, madam. Your rooms are just as you've requested. You and your guests will be residing on the third floor, next to the Bostwick family suites. I trust that's acceptable?"

"Are our suites as large as the Bostwick family suites?" Breezy questioned without a hint of shame.

"Larger," Mr. Beeks whispered conspiratorially, one bushy brow arching ever so slightly.

"And the view?" she pressed.

"Superior to theirs," he assured her, sliding the leatherbound guest book across the desk.

"Very good then. Those rooms will suffice." She picked up the quill to sign, perusing the list before committing her name to the parchment as Trudy grimaced again.

The Bostwick family.

Bother!

It hadn't occurred to her *they'd* be at the hotel, although it should have. Breezy and Constance Bostwick were friends—at least in public—so it made sense that they'd summer on the same posh island—at the same luxurious resort—at the exact same time—because that's how the privileged classes seemed to do things. Together. How else could they judge who was truly preeminent among their elite?

It seemed a strange eccentricity of the wealthy, Trudy mused; the insatiable need to compete with each other, to voluntarily jockey for position within the same tiny bubble of good fortune, as if having more than enough wasn't sufficient. The aim was rather to have more than *everyone else*.

"You need to sign the registry, Gertrude," Breezy said, interrupting Trudy's thoughts. "List all your siblings and remember to use their *proper* names. This isn't a boarding house."

"Of course, Aunt Breezy." Trudy's falsely obedient smile made her face ache. By the end of the summer, her tongue was sure to be numb from all the words *she did not say* but she dipped the quill and set her attention to the registry.

"Have *all* the Bostwicks arrived?" she heard Aunt Breezy ask Mr. Beeks.

"They arrived last week, madam. All but Mr. Bostwick Sr. who I believe will be staying in Chicago this season, just as he did last season."

Trudy glanced up to note the hotel manager's lips pursed in an uncharitable smirk, and realized her aunt was wearing much the same expression.

"Do you mean to say that Mr. *Alexander* Bostwick is here?" Aunt Breezy questioned, lowering her voice and leaning toward the manager.

"Indeed, madam. He arrived with his mother and sister."

Trudy paused in her signing to wonder why her aunt would have asked about Alexander Bostwick in particular. It seemed an odd coincidence. Trudy knew precisely why *she* herself disliked Alex, but she had no notion of why her aunt might not be fond of him.

She slid the book back to the manager.

"Very good," he said, carefully scanning the list of names she'd added as if making certain her spelling was correct. Then he offered an ingratiating smile to her aunt.

"Mrs. VonMeisterburger, our lead porter will show you to your rooms as soon as he returns from assisting another guest. In the meantime, shall I find you a comfortable place to relax while you wait? And bring you a glass of lemonade or champagne?"

"A place to relax? Will the delay be as long as that?"

Her question smacked of rebuke, and Mr. Beeks' already flushed cheeks reddened further. "Only a short while, madam, but as you can see, we are quite busy this afternoon. Everyone seems to be checking in at once. The porters are doing their best to keep up."

Trudy's aunt looked around as if surprised to suddenly see other people in the lobby and gave a small harumph. "Very well. Find me a seat. They can stand." She gestured dismissively toward Trudy and the rest of them.

So much for Breezy's generosity.

Coco caught Trudy's eye and whispered, "I wonder if we'll be allowed to sit at dinner."

"Yes," Trudy whispered back, "but we must share a single chair."

The sisters giggled as they stepped away from the desk to follow, literally and metaphorically, in their aunt's dark shadow.

"Ash," Lucy called out. "Get Poppy and come with us."

Their brother was a few feet away, examining a miniature replica of the hotel displayed on a table near an oversized painting of the same. He glanced their way before performing a cursory search of the area around him. "I don't have Poppy," he called back, moving toward them.

The sisters halted their steps as Aunt Breezy and Mr. Beeks continued on, unaware.

"What do you mean you don't have Poppy? I thought she was with you," Trudy said.

His expression was nonchalant as he ambled closer. "She looked at that display for a minute, but I don't know where she went after that."

"She was just here," Coco said, her eyes surveying the lobby. "She can't have gotten far."

"Unless she fell in the lake," Asher teased.

"Asher, that is not amusing," Trudy scolded.

"I thought it was," he murmured, winking at Coco. Those two shared a similar sense of humor and were often in cahoots. Trudy would do well to keep them apart as much as possible until their parents arrived. Although perhaps Asher's juvenile antics would repel any potential suitors from approaching her sister.

"Maybe she—" Lucy's comment was cut short.

"Is that her basket on the floor?" Coco interrupted, pointing to an area near the front doors. She moved hastily across the lobby, picking up the wicker basket and turning back toward them. She held it aloft.

And upside down.

Oh.

Dear.

"Isn't that basket supposed to have a cat inside of it?" Asher asked, his tone a blend of humor and exasperation given that they all knew the answer.

Yes.

Yes, indeed.

That basket was supposed to have a cat inside of it. A cat which Poppy had *promised* to leave at home in the attentive care of their housekeeper but which she had, instead, cleverly smuggled onto their steamship like a stowaway so that *Sir Chester Von Whiskerton* might *also* enjoy a summertime reprieve at the Imperial Hotel.

And so, it seemed their first mishap was already underway. They hadn't even made it out of the hotel lobby yet and Trudy had already misplaced her little sister and a cat. Still, it was nothing to be too alarmed about. With a bit of expeditious hunting, they'd both be found, and all would be well. The lobby wasn't *that* immense.

"Let's each head toward a different corner," Trudy said, "and then we meet back here in this very spot. One of us is bound to find her."

But they did not.

After ten minutes of searching, they reconnoitered in the center of the lobby.

"Do you suppose the little scamp is hiding with him somewhere? You know how she loves to trick us," Coco said.

"Or... do you suppose the cat ran outside and she followed him?" Lucy added, glancing at the open lobby doors. "If that's the case, they could be anywhere."

Oh, dear.

Oh.

Dear.

Lucy was correct. If Poppy had followed Chester outside, there was no telling which direction they might have gone, but now was not the time to panic. Now was a time for decisive action... if only Trudy knew what to do. Adrenaline was building in her veins as she considered their options while also trying *not* to consider all the potential dangers for a little girl chasing a cat in an unfamiliar place.

"Lucy, check on the front porch, will you?" Trudy said after a brief hesitation. "Coco, you check down that hallway, and Asher, you look down that one. I'll ask Mr. Beeks if he can spare a few porters to help in our search and let Aunt Breezy know what's happened." She turned on her heel, pulses thrumming, nerves tingling as she walked quickly to the sunny corner where Aunt Breezy had settled into a green velvet chair.

The hotel manager lingered by her side, obviously trying to

take his leave as she spoke, but people did not simply walk away from Breezy VonMeisterburger. One must wait to be dismissed.

"Mr. Beeks, we have a bit of a situation," Trudy said quietly, but breathlessly, not caring that *she* had interrupted her aunt's story.

"A situation? What situation?" Breezy exclaimed loudly, making heads turn. *For a woman who favored the utmost in decorum, she certainly didn't practice it.*

"I'm afraid my little sister has wandered off," Trudy answered. "Along with her cat. We've searched the lobby to no avail. Mr. Beeks, might we get some assistance from the hotel staff to look for her? I'm sure she's nearby but there are so many different directions she may have gone…"

"The porters are all very busy, Miss Hart," he answered, seeing his chance to step away.

"Busy?" Breezy exclaimed again, louder this time. "Surely, they're not too busy to find my precious niece and her pet. For shame, Beeks. What kind of a lowbrow establishment is this?"

For once, Trudy appreciated her aunt's condescending tone. It seemed to have a rather powerful effect.

Beeks offered a curt nod. "Of course, Mrs. VonMeisterburger. I'll put every available porter to the task and let the rest of them know to be on the lookout. Might I have a description?"

Breezy frowned quizzically at the little man.

"You need a description?" she barked. "A description? My niece looks like a little girl. And the cat looks like a cat. Do you have so many unattended children and beasts running around this hotel you think you might bring us the wrong ones?"

Trudy might have laughed but for the twitch in the man's eye suggesting his patience was at an end.

"It's a black and white cat, Mr. Beeks," Trudy answered calmly. "And my sister, Poppy, is eight years old with blonde hair and brown eyes. She's wearing a dark blue dress, and the last time we saw her she was near the registration desk."

"Very good, miss." He gave a curt nod and spun away, seeming even smaller than he had before.

Trudy turned back to her aunt, feeling rather small herself for having lost her sister and caused a fuss.

"I'm sorry for the kerfuffle, Aunt Breezy," Trudy said apologetically. "She's likely just sitting somewhere, but I'm concerned the cat might run out those open doors, and she'd go right after him."

"You were quite right to enlist help," Breezy answered with surprising affability. "This hotel is a maze of hallways, and she could have gotten to anywhere."

Goodness. The woman was a study in contrasts. Bombastic one minute, understanding the next.

Then Breezy continued, "Of course, you should have kept an eye on her. I can't be expected to take care of everything. This was very irresponsible of you."

Ah, there was the Breezy she knew.

"I'll be more watchful in the future," Trudy promised, but could not resist adding, "I was distracted by having to list everyone's *proper* names."

Breezy squinted at her, then looked past as a handful of porters began to circulate through the lobby to peer under furniture and shake the silk draperies.

"Hm, it seems as if they're starting with the cat," Trudy mused aloud.

"Yes, so it would seem. Help me out of this chair. I'll handle this."

Trudy grasped her by the elbow and as soon as Aunt Breezy was on her feet she strode across the floor and up the stairs, pausing on the landing. She turned and Trudy nearly jumped out of her shoes as Breezy thwacked her closed parasol against the railing multiple times. "Hello! Hello there, all of you!" she shouted.

The din of conversation stopped abruptly as everyone turned

and Trudy was equally appalled and impressed by her aunt's bravado. The woman simply possessed no self-consciousness.

"My niece, Poppy, and her cat are missing somewhere on the premises," Breezy shouted to the now attentive guests. "I would like them found post-haste so please join in our search."

two

Alexander Bostwick lingered on the steps, drumming his fingertips against the glossy, varnished railing as he surveyed the crowded lobby below. Waiting for his sister, he was more restless than impatient, but Daisy had encountered a friend on their way downstairs and girlish chatter ensued, prompting him to continue on his own. Perhaps he should have waited. Pausing there, where everyone could see him, evoked a sensation he'd only recently become familiar with—vulnerability.

It was early in the summer season with new guests arriving at the Imperial every moment. The lobby hummed with the sounds of rustling silks, porters jostling steamer trunks, and the familiar refrain of society's elite greeting their peers, as if they were allies rather than adversaries. Today, however, the pomp and pageantry of this privileged parade left Alex unimpressed. Especially since it was this very element of society he'd been trying to escape.

There they all were, though, milling about and smiling inscrutably as if *their* lives were entirely free from peccadillos and impropriety. Alex knew better. From this vantage point on the stairs, he could see at least a dozen unfaithful husbands, a few unfaithful wives, a suspected embezzler, a railroad titan about to go bankrupt, a politician on the take, and an octogenarian real estate tycoon whose new bride had once been a woman of ill repute. Certainly, half the men in this room knew her as a sought-after dove from one of Chicago's finer brothels—but of course none could reveal *how* they knew.

It was against this facade of refinement and respectability that the Bostwick family—Alex in particular—found themselves embroiled in the scandal de jour. Actually, there were two concurrent scandals. One which his father had vehemently denied, and another which Alex was refusing to discuss. He saw no point in trying to explain anything to people who had no interest in the truth, just as he knew that if he could be patient and silent on the matter, the gossipmongers would eventually seek another source for their juicy morsels.

In the meantime, he intended to keep his head down, mind his manners, and live a life above reproach. For the next few months, as his relatives and rivals enjoyed the lazy days of summer at this resplendent resort, Alex would mingle with the matriarchs, dally with the doyennes, and mollycoddle the moguls in the hopes that a bit of well-timed sycophancy might save his family from further salacious brouhaha.

And as for the pretty debutantes who swished and swayed and seemed to outnumber the other groups by double? Well, he'd steer well clear of them. That shouldn't prove too difficult a task since—in the brief span of the past five months—he had married *and buried* a bride. Given his current status as both newlywed and widower, the debs were likely to steer clear of *him*.

Cutting short a sigh, Alex cast another glance at the staircase. Still no sign of Daisy. If she didn't hurry, he'd be left to greet the Hart family on his own. He was loath to do so since the missive from Morty VonMeisterburger had contained rather vague instructions. It simply read,

"My cousins arrive at the hotel on Tuesday, but as you know, I am currently on my honeymoon and won't be visiting the island this summer. In my absence, I do hope your family might aid Gertrude, Lucretia, and Cordelia in acclimating to the ambiance of

the hotel. Asher and Prudence are youngsters. They'll be fine, but perhaps you might rescue the older girls from my mother."

Alex's mood lightened slightly as he chuckled at the thought of Morty's mother.

Breezy VonMeisterburger was indeed the type one needed rescuing from. Brash and overbearing, she'd clawed her way to the pinnacle of Chicago society and presided over it like a dragon guarding loot—although Alex's mother might argue that she was *herself* the queen of their coterie. Loyalty dictated he support Constance Bostwick's ambitions, but truth be told, his money was always on Breezy whose shamelessly overt pursuit of power was positively Machiavellian.

That being the case, perhaps Morty's instructions weren't so curious after all. With names like *Gertrude, Lucretia,* and *Cordelia,* these poor relation cousins would surely need an ally when facing down the gauntlet of haughty condescension they'd receive from these hotel guests.

And how well Alex understood that!

He was, at this very moment, receiving pointed stares and dubious glances from his own peers down in the lobby—*because his wife had died!*

Nonetheless, the letter from Morty had been addressed to his sister Daisy and certainly she was the most logical one to assist the Hart sisters. Her reputation had, thus far, remained untainted by the Bostwick family's recent missteps. Perhaps because she was only seventeen, or perhaps because she was young and pretty. But the most likely reason was that Daisy was so effervescently charming even the hardest of hearts seemed disinclined to judge her for their father's ignominy or the calamitous misfortune of Alex's brief marriage.

Five more moments passed and Alex was on the verge of going back upstairs to remind his sister of their purpose when Breezy VonMeisterburger's august tone sluiced through the lobby's din like a foghorn, prompting bystanders to clear a pathway as she glided toward the registration desk, a dozen peacock feathers rising nearly a foot above her cumbersome hat.

It was a wonder none of them curtsied, he thought, as she sailed to the front of the line, pretending not to notice there were others waiting to register. Of course, no one dared to suggest she wait her turn. By silent yet mutual agreement, they let the old battleaxe have her way since arguing with the woman was a pointless endeavor. If Alex had learned anything at all from his mother, it was that Breezy VonMeisterburger must be *handled* at all times, but never *confronted*.

Traveling slowly behind her was a cluster of young ladies—surely the Hart sisters, and Alex chuckled again at fate's fickle nature, and his own faulty assumptions. Based on their social standing and rather frumpish names, he'd expected mousy, bespectacled girls hunched at the shoulders from too much reading, or perhaps stout farming stock with serviceable dun-colored dresses and hands made for digging potatoes.

The Hart sisters were not that.

Nothing like that.

In fact, they appeared quite lovely. They moved gracefully behind their aunt, whispering to one another while attempting to be discreet in their wide-eyed wonder at the hotel's opulent decor. Dressed in various pastel hues, they reminded him of an unpretentious springtime bouquet, and he could not spot a plain or awkward female in the bunch, although he was admittedly standing some distance away. Perhaps up close they'd be pocked or toothy, but from here they looked quite appealing. Judging from the murmurs and side-eyed glances from the other guests, Alex wasn't the only one who thought so. Perhaps these sisters would not need Daisy's guidance after all.

Loping in a few feet behind the young ladies was a coltish boy with a gangly frame and an abject lack of discretion. Alex smiled as the boy turned a full circle, grinning broadly and exclaiming something that made the tallest of his sisters turn around to shush him. And finally, trailing behind him, mimicking her brother's actions, was surely the youngest of the Hart clan. A little blonde girl who spun more slowly than the boy and held a wicker basket close to her chest.

Alex lost sight of the little girl as the crowd shifted, until she came into his view again a few short minutes later. She'd walked away from the rest, sitting down on a tufted footstool and placing the basket in her lap. He watched, intrigued as she carefully lifted the lid to peek inside. But the basket wobbled, falling to the floor, and the next thing Alex saw was a black and white cat determined to gain its freedom. It leapt from the tiny wicker prison and dashed away as if the very hounds of hell were on its heels, around a chair, under a table, over a table, up the stairs, and right past Alex.

No one else seemed aware of what had just occurred. Only Alex and the girl, who now stared up at him, brown eyes wide with surprise and dismay. She paused for only a second, then ran after the freed feline, climbing the steps two at a time, until she was nearly to Alex, and it occurred to him that this was a damsel he could aid, perhaps earning himself some much-needed goodwill.

You know his wife died under very suspicious circumstances...
Yes, but he did save that cat...

"Would you like some help?" he asked as the girl sprinted by.

"Yes, please," she called out.

And off they went on their own sort of parade.

The girl was fast, but she halted at the top of the staircase, uncertain which way to go. There were two long hallways leading in opposite directions, more steps around the corner leading up to the next floor, and a large seating area directly in front of them.

"I don't see him," she said quietly as Alex joined her. "Do you?"

"No. What's his name?" Alex asked softly, as if the cat might hear and be on to them.

"Sir Chester VonWhiskerton."

Her answer prompted a chuckle. He couldn't help it, but he quickly schooled his expression.

"Does he come when he's called?"

The girl had the temerity to give him a withering glance, as if the question were nonsensical.

"Of course not. He's a cat," she answered. And then she shushed him. "Shh. Do you hear that?"

She leaned forward, and Alex did the same, although he had no idea what he was listening for.

"I don't hear anything," he whispered.

"Neither do I," she responded, standing up straight and making him smile again.

"Are you Prudence, by any chance?" he asked.

"Sort of."

"Sort of?"

She huffed, leaning forward again as if to better sense the cat's whereabouts. "It's my name but no one calls me that. I'm Poppy."

"Ah, I see. I'm Alex."

"It's a pleasure to make your acquaintance, sir," she said as if by rote, her eyes darting in each direction.

"Perhaps if you search that area right in front of us while I stand here, I can nab him if he runs out, or at least see which way he's headed," Alex suggested.

She nodded thoughtfully. "Good plan."

Her endorsement was oddly gratifying. Perhaps because no one had commended one of his plans in a rather long time, but after a brief search bore no results, he began to suspect the errant feline had gone in another direction.

"Perhaps we should check these hallways," he said, just as the girl called out, "Ah, I see him!"

She motioned for Alex to approach. "He's on that ledge."

Looking up, Alex saw the black and white cat perched far above his reach and who appeared to have no interest whatsoever in coming down. "How on earth did he get up there?" he asked.

"He's a good jumper," she answered with pride. "Plus, I suspect he's the cause of that."

Alex's gaze followed the direction she pointed to see an armoire against one wall, on top of which were the remnants of a potted plant tipped over and spilling over the sides and onto the rug. Mr. Beeks was going to have a conniption fit, but at least they'd found the cat.

Retrieving him was another matter entirely.

After some conversation with the girl about the peculiar nature of felines and strategizing how they might best lure him within reach, it was agreed that the most logical course of action was to simply sit down on the floor near the entrance of the area and wait for Sir Chester VonWhiskerton to come down of his own accord.

"He likes to cuddle," she said, plopping down and patting her legs. "So, our laps will be the bait. Do you have something tantalizing you might wiggle at him," she added innocently.

He pressed his lips together for a moment, suppressing a smile and then suggested, "Perhaps my necktie? Or your hair ribbon?"

"Your necktie, I think."

She was a decisive little miss, he noted as he sat down next to her. Removing his necktie, he handed it over and observed as she laid it out along the floor and shimmied it in varying patterns and speeds. The cat's ears twitched with keen interest. Sir Chester was intrigued.

"If he ever comes down and gets close enough, we should quickly wrap him in your jacket," she whispered a moment later.

"My jacket?"

"Yes, sometimes he scratches if he's not in a mood to be carried. And he's rather annoyed about being stuffed in the basket."

"Ah, I see. Yes, all right."

Alex shrugged out of his jacket wondering yet again where his sister was. He also wondered if this little imp's family was growing concerned as to her whereabout. By all accounts, none of them had seen her chase after the naughty cat and rescuing him was turning out to be a lengthier and more complicated process than Alex had expected. They'd been away from the lobby for at least fifteen minutes.

"Does anyone know you're upstairs?" he asked in a hushed tone.

"Shh, he's moving," she whispered, ignoring his question because, sure enough, Chester VonWhiskerton was on the prowl. Poppy shifted onto her hands and knees, slowly drawing the necktie along the floor like a snake as her quarry jumped onto the top of the armoire, bumping the overturned plant again and sending more dirt onto the carpet. The mess was a small price to pay, in Alex's opinion, if it meant catching this bandit.

Leaping silently onto a nearby sofa, the animal paused, staring with unblinking eyes as Alex moved onto his own knees, jacket clutched and at the ready. Patience had never been a virtue he'd possessed, and despite his father's best attempts, Alex had never developed into a particularly good hunter. He preferred to enjoy the great outdoors without a rifle in his hand and grew too bored waiting for the quarry. He did, however, know enough about cats to realize any sudden movements could send the beast scuttling away.

And so, they crouched on all fours—the three of them—Alex, Poppy, and the cat, waiting to see who might make the next move. A grandfather clock chimed in the distance and the hum of guests in the lobby swelled and receded. Somewhere down the hall a door opened and closed. And still they crouched.

"Here, kitty, kitty, kitty," Poppy murmured softly. *Shimmy, shimmy, shimmy* with the tie.

"What on earth are you doing?" Daisy whispered from behind him. "I've been look—"

"Shh!" Alex and Poppy hushed in unison, and he pointed at the cat, who had finally jumped to the floor and was easing ever so slowly toward the necktie.

"Oh," Daisy giggled softly, moving back into the hallway but peeking around the corner.

Alex's knees were starting to ache from pressing against the wood floor, his shoulders were tight from the tension of it all, and his sister's snickering from behind them was no doubt due to his undignified posture.

But at last! Chester VonWhiskerton made a leap for the tie, and Alex made a leap for the cat, throwing his jacket over the escapee and wrapping him up securely. He received a few well-timed swipes of sharp claws that left bloodied scratches along one hand, and his captive was now yowling like a banshee, but at least the beast was contained.

"Chester," Poppy cooed, stroking the little bit of cat face Alex dared to expose. "My sweet, sweet boy."

Her sweet, sweet boy was squirming like a crazed lunatic.

"I think we'd best go get that basket before he wiggles away from me," Alex said, rising up clumsily from the floor. "And find your family. Speaking of family, this is my sister, Daisy," he added as she came back around the corner.

"I had no idea you were so agile, brother," she teased. "Perhaps you have a future in pest control."

"Chester isn't a pest," Poppy said indignantly. "He's mine, and he's the best, cleverest cat that ever lived."

"Of course he is," Daisy agreed. "And handsome, too, from the little bit I saw of him. I like his tuxedo. He's very dapper."

"I know," Poppy said primly.

"Daisy, this is Miss Poppy Hart," Alex explained.

"Ah!" Daisy responded, clapping her hands together. "They've arrived then. And you've met them?"

"No, just this one." His tone implied what a misadventure it had been thus far, as if that wasn't patently obvious. "And I suspect her family may be looking for her since they did not see her come this way."

"Well, my goodness, then! We'd best get downstairs to the lobby in that ca—"

"Hello! Hello there, all of you! My niece, Poppy, and her cat are missing somewhere on the premises. I would like them found post-haste so please join in our search."

Above the buzzy din of conversation from the lobby, Breezy's strident bellow rang out loud and clear. Poppy jumped at the sound, her eyes widening as apprehension spread over her face.

"Aunt Breezy scares me," she whispered, staring up at Alex.

"She scares everyone," he responded solemnly. "But think of her like thunder. Noisy but harmless."

"But thunder scares me, too," Poppy argued.

"Now, now," Daisy said, extending her arm. "Take my hand and we'll face your aunt together. She's not so very frightening. Just remember she was once a little girl, too, just like you."

"I don't believe it," Poppy said emphatically. "Asher says she eats naughty children for breakfast, and she won't be very pleased I let Chester get away. I wasn't supposed to bring him. I snuck him onto the ship."

"Asher is your brother, yes?" Daisy asked as they made their way down the stairs. At Poppy's nod she added, "I'm sure he was teasing. Brothers love to tease their little sisters, isn't that right, Alex?"

He'd fallen into step beside them with the yowling bundle still struggling to regain its freedom. "Indeed," said Alex. "In fact, I often wish I had another sister so I'd have more to tease, but I must make do with only Daisy."

It was a short way back down the stairs to the landing where Alex spotted the imposing Breezy VonMeisterburger and the tallest of the Hart sisters, a willowy brunette who turned at the sound of their approach. He nearly missed a step upon seeing her face. No pocks or toothiness there. She was beautiful with long-lashed eyes that shone with relief upon seeing her sister.

"Poppy!" she exclaimed, rushing forward to embrace her. "My goodness, where have you been?"

"Chester got away, and we were catching him."

"We?" The sister looked up, taking in the sight of Daisy in her cheerful flowered frock, and Alex, who suddenly felt rather disheveled given that his necktie was currently lying on the floor somewhere, and his jacket was wadded up in his arms with a squirming cat inside.

"Alexander Bostwick, at your service," he said, hoping to sound dignified despite his rumpled state.

Something flickered past her eyes. Not gratitude or appreciation for his efforts but rather something else entirely.

Disdain.

"And this is my sister, Daisy," he added, hoping he was mistaken.

"Thank you," Poppy's sister said, but her earnest words and tremulous smile were directed at Daisy, leaving Alex to feel oddly dismissed. And almost... annoyed?

Daisy hadn't done anything except leave him impatiently waiting and then show up as the escapade was nearly concluded. He was the one who'd rescued the feline fugitive. And the wandering little sister. Where was his smile? And his thank you? The absence of it stung.

He was being irrational, of course. So many prying eyes had been directed toward him lately it had made him belligerent. Plus, the scratches on his hands were beginning to sting and Chester VonWhiskerton, who showed no signs of fatigue, continued to wriggle. Alex was more than ready to be rid of him.

"My niece is found! Return to your gabbing," Breezy called out to the lobby triggering a mild swell of approval from the guests. Then her imperious gaze landed on him.

"Thank you for your... assistance, Alexander," she said coldly, "but perhaps we should remove ourselves from this staircase."

The air squeezed from his lungs at the veiled reference, and the subtle cruelty of her words. Shame, unfounded and undeserved, washed over him. She was making an accusation though he was the only one to realize it.

"Poppy," he said, more gruffly than he'd intended. "I wonder if I might hand Chester back into your care and be on my way."

"Oh, of course," she said, "But don't you want to meet my family? I'm sure the rest of them will be right along."

"Another time." He forced a smile as he passed the cat and coat to her. "It was a pleasure to make your acquaintance, though."

"But your jacket," she said.

"Return it at your convenience. Or give it to Daisy. She'll get it back to me."

Daisy gazed at him curiously. She'd missed Breezy's discreet barb, but he'd heard it—and the malicious intent behind it. He knew he shouldn't let the pointed jabs of that cantankerous old windbag affect him, but her insinuation wounded nonetheless, and suddenly the warm glow of helping a little girl went cold.

This single good deed was not enough to repair the damage he'd wrought.

three

With elegance extending into every corner of the Imperial Hotel, the dining room was no exception. Pausing at the entrance, Trudy noted the soft glow of crystal-accented gasoliers reflecting off cream-colored walls and gilt-framed mirrors giving the expansive room a dream-like aura enhanced by the strains of Mendelson's *Hebrides Overture* wafting down from the musician's balcony.

"Are you quite certain you can manage without my tutelage?" Breezy asked. "This isn't like the boarding houses in Springfield. Perhaps I should sit with you after all."

"Springfield has sophisticated dining establishments, too, Aunt Breezy," Trudy answered, failing to mask her annoyance. "And Mother has instructed us in proper dining etiquette. Please do join your own companions and trust we'll manage perfectly well on our own."

"Don't fret, Aunt Breezy," Asher chimed in. "If I get confused about all those forks, I'll just eat with my fingers."

Lucy swatted her brother's arm discreetly. "Stop jesting, Ash. She thinks you're serious."

"Don't think he isn't," Coco chimed in while batting her

lashes at a passing waiter. Though her aim was to secure a wealthy husband, Coco seldom missed an opportunity to flirt with any comely male between the ages of eighteen and eighty.

"He will not eat with his fingers, Aunt Breezy. I assure you," Trudy said to their aunt while pinching Coco's elbow. Breezy appeared to waver but as the stern-faced maître d approached, she stepped forward.

"I'm dining with Constance Bostwick this evening, and my guests will be dining at a table of their own."

"Very good, madam. Right this way."

"What is the matter with you," Trudy grumbled to Asher as soon as Breezy was beyond hearing. "The more you behave like a hooligan, the more she's going to loom over us like a vulture. Have you any intellect in that colossal skull of yours?"

"According to the phrenologists, I am a genius," he answered, tapping his temple.

"Ah, I see," she said, nodding slowly. "Well, as a Doctor of Medicine, not a practitioner of quackery, I find your ill-timed humor demonstrates a distinct lack of insight. Stop taunting Aunt Breezy or we will all endure the consequences."

It would be the four of them for dinner, Trudy, Lucy, Coco, and Asher. Poppy had already eaten and was tucked into bed with Sir Chester laying across her pillow and one of Breezy's maids keeping watch. With the tables large enough for eight, they'd be sitting with other guests, and Trudy hoped they wouldn't be saddled with anyone as pretentious as their aunt—although few could be. Regardless, she hoped it was someone with whom they could easily converse, and with any real luck, it would be someone who'd missed out on their calamitous arrival in the lobby earlier in the day.

The maître d returned, unsmiling, his posture so rigid one could hammer a nail with it.

"You are Miss Hart, yes?"

"Dr. Hart. Yes," she responded.

If he was impressed by that, his expression failed to show it. "Follow me," he said, turning and guiding them to the center of the vast dining room.

"You're here!" Daisy exclaimed brightly, already seated at a large, linen-draped table. "I told them to seat us together."

Trudy's relief at seeing Daisy Bostwick was short-lived. The girl was charming and had endeared herself to each of them by helping Poppy find her cat, but also at the table and rising from their chairs were her twin brothers, Alex and Chase. Trudy couldn't tell which was which. She'd only seen Alex for a moment as he'd abruptly dumped Chester into her sister's arms before exiting the lobby. As if he could not get away from them fast enough. It was insulting, the superior way he'd eluded introduction. His dismissive manner told Trudy he'd not changed a bit since childhood, in spite of the kind smile he offered now.

Or perhaps that was Chase who was smiling?

Actually, they were both smiling.

It was disconcerting. No two people should look so similar—especially two such damnably handsome men.

There.

She'd admitted it.

They were unnervingly handsome with wavy brown hair, angular jaws, and ridiculously broad shoulders. One seemed slightly taller, perhaps? Or was he simply bowing more deeply as introductions were made? Regardless, they were both tall, and imposing, and... *damn it...* handsome.

Ah, the slightly taller one was Alex, after all. The other was Chase, and next to him was his wife, Jo.

"Do come sit by me," Jo said to Trudy, patting the chair next to her. "I want to hear all about the adventures of attending medical school. Unless you're tired of discussing it."

Trudy never wearied of discussing the intricacies of medicine or her experiences at the University of Michigan, so she accepted the invitation with a smile, determined to make the best of things. At least she wouldn't be sitting next to Alex. Coco had connivingly maneuvered her way to his side with all the subtle grace of a locomotive speeding downhill, and Lucy, through no machinations of her own, ended up on his other side. Perfect, let her sisters keep him occupied.

Of course, the disadvantage of this seating arrangement was that it put Alexander Bostwick directly across the table from her. She could not lift her gaze without seeing his ridiculously blue eyes looking back at her, but she'd manage. She was Dr. Trudy Hart, after all. A woman in a man's world who'd traversed the corridors of academia and halls of medicine with courage and aplomb. Certainly, she could face an arrogant Bostwick for the length of a single meal.

Once settled into her chair, she took note of Jo Bostwick's softly rounded belly. It was hard to avoid, especially given that she, like so many expectant mothers, rested a hand on it as if to provide a little extra protection. It wouldn't be polite to ask questions about the state of her condition, of course, but perhaps once they were better acquainted, Trudy could pry, just a little.

"What's your impression of the hotel, thus far?" Jo inquired as a battalion of servers arrived to fill their glasses with a bubbly Perrier-Jouët. "I myself was quite out of place and overwhelmed when I first arrived last summer," Jo continued. "Thank goodness for Daisy befriending me or I might not have lasted the season."

Trudy smiled at the notion of Jo Bostwick feeling out of place. She exuded style, from her intricately coiffed hair to her glittering jewels, and yet she seemed refreshingly unpretentious. As they conversed, Trudy found Jo to be lacking in artifice with a lighthearted, self-deprecating sense of humor that set them both to giggling into their napkins as they discussed the peculiar eccentricities of those who summered at this exclusive destination.

"Have you met Mrs. Bostwick, yet? My mother-in-law?" Jo asked quietly, some twenty minutes into the evening.

"Once when I was a young girl," Trudy answered. "But not since then."

"Ah, well, word to the wise. Don't waste time being wounded by anything she says. She's sure to hurt your feelings."

"I appreciate the warning, although I've had a good deal of practice interacting with people who say hurtful things," Trudy answered. She was referring to Aunt Breezy and her medical colleagues but could not help but be reminded of her childhood interaction with Alexander Bostwick. Perhaps he'd been cruel to her in their youth because he'd learned it at his mother's knee. If that were the case, she supposed she could understand it, but she didn't have to accept it. People treated you the way you allowed them to treat you.

"A good deal of practice? That's unfortunate," Jo responded. "How do you get on with Mrs. VonMeisterburger, if you don't mind me asking."

"Well enough," Trudy answered neutrally. "She's a bit overbearing, of course, but also generous enough to invite us all to Trillium Bay for the summer."

"Not without prompting, of course," Jo responded with another earnest chuckle.

"Not without prompting? What do you mean?"

Jo's expression froze, her smile suddenly seeming false. "Oh, nothing. Just that she probably wants to *appear* generous, even if she really isn't. Have you seen the gardens yet? They're a work in progress but by the end of the summer, I imagine they'll be lovely."

The abrupt shift in topic did not go unnoticed by Trudy, nor did the tell-tale flush of rosy-pink creeping over Jo's neck and cheeks.

"I haven't seen the gardens yet," Trudy replied after a pause. "We only just arrived this afternoon."

"Oh, yes. Of course," Jo responded, suddenly becoming inordinately focused on buttering a dinner roll. The change in her demeanor was peculiar, and Trudy very much wanted to delve deeper into the matter. Jo, however, ended the conversation by taking a large, rather unladylike bite.

Perplexed, Trudy took a sip of champagne and found herself unexpectedly locked in a gaze with Alexander Bostwick. For the span of a heartbeat, they stared at one another. He smiled, and suddenly Trudy felt her own cheeks flush, and suddenly *she* became inordinately focused on buttering a dinner roll.

He didn't need to waste that smile. She knew what he thought of her.

She looked away and carefully set down the silver butter knife, inwardly admonishing herself for allowing such trivial turmoil to impact her evening. It was nonsense, really, the animosity she felt toward him. Yes, he'd teased her once when they were children. And yes, she'd borne his hurtful words into adulthood like a scar, but perhaps it was time to let that wound heal. She didn't have to *like* the man, of course, but she needed to stop feeling *bothered* by him. If she couldn't do that, her entire summer would be rife with irritation, like a series of bee stings and stubbed toes. She'd suffer and he would not, so, for her own sake, perhaps she should let bygones be bygones.

As waiters arrived with their meals, the room filled with delectable aromas, tenderloin of beef, roasted squab, rosemary pork, and mushroom gravy. The hum of conversation was replaced with the delicate clink of fine China being set down and utensils being lifted. And each plate, it seemed, was meant to be a banquet for the eyes as well as the palette.

"What in tarnation?" Asher exclaimed pointing to a simple tomato that had been pared into the shape of a rose. Trudy might have nudged him for his impolite ebullience but was too busy being amazed by the baked apple on her own plate—manipulated to look like a clam shell!

"Chef Culpepper's wife is the inspiration behind much of the whimsy you'll see at meals, but he is the maestro of flavors. You will never leave a table hungry; I can assure you," Jo said. "And best of all, if by some miracle you do, I can show you where to find more food."

"I cannot imagine any of us will need more to eat after this," Lucy responded. "But how do you know where there's more?"

"As the artist in residence last summer, I often ate with the employees and their lounge always has leftover goodies. The lemon meringue pie is the heavenly."

"You ate with the employees?" Coco asked, seeming appalled yet fascinated.

"I did," Jo said. "I wasn't always a Bostwick, you know. I came from quite humble beginnings."

"Darling, you are many things, but you have never been humble," Chase teased.

Trudy could see Coco filing this information away in the hope that she, too, would one day rise above humble beginnings to become a lady of substantial means.

"And how lucky we are to have you in our family now," Daisy added. "I'm sorry you never made it to Paris but I'm ever so glad you're here for another summer."

"We were there for our honeymoon," Jo said. "And we'll get back again, eventually. We'd be there now," Jo added, turning to Trudy, "But this impertinent baby didn't cooperate. For the first few months I felt as if I were already on a fiercely rocking ship. The idea of getting on an actual one for a journey across the Atlantic was rather more than I could face."

"Are you feeling better now?" Trudy inquired.

Jo nodded, hesitating before saying, "Yes, for the most part. Except for the burping. I cannot seem to control it."

Trudy smiled. "Ginger might help."

"I must find some, then."

Dinner progressed and the conversation circled around the deliciousness of the meal, the lovely ambiance of the opulent dining room, and a detailed review of a tour Daisy and her brothers had taken of the hotel stables. Eventually, Asher tired of those topics and said loudly enough for each of them to hear, "Hey, everyone. Answer me this. What did King George think of the American colonies?"

"Asher, this is not the time," Lucy admonished quietly, but Chase smiled.

"Do tell," he prompted.

"He thought they were revolting."

Trudy winced at the lowbrow humor but thankfully everyone else laughed, even Alex, who by all accounts appeared to be enjoying his conversations with both her sisters—although he did appear to have a slight lean, easing away from Coco and her deliberate attempts to entice his favor.

"Why did the knight always carry a pencil and paper?" Chase challenged in return, arching a dark brow.

"Pff," Asher responded dismissively. "So, he could draw his sword, of course."

Another round of laughter followed and for the next several minutes, the gentlemen, if one could term them as such in this particular circumstance, tried to outdo each other with ridiculous jokes that would not have been so amusing if not for the flowing champagne and comradery brought on by sharing good food. But as their laughter grew louder, Trudy noticed other diners looking askance and felt the hot flush of being at the center of unwanted attention.

"Perhaps we should save our jokes for another venue," she said.

"Who killed the most chickens in Shakespeare?" Asher asked, ignoring her. "Macbeth, because he did murder most foul."

Trudy turned an imploring gaze to Jo. "Can you make them stop? People are staring and we Harts haven't the protection of being well-placed."

Jo smiled, not seeming concerned about the judgmental looks, but said, "Boys, enough. Our merriment is making the other guests lament not sitting with us." But her words were followed by a rather robust belch, sending them all, except Trudy, into peals of laughter. Even Jo laughed as she apologized. "Oh, my goodness, this baby is so rude!"

Chase raised her hand to his lips and brushed a light kiss against her knuckles.

"Which makes me certain it's a boy," he said, his gaze full of love. "But you are right, of course. We're being a bit too loud for this intimate setting. Perhaps we could continue this frivolity at another time and place."

"What is the best way to make a coat last?" Asher whispered, unable to resist. "Make the vest and trousers first."

A round of muffled laughter rippled through their conclave, but Trudy was relieved the volume had subsided. As it was, she was certain to get a scolding from Breezy once they got back to their rooms.

Across the table, Alex was gazing at her once again, a curve to his lips and she wondered at his unpredictable temperament. He was decidedly more cordial and at ease this evening than he'd been in the lobby. Then again, so was she. Apparently, enough champagne could make you friends with anyone. She offered him the smallest acknowledgement, a subtle nod of the head, before turning her attention to Daisy.

∽

Alex shifted in his seat, the glow of their recent laughter warming his veins. It had been an age since he'd enjoyed himself or laughed out loud. Not since before his wedding to Isabella Carnegie, he knew that much.

Oh, they'd enjoyed each other's company at first. Quite a bit, in fact. She was beautiful and sultry, and he'd been utterly captivated, but their laughter had been more of the stuff of naughty innuendo and their speedy courtship meant much of their focus revolved around wedding plans.

Perhaps if he hadn't been in such a hurry to wed, things might have played out differently. But he had been in a hurry, and now he must accept the consequences—and the guilt, for even though she wasn't blameless in their downfall, she'd deserved far better than she got. At least he was still among the living. At least he could sit in the Imperial dining room, laughing too loudly with his brother and sister. At least he was alive and free to make new acquaintances such as the Hart sisters and their shamelessly impolite brother. While Izzy was... somewhere else.

"Have you any interest in astronomy," Lucy asked, drawing him away from his musing.

"Astronomy? I enjoy a bit of star gazing now and then, although my mastery of the constellations is sadly lacking. I'm afraid those lessons Mr. Harris tried to instill in me during school have been pushed aside by other things."

She nodded with understanding. "Yes, thankfully, my knowledge of the night skies has conveniently drummed out any ability to darn socks, so I'm never asked to mend Asher's."

He smiled at her wit. "An excellent trade, I should think."

"Indeed."

"Good evening, ladies. Gentlemen."

Their conversation was interrupted by Hugo Plank, designer, builder, and proud owner of the Imperial Hotel. He was a tall, broad man with a shock of sand-colored hair and a booming voice. Alex had encountered him a handful of times since arriving and found his personality to be as big and as obvious as his nose—which was to say, very big. He was a consummate salesman, and although Alex found him a little pushy, he knew Chase and Jo held him in high regard.

Hugo gave a single nod to each person at their table, saying, "I see some wonderful new faces here this evening. I believe you must be the Harts. Here with Mrs. VonMeisterburger?"

"We are," Trudy spoke up. "I am Dr. Trudy Hart. That's my brother, Asher, along with my sisters, Miss Lucy Hart, and Miss Coco Hart."

"How very wonderful to make your acquaintance. Welcome to the Imperial Hotel." He gave a perfunctory bow.

"Thank you. We're pleased to be here," Trudy responded. "Everything is quite impressive."

"Thank you. I pride myself on attention to detail so if there is anything at all that you need, please don't hesitate to ask. I am at your disposal."

"Mr. Plank," Daisy chimed in, "Is it true there's going to be a scavenger hunt?"

"Indeed, there is, Miss Bostwick. Mr. Tippett is putting the final touches on the list of clues as we speak. It's sure to test your wits so choose your team members wisely. We have a plethora of other exhilarating activities in the works as well. A bicycle course, a horse race, canoeing competitions, archery, and a casino night for the gambler in each of us. And, in addition to all of that," he lowered his voice and made a wide sweeping motion over the table as if to ensure their rapt attention, "I've invited a number of spiritualists to spend a few weeks at the hotel. Trance lecturer Ambrose Gibson will be joining us, as well as psychic mediums Madeline Moyen and Greta Watson to name a few. I've even secured the services of Mrs. Delilah Lamb who has the ability to communicate with our beloved pets."

Chase's brows rose in skepticism as he chuckled. "A psychic who talks to pets?"

Hugo eyed him with an indulgent smile. "The Imperial Hotel caters to all its guests, my good man. Not just the two-legged kind. I'm sure your mother would enjoy a reading for her two little dachshunds, or perhaps Mrs. Lamb might converse with that runaway cat who tore through the lobby this afternoon and find out what he thinks of my hotel."

The others joined in Chase's laughter at Hugo's obvious jest, yet Alex noticed the blush stealing over Trudy's cheeks, and her suddenly strained countenance. It didn't take deductive prowess to realize she was embarrassed by the situation, and understandably so. While every guest at the Imperial Hotel vied for attention, they only wanted the *right kind* of attention. He understood that well enough. To be singled out for an achievement was glorious. To be singled out for a blunder, even one not of your own making, was humiliating.

"Sir Chester VonWhiskerton is a cat of discerning tastes, Mr. Plank," Alex remarked casually, adjusting a gold cufflink. "He simply wanted to explore your elegant premises. Isn't that so, Daisy?"

"I believe that is the case," she agreed emphatically. "And seeing my brother on his hands and knees with his rump up in the air trying to capture the little beast is a memory I shall cherish forever."

All eyes turned to Alex, their amusement evident. His sister might have skipped that part for the sake of his dignity but seeing Trudy's expression go from concerned to relieved to amused was worth it, even if it was at his expense. She glanced over at him, the telltale hint of a smile playing at the corners of her mouth. He'd felt throughout the meal she'd been avoiding his gaze, but now she knew he'd been instrumental in the return of both her sister and the cat, and she appreciated it.

Why her acknowledgment of his efforts felt so pleasant, he could not discern. But it did.

After a few more moments of conversation, Mr. Plank moved away to regale another table with the hotel's offerings, and Coco leaned forward, saying excitedly, "I've read about Madame Moyen. She's well known in Chicago, isn't she?"

"I've heard of her," Daisy responded. "My maid says she very accurate with her readings."

"And she can communicate with the deceased. Can you imagine? What would it be like to converse with a real live ghost?" Coco looked around the table, hoping for the same enthusiasm from the rest of them, but Alex had no interest in talking about spirits or the departed. For a variety of reasons.

From across the table, Trudy offered a small, patient smile at her sister. "There's no such thing as a real *live ghost,* Coco. Ghosts, by their very definition are not alive."

"Oh, Tru," her sister scoffed. "You know what I mean. Can't you just enjoy the mystery of it?"

"I'm fascinated by mysteries of every nature," Trudy continued. "But if our souls truly move on after death, and if heaven is as rapturous as people say, why would any spirit linger here in its earthly visage rapping on walls in the hopes that we might understand their message?"

"But that's why mediums are so essential. They are able interpret the messages," Coco said.

"According to them. Who's to say they're accurate? They're likely more magicians than mediums."

But Coco persisted. "Therese Deveraux was told she was doomed to suffer an injury and just two days later she twisted her ankle. How do you explain that?"

"By pointing out that Therese Deveraux is clumsy and never looks where she's stepping," Trudy responded. "And anyway, now you're talking about a clairvoyant prediction, not a message from beyond. There's a difference."

"And yet you refuse to believe in any of it. You are so very dull." Coco crossed her arms and fell back against her chair.

No one spoke and Alex saw Trudy blush once again, more deeply this time because not only had she been insulted by her sister in front of the rest of them, but because the two of them had just committed a social faux pas. Arguing in public.

"You are entitled to your beliefs and opinions, Coco, and I am entitled to mine," Trudy said quietly. "If trusting in science and evidence and things I can witness with my own two eyes makes me dull, then so be it."

"Of course you're not dull," Daisy responded. "You're brilliant. I don't imagine any one of us could have graduated from medical school the way you did. Certainly, my brothers couldn't have done it."

Daisy's attempt at levity was followed by polite laughter but the joyful mood at the table had dissipated like the bubbles in their champagne, and for Alex, all this talk of spectral visits and ghostly messages had flooded him with inexplicable emotions and unanswerable questions. If you'd asked his thoughts on the occult before Izzy died, he would have parroted Trudy's words. He believed in what he could see. He believed in evidence, not fancy. But lately he'd seen evidence of things he certainly could not explain.

He cast a glance at his sister-in-law, and bless her heart, she understood his silent entreaty.

"Enough talk of the macabre. Shall we discuss something brighter?" she asked the group. "Perhaps we should form a team for the Scavenger hunt."

Later that evening, after the others had retired for bed, Alex and his brother were sipping bourbon on the front porch. The breeze off the lake was nearly cold, and only a smattering of stars and a crescent moon attempted to brighten the midnight sky. The musicians were gone, and the muffled bangs of chairs stacked, and windows being closed indicated the hotel was settling in for the night.

Without the ever-present music and chatter of so many guests, Alex could actually hear the waves lapping on the shore, and the wind stirring the trees. He much preferred the soothing sounds of nature to those of mankind. It allowed him to think, although thinking these days—and remembering—seemed to lead to dark places.

"This isn't bad for a Kentucky bourbon," Chase said, eying the amber liquid in his glass. "Old Forester, Hugo called it."

"It's pleasant," Alex agreed, appreciating its flavor as much as its burn. The sensation was a useful distraction.

"So was dinner," Chase added. "Pleasant until that business at the end."

Alex took a long, slow breath. "Miss Hart has rather strong opinions."

"Which one?"

They chuckled in unison, alike in so many ways yet full of differences, too.

"Both," Alex answered. "Coco is rather… forthright."

"She seemed quite taken with you."

"Quite. She also seemed to think her napkin was in my lap."

Chase let out a bark of amusement. "You jest!"

"I do, but only a little. Her manner is… coquettish."

"Unlike her sisters, then. They seem rather earnest."

"Yes. Lucy is a delightful conversationalist. Congenial. Inquisitive. And Trudy is…" He paused, searching his vocabulary for just the right word.

"Self-possessed?" Chase offered.

"Enigmatic," Alex answered after another pause. "I rather think she doesn't like me, although we've never met. Undoubtedly, she's heard the rumors."

"I think we her once, long ago," Chase said. "When we were children. The Harts were staying with the VonMeisterburgers and Mother took us there to spend the day. Do you recall?"

Alex shook his head. "I don't. It must have been a great while ago."

"It was. The only reason the day snagged in my memory is because of the thrashing we got from Mother for swimming in our underclothes. In mixed company, no less."

Alex shook his head again with a chuckle. "I have no memory of it at all."

"Regardless," his brother continued. "I'm sure Trudy has no cause to dislike you, and she doesn't seem the type to be influenced by ridiculous gossip. Perhaps she simply has a reticent nature. I can't imagine what it must have been like for her in medical school, although it seems she has no qualms in stating her convictions when prompted. Perhaps you should just ask her."

"Ask her why she dislikes me? Good heavens, if I queried every person at this hotel who seems to hold me in contempt these days, I'd be busy until the end of summer."

"You exaggerate. No one blames you for Izzy's death, Alex," Chase replied quietly.

Alex looked askance at his brother. "Now it's you who exaggerates."

Chase shrugged. "Well, certainly no one who knows you believes you had anything to do with it. As for the rest of them, they can go to hell. One thing I've learned since my marriage to Jo is that life gets easier once you stop concerning yourself about the opinions of others."

"I don't disagree with what you're saying, Chase, but we are hardly in the same situation," Alex argued, frowning at his glass. "They judge you for marrying an artist of no social standing. Hardly a crime. They're judging me because they think I murdered my wife for her fortune."

Chase took a hearty swig of bourbon before responding. "It's such unjust nonsense and I'm sorry for it. I wish I could relieve you of the burden, or at least find out who is spreading such vile lies."

"Thank you. I do appreciate that, and I suppose you're correct in thinking I must set aside my concern over what others think. I just..."

"What?" Chase prompted.

"The suggestion that I married Isabella for her wealth is not entirely far-fetched."

"Ah," Chase said as if he'd already considered that. "I can't think of any man who wouldn't be seduced by that kind of money, but you did care for her. You told me so."

Alex nodded slowly. "I did. I genuinely thought I loved her when I proposed, but we'd known each other for such a short time, and I can't deny her wealth may have influenced my... optimism. As the months of our engagement passed, I grew uncertain of our success, but I convinced myself that once the extravaganza of the wedding was behind us, once we were married and she got away from her parents, we'd have a chance to rekindle what we'd started and all would be well. Perhaps if we'd had more time..."

"I'm sorry you didn't have it."

Alex was sorry, too.

For many things.

Distant thunder rumbled from across the lake, and a boisterous group of gentlemen well into their cups at the far end of the porch laughed uproariously as one of them fell off a chair, and suddenly Alex longed to share more about his marriage. And its downfall. But he didn't. Not because he didn't trust his brother, or because he didn't appreciate Chase's insights. He did. Immensely. But what good would come from divulging all the secrets of his time with Isabella? Of revealing all the hurtful things she'd said, or all the ways he'd failed her. Nothing could change the past, and nothing he said or did now would bring her back to life.

"You must forgive me," Alex said, more brightly than he felt. "Too much bourbon has made me morose. I shouldn't be saddling you with this. Not when you are in the throes of wedded bliss."

"Nonsense. I'm your brother."

"My younger brother," Alex responded wryly. "By nearly fifteen minutes, but I'd rather discuss how wonderful it is to see you happy. Jo is a delight, although I question her judgment in accepting you."

Chase's smile was slow and full of contentment. "She is a delight and far too good for me."

"She is too good for you. No question there, and soon you'll be a father."

"I cannot fathom it."

"Nor I, but speaking of your fine wife and impending parenthood, you should bid my sorry self a goodnight and go to bed." He didn't begrudge Chase such happiness but the stark contrast to his own emotions was, at times, acutely painful.

"I can visit with you a while longer," Chase responded, but Alex could see the drowsiness in his brother's eyes.

"Nonsense. I value your council, but your glass is empty, and I think I'd like to take a walk to clear my mind. You go on up. I'll see you tomorrow."

Chase paused, regarding him carefully before saying, "Very well. Tomorrow, then. Don't stay up too late."

"I won't," Alex promised, but he knew he would.

Sleep had become an elusive mistress of late. Each night he'd lie alone in bed and contemplate his situation. He'd recall all the things that happened leading up to Izzy's death.

And all the things that had happened since.

And all the things that were happening still...

His mind would churn with unanswerable questions—along with the growing unease that somehow, Izzy wasn't quite finished with him yet.

four

"Is it far to the West Bluff, Aunt Breezy?" Trudy asked. "I might rather like to walk."

"Walk?" Breezy exclaimed, as if Trudy had said she'd rather *fly*.

"Yes, I enjoy walking. It increases one's vitality."

"It increases one's perspiration," Breezy responded dismissively. "Get in the carriage."

"If you'd rather ride, I'm sure we have a lively mare in the stable eager for some exercise," Mr. Plank said from astride a dappled palfrey. Trudy's pulse quickened at the suggestion, but her hopes of riding alongside Mr. Plank and Asher were quickly dashed.

"We haven't time for that, girl. Get in the carriage," Breezy snapped. "I want to see what progress has been made on my cottage. Mr. VonMeisterburger is expecting a full report as soon as possible."

"Why didn't Uncle Albert come with us from Chicago?" Poppy asked, sitting across from her aunt in the open-topped landau with a securely harnessed Chester VonWhiskerton snoozing in her lap.

"Your Uncle Albert will arrive later in the summer. Unfortunately, your cousin Mortimer won't be coming at all. Apparently his honeymoon is more important to him than I am."

Mortimer VonMeisterburger was Breezy's one and only son upon whom she doted and derided in equal measure. In conversation, he tended to be singularly focused on subjects which interested him alone, but Trudy found him endearing. Perhaps because she was also known to be rather singularly focused.

She was disappointed he wouldn't be joining them. She would have happily endured his avian-laden tangents about *fluffy-backed tit babblers* and *red-rumped bush tyrants* if his presence provided a cushion between herself and his mother who had, earlier that morning, declared Trudy's *sallow complexion* would surely benefit from the use of *Dr. Campbell's Arsenic Complexion Wafers*, and that a *vigorous daily rubbing of her breasts* with elderflower water might enhance their lackluster growth.

"Or perhaps a bust food cream," Breezy had added at Trudy's dismayed look. "We can order some from the Montgomery Ward catalogue and have it sent to the Imperial straight away. It will come in a brown paper wrapper, and no one need ever know."

"I do not need *bust food cream*, Aunt Breezy. I am quite satisfied with my figure," Trudy had responded sharply.

"Well, you needn't get tetchy with me, young lady. I am only suggesting that a larger bosom would distract potential suitors from noticing your *age* and how very *tall* you are."

That had brought the conversation to an abrupt halt.

Because Trudy was not old. Nor was she *too* tall. She was a perfectly acceptable age and a perfectly acceptable height. In fact, it was her *advanced years* which gave her the wisdom to embrace her stature, knowing that the extra inches gave her more gravitas with patients who might otherwise be reluctant to trust a physician who was *just a girl*.

Trudy also had no intention of discussing matrimonial prospects with Aunt Breezy because Trudy had no inclination to get married.

Ever.

She'd worked too diligently at earning her medical degree, and too tirelessly at establishing herself as a qualified physician. She was not about to renounce her hard-won achievements in trade for a husband who would undoubtedly demand she forsake her vocation for the *blessed opportunity* of tending to his home and bearing his children.

No.

Thank you, but no.

It wasn't that she had anything against husbands *conceptually*. She just didn't have a practical use for one of her own. She felt much the same about children, too. She adored her brother and sisters, and upon occasion, did wonder what it might be like to have a family of her own, but Trudy had recognized long ago she lacked the patience and selflessness required to be a good wife, as well as the nurturing, maternal qualities necessary to be a good parent. *Trudy's mother would never have lost Poppy in the chaos of a bustling hotel!*

"Have you no care at all for your complexion?" Breezy scolded as Trudy clamored into the carriage and plunked down ungracefully between Poppy and Lucy. "Didn't you bring a parasol?"

"No," Trudy said peevishly. And then she turned her face up to the sun and silently begged for freckles.

"I have a parasol," Coco said demurely, smiling at Aunt Breezy. "And I was hoping you might tell me more about Chicago. Life in Springfield is so dreadfully monotonous. I just know I am destined to live in a big city."

Whether Coco's intent had been to distract Breezy for Trudy's sake, or if she was genuinely interested, the question successfully occupied their aunt for the duration of the scenic carriage ride to the site of the VonMeisterburger's new summer cottage.

Once there, they disembarked with the aid of a gallant Mr. Plank, and Trudy felt her irritation evaporating like springtime dew. She breathed deeply, inhaling the soul-nourishing scent of pine trees, blossoming lilacs, and fresh cut lumber. Walking to the crest of the bluff and looking out, she found a view of Lake Huron stretching all the way to the horizon, like a painting done in shades of emerald and turquoise as golden sunlight bounced off the smooth surface of the water and dappled the ground through the branches.

To Trudy's right, along the bluff, sat a long row of building sites, each at the skeleton stage but already hinting at future grandeur as the noisy *tap, tap, tap* of busy hammers competed with the gentle sounds of rolling waves below and happy birds chirping overhead.

"It's so serene," Lucy murmured, coming to stand next to Trudy as she peered out at the beautiful vista.

"Breathtaking," Trudy responded.

"It's wasted on her," Lucy added with a wistful sigh, referring to their aunt. "She won't appreciate it."

"Probably not. But we can. At least while we're here." Trudy slid an arm around her sister's waist, enjoying the comradery before abruptly exclaiming, "Oh, good heavens! Where is Poppy?"

"She's fine. She's introducing Chester to Mr. Plank."

"I am the shoddiest guardian imaginable," Trudy said with a huff before turning away from the lake to walk back toward the others.

"You're not," Lucy replied with amusement, following her. "And anyway, isn't Aunt Breezy supposed to be in charge of her? Of all of us?"

Trudy gave a tiny shake of the head. "Mother bade me to keep an eye on everyone. Including her own sister. I suspect she thinks Aunt Breezy could be a poor influence."

"I sincerely doubt that." Lucy reassured her as they walked. "The only one she has any sway over is Coco, and we both know Coco was spoiled long before this trip."

"That's true enough. And she's far too fond of boys."

"*And* she has her eye on Mr. Bostwick," Lucy whispered.

"Hmm," Trudy responded vaguely. They'd nearly reached the

others and what she wanted to add couldn't be said in front of anyone but Lucy.

"You're certain my cottage will be larger than the Bostwick's, correct?" Breezy demanded as she stared down a short, pug-faced man who, judging from his blunt, misshapen nose, was no stranger to physical altercations. His menacing features did nothing to smooth her aunt's rough edges.

"I don't know the square footage of no other houses, ma'am," he said impatiently. "I ain't building those ones. I'm building this one."

"Well, certainly all you building men are acquainted. Can't you just go and inquire?"

He twisted the tattered, tweed cap in his hands, then looked up gratefully at Mr. Plank who had just stepped forward to join their discussion *(if one could call Breezy's rude interrogation a discussion.)*

Trudy gave a chuff of laughter as she realized Poppy was clasping Mr. Plank's right hand while he held Chester's leash in the other. Perhaps he and the cat would not need the aid of a pet psychic to make friends, after all.

"How goes it, Davenport?" Mr. Plank asked the visibly flustered man.

"Fine, sir. We're on schedule, right enough, but Mrs. Von... mer... Von burg..."

"Mrs. VonMeisterburger," Mr. Plank said.

"Yes, sir. Well—"

"My cottage needs to be the largest," Breezy interjected. "It's the first one people will see when they come up this boulevard and I won't have it dwarfed by some ghastly monstrosity the Bostwicks aim to build."

Mr. Davenport stared drolly at Mr. Plank, as if to say, *"Do you see what I am up against?"*

"Your cottage is sure to be the finest, Mrs. VonMeisterburger," Mr. Plank said diplomatically. "Like Mr. Davenport, I am also familiar with all these builders. Most of them worked on my fine establishment, and I assure you he's the very best."

"Well, of course, I expect the craftsmanship to be of the highest caliber. That goes without saying, but I'm asking about the size," she said.

Mr. Plank nodded patiently. "Yes, I understand, and while I don't know the precise measurements of the Bostwick's cottage, I do have it on very good authority that yours is larger. And," he leaned forward as if to impart a great truth, "your lot size is bigger. It always will be, and nothing the Bostwicks do can ever change that."

He followed his comment with a definitive nod of approval and Trudy nearly laughed out loud. It seemed Mr. Plank, like his hotel manager Mr. Beeks, knew just how to coddle her aunt into submission. Trudy could learn a thing or two from them.

"But how much larger?" Breezy asked insistently.

Mr. Plank hesitated for a fraction of a second before stating what was clearly a guess, saying, "Substantially larger."

"All right then," Breezy said after a moment, smoothing the hair at her temples. "Carry on then, Davenport, but hurry. If you're on schedule, as you say, then you can speed things up and finish sooner. I'd like to move in as soon as possible."

Mr. Plank gave a tilt of the head toward the wilting Mr. Davenport, excusing him, and turned to Breezy. "Mrs. VonMeisterburger, you wound me. Aren't you happy at my hotel?"

"Of course, Mr. Plank, but I am eager to set up my own household here, as well. You know we'll still dine at the Imperial most evenings and participate in the activities."

"Well... If you promise. The hotel would be so drab without the effervescent glow of your company. Now, let's all take a walk through your cottage to see what's been done so far."

Trudy and Lucy exchanged wry glances at his preposterous compliment but Aunt Breezy was practically preening as everyone traipsed across the grass to the steps leading up to a grand porch and the framed doorway of the cottage.

"I would normally say ladies first," Mr. Plank commented as he paused at the threshold, "but perhaps I should lead the way since it's an active work site. I'd hate for any of you to take a tumble so please watch your step."

Breezy nodded, and they followed carefully, one by one, through the construction, dodging loose nails and rough-edged pieces of lumber. Even in its unfinished state, Trudy could see it was the largest home she'd ever been in, including the VonMeisterburgers' home in Chicago. And that was a mansion! Calling this anything less was a gross misnomer.

In spite of the vast size, or perhaps because of it, Asher quickly grew bored of looking at the exposed trusses and unfinished rooms. He offered to take Poppy back out onto the grass where Chester might sniff to his heart's content, and Trudy was relieved by their departure given the perilous environment, not to mention the barrage of vulgar expletives currently being shouted by a tool-wielding workman who'd accidentally smashed his own thumb with a hammer. She knew for certain Asher would be repeating that crass language at his first opportunity.

Dear Mother and Father,

On the first day, I lost Poppy, and on the second, Asher learned a dozen new words that you never want him to say.

Meanwhile, Coco kept Breezy engaged by asking about furnishings. There was talk of Aubusson rugs, velvet and brocade draperies, stained glass windows, and furniture pieces by Phyfe, Stickley, Chippendale, and the Herter Brothers. Trudy stopped listening after the first room, not knowing *(or much caring about)* the difference between an inlaid maple table and a satinwood writing desk. As long as a seat was comfortable, it didn't matter to Trudy if it was a Queen Anne or a Morris chair. Her uncultured backside certainly couldn't tell the difference. She was about to excuse herself under the guise of checking on Poppy when the sound of carriage wheels caught their collective attention, and everyone returned to the yard.

It seemed the Bostwicks had arrived unexpectedly, causing a strange and equally unexpected tightness in Trudy's chest.

She'd enjoyed herself well enough at dinner last night. Jo and Daisy were warm and engaging. Both the Bostwick brothers had been cordial and amusing, and while Trudy had even come to the mature realization that she should give Alexander Bostwick another chance to earn her good opinion, somehow... thoughts of him made her edgy, and his presence here now made her... inexplicably nervous.

She didn't understand why. There was no reason to be intimidated by him. He was no better—or worse—than any other person she'd encountered throughout her lifetime, and yet, something about the way he'd looked at her last night made her feel... peculiar and uncertain.

It wasn't an altogether unpleasant feeling... but it was... unfamiliar. Unfamiliar things usually piqued her curiosity and begged exploration, but in this case, she felt avoidance was her better option. Of course, it didn't help that Coco had waxed poetic about the man for an hour once they'd gotten back to their rooms and were preparing for bed.

Did you notice Alexander Bostwick's shoulders?
His voice is like velvet.
His hair is so thick. I imagine it's soft. Do you imagine it's soft?

Her sister had gone on so long in such pointless rapture that even Lucy, who never got annoyed by anyone, finally told Coco to shush.

And now, here they all were again. The Bostwicks. And they had increased in number, as if there weren't already too many of them.

Alex and Chase climbed from the carriage first, looking as dashing as expected in casual linen suits which on them looked anything but casual, then down floated Daisy in a pink dotted dress with fringed trim. Behind her was Constance Bostwick, their mother. She did not float. She descended—without moving a muscle if one judged from the ramrod stiffness of her posture. And behind Mrs. Bostwick came a very tall, dark-haired young man who appeared to be close to Lucy's age, and a sandy-haired, freckle-faced one who could not be more than sixteen.

"My dear Constance," Breezy said, her voice dripping with faux affection as she walked forward, open arms outstretched. "I knew you wouldn't be able to resist seeing what fabulous plans I have for my cottage. How predictable of you to stop by."

Constance leaned stiffly into the embrace without making any point of contact, responding, "How quaint you are for pretending this was our destination when surely you realize we are merely passing by your bungalow on our way to my own grand villa."

"*Ah, ha, ha, ha*," the women twittered in unison as if their words were laced with humor instead of venom.

It was the first time Trudy had ever considered feeling sorry for her aunt. While Breezy was a bombastic force of nature carving a path toward what she wanted, Constance Bostwick was more an immovable mountain, forcing others to go around. Her tone was calm, her style understated—the kind of understated that proved she had nothing to prove.

"Perhaps I should make a few introductions," Chase said, stepping forward. "Mother, of course you know Mr. Plank, but allow me to introduce the Hart family, Miss Trudy, Lucy, and Coco Hart, and Mr. Asher Hart. Ladies, gentlemen, this is my mother, Mrs. A.J. Bostwick."

"Hey," said Poppy, stomping her foot.

"Oh, I beg your pardon, miss," Chase continued. "I didn't have the pleasure of making your acquaintance yesterday. Am I to assume you are Miss Poppy Hart?"

"I am," she said superciliously, then held up her now resigned cat by the scruff. "And this is my companion, Sir Chester VonWhiskerton."

Mrs. Bostwick nodded stiffly at Trudy and her siblings with

something that *could* be considered a smile—but that in most cases would *not* be considered a smile. It was more akin to the way one's lip quivered before a good sneeze.

"And these are my cousins," Chase continued. "Ellis and Finn Bostwick, sons of my Uncle Vernon."

Ellis's bright blue eyes had gone directly to Coco, although *she* appeared too occupied with ogling Alexander Bostwick to notice, and Trudy made a mental note to check the location of everyone's bedrooms back at the hotel to ensure there was no inappropriate nocturnal prowling.

Dear Mother and Father,

On the first day, I lost Poppy, on the second day, Asher learned to cuss, and on the third, Coco was compromised by a Bostwick. Not sure which one.

∼

"Is it just my imagination or do those two hens peck at one another incessantly?" Ellis murmured to Alex with a glance toward the older women.

Alex briefly considered rising to his mother's defense, but chose against it since his cousin was entirely correct. He chuckled instead and gave Ellis a single pat on the back.

"It's not your imagination. This campaign they've waged against one another has gone on longer than the crusades. Just ignore it, if you can."

Alex had hung back during Chase's introductions, in part because everyone knew him, but more because he was still agitated with Breezy VonMeisterburger and the mean-spirited comment she'd made to him. The woman was hard to take in the best of circumstances, and these were certainly not the best of circumstances. In fact, he'd have begged off touring the cottages entirely since he and Chase had gone through them just days before, but Daisy insisted he come along.

She was worried about him. She didn't say it outright, but it was obvious in the solicitous way she'd taken to asking questions about his interests, and the way she always made sure he had someone to sit next to. It was kind of her, he supposed, but it was also a bit humiliating, having his 17-year-old sister attempting to play nursemaid to his wounded emotions.

"I suppose, since I'm here, you may as well show me around," Alex's mother said after introductions were concluded. "Of course, my cottage will certainly be finished first, so I know you'll want to tour mine as well."

"I suppose I could if it would make you happy," Breezy responded with indifference, "But I'm sure ours will be finished sooner than yours."

"Shall we resume the tour then?" Mr. Plank interjected quickly before the ladies could begin a new argument about which cottage would be completed first. "Who would like to join us?"

"I think I'll take Poppy down to the shore," Trudy responded, just as quickly. "The cottage isn't quite safe for her with all the construction going on."

"I'll go with you," Lucy said to her sister.

"To the lakeshore!" Asher shouted, nudging Finn before dashing toward the path. "Race ya," he called out.

Finn instantly responded, sprinting forward and passing the other boy with ease. Soon they were out of sight over the crest of the hill, but their laughter rang out among the trees.

Ellis, however, had a more nuanced goal in mind. He sidled up to Coco, asking smoothly, "Which direction might you be heading, Miss Hart?"

Alex nearly chuckled because, just as she had at dinner the evening prior, the girl had been casting coy glances his way from the moment they'd arrived. She only now seemed to notice his cousin's existence—which was surprising given that Ellis was nearly six foot, four inches tall. He was hard to miss.

Coco's pale blue eyes traveled up Ellis's lengthy torso until she met his gaze.

She blinked.

And blushed.

"Uh, I... believe I'll visit the shore," she stammered.

"Wonderful," Ellis replied, offering his arm. "Then I'll escort you. The path may be uneven."

"Uh... thank you." Her eyes darted back to Alex for a scant second. He tamped down a smile at her apparent indecision but since he had no intention of deepening their acquaintance, the sooner her interest was diverted the better. It wasn't vanity that convinced him of her admiration. The girl was not subtle.

Then again, neither was Ellis.

With only Mr. Plank, Breezy, and Constance touring the cottage, Alex and the rest of the entourage ambled down the narrow path leading to the water's edge. At the back of the pack, Trudy, Poppy, and the cat meandered to and fro apparently looking for flowers and pretty rocks along the way, and he paused to wait for them.

"I see Chester is out for another adventure," he said.

Trudy's flickering glance was accompanied by a small, tight smile, and he wondered how two sisters could hold him in such contrary regard. Whatever attraction Coco felt toward him, Trudy was clearly immune.

"Yes. Let's hope he stays on a leash this time," she responded.

"Yes, let's hope. I've no interest in trying to rescue him from a tree."

"He'll behave today," Poppy stated with confidence. "I had a very stern talk with him last night about proper manners."

"Ah, well. That should do the trick," Alex said, smiling at Trudy over the little girl's head. Her expression relaxed—a little.

"Poppy, come see!" Lucy called out excitedly a moment later. "I may have found a Petoskey stone."

Poppy gave a gasp of excitement, promptly scooping up the allegedly obedient cat and scampered toward the lake.

At her departure, Alex heard a small sigh from Trudy—whether one of exasperation or relief, he wasn't certain. He looked over to see she'd removed her hat and was casually swinging it from one hand by its ribbons. The sun had pinkened her cheeks and the ever-present breeze over the lake was doing a delightful job of stirring loose tendrils of hair around her face.

He probably shouldn't notice such things. He was a grieving widower, after all, and had more than enough drama in his life at present, but he found her uniquely pretty with chestnut colored hair and hazel eyes that appeared nearly green in the sunlight. She was willowier than what was currently considered fashionable—*although who decided such things, he certainly didn't know*—and there was something undeniably delicate in the way she plucked a flower from beside the path and examined it in her fingertips.

They walked a moment in silence, until she finally said, "It does seem I owe you a debt of gratitude, Mr. Bostwick. Thank you for helping my sister recapture Chester yesterday."

He was warmed by her words even if it was a most tepid attempt at gratitude. "Of course. It was my pleasure, although the wounds on my hand might suggest otherwise."

She looked over at him with concern. "Oh, goodness. Did he scratch you? I'm sorry. I may have an ointment to remove the sting."

"His opinion on the subject of recapture did leave a mark," Alex replied with a chuckle. "But I hardly blame him. I would feel much the same in his predicament, and I'll recover. I have a brother, you know. I've suffered far worse, and far more deliberate injuries."

A subtle blush deepened the hue of her already pink cheeks. "Well... I am sorry, and I do thank you."

"You are most welcome. Truthfully, I enjoyed the adventure."

Her expression shifted to bemusement. "Then you have an

unusual sense of fun, Mr. Bostwick. I can think of a great many things more entertaining than wrangling a cat."

He laughed at her observation, and at the fact that she was *finally* conversing with him.

"As can I, Dr. Hart, but yesterday's adventure did have a certain originality to it, and your sister was a delightful hunting guide."

"Oh, that girl," Trudy scoffed, shaking her head. "She was not supposed to bring the cat on this trip."

"She mentioned that."

"Did she?" At his nod, she continued as they walked. "Did she also mention stuffing him into a pillowcase—and then into a carpetbag—to smuggle him onto our steamship? I cannot imagine how he got enough oxygen. The poor fellow nearly asphyxiated, and what an ordeal *that* would have been!" She shook her head again, but he sensed the slightest hint of amusement in her tone at the absurdity of it all.

"My goodness. No wonder he jumped from the wicker basket at his first opportunity," Alex concurred. "But at least if he encounters Mr. Plank's pet psychic, Chester will have a fascinating tale to tell."

With an easy shrug, she replied, "I suppose that would've been true whether he'd survived the trip or not."

Then she laughed, and Alex found the sound of it delightful. Perhaps Dr. Hart was not nearly as serious-minded as he'd thought.

five

"Why, he shoved her down a staircase, of course." Breezy's indifferent tone suggested she considered this general knowledge and not at all a shocking allegation that Alexander Bostwick had deliberately harmed his wife.

But it was shocking, of course, and left the Hart sisters quite aghast.

They were in their suite getting dressed for dinner when Lucy asked their aunt how Alex's wife had died. Not out of morbid curiosity, but rather so she might offer the appropriate condolences.

Like the evening before, Poppy had eaten earlier and was in bed while Asher was dressing in his own room, so it was just the four of them putting the finishing touches on their ensembles before going downstairs to the dining room.

"What do you mean he shoved her down a staircase?" Coco asked slowly and carefully, as if she'd certainly misheard, especially given the dispassionate way their aunt had uttered the accusation. As if all she'd said was, *"He wore a brown suit."*

Breezy squinted at Coco. "Have you no understanding of

gravity, my dear? They were standing at the top of the stairs, he pushed and down she tumbled. *Gravity.*"

"That cannot be true, Aunt Breezy," Trudy chided. It wasn't her place to call her aunt a liar, but this was a heinous accusation, and she felt quite confident that the man they'd just spent an afternoon with at the cottage site was not capable of doing anything so diabolical.

"Of course it's true. Everyone knows it's true," Breezy responded, buffing her nails with a lemon wedge.

"But...*why* would he push her down a staircase?" Lucy pressed.

"For the money, naturally," Breezy answered. "Isabella was a Carnegie, you know. Not one of Andrew's children, of course, but a cousin I think. Or a second cousin. Regardless, the girl's father is wealthy enough in his own right and he set her up with a sizeable fortune which became the sole property of Alexander Bostwick the moment the poor girl died."

The Hart sisters exchanged troubled glances, and Lucy sank down onto a velvet ottoman.

"That doesn't make sense. The Bostwicks were already rich," Lucy added. "Why would they need Carnegie money, too?"

"You can never be too rich," Coco replied, nodding sagely, and Trudy wondered if this would be the end of her sister's infatuation with Alexander Bostwick, or if his increased wealth would only serve to make him *more* attractive—the possible murder of his bride notwithstanding.

"The Bostwicks are rich," Breezy said, turning in her chair, obviously thrilled to have their full attention. "But there's been talk of a business investment gone horribly awry. I've heard from a trusted confidante who heard from a very reliable acquaintance that Alexander made a regrettable investment in a northern Michigan copper mine. The thing went bust almost immediately, and cost Bostwick & Sons thousands upon thousands of dollars. I suspect the error might have ruined them had he not married Isabella Carnegie."

"I cannot imagine he'd go to such extreme measures just to rectify a business mistake," Trudy said. *She also happened to know there were far easier and more reliable ways to murder someone, but this hardly seemed the time to mention it.*

"Maybe if it had just been the fall," Breezy responded, annoyed by Trudy's doubt. "But, you see, Isabella was alive when she landed at the bottom of those steps. A little bump on the head, is all. She was fine. It wasn't until later that day, when she and Alexander were alone in her room that she mysteriously died. So, there you have it. It's obvious!"

"What is obvious about that?" Trudy asked.

"It's obvious," Breezy retorted, "that when the fall didn't kill her the way he'd planned, he finished her off some other way once they were alone."

"Oh, good Lord, Aunt Breezy!" Trudy exclaimed, her patience at an end. "That is ludicrous, not to mention malicious. Constance Bostwick is your friend. You have known Alexander his entire life. You can't possibly believe he murdered his wife for money. Shame on you for saying so."

It wasn't that Trudy felt any kind of kinship toward Alexander. She had no reason to defend him in particular, but her aunt was being cruel and unjust, and that she could not tolerate—no matter who it was directed toward, but Breezy reacted as if she'd been slapped, drawing up and lurching back against her chair.

"No, shame on you, Gertrude Hart!" She huffed and puffed and sputtered. "How dare you accuse me of spreading falsities! Lucy asked how his wife died and I'm telling you what I know. Alexander was the only one there when she fell, and he was the only one in the room when she unexpectedly died. How else would you explain it, if you're so smart?"

Trudy took a breath, trying to regain some semblance of calm as her sisters looked on, wide-eyed with uneasy fascination. No one ever spoke to Breezy this way, and perhaps Trudy should not be so harsh, but the woman needed scolding.

"I would explain it," Trudy said slowly, "by pointing out that head injuries are notoriously unpredictable, and that a fall down the stairs could have easily produced a brain injury which caused her skull to fill with blood until the pressure grew so great she finally succumbed."

"Ugh! That is the grisliest thing I have ever heard," Breezy exclaimed, along with more huffing and puffing and sputtering. "I don't know how you can consider yourself a proper young lady when you say such revolting things. A head full of blood, indeed!"

Trudy knew that if a bee was buzzing around her, the best course of action was to simply walk away. To engage with the bee was to invite a sting but she could not let this go.

"So, you're suggesting that it's perfectly acceptable for you to haphazardly accuse someone of *murder* based on the flimsiest of evidence but not for me, as a trained physician, to provide a logical, medical explanation for the cause of death?"

Tiny dots of perspiration had beaded on Breezy's forehead, and her always florid cheeks were nearing a burgundy hue. She looked near to bursting, and Trudy realized she may have actually gone too far.

Dear Mother and Father,

Under my watch, Poppy got lost, Asher learned to cuss, Coco's reputation is sure to be ruined... and I may be responsible for Aunt Breezy's most recent bout of apoplexy. My sincere apologies.

"Even if what you say about the delay in her demise is true," Breezy responded imperiously once she'd regained some of her own composure, "Alexander is still the one who pushed her down the stairs."

"According to whom?"

"I beg your pardon?"

"According to whom? You said he was the only one with her

when she fell so there must not have been any witnesses to the incident. Has he said he pushed her?"

Apparently, Trudy was not *quite* finished.

"Of course not," Breezy retorted. "He said she fell, but someone in that household distinctly heard Isabella say it was all Alexander's fault."

"She said that?" Lucy exclaimed softly.

"Yes." Breezy's chins lifted in vindication.

"Who from the household?" Trudy asked, while silently acknowledging it was an unexpected—and potentially damning—twist.

"Someone," Breezy answered defiantly. "The Bostwicks don't know who. Obviously, it's one of the servants but no one would come forward with details when the police questioned them."

Breezy smoothed her skirts and glowered at them all, as if waiting for the next rebuke, but Trudy had none left. She still didn't believe Alex had anything to do with Isabella Carnegie's death. Not deliberately, anyway... but accidents happened all the time and perhaps he'd pushed her without meaning to. And if he did, how awful for them both.

"Well?" Breezy prompted a moment later. "I'm ready for your apology, Gertrude."

At Trudy's hesitation, Lucy rose from the ottoman and put an arm around her sister's shoulders, squeezing. Rather hard, in fact, indicating in a gentle, sisterly fashion that Trudy must mend this fence before their aunt sent them packing back to Springfield. Even though, in that moment, Trudy would willingly have gone.

"Please understand, Aunt Breezy," Lucy said smoothly. "Our dear Trudy is passionate about injustice, and she'd hate to see poor Mr. Bostwick be blamed for something so nefarious when we don't have firsthand knowledge of the event. I'm sure she didn't mean to offend you. I think we're all just rather shocked by the they entire situation."

"Is that so, Gertrude?"

Lucy squeezed her shoulders again, as if to make an apology pop out of her mouth from the pressure.

"I'm sorry, Aunt Breezy," Trudy murmured. "I only disagreed with you because I believe it's important to give people the benefit of the doubt and not rely on hearsay."

Breezy sniffed. "That's the pot calling the kettle black, don't you think? Perhaps you should give me the benefit of the doubt before casting aspersions toward my good character and accusing me of lying."

"Yes. Of course. I'm sorry," Trudy muttered again although they all knew she was not, in fact, sorry.

"This is all just silly," Coco said, abruptly. She pranced across the room and plucked a fresh lemon wedge from the bowl in front of their aunt. "Of course he didn't do it. Alexander Bostwick is clever and funny and far too handsome to be a murderer. In fact, I may as well tell you now, I love him. Now that he's without a wife, I intend to marry him."

The tension in the room, which had mere seconds before begun to ease, doubled at Coco's flippant declaration.

"I assume you are joking and it's not funny," Breezy responded heatedly. "There are dozens of fine young men here, so I expect you to set your cap for one of them and stay far away from the likes of Alexander Bostwick."

Coco gave a saucy shake of her blonde head. "I don't want to set my cap for someone else, Aunt Breezy. I don't need to. Mother said she knew from the very first moment she saw Father that he was meant to be her husband and that's what happened to me yesterday. The first moment I met Alexander Bostwick, I just knew. He's going to be my husband."

She brought the lemon wedge to her mouth and bit into the flesh, but it was Breezy's expression that puckered, and Trudy wondered how on God's green earth they would survive the summer together intact.

"And I'm telling you to choose someone else," Breezy snapped. "The Bostwick family is riddled with scandals and their business is teetering on the brink of financial disaster. Your mother didn't insist I bring you girls all the way to Trillium Bay to find you husbands just so you could end up with the likes of him."

Breezy's eyes went wide at her own words, and her lips smacked shut as she abruptly turned her back. The ensuing pause was long and heavy as Trudy, Lucy, and Coco exchanged bewildered glances.

"What... did you just say?" Lucy asked, and Trudy took a turn sinking down onto the velvet ottoman.

Breezy returned to her manicure. "I beg your pardon?" Her voice squeaked with innocence, and she refused to look their way.

"What did you just say about our mother?" Lucy asked again.

Another moment passed as Breezy buffed at her nails so aggressively they'd be shiny as mirrors by the time she was finished.

"Aunt Breezy?" Lucy said with more determination.

"Oh, very well!" She flounced back around to face them squarely. "I suppose it's not the worst thing if you know. I was sworn to secrecy by your mother, but since Gertrude has already accused me of being a liar, I suppose it's best to tell the truth." She folded her hands in her lap as if she were about to sing a hymn. "Your mother asked me to bring you girls to the Imperial Hotel for the summer so you might each secure a proposal."

"A proposal?" Trudy gasped. "Of marriage?"

"Naturally, a proposal of marriage," Breezy said. "Any other kind of proposal would be inappropriate. Although I admit I don't hold out much hope for you, Gertrude, what with your age and your height and your freakish fascination with grotesque illnesses."

Two minutes ago, Trudy couldn't fathom how anyone could commit murder. Now she understood.

"Mother asked you to bring us here? To find... husbands?" Lucy asked, as if she still could not believe her ears.

"Yes. I just said so."

"But why here?" Lucy persisted. "And why now?"

"I should think that would be rather obvious. Your mother wants what's best for you and she knows you'll never find suitable husbands in that country hollow you live in, quaint though it may be. She wants you to have a better life than she's had."

"Our mother loves her life," Trudy responded. "She's not concerned with wealth and status."

"Not for herself, perhaps, but she doesn't want to deny you girls a chance to better yourselves."

"We're already bettering ourselves," Trudy exclaimed, losing her patience. Again. "I have a medical degree and Lucy's going to college in the autumn to study astronomy!"

But her point was lost on their aunt as Coco giggled and did a clumsy pirouette in the center of the room. "This is fantastic!" she exclaimed gleefully. "I'm going to write to Mother straight away and tell her I've already found myself the most perfect husband."

"You will do no such thing," Trudy argued. "There has obviously been some kind of misunderstanding. And besides, you are only seventeen. Too young for marriage."

"But not too young for courtship," Coco replied. "Alexander can woo me all summer, and then we'll get married in the winter, when I turn eighteen."

"I appreciate your vigor, girl, but I'm telling you, Alexander Bostwick is not a suitable match," Breezy reminded her. "I will find you someone better. I will find each of you someone with wealth and status who will make a fine husband. Yes, even you, Gertrude," Breezy added at her stunned expression. "I adore a challenge and if I can find someone willing to marry *you*, well, that would be a real feather in my cap. Now, let's go down for dinner. I'm famished."

six

"I will not have my daughter traipsing about the halls of this establishment like some orphaned guttersnipe," Alex's mother stated haughtily from a satin settee in her suite.

The two of them had been engaged in this dispute for a full ten minutes, but Alex knew he'd lose. No one ever won in an argument with Constance Bostwick, but he wasn't yet willing to raise the white flag of surrender.

"Mother," he responded with strained patience. "The theatre is down two flights of stairs and around a single corner. Daisy would hardly be traipsing about, not to mention the fact that she knows virtually every person in this hotel, guests and staff alike. I very much doubt she'd be accosted or mistaken for a beggar and thrown out onto the street."

"Is it really such an enormous imposition to escort your sister to see the trance lecturer perform? What else did you plan to do with your evening?"

His mother could make the most innocent utterance drip with disdain, but this query felt particularly unfair. She knew it was raining. She knew his choices were limited to lounging in the cigar room listening to old men brag of their youthful exploits or lingering in the lobby waiting for someone interested in a game of cards, just as she surely knew his other option was to loll away the evening in his room pondering all the things he'd rather not ponder. Taking Daisy to watch Ambrose Gibson was the only real alternative, and well his mother knew it.

But, oh, how he hated giving in to her perpetual state of annoyance. After all, he wasn't singularly to blame for the scandals currently swirling around their family. It wasn't Alex's fault his libido-driven father had suffered a heart attack while in bed with an opera singer. *(Bostwick family scandal number one.)* Nor was Alex to blame for that salacious bit of information finding its way into the newspapers. In fact, Alex had gone above and beyond trying to protect the Bostwick name by artfully luring the press away from printing that negative tidbit by tantalizing them with a romantic, whirlwind engagement to Isabella Carnegie.

It had worked, for a spell, but then Izzy died, *(thus scandal number two)* and the story of the opera singer went public along with an assortment of malicious accusations insinuating Alex had deliberately pushed her down the stairs. So, if anyone had a right to be cranky tonight, it was him. However, no one could out-crank Constance Bostwick. It was time he waved the white flag.

"Very well, Mother. I'll escort Daisy to the performance, although I'm not sure why Ellis can't do it."

"Ellis and Finn have already gone downstairs, and before you even ask, I didn't bother asking your brother because he's preoccupied with that artist of his."

"That artist of his? You mean… his wife?"

His mother's face twitched as if she'd smelled something foul. "Call her what you will but you'll never convince me that marriage is legitimate. None of us were even invited to their alleged wedding."

"Come now, Mother. You know the only reason they didn't host a grand affair was because they didn't want to detract from mine."

"Yes and look how well that turned out."

His jaw clenched tightly. He wasn't going to argue with her about this anymore.

"Where is Daisy?" he asked instead.

"She's in her room, no doubt giggling over nonsense with that lady's maid we brought along. I really should let the girl go, but she does have a deft touch with styling my hair." His mother leaned forward to admire her reflection in a nearby mirror.

"If you like the way she style's your hair then why let her go?"

"I find her entirely too lively," his mother responded dismissively. "I can't imagine what possessed Wadsworth to hire such a young and pretty maid. She came highly recommended from the agency but she's simply too vivacious for my tastes."

Alex was far removed from the hiring and firing of his parents' household staff and although he had an inkling of why their butler may have hired a young and pretty maid—and why that might create a host of problems—it seemed rather unfair to let one go for such superficial reasons. Leave it to his mother to fault someone for being *too joyful*.

"Perhaps she could keep a bag over her head," he muttered sarcastically as he turned toward Daisy's door.

"Perhaps you could keep a sock in your mouth," his mother quipped in response.

He nearly laughed but refused to give her the satisfaction as he rapped on Daisy's door.

"Come in," his sister called out.

He stepped inside the room, shutting the door firmly behind him, and discovered Daisy placing a delicate necklace around the throat of the aforementioned maid. Both girls were dressed for an evening out. In fact, if he hadn't recognized Lorna from the Bostwick household staff, he might have thought her another guest of the hotel, and he realized then that his mother was right, for once. This maid was young and pretty.

He hadn't paid much attention to her before and had likely only crossed paths with her a few times, but in a fine dress and her hair arranged just so, he could see how she might cause trouble, even if unwittingly. With her blonde hair and pale blue eyes, her coloring reminded him of Isabella, a fact he found distressing in a variety of ways.

"What... have we here?" he asked.

"Lorna's coming with us," Daisy answered brightly. "She's heard so much about Ambrose Gibson, I thought it would be a shame for her to miss this evening's show."

Lorna glanced at him then looked away, a blush stealing over her cheeks.

"Unless you think it isn't proper," Lorna said demurely. "I don't want to be a bother."

"Of course you're not a bother," Daisy answered though the maid was obviously speaking to him. "You must come with us. I won't hear another word about it. But let's go out this door," Daisy added hastily, pulling the girl into the hallway rather than walking though the sitting area of the suite. Alex realized then that his mother was in no way privy to Daisy's plan.

Lorna looked back at him, uncertainty etched across her features, but his sister gave another hearty tug on her arm.

"Come along or we'll be late," Daisy said. "I don't want to miss anything."

And down the stairs they went to the Imperial Hotel theater.

In the reception area just outside the doors, waiters in blue jackets served champagne and lemonade from silver trays while finely clad guests gathered in predictable groups; the Goodmans with the Armors and the Marshalls, the Adlers with the Renfroes and the Mooreheads, the Baldwins with the Hobbs. Alex spotted Breezy VonMeisterburger with the Palmers and the Pullmans and promptly steered Daisy and Lorna in the opposite direction toward the entrance of the theater.

Inside was a vast sea of crimson velvet seats, some already occupied but most still empty. The walls of the theater were adorned with gold-flecked paper that seemed to flicker along with the gasoliers, and off to one side of the large stage, a woman in a flowing white dress plucked the strings of a harp with an appropriately haunting melody. Her presence, along with the ethereal music, created a distinctly celestial atmosphere within the room.

From somewhere hidden, a gong sounded, and guests from the reception area began rapidly streaming in to secure their seats. A gentleman Alex didn't recognize all but elbowed his way around them in his apparent haste, nearly knocking poor Lorna to the floor. Alex caught her arm and offered a reassuring smile.

She smiled back weakly but could hardly meet his gaze, and no wonder. She was obviously nervous. She knew she didn't belong here. It was a discomfort he could now relate to, that sense of being surrounded by those who thrived on feeling superior. People determined to diminish another's worth, and the injustice of it rankled him—even though, or perhaps because—he was one of them. He'd been born into privilege and enjoyed every advantage it offered.

Meanwhile, this maid undoubtedly worked as hard—or harder—than virtually anyone in this room. Was she less deserving of a night of entertainment because of her circumstances? He didn't think so, but knew few others would agree. His mother certainly wouldn't, and if she learned of this excursion, the girl would be tossed into the cargo hold of the next ship back to Chicago.

That should have occurred to him when they were still upstairs. Daisy's invitation was born of her own innate generosity, an endearing quality, but one with the potential to create unexpected repercussions. Her kind gesture might very well get the poor girl sacked. Perhaps it was not too late to send her back upstairs.

"There you are!" Daisy exclaimed as she spotted the Hart sisters standing at the end of an aisle.

Now... it was too late.

Daisy moved toward the sisters quickly with Lorna and Alex trailing behind. As they approached, Lucy waved, Trudy offered a polite nod, and Coco's eyes roved over Alex in much the same way one might inspect a horse for stud services. He nearly thought she was going to check his flanks and teeth. Egad, Ellis would need to improve his game to win the girl's affection.

"Good evening, Miss Hart. Miss Hart. Dr. Hart." He nodded at each of them in turn but saved his smile for Trudy.

"Mr. Bostwick," they responded in unison.

"This is Lorna Albright," Daisy added.

Alex tamped down the urge to reveal the girl was a Bostwick maid, for her own sake, but held his tongue. This was Daisy's misadventure. In fact, he suddenly realized with no small amount of relief, he wasn't actually obligated to stay for the show. His mother had asked him to escort his sister to the theater and he'd done that. His task was complete.

"I've delivered you safely," he whispered to Daisy a moment later as the girls moved toward some empty seats very near the front of the stage. "Come find me in the lobby when it's over and I'll take you back upstairs."

"You're not staying?" she whispered back with dismay, reaching out to clasp his forearm. "I wish you would. I think it might be good for you."

"Good for me? Why?"

She gazed up at him earnestly. "You know why. Perhaps you'll receive a message. Or an explanation."

"Daisy—" He didn't want either of those and would have told her so if Dr. Hart had not inadvertently interrupted.

"Ladies, it seems there are not enough seats up front to accommodate us all, but not to worry. I'd rather sit farther back anyway," she said.

"But you can't sit by yourself," Lucy responded.

"I'll join you in the back," Alex heard himself say, and was as surprised by his words as Trudy appeared to be. Why had he just made such a foolish offer? He was halfway out the door but just committed to staying for the entire show. Perhaps it was Daisy's grip on his arm, or his own sense of chivalry, but nonetheless, he'd said what he'd said.

Trudy regarded him carefully before responding.

"Thank you, Mr. Bostwick."

"I can move back, too," Coco added quickly, but she was already seated, and Alex was grateful when her sister waved her off.

"Keep your seat, Coco," Trudy quipped. "The back is where the dull people sit."

Alex chuckled, his mood lifting as they turned and made their way up the aisle. The place was nearly full now, and ushers were moving along the row of gasoliers, dimming their brightness.

"I'm afraid we may end up quite far back," he said, guiding her by the elbow.

"Good. That's where I wanted to be anyway," she answered.

They found two seats, in the very last row, in the farthest corner of the room, and Trudy's satisfied amusement showed in her expression as she sat down.

"We're so far from the front, we're nearly outside," she said.

"Just through that exit," he answered, pointing to a service door nearly covered by a curtain.

For some reason, knowing he could dash through it and be free from this crush of people and whatever might happen on that stage made the thudding of his heart a little less erratic. Truthfully, the idea of sitting in a darkened theater with a spiritualist who could potentially read his mind left Alex clammy and flooded with dread, but sitting next to Trudy offered a modicum of comfort.

"I must confess I'm a bit surprised to see you here at all, Dr. Hart," he said once they were seated. He spoke quietly although the din of the theater was loud enough to conceal any words they might exchange. "I didn't think the occult held any interest for you."

"It interests me, but perhaps not in the conventional manner."

"In what manner, then?"

He was genuinely interested in her answer. She was an educated woman of science, after all, and seemed a sensible sort not easily influenced by societal trends or superstition. He'd always considered himself to be a sensible sort, too, but given recent events, he'd begun to question the reliability of his own judgment.

"Studying medicine has taught me to rely upon established empirical facts," she said. "But it's also shown me there are a great many things occurring all around us that we have yet to comprehend. Just because something may be intangible to our senses, or beyond our current comprehension, that doesn't negate the possibility of its existence."

"Please, do continue," he prompted as she paused.

She turned toward him slightly. "Well, take germ theory, for example. A generation ago, we had little understanding of microbes because they cannot be seen without a microscope, but now we know they're everywhere. We understand some of the ways they impact our lives but certainly ten years from now, we'll know so much more."

"That does make sense," he said with a contemplative nod. "But how does that relate to the occult? Do you suspect one day we'll be able to see spirits using some sort of spectral lens?" He was partially teasing, and yet...

She chuckled at his question. "I think that's unlikely, but my education has taught me to keep an open mind and not let old beliefs hinder potential new discoveries."

"Old beliefs?"

"The medical community is often slow to accept new information, especially if it flies in the face of universally accepted treatments. It's as if new ideas somehow threaten the status quo." She gave a tiny shake of her head before continuing. "It's 1889, and we're making scientific breakthroughs every day, yet there are still physicians who refuse to sanitize their hands before laying them on patients because they consider germ theory to be a passing fad. It's ridiculous. My father always says the only certainty in life is that we will never know all there is to know, and that personal arrogance should never prevent us from seeking out new information. So, I suppose that's why I'm here. I cannot let my current opinions about the occult prevent me from learning something new—even when it's about something as silly as ghosts trying to communicate with the living." She smiled shyly, in spite of her confident words, and his already high opinion of her intelligence rose further.

"What a wise perspective, Dr. Hart. I suppose it is rather arrogant to believe knowledge is finite and unchanging."

"Precisely, Mr. Bostwick. So, although I may be a skeptic, I try to engage an open mind."

She leaned toward him, and he caught the twinkle in her eye as she added quietly, "On the other hand, I also want to know what gibberish my sister hears from Mr. Gibson tonight so I might be prepared with a logical, scientific argument when she tries to convince me of its validity."

The conspiratorial nature of her comment made him laugh out loud, and he was suddenly glad he'd decided to stay.

"In truth, Mr. Bostwick," she continued when their laughter subsided, "my parents raised us to question everything and to decide for ourselves what we believe. As for the supernatural, I honestly don't know what happens after we depart this earth. I've witnessed inexplicable things that seem divinely orchestrated, and I do hope there's some place more enlightened waiting for us after we perish, but as of yet, there's nothing in science to suggest that death isn't final."

As soon as the words left her mouth, an expression of uncertainty passed over her face as if she'd realized how that must sound to a recently widowed husband.

"Oh, my goodness. Please forgive me. I'm speaking out of turn and being terribly insensitive."

But she had not offended him. "On the contrary, Dr. Hart. I find your comments thought-provoking and intriguing. I confess I find myself rather consumed by similar questions these days about this life and whatever happens next." *And whether or not communication continues...*

Her uncertainty shifted to sympathy. "Of course you are, Mr. Bostwick. That's entirely understandable. Please know I'm so very sorry for your loss. I cannot imagine how difficult these past few months have been for you."

Alex wasn't sure if she was referring exclusively to the death of his wife, or if she'd heard the rumors, too, but either way, her sincerity tugged at his composure. Kindness seemed in short supply these days, and he appreciated her compassion.

"Thank you, Dr. Hart. I am... managing." *He wasn't, really, but it was the polite answer.*

"Is that why you're here this evening?" she asked quietly. "To get answers to some of those questions?"

He paused.

And pondered.

She'd been honest and frank with him. Perhaps he owed her the same, but this was not the place to share his story. It was simply too long and complicated, and if he told her all of it, she'd think him mad.

"I'm afraid the answers to my questions might actually make me feel worse," he said, trying to sound flippant but instead, he sounded melancholy as he added, "But if there's peace to be found, I would relish some of that."

She nodded solemnly. "Then I hope tonight you receive whatever will serve you best."

"Thank you, Dr. Hart." He stared at her for a moment, perhaps longer than was proper, but she held his gaze. From any other woman that might have seemed brazen, but Trudy Hart lacked artifice. She wasn't flirting with him. She was just being earnest. Still... his heart thumped a little faster.

Then half a second later it nearly leapt from his chest as Hugo Plank's voice rang out like a carnival barker from the center of the stage. Alex had been so engrossed in conversation with Dr. Hart he hadn't even notice the man arriving.

"Good evening, one and all! Welcome to the Imperial Hotel theater!" Hugo nearly shouted. "It's my great pleasure to formally invite you on a voyage beyond the realm of our understanding, to a place of mysticism and magic, where messages from our dearly departed long to be heard." He gestured outward as if reaching for something enticing yet elusive, his voice filling the room. "Take a journey into the intangible as the veil is lifted to reveal the unknown. The unseen. The unheard. And the inexplicable."

Alex smiled as Trudy leaned close again and whispered, "Mr. Plank has missed his calling. He's quite the showman."

"Indeed. I wonder if this trance lecturer can equal his flair."

"Or his fervor." They chuckled and the woman next to Trudy shushed them.

"And now, ladies and gentlemen," Hugo said, "It is my great honor to introduce to you a man who has astonished European royalty, astounded the British aristocracy, and amazed American audiences all across our great nation. I give you gifted, the mesmerizing, the ahhhhh-mazing Mr. Ambrose Gibson."

The harp music swelled, and yet despite Hugo's overly zealous introduction, the applause was more polite than enthusiastic as Mr. Gibson ambled onto the stage. Alex felt both a twinge of disappointment and a surge of relief. He'd expected someone more...imposing. More mystical. More... dangerous, but Ambrose Gibson was slight of build and dressed in a tuxedo several seasons out of fashion. A long white scarf draped around his neck and jet-black hair falling well past his shoulders lent the only bit of eccentricity to his otherwise average appearance.

"Good evening, ladies, gentlemen, spirits, and guides," he said as the applause in the theater waned. He had an accent Alex couldn't place, and although he spoke quietly, the audience had hushed to hear him. "I'm pleased and grateful to be here among you this evening. I am Ambrose Gibson, a simple man, but one blessed with a miraculous and cherished gift. God has given me the ability to commune with your beloved dear ones who have passed over to the other side."

The harpist continued playing an enchanted melody as Mr. Gibson continued. "Tonight, we seek messages of love and lightness, so fear not, fellow travelers. Nothing that comes forth this evening can harm you. I am here to serve as your guide. You may choose to trust in me, to celebrate my gifts, or you may choose to doubt my words, my intentions, my abilities. The decision is entirely yours. And now, let us begin with an experiment."

The harpist plucked at the strings, shifting to a tune that seemed almost discordant, and Alex felt the back of his neck prickle with apprehension.

"I need approximately ten volunteers from the audience," Mr. Gibson said, "but I will let the spirits in the room decide who is to join me on the stage. Willing participants only so those who'd like to assist me, please stand while I put on this blindfold."

He removed the scarf from his neck and tied it over his eyes as a rumble of excitement circulated around the theater. Alex watched as some guests rose instantaneously and others stood more slowly, awkwardly, smiling at those around them who'd kept their seats.

"It's tempting to participate, if only to prove him a charlatan," Trudy whispered, "But I prefer the view from here."

"As do I," Alex replied as his hands grew clammy. His nerves were taut and there was simply no reason for it. He was letting his imagination get the better of him. Perhaps he should've had a dram of whiskey before the event, like some high-strung dowager.

Damnation! When had he become such a coward?

Alex cleared his throat and sat up straighter, silently reminding himself that nothing here could harm him. *Unless Izzy did somehow send a message...*

More than half the audience was now on their feet, but as Mr. Gibson—allegedly guided by benevolent phantoms—listed his requirements, one by one, they sat back down.

Remain standing if your mother's name begins with the letter M.

Remain standing if you've ever suffered the loss of a beloved pet.

Remain standing if your shoes are currently pinching your feet.

Alex looked askance as he heard Trudy softly snort at that last question, a bemused smile on her face.

"Are you already taking issue with his talents?" Alex whispered, his tone light-hearted even though his concerns were not.

"Not at all," she answered, although her expression said otherwise. "Although a skeptic might suggest no spirit guides are necessary when a simple process of elimination is all this is."

Alex nodded. "But the blindfold. How will he know when there are only ten people are left standing?"

"I suspect the harpist may have something to do with that."

A chuckle overtook him, and his tension eased. She was right, of course. Thus far, there was nothing otherworldly about this show, and an especially sharp note from the musician when ten participants remained on their feet proved Dr. Hart's theory correct. Nonetheless, a murmur of approval swept over the crowd as Ambrose yanked the blindfold from his eyes and exclaimed, "The spirits have made their choices!"

Dr. Hart giggled at the theatrics, and he nearly laughed alongside her—until he spotted Lorna walking toward the stage.

"Oh, good heavens," he muttered.

"What is it?"

"Lorna," he replied. The maid was looking around with uncertainty, a pained, awkward expression on her face.

"Daisy's friend?" Dr. Hart asked.

"Daisy's maid," he answered quietly.

"Lorna is her maid?" Trudy craned her neck to get a better view. "She doesn't look very happy to be participating."

"Nor should she," he said tersely. "I suspect, much like Poppy's cat, this girl has been dragged along on an excursion she didn't ask for. And if this fortune teller is worth an ounce of salt, he'll be on to her in no time."

This was most unfortunate. Alex *should* have sent the girl back to her room when he'd had the chance, but now the die was cast. She was on the stage and in front of an audience of his peers who would love nothing more than to learn her secrets, not to mention secrets about his family and their private struggles. His neck began to prickle again, in earnest this time. Suddenly a message from Isabella was the least of his concerns.

"Dear friends," Ambrose called out to the audience once the volunteers were seated in a row on stage. "Rather than calling forth your loved ones on my own, I will endeavor to send these intrepid voyagers into another realm." He gestured to the volunteers who were now glancing at one another with uncertainty. "Once they've reached a transcendental state, they will serve as conduits for messages from the great beyond."

Alex crossed his arms as Ambrose turned his back to the audience and spoke quietly to the wide-eyed participants. There were seven women and four men with Lorna surely being the youngest.

Ah, Lorna. What a foolish girl she was for having volunteered. And what a foolish sister Daisy was for inviting her in the first place. And... what a foolish man Alex was for allowing it. This entire scenario was avoidable. If he'd had the stamina to refuse his mother, he'd be in his room right now, minding his own business, and his sister and her maid would be in theirs.

But... perhaps he was worrying over nothing. Perhaps it would all be fine. Then he chuckled again at his frail optimism even though nothing about this was comical.

Moments passed. Ambrose Gibson continued to murmur, pacing back and forth in front of the *intrepid voyagers*, and the audience remained hushed, as one by one, the participants slumped in their chairs. First their face would go slack, they'd slowly blink, and then their shoulders and chin would droop until, finally, they appeared to be deep in sleep.

Lorna was the last to fall.

∽

To the uninformed this surely looked miraculous and mystical, but Trudy was familiar with the tenants of hypnosis. Ambrose Gibson was a skilled practitioner of mesmerism to be sure, but that didn't mean he could read minds or consult with the deceased. This was a clever parlor trick and nothing more.

Beside her, Alexander Bostwick fidgeted, and she could not tell if it was from nervousness or boredom. Regardless, she suspected his disquiet had little to do with what was happening on the stage and was instead symptomatic of what was going on inside his mind. He was likely thinking of his wife, and Trudy flushed with regret.

Had she really suggested to the man his dearly departed bride was nothing more than worm food? Had she left every iota of her bedside manner back at her father's clinic? She shook her head in the darkened theater and wondered how to apologize to him again without sounding even more insensitive.

He'd been gracious, though, just as he'd been a few days ago at the cottage site, and during every brief encounter they'd had since. The truth was, Mr. Bostwick was a far kinder man than she'd given him credit for on that first day at the hotel. She'd boasted tonight of having an open mind, and yet she'd carried a grudge for all these years simply because of something he'd said to her when they were children.

Granted, what he'd said had been cruel and had rung in her ears for years afterward, but he'd been ten years old at the time, and ten-year-old boys (or boys in general) were not known for their sensitivity. If she'd learned anything at all from Asher, it was that!

"Rejoice. Their journey is complete," Ambrose said as Lorna finally succumbed to the slumber of hypnosis. Then, speaking to the participants, he said softly, "My dear friends, I'd like you all to sit up straight and open your eyes."

They promptly responded, their collective gazes locked on him, sending a chill through Trudy. She understood how the process of hypnosis worked, but Ambrose's influence was unnerving. Beside her, Alex gripped the armrests, his knee bouncing slightly, and Trudy wished they were better acquainted so she might lay a calming hand over his arm. But they weren't, and so she didn't.

"Are you well?" she whispered instead.

"I'm fine," he answered without looking her way.

"I've guided you into another realm," Ambrose continued from the stage, his voice soothing in the quiet theater. "A place where our loved ones linger in peace and harmony. With your consent, they'll share their messages through you. If you have a message to deliver, please raise your right hand."

The audience buzzed with excitement as each participant slowly lifted a hand. Another chill tingled through Trudy's limbs. Again, she understood how hypnosis influenced behavior, but the man was a convincing entertainer!

"Very good," Ambrose said. "Lower your hands. When I touch your shoulder, please stand and I will guide you."

A plump woman in a burgundy dress was the first to rise.

"What is your name, my dear?" Ambrose asked.

"Mrs. Robert Turnham."

"Who has given you a message?"

"My brother-in-law, Edgar. For his wife."

A tiny gasp came from the audience, no doubt from Edgar's wife.

"What does Edgar want to say to his wife?" Ambrose prompted.

Her voice lowered as she said, "Bitsy, honey, I love you. I don't want you to be alone. Move in with Cousin Lilly. Sell the house. Bobbie will give you a good price for it."

Another gasp, followed by murmurs of amazement, but Trudy smiled. Whether cognitively aware of it or not, Mrs. Robert "Bobbie" Turnham was angling to scoop her sister's house right out from under her, and all with dear, old, dead Edgar's blessing.

But as other *voyagers* stood and delivered equally convenient messages, Trudy sensed those around her being thoroughly seduced by Ambrose's skillful manipulation. He knew how to cleverly lead the speaker with vague questions, then steer them with more pointed suggestions, and even redirect a *message* if it took an irrelevant turn. But he wasn't a psychic, in Trudy's opinion. He was an adept magician disarming these people with hypnotism.

Then Lorna's turn came, and Alex went from fidgety to motionless.

"What is your name, my dear?" Ambrose asked.

"Lorna Albright."

"And what message have you been asked to deliver?"

She frowned and twisted the fabric of her skirt in clenched fists. "I'm not... sure."

"You're not sure?" Ambrose asked.

Lorna shook her head, and Alex shifted uneasily in his seat.

"Who is the message from? Can you name them?" Ambrose prodded.

Lorna hesitated again. "No. I can't tell."

A ripple of curiosity circled the room, and Trudy heard Alex exhale slowly.

"Take my hands, dear child," Ambrose said. "Allow me to look into your eyes and sense what message you've been asked to deliver. I can help you." He clasped her hands and held her gaze for what seemed an eternity. The tension in the room compounded with every second as Lorna's apparent discomfort increased.

Even Trudy set aside her skepticism for the moment and leaned forward. Whatever the meaning of this, she was captivated, but if she discerned that Ambrose Gibson was manipulating a young girl for the sake of showmanship and this audience's entertainment, she'd leave no stone unturned to expose him as a fraud.

Sixty seconds seemed like sixty minutes, and then Lorna abruptly pulled her hands free and jerked backwards as if shoved.

"I can't say it!" Lorna said stridently. "It's too cruel."

The audience gasped as one, and Trudy sat back in her seat, glancing discreetly at Alex. He reached into his jacket pocket, pulled out a handkerchief, and dabbed at his forehead with an unsteady hand, then he stared down at the fabric in his fingers. With a quietly muttered curse, he rose from his seat and strode out of the theater through the nearby service door.

Trudy watched his departure, while on the stage, Ambrose had placed a hand on Lorna's forehead.

"No woebegone spirits are welcome here. I cast you out. Leave this young woman and never return." More murmurs rippled through the crowd as he continued. "Miss Albright, you'll remember none of this. You'll feel refreshed and alert when I count back from three, two, one..." Then he snapped his fingers, and her body twitched. She blinked rapidly, shaking her head and looking around, her previously pained expression shifting instantly to relaxed but bewildered. She smiled shyly.

"Are we starting now?" she asked, and it seemed everyone in the audience began to speak at once.

Trudy was flummoxed. Should she check on the girl? Probably, but her greater concern was Alex, so after the briefest hesitation, she rose to her feet and followed him. Exiting through the same door and looking in both directions, she caught a glimpse of his retreating form at the end of a long corridor leading toward the back of the hotel.

"Mr. Bostwick," she called out, but his pace only increased. She lost sight of him as he rounded a corner, and she heard another door open and shut. Walking as briskly as her skirts would allow, she found herself a moment later stepping outside and into a misty rain. A nearby lamppost illuminated the area, casting gloomy shadows, and she spotted him not far from it, leaning against the building.

"Mr. Bostwick?" she said again.

"Go back inside, Dr. Hart. It's raining," he said quietly.

"I might offer you the same advice," she said, letting the door shut behind her.

"I just needed some air."

"And so you've found some."

He frowned at her for a moment, brows furrowed. "You must think me quite unstable."

"On the contrary. I think it was courageous of you to sit through a show that obviously made you uncomfortable."

"Obvious, was it?"

There was her excellent bedside manner again. What was wrong with her?

"Not at all," she lied. "Until the very end, and I daresay the entire audience was distressed by that demonstration. I know I was."

He leaned his head back against the wood, closing his eyes. "Would you please go back inside? I can't be responsible for you falling ill from standing outside in inclement weather."

She held her hand out, palm up. "Hardly inclement, sir. This isn't enough moisture to water a fern. And besides, I'm made of sturdy stuff."

"So, it would seem," he said on a sigh.

He appeared rather despondent, and she was at a loss. She didn't want to intrude upon his solitude, but it seemed perhaps he could use a friend. She stepped closer and took a place beside him, leaning against the rain-dampened wooden siding. A slight awning overhead protected them from some of the rain, but not all of it.

"How long do you plan to stay out here," she asked casually.

"I haven't really formulated a plan, as of yet. My primary purpose was merely to escape the theater."

She nodded, wiping raindrops from her cheek. "In that case, well done. You did indeed escape the theater."

She was rewarded with a rueful chuckle. "Rather out of the frying pan, into the fire, wouldn't you say?" he asked.

"Something akin to that. More like out of a leaky boat and into the lake."

They lingered a moment in silence, Trudy wondering just how she might convince him to go back inside. She didn't relish the idea of her gown getting wet, but neither did she relish the idea of leaving him out here alone when he was in some sort of distress. She was a physician, after all. It was her obligation to help him heal from whatever ailed him.

"Are you familiar with hypnotism, Mr. Bostwick?"

"Not particularly."

"It's when a practitioner, such as Mr. Gibson, coaxes people into a kind of half-sleep. A state of lucid dreaming, if you will, and in that state, people become very susceptible to the power of suggestion."

"And?"

"And it's my hypothesis that no one on that stage actually communed with otherworldly spirits but were instead delivering messages they *imagined* their loved ones would want to share, if they could."

"Are you saying every person on that stage conspired to deceive us?"

"No, not the participants. Only Mr. Gibson. Under his spell of hypnosis, they were freed from inhibition and spoke without fear of judgment or reprisal. With his subtle coaxing, they were compelled to reveal thoughts and longings they may have otherwise kept buried. Thoughts they may not have even realized they had."

"Hm," he said, seeming neither relieved nor impressed by her observation.

"And what do you suppose happened with Lorna?" he asked.

"I cannot say for certain, but I suspect whatever thoughts or perhaps even memories she was experiencing distressed her. Our mind will go to great lengths to protect us, so it's possible that something in her past or her worry at being discovered as a lady's maid prevented her from sharing."

He nodded slowly. "I suppose that's a possibility."

She'd thought to ease his tension with her explanation, but he remained unmoved. Meanwhile, her dress was getting damper by the minute, she had no hat and so her hair was certainly getting soggy, and the wind had picked up causing her a chill. Perhaps she could—and probably should—leave him outside to work through his own musings. Her company did not seem to be improving his mood. She was about to say as much when he spoke again.

"I don't believe in ghosts, Dr. Hart," he said, his tone definitive, almost defiant.

"Don't you?"

"No. I don't believe in spirits or phantoms or things that go bump in the night. I don't believe in soothsayers or mentalists or anyone who claims to have an ability to speak with the dead. None of it."

"I see."

"Except…" he tilted his head forward and looked down at the ground.

"Except… what?"

"Except that my wife is haunting me."

Her heart flooded with sympathy, and she forgot her wet hair and soggy dress. "Oh, Mr. Bostwick. It's entirely understandable that you feel that way. When we lose someone dear to us, grief plays tricks. Our longings and our memories can be so powerful we're convinced our dearly departed linger nearby. There's nothing wrong with that. In time, you'll be able to say goodbye and let her go."

He shook his head slowly, his sigh heavy.

"No, you don't understand." He pulled the handkerchief from his pocket again, just as he'd done a few moments ago in the theater.

"Do you see this?" he asked.

"Your handkerchief?"

"Isabella's handkerchief. It belonged to her."

Now they were getting somewhere. "You carry a token to remember her by. I think that's lovely and not at all unusual."

"It was in my pocket," he said, as if she still misunderstood.

"Yes, I saw you take it out in the theater."

"But I didn't put it there."

It almost seemed as if he wanted to argue, and she thought it best to just go along. But she was confused. "What do you mean you didn't put it there?"

"I mean exactly that. When I donned this jacket earlier in the evening, my pockets were empty. I know because I've taken to checking. Then I put my own handkerchief inside this one. It's still there. But so was hers."

"I see. Perhaps they were folded together by a careless laundress. Is that possible?"

He pressed his lips together for a moment, as if considering her words—and his— very carefully.

"It would be possible, I suppose, if this were an isolated incident, but it isn't. Dr. Hart, may I share something with you in the strictest confidence? Something you vow not to share with anyone else?"

"Of course, Mr. Bostwick. You can be sure of my discretion. Anything you say will remain entirely between us."

He stared down at her, as if evaluating her trustworthiness. She was on the verge of reminding him she was a physician whose patients trusted her with the most sensitive and intimate information, but at last he spoke.

"Ever since my wife's death, her belongings have been appearing in strange and peculiar places for me to find."

She paused, having expected him to reveal something a bit more... spooky.

"That is peculiar, I suppose, but perhaps someone is simply moving her items to places they think they belong."

"That's what I thought at first," he said. "The morning of her funeral, I found her hair comb under my pillow. I could not imagine how it got there since she'd never dressed in my room, but I pushed my curiosity aside and forgot about it. But then a few days later, I discovered one of her stockings between the pages of a book I'd been reading. Certainly not a logical place for it. And in the months since, there have been dozens of such occurrences. I've found her jewelry among my cufflinks, her brooch pinned inside my overcoat, her glove in the pocket of my trousers, even a letter I'd once written to her stuffed into the toe of one of my riding boots. And tonight, her handkerchief appeared in my jacket pocket."

Odd, indeed, but hardly indicative of anything supernatural.

"I... I don't know what to make of that," she said.

"Nor do I. I'd thought leaving Chicago and coming here, to a place she'd never been, might put an end to these incidents, but they've continued. That's why I suspect she's haunting me—even though I don't believe in such nonsense. And now you must certainly think me unstable. God knows I do."

She wanted to comfort and reassure him but what he said was bizarre and unsettling. She didn't know what to make of it.

"I don't think you're unstable, Mr. Bostwick, but..."

"Perhaps you could call me Alex."

"I beg your pardon?"

"I've just revealed to you my rather dark and shameful secret so perhaps you could call me Alex? I think we've moved beyond formalities."

"Oh, of course. Alex. Then you may call me Trudy, but why do you say shameful? Whatever is happening, it's through no fault of your own."

"Not all would see it that way. I was... an imperfect husband, you see. Perhaps Isabella is taunting me out of spite."

At Trudy's hesitation, he added ruefully, "I did not push her down the stairs, if that's what you're wondering."

She was wondering that... a little bit...

"Of course you didn't," she said, as if to convince them both. "But obviously you're aware of the gossip. Is it possible someone is playing a cruel prank?"

"Believe me, I have set my mind to the task of answering that question on a daily basis, but I cannot think of who would benefit from it. Especially someone with access to her items as well as mine. As I said, my pocket did not contain her handkerchief when I put this jacket on a few hours ago so how did it appear there if not by supernatural means?"

"I cannot imagine. Have you told anyone else of these incidents?"

"Only Daisy, and only then because she was with me when I found a lock of Izzy's hair inside one of my riding gloves."

"What did Daisy think when you revealed it?"

He scoffed lightly. "She thinks my wife is leaving sweet mementos for me to remember her by, but that was not Izzy's nature. My wife was not... sentimental."

"She wasn't?"

"No."

It seemed there was more to say on that particular subject, but a chill ran through Trudy, either from his story or from the fact that she'd been standing in drizzle for half an hour, and she visibly shivered.

"Goodness me," he said, "How selfish I am to make you stand out here in the rain. Let's get you inside." He shrugged out of his jacket, wrapping it around her shoulders before pulling open the door and ushering her back into the brightly lit hallway.

"Trudy, my goodness! There you are!" Coco called out from halfway up the hallway. Her expression of relief soured when she realized who Trudy was with. "Why, Mr. Bostwick. Whatever are you two doing out there in the rain? You'll cause a scandal."

"All the excitement of the trance lecture made me lightheaded," Trudy answered quickly. "Mr. Bostwick was kind enough to escort me outside for a breath of fresh air."

Coco's eyes narrowed with doubt.

"Is my sister nearby?" Alex asked. "I told her to find me after the show."

"The show has only just ended," Coco replied. "But your cousin, Ellis, was on hand to escort Daisy and Miss Albright back upstairs."

"And how is Miss Albright?" Trudy asked, pulling Alex's coat from her shoulders and returning it to him.

"She's fine, so far as I know. Why wouldn't she be?" Coco

answered dismissively, watching Alex as he slid his arms back into his jacket.

"Uh... she had a rather strange experience on the stage, wouldn't you say?" Trudy replied. "A person might be a little shaken up after something like that."

"She doesn't remember any of it," Coco answered. "And Daisy was making such a fuss over her, I think she rather liked the attention."

"She doesn't remember any of it?" Alex asked.

"No," Coco said with a tiny toss of her head. "Personally, I think she was just pretending. She probably didn't receive any sort of message at all and was just too embarrassed to admit it."

"Coco, that's uncharitable," Trudy scolded gently. "You shouldn't say such a thing."

"You also shouldn't pretend to be a person of means when you're not. Did you know she's just a house maid?"

"Yes, I did," Trudy responded curtly. Then she turned toward Alex, adding, "Please forgive my sister, Mr. Bostwick. She's far too concerned with status and position."

"I'm concerned with propriety," Coco responded, "As you should be. If Aunt Breezy discovers you've been loitering outside with a man, she'll have plenty to say about it."

"Ah, Miss Hart," Alex said smoothly, "How thoughtful you are to be concerned over your sister's reputation, but you have my word, as a gentleman, nothing untoward has occurred. Now, I was wondering, will you be attending the dance on Saturday evening?"

That sly dog.

Coco stern expression melted into girlishness. "I... why, yes, of course, Mr. Bostwick. Will you be in attendance as well?"

"I will. I'll look forward to seeing you on the dance floor. In the meantime, perhaps I could escort you both to the lobby before I go check on my sister and her... and Miss Albright."

He stepped forward and held out an arm for Coco.

Trudy nearly laughed aloud at his obvious ploy, but as they

moved together down the hallway, her mind spun with curiosity and the overwhelming question of how to reconcile the many different versions of Alexander Bostwick. There was the obnoxious ten-year-old boy hurling reckless taunts. The feline-rescuing good Samaritan. The solicitous gentleman who seemed interested in her opinions and wrapped her in his jacket. But there was also the handsome, young widower embroiled in scandal. And perhaps even a haunted bridegroom.

Somewhere in all that was ... just Alex.

Like an intriguing puzzle to be assembled, she would need to find more pieces until the final image emerged, and as they made their way toward the lobby, the challenge filled her with uneasy yet irresistible anticipation.

seven

"You do realize if you fracture a limb, I am in no condition to assist you," Jo said as Chase gazed at her in what Alex could only describe as *naïve optimism*.

"I've ridden a bicycle before, my darling," his brother replied. "There's no reason to think I'll fall and injure myself."

"That's right, Jo," added ginger-haired Harlan Callaghan. "Let the man have some fun. He's not *that* clumsy."

Alex chuckled at the young man's impertinence.

As a hotel employee, Harlan was expected to be deferential to the guests. However, he also happened to be friends with Jo and Chase, and frankly, anyone willing to tease his brother was a good enough chap in Alex's book. Besides, old friends had been scarce of late. Perhaps it was time for Alex to find some new ones.

Last night's rain had given way to a gloriously sunny afternoon, and the expansive front lawn of the Imperial Hotel was alive with activities. Archery, croquet, badminton, and tennis on the new clay courts had virtually every guest taking part in some sort of sport, and those who didn't engage were still outside, picnicking on quilts in the shade, or perhaps enjoying juleps on the porch.

In this remote corner of the lawn, however, an assortment of bicycles had lured men of various ages, girth, and athleticism toward Harlan Callaghan and his sturdy clipboard. It seemed there was to be a race, and apparently Chase was determined to participate.

"I'm not at all clumsy," Chase responded to Harlan's good-natured insult. "In fact, I intend to ride this fine contraption with the skill of a Belmont Stakes jockey. I might even win."

"Perhaps your aim should simply be to finish," Alex responded dryly.

His brother scowled. "I'm certain I could best you. Care for a little wager, big brother?"

"Me?" Alex asked with a dismissive chuckle. "So we can both be fools? No, thank you. I'll cheer you on from a safe distance, though."

"That's a mistake," Harlan murmured to Alex. "If my brother threw a gauntlet down at my feet, and I didn't pick it up, I'd never hear the end of it. He'd spend the rest of his days saying I was chicken."

Alex bristled slightly although knowing it was a harmless, good-natured jest. Perhaps because at any previous time in his life, he would've risen to the occasion without hesitation. Brotherly competition was as much a part of his relationship with Chase as sharing a ribald joke, enjoying a glass of fine whiskey, or sitting near a roaring fire and extolling upon the merits of being tall, handsome, and rich.

But Alex didn't feel like himself these days. He was distracted, especially this afternoon. His mind was consumed with regret at having told Trudy Hart about his... predicament.

It wasn't that he thought she'd share his story with anyone. He felt he could trust her with the information because she was clearly a woman of great integrity. But she was also a woman of common sense. An analytical thinker who, by her own admission, relied on evidence, and every comment she'd made last night revealed her belief that Isabella's belongings were being placed in his path by a human hand, not a spectral one.

And that made him feel foolish.

But he wasn't foolish.

He wasn't gullible, or fanciful, or prone to bouts of hysteria. He wasn't being deceived by his grief or letting his mind play tricks on him. He knew what he'd experienced. He knew no living person could be privy to the details that Izzy knew.

That letter she'd left in his boot? It was an apology he'd once written to her, and it had been torn to shreds. Her distinctly embroidered stocking had been left in a book of poems—between the pages of a verse he'd once recited. He remembered it clearly because it had taken him a week to memorize the damn prose and another week to muster the courage to say it to her—and then she'd giggled at his bungled elocution.

And the comb he'd discovered under his bed pillow—on the morning of her funeral—was the very same comb he'd given to her on the morning of their wedding. It was bejeweled, encrusted with garnets in the shape of a rose, but she'd never worn it because *she preferred gardenias* and thought an *attentive* husband should have known that.

In life, Isabella Carnegie hadn't been hard to please. She'd been *impossible* to please, but heaven knew he had tried. Oh, how he had tried—until he simply could not try anymore, and something had to be done about it.

"I won't say you're chicken," Chase teased, pulling Alex to the present. "I'll simply say you knew I'd wallop you given my certain victory."

"Certain victory? That's a lark. I could beat you in a bicycle race with one leg tied behind my back," Alex replied, feeling that old sense of sibling rivalry stir at his brother's words.

"No, you couldn't."

"Yes, I could."

"Prove it."

Damn it all to hell. They may as well have been twelve years old again. "Fine. I'll race you."

Chase clapped his hands together in a single motion. "Excellent."

"Does anyone care what I think?" Jo asked casually.

"No," the men replied in unison, but Chase immediately leaned over with a grin and kissed her cheek.

"Of course, I do, my darling. What do you think?"

"I think Harlan and I are going to sip lemonade in the shade while the two of you make silly gooses of yourselves. Just please don't break anything."

"I'm willing to give you both a quick lesson," Harlan added magnanimously. "The race doesn't start for another twenty minutes."

Twenty minutes was not enough time to perfect his cycling skills, but Alex had ridden before. He knew it was as much a matter of confidence and commitment as it was of balance and footwork. If you doubted yourself and began to wobble, you were sure to fall, but if you sped up when every instinct told you to slow down, you'd stay upright. And at least the course was fairly level. It ran from one corner of the hotel, down around the edge of the lawn, along the boulevard leading toward downtown Trillium Bay, and then curved back up along the drive, ending near the entrance of the main lobby.

A finish line had been drawn in chalk, and as the racers practiced, some twenty in all, spectators began to gather, many taking seats on the red carpeted steps of the front porch, while others were scattered along the route to cheer their favorite riders.

Alex, meanwhile, was having second—and third—thoughts about his participation. He hadn't expected an audience, but naturally Hugo Plank and Julian Tippett, the Imperial Hotel's social director, were doing their utmost to drum up excitement, even encouraging wagers. Alex spotted Finn and Ellis arriving along with Daisy and a few of her friends, and then the Hart sisters with Asher. Even Sir Chester VonWhiskerton was in attendance, but it was Trudy who caught his eye and waved, sending a strange buzz of anticipation thrumming through him, yet increasing his trepidation.

"I'm sorry," Chase said with an easy smile as they stood near the starting point, holding their bicycles steady by the handlebars.

Alex scoffed in mock exasperation. "For which thing? For taunting me into a bicycle race with all of these people watching? Or for most assuredly beating me to the finish line?"

His brother shrugged. "Both I suppose."

"At least promise me that this one will be a fair fight," Alex replied. "Last time we raced on foot, you tripped me."

"I had to. You were winning."

Alex bit back a smile and shook his head.

"Good afternoon, ladies and gentlemen!" Hugo Plank shouted from in front of the steps. "Welcome to the First Annual Imperial Hotel Bicycle Battle. The rules are simple. When Mr. Callaghan lowers the flag, our cyclists will begin the race over there." He pointed to the group of them and then continued.

"The first rider to complete the entire route and cross this finish line wins." He tapped his large foot against the chalk to mark the spot. "Any rider who falls over is out of the race, but the gentlemen may touch their feet to the ground if necessary. Most importantly, there is to be no deliberate contact between cyclists."

"Did you hear what he just said?" Alex glared at his brother. "No deliberate contact."

"I didn't hear anything. Must've been the wind."

"The winner," Hugo added, "will receive ten dollars and a bottle of his choice from the top shelf of the bar."

"A top shelf bottle? Glad to know I'm not risking life and limb for nothing," Chase remarked.

"Well, regardless of the outcome, at least you'll always have your wife's derision," Alex replied.

There was a moment of conferring between Hugo, Harlan, and Mr. Tippett, then Harlan sprinted over to stand before them.

"Gentlemen, on your marks!" Harlan called out.

Everyone scrambled onto their bicycles. Most had removed

their jackets, and a few, like Alex, had rolled up their shirtsleeves. Some had gone so far as to don goggles, clearly expecting the ride to go much faster than was likely.

"Get set!" Harlan shouted. "And go!"

He waved a red scarf and Alex pushed forward with one foot before focusing all his attention on simply pedaling the bike amidst the fray of other unsteady riders. There was laughter and shouting as the racers left the starting line en masse, but it died away as the group spread out along the route.

Alex felt a faint acknowledgement that the crowd was cheering, but he paid little heed to it. The only thoughts on his mind at present were to stay upright, keep moving forward, not be last of the pack... and that somewhere in that cacophony of onlookers, Trudy Hart was watching him race. He didn't know why that mattered, but it did.

Rounding the first curve, the finish line felt miles away. To his left, Chase was keeping pace with him but the number of riders in front of them was thinning incrementally. A pudgy man in striped trousers veered off into the grass and tumbled over. To the right, three riders collided, and landed in a heap, and Alex recommitted himself to simply *finishing*.

The wind brushed against his face. His heart rate increased from both excitement and exertion as he passed one rider, and then another. Chase was still beside him, but they were leaving the others behind, and he dared to wonder if perhaps they might finish together near the front of the pack. That would be satisfying. He'd already made enough progress in the race to not completely humiliate himself and he was content with that.

But as they sped onward, as they passed one cyclist, and then another, Alex wondered if perhaps—just perhaps—they might be able to take the lead. They were among the most fit of the participants, and seemed to have mastered some technique. As the possibility took hold, it became his purpose. His mission. He wanted to finish with the best of the riders.

He lowered his head and pumped his legs. Chase moved

ahead of him by a nose, or a wheel as it were, and suddenly a lifetime of his brother always claiming victory at the final moment, of always defeating Alex either by luck or skill or questionable strategy, filled Alex with a need to *win*.

He wanted to win, and he *could*. There was no one else in front of them now. It was just Alex and Chase.

Rounding the final bend, he saw Hugo up ahead. The noise of the crowd was a dull roar drowned out by the relentless *thump-bump* of his heart beating in his ears. Chase was mere inches ahead, but Alex doubled his efforts and passed him. The finish line was right there. He ignored the burning in his legs, the ache in his shoulders, the pounding in his chest. Alex pedaled with every ounce of remaining strength he had. He sped past Hugo with Chase nowhere in sight.

By Jove! He had done it! He had won!

Silly schoolboy elation flooded through him at the victory… and then he felt a jolt… and his jubilation was overtaken by the alarming and rather confusing sensation of flying through the air with no bicycle beneath him. He had the presence of mind to realize this was an inauspicious twist to his triumph, but at least he'd *won*.

He had won *and* he had beaten his brother.

Then he landed on the hard, solid ground with a whump and an oof and pain shot up his left arm. Noises and colors blended together as he lay there in the dirt, dazed, bewildered, and breathless. A strong hand rolled him over onto his back.

"Good God, man! Are you all right?" Hugo asked, bending over him. The sun overhead was bright, and Alex blinked.

"Did I cross the line first?" he asked on a wheeze.

"In a manner of speaking," Hugo answered.

"Then I'm all right."

Chase was next to him a second later. "Land sakes, Alex. Are you hurt?"

"I don't think so. Help me sit up."

"Maybe you should just lay still for a moment," his brother responded. "You've likely had the wind knocked out of you."

"Help me sit up," Alex said again. "I'm fine."

He didn't actually feel fine. In fact, his head was spinning, and it was hard to breathe, but the lovely Dr. Hart had just arrived, and he didn't want to seem frail with her staring at him like that.

"That was quite a spill," she said, kneeling beside him without a care for her dress. "Can you look at me."

"Gladly."

He was upright now, sort of, and not so addled from the fall he didn't realize her intense gaze at his face was diagnostic in nature, and yet he was senseless enough to enjoy this opportunity to stare into her lovely hazel eyes. He took note of the smattering of pale freckles sprinkled across her nose and the tiniest little scar near the corner of her mouth. So tiny only a lover would ever be close enough to notice it.

A lover, or a foolish oaf who'd just flown off a bicycle.

"You're very pretty," he whispered for her alone to hear.

She frowned. "Did you bump your head, Mr. Bostwick?"

"I don't think so. And I won the race," he said smugly.

"Mmm... did you?" She glanced up at Hugo.

"Hugo?" Alex looked up at him, too. "You did say I won, didn't you?."

"Not exactly, son," Hugo said sympathetically. "You asked if you crossed the finish line first, and well, your body did but your bike still hasn't. Technically, I think your brother won this race."

"Damn it!" Alex's frustration was quickly displaced by a woozy light-headedness and the pain radiating up his arm. He lifted his hand to see why it was throbbing to find his pinky finger bent at an unnatural angle and already turning purple.

"Well, that's definitely broken," Trudy said. "Do you mind if I check to see if you have any other injuries?"

"Go ahead," he said with resignation, fairly certain everything else was intact and that only his finger and his dignity were wounded.

"A little privacy is in order, Mr. Plank," Trudy said. "Might you shoo away the gawkers?"

"What? Oh, yes. Of course, Miss Hart."

"Doctor Hart," she said automatically, although she knew he meant no disrespect.

"Friends, if you would all kindly disperse," Hugo called out. "Let's give Mr. Bostwick a moment to recover. Refreshments are available on the lawn or in the tearoom if you'd rather take respite from the sun."

People slowly drifted away as Finn, Ellis, and Daisy appeared nearby, concern etched on their faces. Alex caught a glimpse of Lucy Hart embracing a tearful Coco some distance away, and even little Poppy looked upset.

Goodness. His voyage over the handlebars must have been quite spectacular for everyone to seem so worried, but thankfully, he was already regaining his equilibrium. He glanced up at his brother.

"You didn't knock me over this time, did you?"

Even Chase's smile was full of apprehension, yet still his brother teased. "I didn't need to knock you over. You hit that rock in the path all on your own. I'll split the winnings with you, though."

"Keep your pity money. I don't want it. I'll win fair and square next time."

"There had better not be a next time," Jo said, at last arriving to the scene, her face flushed. "I told you fools you'd break something."

"That you did," Alex said with a slow nod. "But must you all stare at me as if I'd been pitched from a speeding locomotive rather than a bicycle? Do you really think me so breakable?"

"You did travel some distance through the air," Ellis responded matter-of-factly. "It was impressive."

"But not very dignified," Finn added with a small grin. "Rather like a chicken trying to fly."

"Not like a chicken at all," Daisy argued. "More like an acrobat. But Alex, are you hurt?"

"I'm fine," he said again, wishing they'd all go away and let him catch his breath in peace. Their fussing was embarrassing and entirely unnecessary.

Meanwhile, however, Trudy was running her hands down his arms, giving little squeezes and bending his joints this way and that. She proceeded to do the same with his legs and in spite of his embarrassment and the significant pain coming from his mangled finger, the rest of him was starting to feel rather fine. Perhaps he should fall down more often if her attentive ministrations were the result. He smiled at her again and felt vindicated when she blushed in response.

∽

"Out of my way! Out my way, now! I'm the doctor," a gruff, booming voice called out from the upper slope of the lawn, and Trudy turned to see a bespeckled, bewhiskered man with frizzy grey hair and a ruddy complexion push his way through the remaining onlookers. He elbowed his way next to Hugo, and she felt her pulse quicken in preparation for a fight. She knew this man's type just by his belligerent expression and the fact that his complexion indicated he enjoyed *drinking* elixirs as much as he enjoyed prescribing them.

"Which one is the patient?" he demanded, as if it weren't obvious since Alex was the one sitting in the dirt in a torn shirt and holding up a hand with a clearly broken finger.

"This is the injured party, and I am Dr. Hart," she answered calmly. "Did you witness the accident?"

The man's eyes narrowed. "I beg your pardon?"

"Did you witness the accident? If not, I can describe what happened so you might assess his injuries."

He scoffed. "I don't need any assistance in assessing his injuries, missy. Move aside please."

Alex grasped her wrist with his uninjured hand, keeping her by his side. "Who might you be, sir?" he asked.

"I am Dr. Aloysius Prescott, M.D.," he answered with self-importance. "I'm the Imperial Hotel physician and I've come to ensure your well-being."

Trudy looked back at Alex. It was possible he'd prefer this man's care over hers, and if that were the case, she'd try not to take it personally. *She'd fail... but she'd try.*

"Thank you, doctor, but I'm already being well tended to." Alex squeezed her wrist, and she felt herself blushing.

Again.

And then she felt annoyed by all her blushing which only served to make her cheeks burn that much hotter. It was his hand on her wrist causing the issue, but why such a simple touch should elicit this reaction within her was a mystery.

Dr. Prescott looked around the area, his tumbleweed brows coming together in consternation. "You're being tended to? Has Dr. Hargrove already been here? Has he examined you?"

"I believe Mr. Bostwick is referring to Dr. Hart," Hugo explained. "She is one of our guests and a graduate of the University of Michigan Medical College."

Dr. Prescott looked back at her with an expression she was all too familiar with. *Patronizing indulgence.* As if her degree in medicine was a quaint, adorable thing but certainly nothing of actual value.

"This man didn't faint from hysteria onto a chaise lounge, Mr. Plank. He was flung from a speeding bicycle and needs a proper examination. Best let me get a look."

He stepped closer, but Chase rose to his feet as Alex replied, "Thank you, no."

"I beg your pardon?"

"Thank you, but your care won't be necessary. I have my own physician," Alex said.

His confidence in Trudy was validating, but in spite of the boost to her ego, his health was her main concern.

"Dr. Prescott likely has supplies that I do not," she said quietly to Alex. "And you need to get that finger set."

"Surely, you can set a broken finger," he replied, just as quietly.

"I can," she nodded, "but I'm not sure what I have on hand for pain management."

He laughed out loud at her concern. "I've had the wind knocked out of me and broke an essentially useless finger. Otherwise, I'm fine. What I'd really like is to stand up now and collect that half a bottle of liquor Hugo promised me."

"I thought you didn't want pity winnings," Chase said as he helped Alex slowly clamor to his feet.

"I guess I've come to my senses."

"Well," Dr. Prescott scoffed. "When you come to your senses about proper medical care, my office is at the back of the hotel. Until then, good day to you, sirs." He stomped off as Chase extended a hand to Trudy, helping her rise. She tried to brush the dirt from her skirts and turned to Mr. Plank.

"Do you have any supplies on hand?" she asked. "Anywhere other than in Dr. Prescott's office?"

"I do," Mr. Plank replied. "My private study is just off the lobby if you'd like to go there. I can fetch whatever you need. Please follow me."

Some twenty minutes later, Trudy had set Alex's finger with a splint and clean bandages and checked him for signs of concussion, thankfully finding none. Had he been any other patient, she might have also asked him to remove his shirt and trousers so she could check for serious contusions, but working at her father's clinic, she'd grown accustomed to treating the old, the infirmed, the malnourished, even the odorific.

Alexander Bostwick was none of those things.

He was hearty and hale, made of muscle and strength. He even *smelled* good in spite of the dirt clinging to his clothes. It was... befuddling, and although she should not alter her treatment simply because her patient was *pleasantly scented and muscular*, all things considered, it seemed prudent to leave well enough alone.

And to leave *him* alone.

He'd be fine.

"Don't be surprised if you suffer some muscle aches and pains over the next few days," Trudy said as she avoided his gaze and tidied up the supplies while he sat on a small sofa in Mr. Plank's study. "But I think, overall, you should consider yourself fortunate. You could have broken far worse than a finger."

"Yes, I believe Jo made that quite clear during her tirade. My ears are still scorched from her scolding."

His sister-in-law *had* gone on at some length once they'd reached the privacy of the office, telling both of the Bostwick brothers in no uncertain terms they were to behave themselves from this day forward. Trudy had found Jo's overly zealous diatribe justified yet distracting and had ultimately sent everyone from the room, except for herself and Alex.

"I think you frightened her," Trudy replied to Alex's comment.

"I frightened Jo?" He shook his head. "Jo's not afraid of anything."

Trudy looked over at him. "Don't confuse fear with courage, Mr. Bostwick. Jo is certainly courageous, but that doesn't mean she's not afraid of things, such as someone she cares about getting injured. And women are especially sensitive to that sort of concern when they're expecting."

He looked down sheepishly at his bandaged hand. "Truly, no one expected this to happen. I certainly didn't expect a rock in my path."

"No one ever expects a rock in their path Mr. Bostwick and yet they are there all the time, in one form or another."

He nodded slowly. "Are you back to calling me Mr. Bostwick, now? I rather prefer Alex."

So did she.

"When you're my patient, you are Mr. Bostwick," she replied. "But now that I've finished trussing up that finger, Alex it is."

He smiled, reminding her—as if she could forget—that he was disarmingly handsome.

"Good," he replied. "And may I say, I'm glad to see you haven't caught a cold."

"Caught a cold?"

"Yes, from being in the rain last evening."

"Ah, of course."

"I shouldn't have let you linger out in the chilly night air."

His words prompted her laughter. "I am quite capable of making my own decisions, Alex. I chose to remain outside with you."

"But had I not bolted from the theater like Henny Penny, you wouldn't have been outside at all."

"I suppose not, but I have no regrets. Except, perhaps, for one."

His gaze clouded. "And what regret is that?"

She regarded him carefully. "I'm not sure how to help with your... other predicament."

He straightened his shoulders. "I shared what I did out of an absence of good sense. Not so you'd feel obligated to help me."

"I don't feel obligated, but as a physician, as *your* physician—and dare I say your friend—I would like to be of service. To help find a cure, as it were, to your peculiar malady." She was teasing now, but her smile seemed to catch him off guard. "Unless, of course, I'm being presumptuous. If you'd rather not discuss it with me further, I'll respect your privacy."

He was silent for a moment, then shook his head. "Not presumptuous at all. I'd welcome your insight, but do you truly consider this a malady? Some illness of my mind, perhaps?"

"Oh, my goodness. No, Alex, that's not what I meant."

Why did she always phrase things so poorly around him?

"I only meant that, if it were up to me, I'd try to uncover the source behind the appearances of your wife's items using a scientific method, the same way we try to find cures for diseases."

"And how might one go about that?"

"By gathering evidence, I suppose. Using observation, testing theories, interviewing experts if we can find any." Although any so-called experts in the realm of the supernatural would have to be carefully vetted, and how *that* might be accomplished, she had no idea. It would be like trying to solve a robbery by only interviewing burglars and thugs.

"That process sounds rather labor intensive. Are you sure you have the time?"

She smiled again." I'm accustomed to hectic days at my father's clinic and thrive on keeping busy. Truthfully, I don't relish the idea of spending this entire summer at leisure, discussing fashion and home furnishings. If I can't see patients, I'd much prefer to focus on solving a riddle, especially one as unique as yours. That is, of course, only if you genuinely want my participation."

His smile was slow, and she sensed that tumble from his bicycle had sapped more energy from him than he'd realized, but he nodded at her words.

"Your participation, however much you care to give, would be most appreciated. I fear my objectivity in this matter may be faulty and I haven't wanted to alarm my family. Perhaps you will see things through a different lens."

"Perhaps, but either way, two heads are better than one. We'll work on this together, but for now, *Mr. Bostwick*, I'm going to be your doctor again and advise you to go upstairs and rest. I'll have some tea sent to your room that should help with any discomfort."

He looked, for a moment, as if he might argue because men always seemed to equate *rest* with *weakness*. They didn't realize that, although their body might be motionless, on the inside, it was working hard at healing. Fortunately, he nodded again and rose, slowly, from the sofa. He looked over at her, his expression somber.

"Thank you, Trudy."

His words were simple, but his tone said more. It said he appreciated her, and he trusted her. As a doctor, that was the best compliment she could receive.

eight

"I like the blue gown but rather think this pink one does even more wonderful things for my complexion. Wouldn't you agree?" Coco asked, pressing the satin skirt against her cheek for Daisy's inspection.

"I do agree," Daisy replied, and Trudy was duly impressed by the girl's diplomatic patience.

The three of them, along with Lucy, were in the Hart family suite. While Trudy was trying valiantly to focus on her medical textbook and Lucy flipped through the pages of an astronomy journal, the two older sisters had exchanged frequent, exasperated glances brought on by Coco's endless prattle about the upcoming dance and her relentless need for adoration. Even little Poppy demonstrated less self-absorption than Coco. It was exhausting.

"You're right. I should wear the pink. Although your brother's eyes are blue, so..." Coco giggled, and Daisy's smile turned to bemusement.

"My brother's eyes?"

"Mm, yes," Lucy responded absently, flipping another page. "She's intent upon marrying your brother. Hasn't she told you? It's all we've heard about for days."

"Lucy!" exclaimed Coco. "That was private."

Lucy snorted with amusement. "Hardly private, Coco. You squirm around like a puppy every time he's near, and nearly fainted from distress yesterday when he fell from his bicycle."

"Well, of course I was distressed," Coco snapped. "Are you so heartless his accident didn't upset you?"

Lucy shifted from a reclined position to sit up tall. "Of course it upset me, but Daisy is his own sister and even she didn't make as much of a fuss as you did."

"I did have a little tear in my eye," Daisy said generously, patting Coco's arm. "But I was so relieved your sister was there to take care of him, crying didn't seem necessary."

Coco glared over at Trudy, as if her treating Alex's injuries was somehow a betrayal.

"Ah, yes," Coco said dryly. "The doctor saves the day."

"Yes, and thank goodness," Daisy responded effusively, as if the sarcasm was lost on her. It wasn't, though. Trudy could tell by the sympathetic gaze Daisy cast her way.

"But I rather think..." Daisy said, and then paused, twisting the fringe of her dress. "Well... Coco, if you hope to marry Alex, I think you'll have to wait a good long time."

"I'll be eighteen this winter," Coco replied.

"Um, yes, well... it's not your age that may be the problem. I'm just not sure my brother is considering remarriage any time soon. His wife only died a few months ago."

"And what a tragedy," Coco replied with a practiced tremor of sympathy in her voice. "But how better to mend a broken heart than to find love again?"

Trudy scoffed. "Coco, let the man grieve properly. He's in mourning. He doesn't need to be tripping over you every time he steps from his room."

"He doesn't need to be tripping over you, either," she replied tersely. "Since when does a spiritualist show make you lightheaded? You've never been lightheaded in your life and yet Mr. Bostwick suddenly had to escort you outside? In the rain?"

Daisy looked over at Trudy once more, her bemusement now laced with humor.

"It was stuffy in that theater," Trudy responded. "And you'd insisted I tighten my laces that night so could barely breathe."

"It was stuffy in the theater," Lucy agreed. "And then when Lorna got so agitated? Well, I felt a little off kilter after that, as well. How is she, by the way?" She directed the question to Daisy.

"She's fine. Entirely fine. She remembers going up on the stage, and then Mr. Gibson telling her they were all finished and that she should go sit back down."

"She doesn't recall anything that happened in between?" Trudy asked, glad the subject was no longer Alexander Bostwick and who might be tripping over whom.

"Nothing at all. In fact, when I told her what I'd seen, she didn't believe me," Daisy said.

"What a strange thing indeed," Lucy murmured.

"She's a little disappointed, if truth be told," Daisy added. "She volunteered to participate and in a sense, she missed the first half of the show."

"She should just be glad she got to see any of it," Coco commented, and Daisy frowned.

"Why would you say that?"

"Well, I mean, because she's your maid. I can't think of any other lady's maids who were allowed to attend. At least she got to see a bit."

Daisy's smile turned strained. "I suppose, but Lorna is my friend as much as she is my maid, and she knows far more about the supernatural than I do. She was so excited to meet Mr. Gibson, and now my mother has forbidden her to speak to any of the other occultists for the rest of the summer."

"Why?" Lucy asked.

"It's my fault, really," Daisy said, turning forlorn. "I didn't ask for permission before bringing Lorna to the theater. My mother was furious when she found out, especially the part about Lorna going up on stage."

"How did your mother find out?" Lucy inquired.

"My cousin Ellis told her everything. He couldn't very well avoid it. He was escorting Lorna back to her room after the show and Mother saw them. Naturally he had to explain why they were together. If he hadn't, she would have made all sorts of uncharitable assumptions."

"Hmm. So, should I wear the blue dress, then?" Coco asked, eager to bring the topic back to herself.

Trudy looked over at her sister and Daisy, two girls who, from all outward appearances, had much in common. They were both pretty and witty and full of vivacious energy, but Coco was like a simple watercolor. A splash of vibrant but translucent hues creating a picture you could absorb with a single glance while Daisy was a captivating Rococo full of bold, unexpected colors and rich contrasts. The kind of painting that revealed something new every time you looked at it. As disloyal as it might be to think, Daisy had a depth and maturity Coco lacked and would likely never develop.

"Wear the pink or the blue," Daisy answered, standing up. "You're sure to look lovely in either, but just so you know, I don't think my brother will be at the dance tonight. His hand is bothering him. In fact, Trudy, I was wondering if you might check on him this afternoon to make sure it's setting properly."

"Yes, of course. I'll just finish reading this article and go see him in a few minutes," Trudy answered. She'd been planning to do that anyway but was glad to have Daisy's endorsement. She didn't want anyone to think she was stopping by his room for no good reason.

"Thank you. I'm sure he'd appreciate it."

Coco frowned as Daisy picked up the hat and gloves she'd been wearing when she arrived.

"Are you leaving? Already?"

"Yes, I'm afraid so. My mother wants me to have tea with her and I'd like to finish some correspondence before that. I'll see you all this evening at the dance, though, yes?" She smiled at each of them and after a chorus of goodbyes, made her exit.

Coco spun toward Lucy the moment the latch of the door clicked shut. "You didn't need to tell her about me and Mr. Bostwick, Lucy."

"I thought she knew."

"Of course she didn't know. *He* doesn't even know. Not yet anyway, but he will soon enough."

"Because you'll be wearing a dress that matches his eyes?" Trudy asked dryly, prompting Lucy to giggle.

"Because I will charm him," Coco replied defiantly. "And just because you two never put any thought into your appearance doesn't mean I shouldn't. This is the first dance of the season and it's imperative we make good impressions. Mother is counting on us to secure proposals, and I intend to do just that!"

Trudy slammed her book shut but said nothing. Because there was nothing to say. Coco was determined to proceed with this ridiculous caper of finding a husband, but Trudy was not, and every time she thought about it, it rattled her senses.

How could their mother have sent them to Trillium Bay with such a preposterous goal without even discussing it with them? Especially knowing Trudy's personal stance on matrimony? It made no sense, and she would not participate.

Dear Mother,

During our first week at the Imperial Hotel, Poppy has made several new friends, Asher has learned several inappropriate words, and Coco, who, as you well know, has never been bound by the tenants of good judgment, has made several overtures toward the one and only suitor Aunt Breezy deems wholly unacceptable.

Oh, and speaking of Aunt Breezy, she cannot keep a secret. She's revealed your scheme, Mother, and I am not in favor of it. Therefore, please note, I will NOT be coming home with a proposal of marriage—while Coco may be coming home with one you cannot abide.

Trudy tamped down a sigh, wishing she could actually post such a letter. She could not, of course. But she wanted to.

∼

"Ah, there you are," Daisy said, rising from a bench in the hallway not too far from Alex's hotel room door.

"Daisy?" Trudy asked. "Have you been waiting for me?"

"I have. I was hoping we might exchange a private word."

"Of course, but should I check on your brother first? You said his hand was troubling him."

Daisy waved her own hand dismissively. "Oh, I only said that so you'd come into the hallway, and I might see you. Forgive the subterfuge, but I think it's imperative you and I have a conversation. Do you mind?"

Trudy would have chuckled at the ploy if not for Daisy's solemn expression. "Of course I don't mind."

"Good. There's a sitting room at the end of the hall. We'll go there."

Daisy looped her arm through Trudy's, guiding her some distance away, to an alcove near the back staircase. Two upholstered chairs with matching tufted ottomans were tucked against the curve of the wall, creating an informal, inviting spot to linger.

"You've piqued my curiosity, Daisy. What's on your mind?" Trudy asked, once they were settled.

Daisy fidgeted for a moment, plucking again at the fringed trim adorning the ruffles of her dress, prompting Trudy to wonder if this discussion might pertain to Coco's infatuation with Alex, or perhaps a concern that Trudy had her eye on him as well. She didn't, of course, but Daisy might think she did.

"What I have to say, I don't say lightly," Daisy said quietly. "But Alex told me you're aware he's being haunted by Isabella."

Ah, so not about Coco, then.

Although given this as the alternative, the former may have been a simpler conversation since Trudy didn't actually *believe* Alex was being *haunted*. If items were being placed in his path, it was undoubtedly the work of a living, breathing person, not the phantom of a deceased one.

"Alex has told me he's come upon some of her personal belongings in peculiar places," Trudy responded neutrally.

"Numerous personal items and very peculiar places," Daisy replied, a worry line creasing her usually smooth forehead. "And I don't think he's told me everything that's happened since she died. That's why I'm so concerned about him."

This was an uncharted voyage. Trudy had promised Alex confidentiality, a promise she intended to keep.

"I'm sure he appreciates your concern, Daisy, but I'm not comfortable discussing this without Alex's permission. I've only just learned of the situation myself and anything I say would be pure speculation anyway."

"I understand that, and please know I'm not trying to gossip about my brother behind his back," Daisy assured her. "But he must trust you a great deal if he's told you anything at all. I only want to help, and so I have to say this." She leaned forward and lowered her voice. "I don't think they're love tokens."

Daisy's hushed tone sent a ripple of curiosity through Trudy's limbs. Perhaps she wasn't the only skeptic. "You don't?"

"No. I only said that to Alex because he's so unsettled by these occurrences." Daisy paused, and frowned, and twisted another tassel. "In fact, I think Isabella's intentions are exactly the opposite of love."

Oh. So not a skeptic then.

"What do you mean 'the opposite of love?'"

"I think Isabella is angry. I don't know many details, but I do know that whatever happened between her and my brother wasn't good. Especially towards the end."

Trudy's curiosity shifted to discomfort. She had no business hearing about Alex's marriage. Especially from someone other than him, but Daisy looked around furtively, as if she feared someone—or some*thing*—might be eavesdropping, and her voice dropped to the faintest of whispers.

"I blame Izzy for their discontent. Alex is no saint, mind you, but he has always been true to his own nature. He didn't pretend to be someone he wasn't, but she certainly did."

"How so?" Trudy could not resist asking.

"She was gracious at first and seemed genuinely enamored of my brother, but I always sensed that underneath her agreeable facade, she was actually quite dreadful. She reminded me of a beautiful, exotic flower but the kind that emanates poison. The better I got to know her, the more I noticed the calculating ways she manipulated things to satisfy her own whims. And although she was never directly unkind to me, I once saw her being very harsh with one of our staff."

"Did anyone else notice this change in her demeanor?"

Daisy almost smiled but held it at bay. "Everyone *noticed* but noticing something and acknowledging it are two very different things in my family. I did tell my mother Izzy had been cruel to our butler, but other than that, no one ever spoke of it. She was Alex's problem to deal with but given her propensity for nastiness, it does make me wonder…"

"Wonder what?" Trudy prompted at her hesitation.

Daisy leaned closer still, and whispered, "I wonder if Isabella is the angry spirit who tried to communicate through Lorna."

Trudy attempted to school her expression—the way she'd learned to do when patients shared overly intimate yet irrelevant details she'd rather not hear. She nodded slowly at Daisy. Not in agreement, but rather in simple understanding because, at the moment, it didn't matter what Trudy believed.

Eventually, of course, Trudy would have to find a way to differentiate the facts from the fantastical and was beginning to realize how difficult a task that may be since her two best suppliers of information—Alex and Daisy—were equally unreliable sources.

"I wouldn't be too alarmed about that, Daisy. I don't think that's what happened," Trudy said softly. "And it may not be in your brother's best interest to suggest that to him. Unless you already have?"

Daisy shook her head. "No, I haven't. It would only upset him. I let him think I'm just a silly girl who believes in romantic fairy tales the same way he tries to shield me from the misery of his marriage. He seems to forget we grew up in the same household, watching our parents be subtly despicable to one another. I know the signs."

Daisy's words tugged unexpectedly at Trudy's heart. She was blessed with parents who loved and respected each other as individuals, and who somehow, when together, made one another *better*. Perhaps she'd taken that for granted. And perhaps that was, ironically, why she never planned to marry. Trudy had yet to meet a man who didn't think making her *better* meant making her *different*.

"But why don't you think it was Isabella trying to communicate through Lorna?" Daisy added.

Trudy carefully considered her words. She didn't want to insult Daisy with her continued skepticism, nor did she want to be dishonest.

"Truthfully, I'm not convinced Mr. Gibson possesses the gifts he claims to have. All I witnessed during his performance was skillful hypnotism. I've said as much to your brother."

"But didn't you leave halfway through the show? You didn't see the second half of Mr. Gibson's demonstration."

"That's true, I didn't."

"He was quite amazing when it was just him on the stage. He revealed dozens of messages and even brought a few audience members to tears with what he shared. It was incredibly moving."

"Perhaps he is more skilled than I give him credit for," Trudy replied noncommittally.

"But you're still dubious?" Daisy pressed.

"I am. You know I rely on proven facts and reliable evidence, and I've yet to see anything credible to convince me that Mr. Gibson, or anyone else for that matter, has the ability to converse with the departed. And even if there were such a skilled and gifted oracle, it seems highly unlikely they'd be spending their summer at the Imperial Hotel giving tarot card readings for one dollar a session."

"What should they be doing?" Daisy asked.

"What do you mean?"

"If not visiting a resort full of guests interested in their talents, what should they be doing? Surely you're aware many respected psychics and trance lecturers travel around the country giving demonstrations and offering readings so they can reach the people who need them."

"I... have heard that, yes."

Daisy smiled at her indulgently, as if sorry for Trudy's lack of faith and imagination. "Perhaps Mr. Gibson is not who we need," Daisy continued, "but what if you met a psychic medium who could convince you of her abilities? Would you consider the possibility that she was such an oracle?"

This question seemed like a trap. "I suppose I'd have to, if she could convince me."

Daisy pondered this for a moment, her expression slowly shifting toward optimism. "I think may I know of someone."

Trudy sincerely doubted it, but by God, Daisy Bostwick was a dog with a bone. "And who might that be?"

"Madame Moyen," Daisy answered. "She's already done a number of readings for guests at the hotel, and everyone says she's extraordinary. Lorna heard from one of the other maids that she helped Mrs. Endicott communicate with her son who died last year, and Pearl Mahoney's mother saw Madame Moyen and was left speechless. If you knew Pearl Mahoney's mother you would understand how very remarkable that is."

Trudy chuckled at the comment, but asked, "Why is it so important to you that I'm convinced?"

Daisy sat up tall. "Because...I think Madame Moyen could guide us in a séance."

"A séance?" *What a fascinating yet ludicrous suggestion.*

"Yes, think of it. We could summon Isabella. If she has an opportunity to express whatever it is she's been trying to tell Alex, perhaps she'd be satisfied and would finally leave him alone. With luck, he could say what he needs to say, too, and be free of all his misplaced guilt."

Curiosity and caution clashed inside Trudy's intellect. She did not believe séances could open a portal between the living and the dead. Participating in one would likely be a waste of time, not to mention potentially unsettling for everyone involved. And in the end, they'd be no closer to discovering who was leaving Isabella's items for Alex to find. What would be the point?

And yet... *what if she was wrong?*

What if Trudy was doggedly clinging to a faulty conviction because of old beliefs? She knew science had its limits, and that there were a great many inexplicable things occurring and existing in the world that no amount of logic could currently explain. So, perhaps she had to at least contemplate the possibility of communication with other realms of consciousness.

But a séance? *Good Lord.*

"It's an interesting idea, Daisy. Certainly, something to think about."

"So, you'll consider it?"

"I'll consider considering it," she replied slowly, smiling at Daisy's eager expression.

"Do you think we should mention the idea to Alex?" Daisy asked.

"I do not," Trudy responded quickly.

The thought of Alex telling a potential charlatan his wife was haunting him left Trudy feeling all sorts of uneasy. In fact, this entire conversation seemed far outside the sphere of her mission.

She'd told Alex she enjoyed solving a riddle...and she did, but dabbling in the occult was another thing entirely. Things were spiraling in the wrong direction.

"You're right, of course," Daisy responded. "It's too soon to include him, and I'm sorry to pull you into our current misfortune. It's just that, other than me, you're the first person Alex has shared this with and quite frankly, I've been bursting at the seams to discuss it with someone."

"I'm sure it's a heavy burden to shoulder alone, and I'll help in whatever way I can. But for now, I do think the best thing I can do is go check on your brother's hand."

nine

"Brace yourself, Mother. It's time to feed the wolves," Alex murmured as they paused at the entrance of the Imperial Hotel's grand ballroom.

It was the first dance of the season and every guest over the age of sixteen was sure to be in attendance. Beside him, Daisy smiled with eagerness in a shimmering ivory gown, Ellis smoothed his carefully combed hair and straightened his necktie, while Finn tugged at his collar and twitched uncomfortably in a borrowed tuxedo. Alex's mother, of course, surveyed the crowd in front of them imperiously as if they were her unruly subjects.

Inside the vast, mirrored room gasoliers and candlelight competed for the brightest glow while on the dance floor, ladies, resplendent in their pastel silks and jewel-toned satins, twirled around the dance floor led by attentive tuxedo-clad swains. The air around them seemed to swirl as well, thick with the strains of a Viennese waltz, the cloying scent of expensive French perfume, and the undeniable sparkle of expectation. Hugo Plank certainly knew how to host a ball.

"I told you we should've come downstairs earlier," Alex's mother said. "Breezy has already set up court. Now I'll have to catch up."

"Or," Daisy suggested, "since you two are friends, perhaps you could stand next to each other and *share* the court."

"Share?" His mother arched a brow, clearly finding that suggestion both preposterous and demeaning. Sharing was the purview of children and charity workers, not the likes of Constance Bostwick.

With a subtle shake of the head toward Daisy, Alex held out an arm to escort their mother into the fray, hearing her subtle *tsk, tsk, tsk* at the bandage wrapped around his fingers. His accident had embarrassed her, as had his dismissal of Dr. Prescott—an action which had all but drowned out any other aspect of his spectacular fall. Apparently, in choosing to be treated by *some random woman* instead of the hotel physician, Alex had bucked protocol and tradition. And Mrs. A.J. Bostwick was nothing if not a traditionalist.

"You look very lovely tonight, Mother," Alex said, hoping to steer the evening toward pleasantry in spite of her ever-present disdain.

"Of course I look lovely," she replied, the barest hint of a smile playing around her mouth. "I spent an exorbitant amount of your father's money on this Parisian gown. I'll be the most exquisitely dressed woman in the room."

Her tone was tinged with humor, and Alex considered that a victory. A tiny one, yes, but a victory, nonetheless.

"I'm sure you will be," he agreed. "You always are. Shall we take a turn about the room to show you off and make the other women envious?"

"Naturally."

As they descended the staircase leading into the crowded ballroom, Ellis leaned toward Daisy.

"You must introduce me to all your pretty friends," he said. "I intend to dance every dance."

"Not me," Finn said. "I don't intend to dance at all, but I do see a table of food over there I'd like to get better acquainted with."

"Oh, but you must dance, Finn," Daisy replied. "There are so many more young ladies in attendance than there are young gentlemen, and there's nothing so disheartening to a girl in a new dress than to not be asked."

"Only the homely girls don't get asked," Ellis remarked. "That's why I said introduce me to your 'pretty friends.'"

The younger boys laughed, but Daisy was not amused. "Shame on you both. Now, I won't introduce you to a single girl."

"Fine," Ellis responded with indifference. "I can manage well enough on my own."

"No, you cannot. You can't dance with anyone you haven't been properly introduced to," Daisy argued. "But if you promise to dance with *all* my friends, not just the pretty ones, then I shall introduce you."

Alex glanced over at his cousin who appeared to be weighing his options.

"You've already met Coco Hart," Alex said pleasantly. "I'm sure she'd be happy to dance with you,"

Ellis smirked. "I'm sure she'd be happy to dance with *you*, cousin."

"Coco Hart?" Constance whispered. "Surely you're not referring to one of Breezy's homespun nieces. You must stay far, far from the clutches of those girls."

"Mother, why would you say that?" Daisy asked.

"Because they're all on a determined husband hunt, that's why. Breezy told me so herself, but no self-respecting man would accept a bride who has so little to offer. And certainly not a *Bostwick* man."

Alex was only partially surprised by this news since Daisy had —thankfully—alerted him to Coco Bostwick's aim of enticing him down the aisle *(which was absolutely not going to happen)* but he hadn't gotten the impression that either Lucy or Trudy were similarly focused on finding a husband. Not that it mattered to him one way or another. He wasn't in the market for a wife, and the Hart sisters were certainly not the only young ladies at the

Imperial hoping to make a successful match this summer. His cousin, however, seemed disheartened by Constance's declaration.

"What do you mean, 'so little to offer?'" Ellis asked. "I thought Albert VonMeisterburger was rich as Midas?"

"He is," Constance quipped. "But the Hart girls' mother is Breezy's sister, so Albert VonMeisterburger is their uncle only through marriage, and their father is nothing but a simple country doctor in Springfield. I can only imagine how he's paid. Probably with rhubarb pie and chickens."

"The Harts are very nice, though," Daisy said, rising to their defense.

"So are most shopkeepers, but that doesn't mean you want to marry one," Constance stated, effectively ending that conversation.

They moved onward, through the throngs of well-dressed guests, and Alex began to relax as one acquaintance after another greeted them cordially. While not all the exchanges were warm, per se, neither were they cold, and he wondered if perhaps the cloud of scandal that had been lingering over the Bostwick family was finally beginning to dissipate. Or perhaps it was merely that his flight over the handlebars into the dirt yesterday had earned him some sympathy if not outright pity. Whatever the reason, he was glad for their hospitable reception.

Eventually, Finn left their group to explore on his own and Daisy—somewhat reluctantly—led Ellis toward a cluster of her own acquaintances while Alex guided his mother in the direction of Breezy VonMeisterburger. En route, they encountered a spirited yet playful debate between Mrs. Alvah Roebuck and Mrs. Richard Sears regarding which of their husbands was the true genius behind the success of their mail-order watch company, and Alex saw his chance to escape. His mother could easily fend for herself in this environment so under the guise of ensuring Finn wasn't making a beast of himself at the refreshment table, Alex took his leave.

In truth, he wasn't worried about Finn. He simply wanted a

moment to himself. He hadn't attended a dance since before Isabella's death and the atmosphere of this one was stirring up a myriad of memories, both pleasant and painful. As he wound his way around the periphery of the room, one song ended and dancers left the floor, but just as quickly another melody began, and the floor filled again. Like a gentle wave lapping at the shore to and fro, this familiar motion filled him with nostalgia.

He'd always enjoyed this sort of ambiance in the past. In fact, in earlier days, he'd loved the communion and commotion of a complicated quadrille, or the joyful hop and skip of a lively polka. But, ahh…nothing could surpass the enchanting thrill of an intimate waltz. To have a woman in his arms, to spin and sway together as one to a lilting melody that stirred the senses. He missed that.

His wife had been an elegant dancer. He might even go so far as to say he'd fallen in love with her during a waltz at a ball very much like this one—at the Palmer House Hotel in Chicago last March. A memory rose unbidden in his mind of the first time he'd kissed her—it was that very same night. He'd proposed the next day and thought himself the luckiest man in the world to have won the affection of a woman such as Isabella Carnegie. Their rapid engagement had been the talk of Chicago. A love match, people had said, albeit a well-funded one. A case of *good fortune* coming to those in possession of *a good fortune*, and Alex had laughed at the seemingly harmless turn of phrase.

Now that all seemed decades in the past but, he realized with a start, it had been barely over a year ago that'd he'd met Izzy. How drastically things had changed. And how strange to find himself suddenly missing her so acutely, even after all that had occurred.

Then again, perhaps it wasn't Izzy he was missing so much as he was missing *the idea* of her, and the way she'd made him feel in those first few weeks. He missed the promise and the potential of what they'd had. Or at least, what he'd thought they'd had. He missed being joyful. He missed being in love—although he could not imagine ever trusting in that emotion again.

"Mr. Bostwick! Oh, Mr. Bostwick!"

His jaw clenched reflexively at the enthusiastic call, and he turned to see Coco Hart virtually careening his way. His bittersweet memories evaporated like the misty fog of a lovely dream. The kind you weren't yet ready to awaken from, leaving him doubly annoyed by her arrival. He was in no mood to navigate her adoration, especially after what Daisy had told him that afternoon. He wondered if he might melt into the crowd and disappear, but there was no escaping her. She'd obviously spotted him.

"Good evening, Miss Hart," he said as she reached his side, her cheeks flushed with excitement. She giggled, batting her lashes as if a cinder had just landed in her eye.

"And good evening to you, sir. I'm so pleased to see you here. Daisy said you might not be in attendance."

"I had considered a quiet evening of solitude, but encountered Mr. Plank at luncheon, and he insisted I put in an appearance. *(That much was true.)* It seems there's something he wishes to discuss with me. *(Also, true.)* In fact, I just spotted him across the room and am on my way to join him now. *(Not remotely true.)* So, if you'll excuse me, Miss Hart."

"But wait! Mr. Bostwick?"

He halted with an audible sigh. "Yes, Miss Hart?"

"You do intend to dance with me this evening, don't you?" Her eyes looked up at him imploringly.

"Alas, my injured hand has rendered me an incapable dance partner."

"Then... perhaps next Saturday? Or perhaps we could go for a buggy ride tomorrow? Oh, but silly me. Of course you cannot hold the reins. A walk, perhaps?"

Alex lingered for a moment, pondering how best to respond to this list of activities in which he had no interest.

Coco Hart was a pretty girl and might even be sweet if she received the copious amounts of attention she so desperately craved, but dancing with her at any time, or going for a buggy ride, or taking a walk together, would only give her a false impression of his intentions. Worse than that, it might give *others* a false impression. He had neither the energy nor the inclination to stir up more gossip.

With those poignant memories of Isabella still hovering in the recesses of his mind, he knew he needed to be honest with this impressionable young girl. Perhaps if he'd been more honest with his wife, things might have turned out differently. He took a step closer toward Coco and her smile brightened, only serving to make him feel worse. But he knew he was doing the correct thing.

"Miss Hart," he said quietly. "I do hope I have not in any way misled you. You are a delightful young woman, and I am certain there are any number of fine, eligible gentlemen here at the hotel who would be easily captivated by your smile and would love to dance, or ride, or walk with you, but alas, I am not such a man. Therefore, I must beseech you to direct your attentions elsewhere. I do wish you every happiness, but I must bid you a good evening and be on my way."

With a curt bow, he strode away feeling every inch the heel. His words had sounded far harsher to his ears than he'd intended. He should have chosen them more carefully. Or perhaps he should have just danced with her. But... no. The truth was the truth and allowing her to think he had any designs on her whatsoever would be the true injustice.

∼

"My goodness, Coco. Whatever is the matter?" Trudy asked as her sister stumbled toward the corner where she and Lucy had been enjoying their glasses of champagne.

"He's despicable," Coco cried. "Detestable, even. I never met such a horrible brute."

Alarm propelled Trudy forward. She wrapped both arms around her sobbing sister, and pulled her farther into the corner, away from prying eyes.

"Coco, darling," Lucy murmured. "Who is despicable?"

Coco snuffled and hiccupped against Trudy's bodice before blurting out, "Alexander Bostwick."

"Alexander Bostwick?" Trudy replied.

"What did he do?" Lucy asked.

"He said he isn't captivated by my smile," Coco wailed, and Trudy pressed her lips together tightly to prevent her own smile from showing.

"Despicable," Lucy said, her eyes meeting Trudy's, their collective distress easing.

This was hardly the first time they'd consoled Coco over some hinted slight or perceived offense, and while it was certainly possible Alexander Bostwick may have been unduly rude, Trudy knew it was equally possible her sister was overreacting. Coco was prone to melodramatics, after all. She'd been inconsolable just a few days ago because no one had complimented her new hat, and last month, when her music teacher suggested she had not practiced the piece he'd assigned, she'd wept for an entire afternoon. No matter that virtually no one had even *seen* her new hat, or that she had *not*, in fact, practiced her music.

"What exactly did he say, dear?" Lucy asked, patting Coco's back.

"He said he didn't want to dance, or ride, or walk with me, and that I should direct my attentions elsewhere."

"Did he say anything else?"

"Isn't that enough?" Coco wailed, pressing her face back against Trudy's décolletage.

"Yes, of course, it is," Trudy murmured as she felt the heat of her sister's tears soak into the fabric of her gown.

When Coco was on a tear, it was usually best to go along. Pointing out her own errors, or her potential misinterpretation of a situation only served to add fuel to the fire of her discontent. Letting her cry it out was typically the most expedient solution. Perhaps they could discuss the matter more rationally tomorrow.

Hugging her sister close once again, Trudy gazed across the ballroom, spotting the offender in question. Alex was standing some twenty feet away and staring at them, an expression of bemused dismay splashed across his face.

He took a step in their direction as if in hopes of rectifying the situation, but Trudy held up a hand and gave a tiny shake of her head. She'd confer with him later.

"Coco?" Daisy Bostwick asked breathlessly as she joined them. "I saw you rushing this way. What's wrong?"

Coco sniffled again, and lifted her face from Trudy's now thoroughly tear-stained gown.

"Nothing's wrong," Coco said. "Only that your brother is a cad."

"Coco, you can't say that to Daisy. She's his sister," Lucy chided gently.

Fortunately, Daisy appeared nonplused by this news.

"Well, respectfully, I disagree, but if you think he's a cad, isn't it better for you to know now instead of wasting an entire summer pining for him?"

Coco considered this comment with a tearful hiccup. "I suppose."

"Of course it is. So that's settled then. Now quickly, wipe your face and smile. I cannot imagine why four such beautiful woman are loitering over here when there is music playing and dancing to be done. No gentlemen will find us in this corner, though. We must promenade so the men will covet us as partners and come running."

Trudy pulled a linen napkin from a nearby table and handed it to Coco so she might dry her eyes—on something other than Trudy's dress.

"Perhaps the three of you could promenade without me," Trudy said, once Coco had regained her composure. "I must repair the stains on my dress before I can mingle."

"Oh, goodness, Tru," Coco giggled, her mood already brightening, "How did you stain your dress already? We've hardly been here an hour."

"Really, Tru, how did you?" Lucy whispered wryly, winking

as she looped her arm through Daisy's, and Trudy watched as the three of them moved toward the dance floor. She sighed with familiar resignation.

> *Dear Mother and Father,*
>
> *It seems Coco's dreams of ensnaring Alexander Bostwick in holy matrimony have crumbled like day-old teacakes. She won't be coming home with a proposal of marriage after all. I, however, will be returning home with a ruined dress.*

Perhaps the tear marks on her bodice weren't that noticeable. The ballroom was shadowy enough. She might pretend they weren't even there. No one should be staring at her bosom anyway. She brushed her hand against the fabric. To no avail. Looking down, she wondered what to do, and when two finely buffed men's shoes came into her field of vision, pointing directly at the hem of her gown, well, she wondered what to do then, too.

Looking up slowly, she found herself staring into the sapphire blue depths of Alexander Bostwick's eyes. He was standing directly in front of her, the inky blackness of his finely cut tuxedo in stark contrast to the starched crisp brightness of his shirt. He'd grown tan over this past week and his darker complexion only served to make those eyes of his that much deeper a hue.

Not that any of this mattered, of course. As a physician, she was trained to notice such things. *It was simply an observation.*

"I sorry, Trudy. I didn't intend to make your sister cry," he said, brow furrowed with consternation.

"I know you didn't."

"Do you? I'd hate for you to think I'd been careless with her feelings."

"I don't think that, but whatever you said to her, I'm quite certain she won't be nipping at your heels any longer."

"I'm..." He sighed. "I only asked her to direct her attentions elsewhere. I'm in no place to entertain the idea of another wife."

"Another wife? How did you...?Oh, Daisy told you." She felt a wave of both annoyance and relief, followed quickly by embarrassment.

"I'm sorry Coco has been such a pest. I do hope her impetuous nature doesn't influence your impression of the rest of us."

"Of course it won't," he said with a chuckle, seeming relieved at her response. "You know I hold you in the highest esteem. I should think that much is obvious."

Trudy gazed back at him. She wasn't sure what to say to that. The highest esteem was... rather high, and his words flustered her even though she knew he only offered them in *friendship*. There was nothing romantic in his tone or his expression, so why did she suddenly feel so... vulnerable?

"You didn't always hold me in the highest esteem," she heard herself say.

"I didn't? What are you talking about?"

"When we were children."

He frowned. "When we were children? I didn't know you when we were children."

Oh, good gracious, Gertrude!

Why had she just said that? Why mention it now? She had well and truly forgiven that ten-year-old version of Alexander Bostwick and dredging up this story served no one. She laughed self-consciously as her vulnerability seemed to multiply. Perhaps she could blame her mindless blathering on his finely cut tuxedo. It seemed to be causing some sort of fluttery business to her insides—and apparently forcing stupid words from her mouth.

She waved her comment away with a gloved hand. "Oh, it's nothing, really. Just a silly misunderstanding. Are your brother and his wife here this evening? I'd love to visit with Jo."

"They were planning to attend but I haven't seen them yet. What misunderstanding?"

Trudy's brain began sifting through various scenarios, ways in which to cleverly change the subject but his gaze had turned curious and intense, and for better or worse, she had never been one to shy away from stating the facts. Although, at this moment, she wished her skills of obfuscation were more adept. She also wished her smile didn't feel so strained as she replied, "You hurt my feelings once, when we were children, but I assure you, I've long since recovered."*(Long since? Not exactly, but it had been at least a few days.)*

"I hurt your feelings? I'm terribly sorry. What did I do?"

"It doesn't matter now. I shouldn't have even mentioned it."

"Tell me." His tone was determined, almost bossy, and all that fluttering business inside her body made it hard for her to breathe. *What to do? What to do? Nothing to do but tell him, she supposed.*

"Oh, very well. Do you recall the time several of us children went swimming at my aunt's house?" she said.

"I don't," he replied. "Chase mentioned that to me the other day, but I have no recollection of it. He said we swam in our underclothes and that our mother tanned our hides because of it, yet somehow the memory has escaped me."

Trudy felt an ironic chuckle bubbling up at her own expense. All those years she'd spent feeling wounded by him from a distance and he didn't even remember it. There must be a lesson for her in there, somewhere, but she'd have to decide later what it might be.

"Yes, we swam in our underclothes," she replied after a pause. "I was thirteen. A late bloomer in every way except for my height, and when I came out of the water in my wet chemise... you called me... a scrawny scarecrow."

She said it with no heat because there was none to be had but confusion and discomfort co-mingled in his expression as he tried to bring forth the memory while contemplating what he'd allegedly said.

"I called you a scrawny scarecrow?" he repeated quietly.

"You did." Her nod was matter-of-fact.

"How terribly unkind of me. I can certainly understand why

that would've hurt your feelings. Please tell me I apologized at the time."

Her smile slowly turned genuine because, now that she was an adult, it all seemed rather funny. In retrospect. Especially since she now knew him to be kind. But since she *had* waited fifteen years to confront him, perhaps she'd be justified in enjoying his dismay, just a little.

"No, you did not apologize," she said, tapping her chin as if to remember. "In fact, you pointed at me and laughed and then if I recall correctly, you danced a little scarecrow jig."

His face blanched even as she smiled. "Say it isn't so," he said solemnly. "You're teasing me right now, aren't you?"

She shook her head. "I'm not. You were positively beastly to me that day, but I'm happy to see you've outgrown such ungentlemanly behavior."

"Have I?" he asked, more earnestly than she'd expected. "I just made your sister cry."

Oh, goodness. She hadn't meant to make him feel *worse*. She'd meant to make him snicker at an awkward boyhood blunder.

"Did you call her a scrawny scarecrow?" she asked in mock seriousness.

He shook his head—in serious seriousness.

"Then whatever you said to her was probably something she needed to hear but didn't want to. Coco is obstinate and willful, but she'll recover. Probably by the end of the evening if enough men ask her to dance."

Trudy nodded toward the dance floor where her sisters were already laughing their way through the steps of a lively polonaise, attentive partners by their sides. The sight was charming but caused Trudy's heart to twitch with the tiniest sense of unexpected longing.

She never felt *that* much older than Lucy and Coco, but she'd spent so much time studying medicine and working at the clinic with her father, she'd missed out on many evenings such as this. Now, at twenty-eight, with no intention of getting married, society had placed her firmly on the shelf. Her dancing days, brief as they were, seemed far behind.

Oh, she might be asked to dance by the occasional neighbor or kindly old man, but few would seek her out. She was already relegated to the periphery of the activity, left to tap her foot to the music and watch others having fun.

Perhaps that was why her sister had suggested they sip their champagne here in this corner. Because Lucy knew she'd likely be asked to dance, while Trudy wouldn't. It was meant to be a thoughtful gesture, but the notion of it stung like a needle prick. Trudy didn't want anyone's *pity*.

And since when had she cared about dancing, anyway?

Alex gazed out over the dance floor but must have noticed something wistful in her expression.

"Once my hand has mended we must take a turn," he said.

"Mm, perhaps," she murmured.

No, she didn't want anyone's pity.

ten

"Ah, there you are, Dr. Hart."

Trudy looked up from her copy of the *Journal of the American Medical Association* which she—at Aunt Breezy's insistence—had started hiding inside the latest edition of *Harper's Bazaar Magazine*. Standing beside her chair was one of the Mr. Bostwicks, but judging from his greeting, she knew it must be Chase.

It was early Sunday morning, and Trudy was enjoying the peace and tranquility of the front porch while most of the other guests were either sleeping off last night's festivities or attending church services in town. Her sisters were among the former while Asher and Poppy were, reluctantly, with the latter.

"Why don't the older girls have to go to church with us?" Asher had grumbled to Aunt Breezy an hour prior as Trudy listened through the bedroom door. "It's not fair. Maybe Poppy and I wanted to sleep all day like them."

"Because, young man," Trudy heard Breezy respond. "It's my Christian duty to take you to church. You want to get into heaven, don't you?"

"Sure, but do you really think my going to church will be enough?"

"For you? Probably not, but my taking you might at least help me get in."

Trudy heard Asher chuckle good naturedly as he said, "If that's the case, getting my sisters to go would earn you some real points with the Almighty."

Breezy scoffed. "Even God doesn't expect miracles, boy."

Trudy had stifled a giggle and jumped back into bed lest her aunt realize she was awake. It wasn't that she minded going to church. In fact, she rather liked parts of it, but sitting on the porch of the Imperial Hotel, watching the sun dry dew drops off the morning grass was every bit as spiritual as a sermon, as far as Trudy was concerned. And having some uninterrupted time to read? *Now that was a miracle.*

But it seemed she *was* to be interrupted.

"Good morning, Mr. Bostwick," she answered, raising her hand to shield her eyes from the sun. "I was hoping to see your wife at the dance last night. Did I miss you in the crush?"

He shook his head and sat down in the chair next to her.

"No, we weren't able to make it. Jo wasn't feeling well."

"She wasn't? Oh, I'm sorry to hear that. Is she better this morning?"

His nod was half-hearted. "She says she is, but I'm not convinced. Truthfully, that's why I came to find you. I do hate to impose, but I was wondering if you might stop by and see her today."

"Of course, I'd be happy to. What seems to be the problem?"

His relief at her response was clouded by his concern.

"I'm not sure," he answered. "As you can imagine, I'm quite out to sea in this matter. She keeps insisting she's fine, but I sense she's more uncomfortable than she's willing to admit. She was too fatigued to attend last's night's ball, and this morning she's complaining of a headache."

"I see. In that case, I can go see her now, if that's convenient."

His expression brightened. "Most convenient. Thank you! Only…"

"Only?"

"She doesn't know I've come to find you."

Trudy crooked an eyebrow, and he smiled sheepishly. "She told me not to bother you, and I told her I wouldn't, but she knew I would. She doesn't want to take advantage of your generosity, especially since we've already imposed upon you to treat Alex's finger."

"Don't be silly. It's no imposition at all. In fact, I'm sorry she's not feeling well but I miss seeing patients. I feel rather rudderless without something purposeful to do."

"If you're sure it isn't too much trouble," he said.

She closed her periodical and rose from the chair. "No trouble at all. Lead the way, Mr. Bostwick."

Some fifteen minutes later they were standing outside a second-floor suite.

"Just go ahead and knock," Mr. Bostwick said. "And if she asks, you never saw me."

Trudy looked at him askance. "And am I supposed to fabricate a reason for my visit then?" she asked dryly. "Good morning, Mrs. Bostwick. I just happened to be wandering around on this floor and wondered if you'd like some unsolicited medical care?"

He chuckled at her humor. "Yes. Perfect. Say exactly that."

"I will not say that. Come inside with me and confess your intervention or I'll be on my way."

He hesitated for only a moment then with a subtle shake of his head, he turned the crystal knob and slowly opened the door. "You drive a hard bargain, Dr. Hart," he said quietly before calling out, "Darling? I've brought you some company."

They stepped into the room and Trudy saw Jo leaning back in an upholstered chair with a cloth pressed against her forehead.

"Oh, you silly man," Jo muttered, setting the cloth on a side table and straightening in the chair as if to rise.

"Please don't get up. It's not necessary," Trudy said quickly, walking closer.

"Good, then I won't. You may blame my poor manners on

this impertinent baby," she answered with a wan chuckle. "And please pardon the mess. We've forbidden the maid to tidy in this room since she cannot tell our trash from our treasures."

The room was a standard hotel design, but with the bed removed to make space for a large walnut desk currently littered with official looking documents. Surrounding that was a collection of easels, and more painting supplies than Trudy had ever seen in one place. She marveled at the array of tubes and pots and brushes, as well as the numerous canvases, some blank, and some in various stages of creation.

"My wife is finishing some commissioned pieces for the hotel," Chase explained. "So, Hugo was kind enough to provide us with an extra room where we might work together."

"It's not exactly Paris," Jo said. "But at least it doesn't require an ocean voyage to get to."

Chase crossed the room to her side. "Darling, can I get you anything? Some tea, perhaps, for you and Dr. Hart?"

"Yes, some tea, please. And if you truly love me, you might see if Mrs. Culpepper has any cucumber sandwiches."

"I do, and I will."

"Thank you."

"Can I get anything for you, Dr. Hart? Besides the tea?" he asked as he turned.

"No, I'm fine, but thank you."

"Of course."

He crossed back to the door, and as it shut behind him Jo gazed over at Trudy, an expression of mild exasperation on her face.

"I don't really want cucumber sandwiches," she said, "but he needs to be *doing* something, and his hovering is driving me mad. I'm sorry he bothered you."

Trudy chuckled. "It's truly no bother. I was reading on the porch and have very few plans for the day. I'm sorry you're not feeling well." She took a seat in another upholstered chair not far from Jo's and gazed around the room.

"It rather looks like a herd of cattle stampeded through here, doesn't it?" Jo said. "I'm usually quite tidy but it doesn't take much for this small space to look cluttered."

"I rather like it in here," Trudy responded. "The mess feels more at home to me than all the opulent décor. And your paintings are marvelous."

"Well, hopefully they will be when I'm finished. Do you paint?" Jo asked.

"No. I draw a bit but mostly things of a clinical nature. Injuries, curious anatomical anomalies, ideas I have for new medical equipment. Things like that."

"That's rather fascinating. I'd love to see your work," Jo replied politely causing Trudy to chuckle.

"No, I don't believe you would, but I appreciate you saying so."

Jo's smile appeared sincere, although Trudy could see lines of fatigue around her eyes.

"Perhaps one day you might take one of my painting classes and try your hand at something more lighthearted. A bowl of fruit perhaps? Or a bouquet of flowers?"

"My sisters are far more artistic than I, but I'm willing to make an attempt, as long as you won't think less of me for my inability to properly render a daffodil."

"I assure you, I would not. And may I add, I am entirely daunted by your other skills. Your deft handling of that incident with Alex was inspiring."

Trudy laughed again. "It isn't much to set a broken finger."

"But it wasn't just that. You kept everyone calm. Well, everyone except for me when I lambasted the boys for their foolishness while we were in Hugo's office, but even then, you had the good sense to send me from the room."

"My apologies for that."

"Don't apologize. It was the correct decision. You knew just what to say, even to Alex and that's no small thing."

Trudy warmed at the compliment. "Thank you. I appreciate

your kind words, but let's talk about what's troubling you. If you'd like to, that is. I realize I am here at your husband's request, not yours."

"I will happily accept any medical advice you offer. We are over the moon with joy about this baby, but I admit I did not expect pregnancy to be such an ordeal."

"You did mention at dinner that first evening you'd suffered from some dyspepsia. Is that still the case?"

"No, that's abated for the most part, thank goodness, although it does come back occasionally."

"Then may I inquire what unpleasantness has you worried?"

"I suspect my husband is more worried than I am, but occasionally I get light-headed or dizzy, my back aches, my legs sometimes cramp, I can't sleep so I'm tired all the time, and as you've already witnessed, I burp indiscriminately. Perhaps these issues are commonplace, but my mother passed away when I was young, and I had a rather unconventional upbringing. I wasn't around women who were expecting so this is all very new for me. And of course, every time I ask Dr. Prescott about any of it, he just pats my hand and tells me I'm being hysterical." Her eyes widened as if a thought was just now occurring to her. She gazed over at Trudy and said, "Oh, my goodness. Am I being hysterical?"

"Of course not," Trudy assured her. "Please don't ever let the dismissive nature of my male colleagues make you question your own judgment. Especially one such as Dr. Prescott." She could not disguise the disdain in her voice. She didn't even attempt to.

"He's horrible," Jo said in agreement. "Which you probably discerned from your encounter with him after the bicycle race."

"He was certainly patronizing, and I can only imagine how much worse he is regarding matters of the female condition."

"Horrible," Jo said again. "Most of the female employees of the hotel refuse to see him. They try to see Dr. Hargrove instead but he's in town and always busy, so they're often left to their own devices. Chef Culpepper is adept at sewing stitches. He says it's from trussing up turkeys for roasting, but for other medical matters, the women tend to rely on one another."

"That's not ideal. Has anyone mentioned their dislike of Dr. Prescott to Mr. Plank?"

"I don't think so. No one wants to be seen as a rabble rouser, but that's a good suggestion. Hugo can't fix the problem if he doesn't know it exists. It's less of an issue in the winter, of course, because there are fewer of us here, but even then, the general opinion is that being treated by Dr. Prescott is oftentimes worse than having no physician at all."

Trudy felt her ire rise. In this day and age, there was simply no excuse for shoddy medical care.

"That's infuriating," she said. "And all too common, I'm afraid. I've encountered innumerable physicians who let their egos cloud their judgment, and many who dismiss a woman's concerns simply because the medical community insists on keeping the mechanics of our female bodies a mystery. Society does everything it can to keep us weak and mild, yet when women are faced with something as complicated and difficult as bringing new life into the world, we're accused of being hysterical. It's maddening!"

"Here! Here!" Jo replied enthusiastically, making Trudy blush.

"My apologies. I'm rather passionate about broadening the scope of knowledge regarding what women need from their physicians."

"And how fortunate we are that you do," Jo responded. "Powerful voices are necessary to bring about meaningful change in any area. As an artist, I've witnessed what obstacles society puts in my path as I strive to be acknowledged, but I can only imagine how much more difficult it is in the field of medicine."

"It hasn't been easy," Trudy admitted. "Progress and acceptance swing like a pendulum. A new sensibility moves things forward but oftentimes those in charge send us backward because they can't adapt. I realize a female physician is a novelty to many, but I do hope to change that perception."

"I believe you will."

"Let's hope, but perhaps I should begin by helping you. I do have a number of suggestions to ease your discomfort, but I must ask, have you consulted with a midwife?"

Jo's cheeks flushed. "I had one who I liked very much but my mother-in-law made her cry, and she hasn't returned."

"How did she make her cry?" The question was not medically relevant, but Trudy *was* curious.

"I believe she called the woman slovenly and ignorant. Or perhaps it was... slatternly and incompetent? She definitely called her unkempt and bedraggled, not seeming to realize the poor woman had been up all night attending to a very difficult birth."

Having met the other Mrs. Bostwick, Trudy wasn't surprised. Those seemed like the kind of words Constance might use. Hopefully she'd never use them on Trudy.

"Your mother-in-law seems to be a woman of strong opinions," Trudy replied.

"You have no idea. When Chase and I first married, I was certain I could bring her around to liking me but so far I've not had much luck. I'm hoping maybe a grandchild will soften her."

"Babies do have a way of melting hearts."

Trudy's heartstrings tugged at her own words—an inexplicable reaction given her decision to remain childless. It was a choice she'd made pragmatically and rationally, and not one that often triggered doubt. Yet suddenly, the idea of holding a baby in her arms sounded very appealing. She must be feeling sentimental since Jo was so near her time.

"When do you expect the arrival?" she asked.

Jo's smile was hesitant. "Well, based on when we got married, Dr. Prescott has said to expect the child in August but..." Her voice dropped off and Trudy nodded with comprehension.

"Ah, I see. You suspect you may be further along than that?"

"I'm certain of it. In fact, I think that may be what the midwife said that caused my mother-in-law to shred her to pieces.

That's the reason I haven't reached out to her. I'm too embarrassed."

"Being surrounded by people you trust when your time comes is the most important thing," Trudy said. "If you'd like me to contact this midwife on your behalf, I'll happily do so."

"Would you? Oh, but that's silly. I should write to her myself. I owe her an apology, at the very least."

"It sounds more as if it's your mother-in-law owes her an apology."

"That will happen when pigs fly," Jo responded.

"What will happen when pigs fly?" Chase asked, coming in through the doorway with a heavily laden tea tray.

"Um..." Jo replied. "Hugo Plank passing up an opportunity to promote the hotel."

Trudy turned her face to hide her smile. Some little white lies were in everyone's best interest.

"Ah," he said, setting down the tray on the table near his wife. "Mrs. Culpepper made these sandwiches just for you. Harlan has apparently been fiddling with things in the greenhouse and she said these cucumbers are something special. Although if you ask me, the only way to make a cucumber interesting is to turn it into a pickle." He smiled, reminding Trudy just how much he looked like his brother. She found that fascinating from a biological standpoint—and rather distracting from a personal standpoint.

"Thank you, darling," Jo said. "Now why don't you run along and meet Alex like you'd planned. I have Trudy to keep me company and once we're finished chatting, I intend to spend my afternoon in the rigorous pursuit of reading and napping."

He glanced at his wife, and Trudy sensed his hesitation.

"I have no plans today," she said. "I can stay as long as Mrs. Bostwick would like me too."

"Oh, good heavens. You must call me Jo, and although I'll certainly enjoy your company, please don't think I need a nurse, or in this case, a doctor, to watch over me. It's a headache and it's nearly dissipated." She turned to Chase, adding, "I love you, but you have to stop fussing. Go bother your brother. He's the one with the broken finger."

Trudy and Chase exchanged smiles, and he set down the teapot.

"Very well," he said. "As my services are not currently required, I shall vacate the premises." He leaned over, kissed Jo's cheek, picked up a hat sitting on his desk, and departed.

"Has your headache truly dissipated our were you just trying to be rid of him?" Trudy asked as the door shut behind him.

"No, it's nearly gone," Jo assured her as she poured them tea from a Lenox pot.

As they sipped from the elegant cups and ate tiny, delicious sandwiches, they discussed Jo's symptoms and Trudy's suggested treatments. They spoke of chamomile, ginger, and peppermint, along with stinging nettle, raspberry leaf, and Partridge berry, and all the while Trudy felt a kinship growing between them. She liked Jo Bostwick. With her, Trudy felt she could be entirely herself, and that was a blessing.

"When you get closer to your confinement, you may try some blue cohosh tea to ease your back pain but be aware it can bring on early labor. That's something to ask the midwife about."

Jo stirred her tea, looking thoughtful for a moment.

"I will write a note to the midwife, and I'd like her with me when it's time, but..." She looked up at Trudy. "Do you think you could be there, too? In fact, would you consider being my physician until after the baby is born?"

Trudy felt her eyes get misty with emotion—which was utter silliness. It made sense Jo would want a doctor she could be honest with and who could answer her questions—and one who *wasn't* Dr. Prescott.

Still, it meant *something* that Jo trusted her.

"Of course, I will. I'd be honored."

eleven

In spite of his bandaged finger, Alex had been looking forward to a relaxing afternoon ride with his brother—on fine horses this time, not those bicycle contraptions—but to his dismay, when Chase entered the stables, he was accompanied by the ever-boisterous Hugo Plank. The two men were guffawing like drunkards over some story pertaining to a dog race last summer, but the more they tried to explain it to him, the greater their mirth, and the less understandable they became.

"I'm sorry, Alex," Chase finally said, clapping him on the back. "I wish you'd been there. Flossie and Regina just kept paddling around in circles in the lake and Mother was so irate."

"I had pictured the race going much differently," Hugo added, wiping a tear of humor from his eye. "Tippett was horrified."

"It must have been amusing to have you both in such a state," Alex said, impatience lacing his voice. "Shall we ride now?"

It wasn't that he disliked Hugo or wanted to avoid his companionship, but there were things Alex had hoped to discuss with his brother today. Topics he did not want to share in front of anyone else and certainly not in front of Mr. Plank. But it seemed he'd have to wait.

"Yes, of course. Of course, my boy," Hugo responded with a nod. "Let's ride and not keep you waiting any longer. I assume you're as skilled an equestrian as your brother?"

"Naturally," Alex replied automatically.

"And you can still manage with that broken paw?" He nodded at Alex's bandaged hand.

"I will manage just fine."

"Excellent," Hugo answered before stepping away to speak to one of the grooms.

"He invited himself," Chase whispered. "I could hardly turn him down. Do you mind?"

"Of course not," Alex lied.

"Good because the two of you should get better acquainted. Once you get past all the bluster and showmanship, you'll see Hugo is an honorable, dependable man. I trust him, and I suspect he has some business he wants to discuss."

"With both of us?"

Chase nodded. "It may not be anything of interest to you, but just hear him out. Let's see what he has to say."

Hugo had, of course, mentioned wanting to speak to Alex yesterday, but there had been no opportunity at the dance last evening. Although, in truth, Alex hadn't made much of an attempt.

After making Coco Hart weep, and then discovering he'd been horrible to Trudy in their youth, Alex had felt rather out of sorts. Chase and Jo were absent, Ellis was dancing, Daisy was dancing, and even his mother seemed disinclined to engage with him choosing to instead embroil herself in a rigorous debate with Mrs. Bertrand Moseley regarding the superiority of *Haviland china* versus *Syracuse china*. Needless to say, he had no opinion on that matter, and if not for fear of wagging tongues, he would have returned to Trudy's side.

But in the end, he'd cast his lot with a group of bored husbands who didn't *want to* dance with their frowning wives and weren't *allowed* to dance with the smiling young ladies. So instead, like a rafter of gobblers, they milled about near the bar, squawking loudly about politics and whether or not Benjamin Harrison was up to the task of being president *(unlikely),* whether or not the Polish immigrants employed by the *Wayne Cigar Company* in Detroit could produce anything as fine as something rolled in Havana *(possibly),* and whether or not *Brooks Brothers* was the premier haberdasher in all of Chicago. *(Definitely.)* And when talk turned to the recent flooding in Johnstown caused by a faulty dam, they grew animated and belligerent.

"Henry Frick was responsible for the construction and management of that dam," Warner Moorehead said, gesturing so broadly the *Glenlivet* sloshed from his glass. "The fault lies entirely with him."

"Frick is Carnegie's right-hand man. If anyone's to blame for the negligence, it's Andrew Carnegie himself," John Winslow shot back with defiance.

But the argument had dwindled as, one by one, they seemed to recall Alex's wife had been Carnegie. A distant relation, but still, he could see in each man's expression when it dawned on him that Alex might be uncomfortable with this particular debate.

He'd left the ballroom soon after, returning to his suite only to find one of Isabella's calling cards perched precariously above the frame of his balcony door... and his bedsheets smelling of her signature perfume, a scent created exclusively for her by Gabriel Guerlain himself.

So, this afternoon, discussing business with Hugo Plank was the last thing on Alex's mind.

As they guided their mounts down the boulevard leading away from the hotel, he silently reminded himself to appreciate the sun shining down from a cloudless blue sky, and the soft breeze keeping the air fresh and cool. As sounds from the hotel's front lawn faded, and the gentle thud of hooves against the hard-packed dirt became a soothing cadence, he strove to set aside his cares and concerns, at least for the moment. They'd be waiting for him when he returned, but for now, he was going to put them on the shelf and enjoy this ride.

Next to him, Hugo rode the same dappled palfrey he'd ridden that day on the West Bluff, and when Alex realized that he and Chase were seated on nearly identical Morgans, it lifted his good humor, and he chuckled.

"Is it a coincidence my twin brother and I have matching horses or does your groom have a sense of humor?" he asked.

"It's possible," Hugo answered affably, "Although if he had a real sense of humor, we have a very frisky filly in the stable that would have given you some real trouble."

"Aren't frisky fillies always trouble?" Chase joked.

"Well, this one is named after my niece so take from that what you will." Their laughter mingled with the jangle of the bridle as they moseyed forward.

"I'm sorry I wasn't able to speak with you last evening," Hugo said to Alex a moment later. "The first dance of the season is always full of mishaps, so I was rather busy."

"Mishaps? I didn't notice any," Alex responded. *Other than himself making Coco Hart weep, of course. Oh, and finding out he'd once called Trudy a scrawny scarecrow.*

"I'm glad to hear you didn't encounter any mishaps," Hugo replied. "It means Tippett and I did our jobs effectively. I don't recall seeing you there, though, Chase. Did I just miss you?"

"Unfortunately, we had to change our plans at the last minute," Chase answered. "Jo wasn't feeling up to it."

"I'm sorry to hear that. Is she better today?"

"She seems to be. I left her in the capable care of Dr. Hart this afternoon."

"Trudy's with Jo?" Alex asked, surprise evident in his tone.

"Yes, and they seemed to be deep in conversation when I left."

Alex pondered this silently.

The fact that Chase's wife was spending time with Trudy should not impact him in any kind of way, and yet he found himself curious about what they were discussing. It was arrogance, undoubtedly, that made him wonder if he might be a topic for surely there were any number of things the two women would find more interesting, not to mention the fact that Trudy was there in a medical capacity.

And even if his name did come up, what of it?

Still, he wondered...

"Whoa, Sally." Hugo reined in his horse and turned in his saddle to gaze back at the hotel. "Will you look at that, boys," he said reverently. "My first masterpiece."

They turned as instructed. Alex had seen the hotel from the carriage while riding up from the dock. He'd seen it from the lawn, and had been inside of it, too, but from this vantage point, he could see the entire expanse with the crystal waters of Lake Huron behind it. Hugo's pride was understandable.

"I never tire of seeing it from here," Hugo said as if to himself.

"A sight to behold," Chase added almost automatically, and Alex realized with growing humor that Hugo had made his brother gaze at the hotel from this spot before.

"Do you know what that hill looked like two summers ago?" Hugo asked. "It looked like nothing. Nothing but big rocks, a few scraggly trees, a shack here and there. And cows. Cows roaming wherever they pleased. But now look at it. The mansion on the hill. That's what the locals call it."

Alex glanced over at Chase, whose mild expression revealed he had definitely heard this before. More than once. The brothers sat silently, letting Hugo relish his achievement until, at last, he turned back and gave Sally a nudge with his feet.

"The thing about building a hotel," Hugo said as they turned onto a road that would lead them to Main Street of Trillium Bay, "is its permanence. You can see it. Other people can see it. They can experience it and create memories in it. And that's a thing of beauty."

His comments seemed rhetorical in nature, so Alex didn't reply.

"Now, on a grander scale," Hugo continued, "is a town. A

town has various businesses, spots for recreation, places to enjoy a meal, pubs for a drink or two, stores for necessities and frivolities. It's a place of memory making, too, so in my humble opinion, Trillium Bay should be a town that inspires memories that are just as wonderful and magical as the ones created by my hotel. Recollections for people to hold dear for years to come."

Alex looked over at Chase again wondering where this monologue was headed. Chase just smiled and shook his head.

"Trillium Bay is a town on the cusp of greatness..." Hugo added. "But it sure as hell isn't there yet."

As he spoke, they rounded another bend, arriving at the southernmost end of Main Street. It was a wide, mostly muddy strip with a few modest storefronts. O'Doul's grocery, Davey's Hardware, Callaghan's Leather Shoppe, and Persimmon's Candy Emporium (which had taken liberal license with the term emporium) along with a few horse troughs, hitching posts, and a single saloon which was dingy enough to make the horse troughs look to be a superior place to wet one's whistle.

"You see," Hugo said, reining in his horse. "What we have here now offers nothing to inspire folks to spend time in town. However, imagine, if you will, this thoroughfare bustling with boutiques and businesses." He waved his hand across the air as if painting a new vision and continued speaking. "A veritable cornucopia of commerce and community. A destination not only for guests of the Imperial Hotel, but for others visiting the island, as well as our dedicated soldiers stationed at Fort Beaumont. I'm picturing a gentlemen's haberdashery, a ladies' milliner, a dry goods store stocked with everything you might need or want, a jeweler and watch repair, a cigar shoppe, an ice cream parlor, perhaps even a bookseller or a library, and of course, fine dining as well as pubs. Thanks to my hotel, this island is becoming a truly coveted destination, but it needs to offer more."

Hugo's excitement grew with every sentence until he was all but shouting. Then he gazed at them expectantly, as if to gauge their level of captivation.

"I thought your aim was to ensure the Imperial Hotel was the most enticing destination on the island," Chase said. "Won't attractive businesses in town compete with what you already offer?"

Hugo's smile was slow and smug. "Not if I own them," he said confidently. "That's where you boys come in."

Chase laughed out loud, and Alex got the distinct impression Hugo was about to pass them his hat for a big, fat donation to the cause.

"You want *more* money?" his brother asked. "Haven't I already invested enough in your hotel?"

"You've invested in the Imperial?" Alex said to his brother.

This was news to him. Chase hadn't breathed a word of it. Then again, Alex had been rather busy over the past few months, falling in love, getting married, attending his wife's funeral, and more recently, being haunted by her.

"Yes, I invested last summer. With my own funds," Chase responded. "Father doesn't know anything about it so I'd appreciate if you kept that to yourself."

"And what a sound investment it was," Hugo added. "You've witnessed the success of the hotel, Chase. You'll make your money back in ample measure."

"So, you say," Chase replied pleasantly. "But I've yet to see a dime in returns."

Hugo shrugged. "Have you seen the new dormitories being built for the employees?"

"Yes."

"There's your profit. I reinvested it for you."

"Without asking me?" Chase responded. "I have a child on the way, Plank. Maybe I need that money for other things."

"What other things? You have free room and board at my hotel. A stable full of horses to ride, even a physician on call to look after your lovely wife and clumsy brother."

The *clumsy* jest notwithstanding, Alex was flummoxed by the casual way they were discussing Chase's money. Just how much had his brother invested? And why had Alex and their father been kept in the dark about it?

"There are plenty of other things requiring money," Chase said with faux indignation. "And our room and board was negotiated under the terms of my wife's consignment work. We're not staying there for free. We're paying with artwork."

Hugo paused, then said, "There's no need to nitpick over every penny. The point is, I have grand plans for this town. Harry Blackwell, the mayor, is on board with my vision, the Callaghan brothers are chomping at the bit to open up a pub with my backing, and I've been communicating with Percy O'Keefe about improvements to the dock and adding a sufficient marina."

"Percy's in on this?" Chase asked. "He hasn't written to me about it."

"I've sworn him to secrecy, and I must ask for the same discretion from the two of you. I'm not the only one interested in developing the downtown area but I intend to be the first and the largest. Naturally, for that, I'll need dependable partners."

"Partners? Or investors?" Alex asked.

"I'm always looking for investors, but in this case, I'm also looking for partners. Men who are quick-witted, dependable, and above all, trustworthy who share my entrepreneurial spirit. This venture will require architects, financiers, builders, suppliers, restaurateurs, you name it. I intend to build this town from the ground up, and even I realize I cannot do it alone."

"Are you certain you need to do it at all?" Chase asked, looking down the street. "Trillium Bay is rustic but adequate."

Hugo's brows came together. "My boy, when have you ever known me to be satisfied with adequate? And anyway, as I said, I'm not the only one with such plans. Trillium Bay is going to be developed into a tourist mecca one way or another. If I don't act quickly, Ryerson and Harwell will snatch up all the prime waterfront properties and leave me in the dust. They would love nothing more than to drive me out of business. That means time is of the essence. So, what do you say? Are you in?"

Chase burst out laughing again. "Am I in? Give a man a moment to think, Hugo. There's a lot to consider."

Hugo turned to Alex. "What about you, young man? Are you ready to strike while the iron is hot?"

"I must agree with my brother on this, Hugo. It's a lot to consider."

It *was* a lot to consider. In truth, Hugo's proposal *had* lit a spark of curiosity within him, but Alex was a savvy enough businessman to know tempering his interest was essential until he'd done a proper amount of his own investigating. His last major investment, a copper mine in northern Michigan, had proven disastrous and he was not going to make that kind of mistake again.

"Do you trust him?" Alex asked Chase later that afternoon as the two brothers walked back toward the hotel from the stables. Hugo had headed off in another direction but not before making them promise to stop by his office this week to see some preliminary drawings he'd done of his vision for Main Street.

"I trust him to be honest and shoot straight," Chase answered. "But that doesn't mean this new plan is a sound investment of either time or money."

"And yet you invested in the hotel. Why keep that a secret?"

Chase shrugged. "I enjoy working for Father at Bostwick & Sons. I don't take for granted all the avenues he's opened up for us, but I wanted to venture out on my own for once. I wanted to see how it felt to take a bold risk without the safety net of the family company beneath me."

"And now? How does it feel?"

Chase's smile grew. "It feels damn good. Of course, if I'd lost my shirt in the deal I might be singing a different tune, but it's a powerful thing to accept all the risks because now I own the reward. You should try it."

"You think I should invest in Hugo's development plan?" His voice held traces of surprise.

Chase hesitated for a moment, and then said, "If not that,

then do something else. You're languishing, big brother. You need something to stir your senses."

Alex was aware of that, and he didn't disagree. He'd been mired in place for months, not only due to Izzy's untimely demise, but also because of that failed copper mine. His poor judgment had cost Bostwick & Sons a great deal of money. Money which his wife's fortune helped to replenish. But movement just for the sake of movement wasn't logical. He needed to know which direction to head.

"Are you suggesting I blunt the consequences of past mistakes by potentially making a new and different mistake?" Alex asked dryly.

"Of course not. I'm merely suggesting you find something, anything to occupy your mind with besides what happened with Isabella. You're not yourself these days. Even this afternoon, I can tell you're preoccupied. I know you've been floundering in your grief, and I know it takes time, yet I can't help but wonder if a new business venture might be just the thing to help you pull through it."

This would be the ideal time to fill Chase in on all the happenings with Isabella's belongings, but they'd reached the edge of the grassy lawn. Not too far from where they stood, youngsters frolicked, engaged in some game that apparently required a great deal of shrieking while their nannies and mommas sat nearby with parasols to keep the sun at bay. On the porch, guests had gathered for an afternoon concert, while further afield boys were playing a raucous round of tennis as young ladies—ostensibly playing croquet—were surreptitiously watching them.

All around people appeared to be enjoying themselves.

"Did you know that was what Hugo had in mind when he asked to come riding with us?" Alex asked quietly.

"No, this is the first I've heard of his latest plans, but he does have a flair for the dramatic, doesn't he?"

"Indeed."

"And he's quite the salesman."

"That he is. But he has created something special here," Alex admitted, gazing out over the bucolic scene.

"He has," Chase agreed. "That being the case, I suppose it wouldn't do any harm to at least peruse the sketches he's made."

Alex paused, the cogs of his mind beginning to engage, sluggishly at first, like an old engine that had lain dormant for too long. Rusty, in need of oil, but slowly building momentum.

"Sketches are all well and good, but it's the financial figures I'm interested in," Alex said at last. "If Plank is formulating a business plan based on his optimistic projections rather than historical trends, he could be setting himself up for financial ruin. And since half this island is designated as a national park, the property he has his eye on may not even be available for development. Assuming it is, and assuming he secures the legal rights to develop downtown, he'll need to hire a reputable civil engineering firm posthaste. If he wants to attract wealthy guests, they're going to expect modern amenities. Indoor plumbing, electricity, accessibility." Alex shook his head as he stared at the hotel. "It's one thing to build a single resort, posh though it may be. But it's quite another to establish the kind of town he's talking about. I'm not sure he comprehends the enormity of what he aims to accomplish here. He'll need a lot of help."

When Chase did not respond, Alex turned to find his brother with a rather satisfied smirk on his face.

"Have I said something amusing?" Alex asked.

No," his brother replied.

"Is there something you wanted to add?" Alex pressed.

Chase's smile widened. "No. Only... welcome back, big brother."

twelve

"Tell me again, which one is Flossie, and which is Regina?" Trudy asked as she, Lucy, and Poppy followed Daisy through the lobby, past a frowning Mr. Beeks, and out onto the front porch.

They'd been tasked with taking Constance Bostwick's beloved long-haired dachshunds out for a stroll, yet never before had Trudy encountered two less enthusiastic pets. In fact, Lucy was carrying one while Daisy carried the other. Partly because their long bodies had difficulty negotiating the long staircase, but also because of—as Daisy put it—their *sheer, unmitigated laziness.*

"This one is Flossie," Daisy answered, indicating the one in her arms. "They'll perk up a bit when we get to the grass."

"Good," responded Lucy, "because this one is heavier than she looks." The dog peered up at her as she spoke and offered a slow, tentative lick on her chin, making Poppy sigh.

"I wish you would've let me bring Sir Chester along," Poppy said wistfully. "I think he would've enjoyed an outing on such a splendiferous day."

"They would've fought like cats and dogs," Trudy teased. "And then none of us would've enjoyed our day."

"Excuse me? Are you... Dr. Hart?"

Trudy turned to see a woman with blood-shot eyes and a rather frazzled expression on her otherwise lovely face. She looked to be around thirty-years old, or so, and was dressed in the height of fashion despite her rather messy hair.

"Yes, I'm Dr. Hart. May I help you?"

"Land sakes, I hope so! Might I speak with you privately?"

Trudy waved the others on, saying she'd meet them on the lawn, and walked with the woman to a quiet alcove near one end of the lobby.

"What's troubling you," she asked as they sat down on a cushioned bench.

"My husband is troubling me. Well, not him, directly, but he has trouble and that's what's troubling me." She glanced around to make sure no one was near and lowered her voice. "He has not been able to…"

The woman paused and Trudy knew this conversation could go in one of several different directions.

"Evacuate his bowls," the woman said at last, and Trudy wasn't sure if she should be relieved or disappointed.

"He's so miserable neither one of us can sleep," the woman continued. "Dr. Prescott told him to take castor oil, but my husband refuses to take castor oil because it gives him a rash and makes it hard for him to breathe. Dr. Prescott said that was just silly and that a grown man should be able to take his medicine without complaint, but my husband said if he had to choose between being able to…to defecate or being able to breathe, he'd choose breathing, but heavens to Betsy, I'm at my wit's end! Then I remembered seeing you taking care of Mr. Bostwick after he fell from that bicycle, and I thought, there's a woman who knows how to get things accomplished." The woman reached over and clasped Trudy's hand." So, Dr. Hart, do you think you can help my husband… well… expel his excrement?"

All of this was delivered in a single breath, and Trudy paused a moment to see if the woman might add something more, although her description of the issue had been most thorough.

"I'm sorry to hear about his discomfort, Mrs...?"

"Oh, good heavens. Where are my manners? I'm Mrs. Dunlap. Mrs. Grover Dunlap and my husband is, well, obviously, Mr. Grover Dunlap. Please forgive me for interrupting your sojourn outside but we are both desperate."

Trudy smiled. "It's a pleasure to make your acquaintance, Mrs. Dunlap, and believe I might be able to help husband. Let me get a piece of paper and write down some instructions."

Trudy walked over to the registration desk where Mr. Beeks begrudgingly handed over a single sheet of paper and the stub of a pencil after making her wait an interminable five minutes. He had clearly not forgiven her for the disturbance they'd caused on the day of their arrival, but nothing could be done about that now. She moved to the edge of the desk, jotted down a list of ingredients, and returned the pencil nub to the hotel manager.

"Thank you, Mr. Beeks."

She smiled brightly.

He did not.

"Here you are, Mrs. Dunlap," she said, returning to the bench. "Have the kitchen brew a tea with these items. Let it steep for about fifteen minutes before your husband drinks it."

Mrs. Dunlap looked down at the list now in her hands. "Milkweed, bloodroot, fennel, and cinnamon? That's it?"

"He might also eat some figs or an apple, but the tea should do the trick."

"But that's so simple. Why didn't Dr. Prescott suggest it?"

Trudy had many theories on that but disparaging another doctor would serve no purpose here.

"You'd have to ask Dr. Prescott, but in the meantime, I suggest your husband drink at least two cups of the tea this afternoon and if he doesn't have results by tomorrow morning, send me a note and I'll come to see him."

"Milkweed, bloodroot, fennel, and cinnamon?" Mrs. Dunlap repeated, rising from the seat.

"Yes," Trudy said.

"Apples and figs?"

"Yes."

Mrs. Dunlap pushed an errant strand of hair away from her face. "Thank you, Dr. Hart. You're a lifesaver. When my husband is feeling better, you must join us for dinner."

"I'd like that. Thank you, Mrs. Dunlap."

Trudy chuckled to herself as the woman rushed off toward the hotel kitchens. *A lifesaver?* Not exactly in these circumstances but she appreciated the compliment nonetheless, and with a lilt in her step, she headed toward the lawn to find Daisy and her sisters.

Unfortunately, it took some time to reach them since she encountered Aunt Breezy on the porch who sought to interrogate Trudy about why in heaven's name didn't she have her parasol. Or her gloves. Or a hat.

Trudy could have journeyed back to her room, gathered those items, and returned to the porch in less time than it took for her aunt to sufficiently reprimand her for what Breezy stated was *an appalling lack of gentility and an utter absence of refinement.* Eventually, though, Breezy's interest was pulled elsewhere and Trudy finally made it to the lawn.

"There you are," Lucy called out, waving her over.

She and Daisy were sitting on a plaid blanket with another woman Trudy didn't recognize while Poppy and the dogs scampered about happily. "What took so long?" her sister asked.

"A simple medical question. And Aunt Breezy," Trudy answered, then she smiled at the newcomer and said, "Hello."

Daisy quickly proffered introductions. "Trudy, this is Miss Greta Watson. Miss Watson, this is Dr. Trudy Hart."

Trudy leaned over to shake the woman's hand while thinking, *"Greta Watson... Greta Watson... Why does that name sound familiar?"*

"It's a pleasure to meet you, Dr. Hart," she said. "I've been hearing wonderful things about you."

Miss Watson was, by Trudy's estimation, on the far side of sixty with dark, deep-set eyes and a bright, friendly smile. Her loose-fitting, emerald green, gown suggested she was a proponent of the Aesthetic Dress Movement, and while Trudy fully supported their mission of influencing fashion trends toward more movement-friendly clothing for women, she silently acknowledged that Miss Watson's dress bore a striking resemblance to a medieval tunic and seemed very out-of-place at a summer resort such as this.

"You've heard wonderful things about me?" Trudy responded as she sank down onto the blanket. "I'm glad to know these girls haven't been revealing all my imperfections."

"Oh, I haven't been hearing it from them," Miss Watson said with a giggle, gesturing toward Lucy and Daisy. "I've been hearing it from them." She pointed to the sky… and Trudy recalled where she'd heard the name before. Greta Watson was one of the psychic mediums Mr. Plank had invited to the hotel.

"Miss Watson has been telling Lucy and I all about our futures," Daisy said, smiling over at Trudy as if to note her reaction, while Lucy suddenly looked down at the dandelion crown she'd been making. Probably because she knew Trudy's thoughts on fortune tellers.

"But the future is always changing, isn't it?" Trudy asked, quasi-innocently. "We turn left instead of right, and everything shifts in a new direction. Isn't that the way it works?"

"Sometimes," Miss Watson answered, her smile remaining warm. "Some things may be influenced by our actions, but other things are kismet and cannot be altered no matter what we do or how we try to change it."

Trudy might have simply nodded. It would have been the polite thing to do, and yet she could not resist asking, "Doesn't that make us all just victims of circumstance, in that case?"

Miss Watson remained nonplused. "Not at all, Dr. Hart. It only means that the Universe has a purpose for each of us and it's our calling to find out what that is and to choose which path to take to get there. Much like your dedication to pursuing medicine. If medical school had not been available to you, you would have found another way. But what do you think drove you in that direction in the first place?"

"My father is a physician," Trudy answered. "I imagine that's what influenced my interest."

The woman nodded sagely. "A fair assumption and I'm sure that played a role, but if that were the only reason, then why aren't your other siblings following the same path? Why is Lucy fascinated with the stars? Why is Coco so determined to prove her worth? You girls have the same parents and yet you're all very different beings because the Universe has different plans for each of you."

Trudy didn't have a good response for that. And she didn't like not having a good response. She also didn't care for Miss Watson's suggestion that Coco didn't know her own worth. That statement was entirely far-fetched because if anyone was confident in her value and appeal, it was Coco! So, this time, Trudy simply smiled and looked over at the dogs.

"Flossie and Regina certainly have perked up," she remarked.

Daisy chuckled softly. "My apologies, Miss Watson. Trudy is a skeptic."

"Yes, I don't think it requires any psychic ability to discern that," Miss Watson replied amiably. "But it's her role to ask those type of interrogative questions. Some of us are naturally comfortable trusting our own intuition, but not everyone is as spiritually in tune with nature's rhythms. When our head and our heart are not in alignment, it fills us with doubt, but when they are aligned, everything just makes sense, and we are open to receive."

Ah, how cleverly Miss Watson turned Trudy's skepticism around to her own advantage. Now, anything Trudy said or did—or believed or didn't believe—could be chalked up to *misalignment*, not Trudy's own analytical intelligence.

Clever, clever, clever.

"Speaking of questions, Miss Watson, I have one I'd like to ask," Daisy said hesitantly. "What can you tell us about… séances?"

Lucy looked up from the flower crown, her eyes keen with interest, just as Daisy's were, and Trudy realized her *destiny* in that moment was to maintain a level head. The mystical idea of a séance was intriguing, and she could understand people's fascination with it, but again, where was the *proof*?

"Oh, séances," Miss Watson said cautiously, leaning toward them. "Those are a dark, tricky business. I won't participate in those anymore although I led a few in my younger days."

"Tricky? How so?" Lucy whispered, brows lifting.

"It requires a great deal of psychic energy to call someone over from the other side, and the reader must be strong enough to expel the spirit once the séance has ended. Sometimes the spectral visitor doesn't want to depart this earthly domain and will cling to a living being until a way is found to sever the attachment. I attended a séance once as a participant, not even as the guide, and left with the most unfortunate echoes of a very intransigent nun who admonished me relentlessly. It took months for me to be rid of the old bat. After that, I said 'never again.'"

Trudy chuckled at the image of a phantasmagorial Mother Superior berating Miss Watson from over her shoulder, but Daisy and Lucy exchanged enthralled glances.

Looking back at the older woman, Daisy asked quietly, "Is it possible for a spirit to latch on to someone even if they haven't been to a séance?"

"Sometimes," Miss Watson responded. "Those who linger in this sphere of awareness when they should move on to the next are often bound to a location, but occasionally they are tethered to a person. Or an object."

"How fascinating," Lucy murmured.

"What balderdash," Trudy thought.

"If that's the case, how would someone go about freeing themselves from a ... tethered spirit?" Daisy asked.

"It requires a gifted medium," Miss Watson replied. "But if the bond is tightly woven, a séance may be necessary. I once freed a young woman from an exceptionally disruptive phantom. He wasn't malicious, just a pesky childhood friend who always wanted to play, which was fine while she was still young but as she matured, she eventually wanted to be rid of him. She said she didn't relish the idea of him tagging along on her honeymoon, if you know what I mean!" Miss Watson giggled at the naughty innuendo, then added, "But he was a stubborn little gent. After several sessions I realized a séance was the only way to get the task accomplished."

"How intriguing," Lucy said.

What poppycock, Trudy thought.

"Several sessions of what? Daisy asked.

"It's rather hard to explain and depends upon the circumstances."

Trudy considered that to be a very convenient non-answer, and felt a frown form on her face as Daisy said, "But, in theory, if someone wanted to be freed from being haunted, they could come to you, and you might be able to untether them?"

Daisy had no business posing such questions without Alex's permission, but of course, Trudy couldn't say as much in front of everyone. Then again, this was likely all hogwash and hokum. Miss Watson didn't seem capable of untethering a dog from his leash much less wrangling phantoms. Even non-existent phantoms.

"No, I'm afraid I wouldn't be able to help," the woman said. "I'm getting too old for that sort of thing. These days, I limit my exposure to the other side with simple readings. I have my spirit guides whom I trust to protect me, but the nearer I get to crossing over myself, the less influence I have over the departed. I guess I'm getting too close to being one of them!"

She giggled again, but at Daisy's obvious disappointment, she added, "But if you ever do find yourself in need of such services, I might recommend you seek out Madeline Moyen."

"Madame Moyen?" Daisy asked, her expression brightening once again. She cast a glance at Trudy as if to say *I told you she's the one we want.*

"Yes, she's formidable, adept at many things but do be careful with that one. You don't want to open a door that cannot be closed."

"Do you mean by letting someone through who won't go back?" Lucy asked.

"I mean that Madaline Moyen is like a powerful magnet. She attracts the living in much the same way she attracts the dead. Make certain you don't get so near to her you haven't the strength to break free of your own accord."

Daisy was about to question that cryptic comment when Poppy plopped down on the center of the blanket followed by two wiggly dogs. It seemed Flossie and Regina were intent upon greeting everyone with their doggie kisses, and Trudy was relieved that their arrival conveniently shifted the mood to something much brighter.

"Coco is talking to a boy," Poppy said. "Look."

She pointed past them toward the croquet field where a young man wearing striped knickerbockers and a straw hat was leaning on his mallet, his face unnecessarily close to Trudy's sister. Coco, meanwhile, was twirling a strand of hair, her expression beatific as if she'd never had a cross thought in her entire life.

"Who is that?" Lucy asked.

"Patrick Fitzpatrick," Daisy said indifferently. "He's nice enough, I suppose, but he seems to consider himself rather too clever. His father is a political cartoonist for the *Chicago Tribune* and although Patrick is full of opinions, it's clear none of them are his own."

"Hm," Miss Watson said, narrowing her deep-set eyes. "You don't have to worry too much about him."

"What makes you say so?" Lucy replied.

"Your sister will grow bored of his vanity. He's so consumed with thoughts of his own attractiveness that he won't bother to remark upon hers."

An interesting observation, Trudy mused. She might have thought a vain man would be a good counterpart for her equally vain sister, but Miss Watson's words made sense. Coco preferred to have the spotlight pointing at herself and didn't want to share it.

"But you, missy," Miss Watson added, tapping a crooked finger at the air toward Lucy, "There's a gentleman thinking of you right this very minute."

Lucy's eyes rounded and her cheeks suffused with pink. "There is? Who? Where?"

"I don't know yet, but he's somewhere."

The others looked around as if Lucy's mystery man might be staring back at them, but Trudy looked at her sister instead. Somewhere someone probably *was* thinking of Lucy. She was sweet, and smart, and witty, and beautiful, and any man would be lucky to have her. But would *she* be lucky to have *him*?

"Do you think he's someone on the island?" Lucy whispered to Trudy late that night after the lamps had been extinguished and the only light in their room came from the moon.

"Maybe," Trudy answered. "Probably," she added.

Not because she believed in Miss Watson's clairvoyance but because Lucy had danced with scores of men the other night and had caught the eye of several more. There were likely a dozen admirers who had thought of her today, and although Trudy knew she should be glad for her sister—because Lucy didn't mind that their mother had sent them here for husbands—she felt a puzzling pang of preemptive loneliness.

Life was going to change whether Trudy wanted it to or not, and she couldn't help but wonder if at least some of what Miss Watson had said about the future might be true. With resolve and determination, a person could forge their own path, but some things, it seemed, were simply... destiny. Perhaps, in the end, it boiled down to a matter of which was stronger. Fortitude... or fate.

thirteen

I have spines but no bones.
I have words, but no voice.
I have letters but no postage.
I am titled but not royalty.

"It's a book!" Daisy exclaimed. "A book has a spine, letters, words, and a title. It has to be a book. But which one?"

The *First Annual Imperial Hotel Scavenger Hunt* was underway, and Alex's sister was determined to win. So, it seemed, was every person on their team which included himself, Daisy, Trudy, Lucy, and even little Poppy who was not so much a participant as she was their mascot.

"Maybe the hotel registry book?" Lucy asked, gazing over at the mahogany desk where Mr. Beeks was already showing signs of extreme exasperation. This was the man's worst nightmare. People scrambling about, laughing, and God forbid, even *shouting* as they rummaged through his pristine hotel in search of clues.

"The registration book is one everyone would know the location of," Alex agreed.

"But it says spines, not just a single spine, so it must be more than one book," Trudy added.

She caught his eye, and he marveled at her ability to note the tiniest detail.

"Multiple books, then? The reading room?" suggested Lucy excitedly.

They nodded in unison, quickly turning in that direction and all but sprinting across the lobby, past poor, miserable Beeks.

Alex heard the harmony of Trudy's laughter blend with Lucy's and his sister's, and he could not think of another instance in which he'd behaved in such a frivolous manner inside the walls of any hotel, much less one as elegant and respectable as the Imperial. They were like rambunctious puppies, dashing around one another and bumping into things—but they were not the only ones.

Alex had assumed this scavenger hunt would be a quaint diversion, mostly for the children, and that he, along with the other distinguished gentlemen would spend the afternoon smoking cigars and drinking beer on the front porch. But the youngest Miss Hart had marched to his side and demanded he join their team, and while it seemed he had little issue with refusing Coco, he could not refuse Poppy. Still, he had assumed he'd be one of the few adult men in the mix.

He was wrong.

Hugo Plank had, as usual, made the prize too impressive to resist. Fifty dollars to be shared among the members of the team. This, of course, encouraged some to compete as individuals. On their way to the reading room, Alex spotted a solitary Senator Stanford Gould on his hands and knees searching for a clue underneath a sofa while Cyrus Garland, heir to his father's railroad fortune, was running as fast as his stubby legs would allow toward the dining room. Everywhere Alex looked, in every direction, the hotel's elite had shrugged off the mantle of dignity and were racing around as if their tails were on fire. *What a lark!*

Daisy reached the reading room first and pulled open the door, breathless and excited, with Lucy, Trudy, Poppy, and Alex behind her. They entered to find a young, scruffy-headed hotel porter sitting on a stool, an eager smile on his freckled face.

"Yer my first customers!" he exclaimed joyfully. He held up a note and read it loudly and with gusto. "Find a book by Mr. Mark Twain and you will find yer next clue inside of it!"

"Any book by Twain?" Daisy asked.

He glanced at the note as if to verify. "Yup. Any book by Mark Twain, but they ain't in any order on the shelves so good luck."

"Let's divide and conquer," Trudy said. "I'll take the bookshelf near the window."

"Hey, that's not fair. I can't see the high up shelves," Poppy exclaimed.

"You and I can work together," Alex replied. "You look at the lower shelves, and I'll look at the higher ones."

She nodded at his plan while Daisy and Lucy chose their spots, and everyone began to search.

"Got one!" Daisy called out moments later. *"The Prince and the Pauper."*

She flipped it open to find a folded note inside just as another team burst through the doorway.

"Hurry!" Trudy whispered. "What's the clue?"

Daisy pulled out the note and read it. *"Put this bow in your hair and you will never hit the center."*

"What kinds of bows don't go in your hair?" Lucy whispered.

"Musical bows? Bow ties?" Alex conjectured quietly so the other team wouldn't hear.

"Maybe it's not pronounced like bow. Perhaps it means the bow of a boat?" Daisy suggested.

"Or a bow like the kind Flossie and Regina wear around their necks?" Poppy said.

"But you will never hit the center. When do you want to hit the center of something?" Trudy mused aloud.

"A target. You want to hit the center of a target. It means bow and arrow," Lucy said excitedly.

"Shhh!" Daisy teased, glancing at the other team who was hard at work scouring the shelves.

"Yes, I think you're correct. It's an archery reference. The next clue must be out on the lawn," Alex agreed.

"I have to sign yer contest form," the lad said loudly from his stool.

Trudy handed him the piece of paper they'd been given at the start of the hunt, a list of numbers from one to fifteen with nothing else written on it except for their names. The lad signed it with a flourish, handing it back to Trudy along with a wooden token etched with an image of the hotel.

"Yer gonna need this completed contest form and all fifteen tokens to win. Good luck," he said again.

"Tally ho!" Lucy called out with a giggle as they rushed from the peaceful quiet of the reading room back out into the frenzied mayhem of the lobby.

Mr. Tippett had explained that each team would receive their clues in a different order, so as Alex and his boisterous co-conspirators went in one direction, other teams were rushing upstairs, toward the dining room, or onto the porch where a few dignified society mavens were attempting to enjoy a quiet cup of tea *(undoubtedly laced with brandy.)*

Alex spotted his mother with Flossie and Regina lounging ubiquitously on satin cushions at her feet. The dogs appeared blissfully oblivious to the pandemonium, while across from his mother, Breezy VonMeisterburger was eyeing the chaos with such astonishment one would have thought the lobby had been overrun by wooly mammoths.

"Mother. Mrs. VonMeisterburger," Alex said smoothly as he rushed past.

"Mother. Mrs. VonMeisterburger," Daisy added, following fast behind him.

He wondered if Trudy or Lucy might offer their own greetings but a glance over his shoulder told him they were—wisely—remaining silent as down the steps they went toward the lush green expanse of the lawn, their breathless laughter mingling with good natured shouts, calls of encouragement, and the twangy sounds of a jug band playing somewhere in the thick of it all.

"I've never seen anything quite like this," Trudy remarked as they approached the archery area. "I'm without words."

Alex glanced over, taking note of her flushed cheeks and wide smile, and something inside him brightened discernibly. He didn't know exactly what it was or what it meant, but it pleased him, and he smiled back.

"Dr. Hart without words?" he teased. "Can it be?"

She tilted her chin upwards. "Just for that, I shan't speak to you for the rest of the day."

"Ah, there's a challenge you're sure to lose."

In fact, he hoped she'd lose that challenge. He didn't want her to be silent because what she said was always of interest, even when it pertained to him being a horrible boy in his youth. Maybe that was due to the tiny dimples which formed near her mouth when she was trying *not* to smile, or the subtle way her brows knit when she revealed something important, or perhaps it was simply that he found the content of what she said to be noteworthy. Regardless, he didn't want to her stop commenting.

"Welcome to Callaghan's Archery Field," Harlan Callaghan called out as they reached a roped off area full of hay bales with targets attached. "Alex, I'm glad to see you upright again after that fall from grace at the end of your bicycle ride," Harlan added, nodding at Alex's still bandaged hand.

"I'm glad to *be* upright," Alex responded. "And today I'm traveling with my own personal physician, just in case of injury."

"I'd say these arrows will be the most dangerous part of your day," Harlan replied. "Just make sure you point them at the target and not at me. By the way, who are your lovely friends?"

Alex gestured toward his teammates. "Mr. Callaghan, please allow me to introduce you to Dr. Hart and her sisters, Miss Lucy Hart, and Miss Poppy Hart. Of course, you know my sister, Daisy."

"It's a pleasure, ladies. And doctor. Doctor lady." Harlan stumbled over his words prompting more laughter, and Alex noted how the young man's eyes seemed to linger on Lucy.

"We are in a bit a hurry here, Harlan. If you don't mind?" Alex added.

"Oh, yes. Of course. One of you needs to shoot an arrow into the target. You don't need a bull's-eye, but it's not enough to hit the hay bale. You have to be inside the target."

"May I try?" Lucy immediately asked the group.

"Oh, yes. Let Lucy do it," added Trudy. "She can hit a turkey at twenty paces."

Alex chuckled at his vision of the delicate Lucy Hart letting loose on an unsuspecting Tom but cheered enthusiastically with the others when she hit the bull's-eye on her first attempt.

"Well, I'll be damned," he muttered under his breath.

Lucy was blushing furiously as she handed back the bow to Harlan.

"Well done, Miss Hart!" the young man said. "One might think you're Cupid with aim such as that."

Alex chuckled again and caught Trudy's eye, his thought being that Harlan appeared rather smitten with Lucy, but something in Trudy's enigmatic expression hinted at something besides amusement. She'd born a similar expression when her sisters had been dancing the other night when she was not, but she smiled just now, and said, "Well done, indeed, Lucy!"

"Here's our paper to be signed," Daisy added, stepping forward.

"Yes, ma'am," he responded, signing it before pulling a token from one pocket and a slip of paper from the other.

"And your clue, milady," he said, bowing deeply before Lucy. It was clumsy chivalry at best, but Alex couldn't fault the young man for trying.

"Thank you," Lucy nearly whispered, handing it over to Poppy. "Here, sweetie. You read this one."

Poppy unfolded it in a rush and read aloud. *"This room is*

steeped in tradition. Well, that's easy. It's the tearoom. But, egad, that's so far away," she moaned.

"Can she ride on my back?" Alex whispered to Trudy.

"If you don't mind carrying her, but it's not necessary. She's more than capable of walking."

"Yes," he replied. "But she rather *moseys*, and I have grand illusions of winning this hunt."

"Illusions? Or *delusions?*"

"Let me enjoy at least the prospect of being victorious, Dr. Hart. I'm still stinging from my last defeat. Besides, with your uncanny knack for deciphering these clues, I think we stand a chance."

With Poppy soon clinging to his back like a spider monkey, they set off across the lawn once more.

"Has anyone ever accused you of being competitive, Mr. Bostwick?" Trudy asked a moment later.

"Of course, and I make no apology for it. My brother has been—quite literally—chasing my heels since the day we were born. If I weren't competitive he would have run me over by now and figured out some way to be five years older than me. And anyway, I suspect you are just as competitive."

She nodded agreeably. "I suppose I am, at least with my older brother, not that he notices."

"I didn't realize you had an older brother."

"I do. He's a physician in Boston. My parents are visiting him now, before they come to Trillium Bay."

"So, three doctors in the family, but what do you mean your brother doesn't notice?"

He'd lowered his voice so Poppy wouldn't hear, although she was humming a fragmented tune, a blend of *Little Brown Jug* and *Battle Hymn of the Republic* and didn't appear to be paying attention to their conversation.

Trudy's shrug at his question was infinitesimal. "Only that, in his opinion, there is no competition between us because my medical degree and experience will never measure up to his no matter how successful I might be. I could perform the most complicated of surgeries and yet his ability to remove a splinter is somehow more impressive."

"That seems unjust. Why do you suppose he thinks that way?"

"Because he's a man. And in case you haven't noticed, I am woman."

"Oh, I've noticed."

Those telltale dimples appeared around her mouth. She was trying not to smile at his innuendo.

"That's not what I meant," she said primly.

"I know."

He smiled over at her, enjoying the way her cheeks burned. She wasn't sure what to make of his comment, and quite frankly, neither was he. What he *did* know was that he'd once been a consummate flirt, and it felt nice to stretch those muscles again. However, he didn't want her to think he'd dismissed her comment out of hand, and so he said, "Surely your father recognizes your talents, though, doesn't he? He must have encouraged your pursuit of medicine."

"He did, but my father, whom I love dearly, by the way, is diplomatic to a fault. He's so intent upon keeping the family boat steady he fails to acknowledge who is actually causing it to rock, so if I complain that Calvin is being unjust, Father sees it as me creating an unnecessary disturbance."

"Ah, that must be vexing."

"It is, but I've learned to harness my frustration and use it to drive my ambition."

"The ambition to prove yourself as fine a physician as your brother?"

"Pff, no," she scoffed dismissively. "The ambition to prove myself a *superior* physician to my brother."

Alex's laughter burst forth with such gusto it nearly caused Poppy to slide from his back. He hitched the little girl upwards with his arms while silently acknowledging that Trudy Hart was perhaps the boldest woman he had ever encountered, with her frank speaking about ambition and her determination to accomplish any task, be it setting a broken finger, performing a surgery, or solving the clue to a scavenger hunt faster than anyone else on her team. She was a delight, and someday, some man would be most fortunate to win her heart.

Most fortunate indeed.

∽

The tearoom was a frenzy of activity as they stared from the entrance. Three teams were currently filling demitasse cups with water from a bucket then running across the length of the floor to dump it into a teapot while a pianist banged unceremoniously upon the keys of a harpsichord if it were a children's toy.

"Oh, my goodness," Daisy giggled. "That sign on the wall says we have to fill the teapot to overflowing. How many trips do you suppose that's going to take?"

"I guess we're about to find out," Alex answered as he eased Poppy down to the floor.

Across the room, laughter erupted as a middle-aged man with whiskers rivaling those of Johann Strauss, slipped in a puddle, flailed for a moment, and then let out a girlish squawk before landing on the floor with a thud and an *oof*.

"Are you injured, sir?" Trudy called out automatically as she carefully scooted across the wet surface in his direction.

It was the nature of her vocation to do so, as well as the nature of her... nature. She was predisposed to assist others in need. Perhaps that's how she'd allowed herself to be drawn into this business with Alex and his spectral shenanigans.

They hadn't spoken of it since she'd set his broken finger, but it had been first and foremost on her mind. She'd come up with a sort of plan, or rather, she'd come up with a plan as to how they should formulate a plan.

Since she'd never before attempted to catch a ghost, or a

prankster as the case may be, she felt a solid foundation for their investigation was essential. There was no sense in going at it all willy-nilly and making guesses or assumptions. They must start with what they knew was certain to be true and move forward from there. Unfortunately, until she and Alex could find some time alone to discuss things, she was rudderless.

"No, injuries, miss!" said the man who was currently splayed out on the tearoom floor. "I am merely testing the sturdiness of Mr. Plank's hotel." He rolled to his knees, smacked a palm against the polished floor a few times, adding gaily, "And I am pleased to report this floor is as solid as a rock." He looked up grinning as she reached his side, and said, "Oh, I say. Are you that lady doctor everyone's been talking about?"

"I am a doctor," she replied warily, wondering just who he was alluding to. Did he mean *people?* Or, like Miss Watson, was he hearing voices from the great beyond?

"Most excellent," the man said. "Might I impose upon your expertise to evaluate the rash on my son's neck?" he inquired, rising unsteadily from the floor.

"Papa!" a youthful voice cried out. "Hurry up! We're racing!"

"What? Oh, yes. Dear me. Another time, madam doctor!" the man said with a wave before shuffling as fast as he dared back to the bucket and his teammates.

Bemused, Trudy returned to her own team who had obtained their teapot and cups and were about to begin.

"If only we had Jesus on our team," Poppy commented to no one in particular as she gazed at the waterlogged floor. "He could walk right over this."

After the tearoom, they journeyed to the dining room, the ice cream parlor, the stables, and what seemed like innumerable other locations.

"It's important to get your pulses racing at least once per day," Trudy said breathlessly as they climbed yet another staircase. "We must thank Mr. Tippett for seeing to our improved health."

Occasionally, they'd crisscross paths with Coco, Ellis, Finn, and Asher who had formed their own team. As playful taunts and jests were volleyed between the Bostwicks, Trudy silently hoped Coco was having as much fun as the rest of them. She appeared to be, but Trudy wondered if her sister's decision to join them had been influenced by Poppy's insistence that Alex participate on their team. Naturally, Poppy had invited him without consulting anyone else.

Meanwhile, other teams continued to zig and zag, to jog and sprint, and finally to amble and meander around the hotel and grounds as they gathered signatures and tokens. The pace slowed as the day warmed and cheeks grew hot. Alex discarded his jacket and had even rolled up his shirtsleeves while hotel employees circulated through the maze of guests offering cool drinks and flavored ices. Mr. Tippett, the hotel's social director, periodically called out statistics of how many signatures various teams had earned thus far, making sure a sense of urgency remained.

"We have thirteen," Daisy all but squealed as they rushed past him.

"Two more to go," Mr. Tippett shouted back.

But at the putting green, they found no employee to provide a clue or any instructions.

"There's nothing here as far as I can see," Daisy said, looking every which way.

"We must be in the wrong place," Lucy added. But I was so certain this was correct."

"Let me see the note again," Trudy asked, taking it from Alex's proffered fingers.

She read it out loud. "*You have six opportunities to sink a ball on this green.* Six opportunities, a single ball, on green," she mused, tapping her fingers against her chin. "If not this green then—Oh! Eureka!" she shouted, snapping those fingers. "I'd wager it's a billiards table! Green felt, six pockets."

"Land sakes, Trudy, you are a marvel," Alex replied, laughing at her prowess. "To the billiards room, then."

Poppy had abandoned their team somewhere between the

seventh and eighth clue, choosing instead to join Jo Bostwick who was showing a group of children how to create art using stones, twigs, and feathers in the center of the lawn while Chase helped a few others launch brightly colored kites with long, ribbon tails. The scene might have been bucolic if not for all the hotel guests rushing hastily around them.

Reaching the billiards room at last, Alex made quick work of sinking a single ball into a corner pocket, in spite of his bandaged hand, and earned them their final clue. While Trudy was glad the scavenger hunt was drawing to a close—because she was hot and thirsty and certain her hair was an unmitigated mess—she did wish he'd taken more time at the task. She'd enjoyed observing the look of concentration on his face as he calculated where to strike the ball, just as she'd enjoyed observing the musculature of his forearms as he gripped the cue.

Not because there was anything particularly alluring about his face or his forearms... but as a physician, she had an appreciation for such things. It was her *job* to notice.

Reaching out to the bored-looking porter leaning against the billiards room wall, Lucy accepted the token and clue from his hand, smiling politely as she gave him their contest form.

"I don't imagine this has been much fun for you," she said sympathetically. "Watching the rest of us run around while you're stuck in here all day."

He smiled wanly and handed back the signed paper. "'Bout as dull as sittin' on a fence watchin' cows masticate, miss, but I guess I'd rather be in here 'stead of standin' outside in the hot sun watchin' folks try to hit a bale o' hay with an arrow." His eyes brightened as he added, "Though I did hear tell o' one gal who hit the bull's-eye on her first try! Ain't that something?"

Daisy laughed delightedly, "That was—"

"Amazing," Lucy interrupted. "That must have been a sight to see." She turned away from him, her cheeks pink and handed the clue to Trudy.

"I think it's your turn to read," she said.

Trudy accepted it with a smile, noting that, while Coco loved attention, Lucy avoided it at all costs. She wasn't shy, necessarily. She just preferred to keep the focus on other people.

"All right, everyone. This is it. Our final clue." Trudy said. She took a breath, then read aloud.

"You may enjoy this original view of the front porch, but you cannot walk on it."

Daisy frowned. "There must be a dozen places you can see the front porch from that you can't walk on."

"Read it again, would you?" Alex asked. "I've learned from Trudy today that paying attention to the exact wording is key to solving the riddle."

Trudy felt herself smiling at his compliment, and if her cheeks hadn't already been flushed from the heat, they would be now from his words.

"You may enjoy this original view of the front porch, but you cannot walk on it."

"It's not saying you can't walk on the front porch," Alex said. "It's saying it's a *view* of the porch that you cannot walk on. A view, like an image. I think it's a painting."

He looked at them eagerly and Trudy nearly chuckled at his apparent pride in having solved this clue before the rest of them. And he should be proud. She would not have made such a connection.

"A painting?" Daisy asked.

"Yes," he replied to his sister. "It's Jo's painting of the hotel. The one hanging in the lobby."

"I've seen that painting," Lucy said. "You must be right because it's a *view* of the front porch—"

"That you cannot walk on," they said in unison as laughter overtook them.

The disinterested porter sighed aloud at their silliness, but soon they were standing in the lobby once again, staring at the large painting which hung above the model replica of the hotel.

"It's got to be one of these two," Trudy said, as they looked over it and under it and beside it.

After a moment, Mr. Beeks cleared his throat. And then he cleared his throat again. And then he coughed.

Trudy wondered if a medical intervention was in order, but when she glanced his way, he gave a subtle bob of his head, as if to draw her closer.

"Oh, that's sneaky," she heard Alex say as he walked past her toward the hotel manager and pointed at the wall behind him. "It's *this* painting of the hotel. Jo did the smaller one first. It's the original view."

"Very good, sir," Mr. Beeks said dryly. "You have successfully deciphered the final clue. May I count your tokens, please?"

Alex emptied his pockets, setting the wooden disks onto the desk. The hotel manager counted them carefully, then nodded. "You have successfully accumulated the correct number of tokens. May I review your form?"

Trudy giggled at his formality. She'd seen less rigid protocols in an operating theater.

Daisy rushed over and handed the paper to Mr. Beeks who adjusted his spectacles and perused it as if it were a binding, legal document. Trudy wasn't certain whether he was trying to build suspense, annoy the dickens out of them, or if Mr. Beeks really was that fastidious, but at last, he set the paper upon the desk, and signed his name. Then he took out his pocket watch, checked it carefully, and jotted the time down next to his name. 3:05 p.m.

"Did we win?" asked Lucy with an eager yet breathless sigh. "Are we the first to finish?"

"I'm not at liberty to divulge such information, miss," Beeks answered formally. "But you have completed every task, and I have been instructed to direct you to the grand ballroom."

Trudy looked around at each of them and smiled. "Win or lose, I know we all did our best."

"Hear, hear," Alex agreed. "I could not have been compelled to join a finer team."

"I agree," Daisy said impatiently, "Now, let's go see if we won."

Walking quickly to the far side of the lobby, they entered the ballroom to find Mr. Plank standing at the bottom of the steps.

"Well done, my fine competitors," he called out. "I commend your worthy effort!"

Trudy heard a smattering of applause as he continued. "Alas, you did not finish in first place but be proud! You are the fourth team to arrive and there are still prizes a plenty. Once everyone is in the ballroom, we'll be announcing various categories, and you may win something yet. In the meantime, please enjoy some well-earned refreshments."

Mr. Plank gestured toward a few long tables laden with delectable treats and refreshing beverages, and as she looked around, Trudy saw at least twenty scavenger hunt participants already in the ballroom. Each one was as flushed and disheveled as she was, and most were smiling wide from an afternoon full of fun and frivolity. She allowed herself to feel only a twinge of disappointment for not having finished first. Not so much for herself, but for her team in general, yet just as quickly replaced that emotion with her enjoyment of the pursuit. It had been a delightful afternoon.

"Fourth place is nothing to sneeze at," Daisy said brightly, "and right now, the only prize I truly want is some of that lemonade. I'm parched." She trotted down the short staircase.

"Lemonade and cookies," Lucy added, following behind her. "I am satisfied."

Alex turned to Trudy, his smile tired but content. "As one fierce competitor to another, Dr. Hart, I am sorry we didn't win. I would've enjoyed sharing that fifty-dollar prize with you."

"As would I, with you," she said. "But for now, it seems we must drown our sorrows in lemonade."

He chuckled as they descended the steps. "I sincerely hope Plank has something a little stronger than lemonade over there."

She laughed in response, but her good humor faded as she

looked to the far side of the room and spotted a sullen looking Ellis, a forlorn Coco, Finn—who was pressing a blood-stained cloth to his nose, and Asher—who was holding an equally bloody cloth against the corner of his mouth. From this distance, it was hard to tell the extent of their injuries, but they were definitely wounded.

Her footsteps faltered at the sight, and Alex caught her by the arm. "Trudy?"

Then he followed her gaze and muttered a quiet curse. "What in the devil's name do you suppose that's about?" he murmured.

"I'm certain I don't want to know," she replied. "But there's blood so I suppose I should go over there and find out." *She was a doctor, after all.*

She and Alex approached the table where the others sat.

"Asher? Finn?" she asked as she reached them. "What happened?"

All the boys exchanged heated stares, Coco sniffled, yet no one spoke.

"She asked you boys a question," Alex said sternly. "Do not disrespect her with silence."

"It was just a stupid game," Ellis said dismissively, pointing at Asher and Finn. "They got upset over nothing."

"It wasn't nothing. It was cheating," Asher responded hotly. "And I'm not a cheater." He pulled the cloth away as he spoke, and Trudy could see he'd split his lip. She moved to his side to examine it more closely.

"Who cheated?" Trudy demanded as she pressed carefully around her brother's mouth.

Both the younger boys pointed back at Ellis.

"Oh, so this is my fault?" Ellis snapped. "Maybe if you morons could have figured out a few clues we wouldn't have had to cheat."

"No one ever has to cheat, Ellis. It's a choice." Alex responded. His voice was low but there was nothing flexible or tentative about it, and Trudy sensed his frustration. She turned to her sister.

"Coco, please tell us what happened."

Coco looked up, her face splotchy, tears puddling, but she dashed them away with her fingertips.

"Ellis found some tokens on the ground that someone must have dropped. He put them in his pocket, and we didn't think much of it. We just kept on with the hunt. After a while he said we'd done everything and that we were finished." She sniffled again but kept talking.

"When we got to the ballroom, we were the first ones here, and I thought we'd won. We were all so excited. But then Mr. Plank said something was wrong with our contest sheet because Mr. Beeks hadn't signed it or recorded our completion time."

Now she glared over at Ellis. "That's when Asher, Finn, and I realized Ellis had forged signatures on the last three challenges. We never did them. Mr. Plank figured that out, too, and disqualified us."

"Damn it, Ellis," Alex said tersely. "Why would you do such a reckless thing?"

"It was just a game," his cousin responded emphatically. "A silly, pointless game."

"Exactly! And since it was a silly, pointless game, why cheat?" Alex asked, his ire visibly growing.

Ellis snorted as if the question was nonsensical.

"For fifty dollars," he snapped. "Are you trying to tell me you wouldn't cheat a little for fifty dollars?"

"No, I wouldn't cheat for fifty dollars. I wouldn't cheat for any amount of money," Alex responded.

"That's because you already have it!" Ellis bit back, crossing his arms and slouching farther down into his chair.

Trudy saw the muscles in Alex's jaw clench at his cousin's words. "It's never acceptable to cheat," Alex said quietly.

"And the cheating doesn't explain why two of you are bleeding," Trudy added moving over to Finn to see what he was hiding behind that cloth.

Coco spoke up again. "When Finn realized what Ellis had done, he was so mad he tried to punch him in the face, only he missed and hit Asher by mistake, then Finn tried to hit Ellis again and Ellis punched him in the nose."

"Ellis," Alex said, his quiet voice full of disappointment and exasperation. "You are twenty-one years old. What is the matter with you. You're supposed to set a better example."

Ellis said nothing as he stared off into the distance.

"I think your nose may be broken," Trudy said to Finn. "We need to get cold compresses on both of you boys, and Finn, don't tip your head back. Lean forward."

"I didn't hit him that hard," Ellis said. "He moved forward when I was trying to defend myself."

"Defend yourself?" Alex said. "You're a foot taller than he is. I'm sure you could have kept him at bay without punching him in the nose."

"It was an accident. All of it was just one big accident," Ellis muttered, but Trudy could see his words were not alleviating Alex's ire.

"The cheating wasn't accidental, and it was your cheating that caused them to get hurt. This is your fault, Ellis. Yours, and yours alone. Go upstairs, now."

Ellis glared at him. "You can't send me to my room like some recalcitrant child, Alex."

But Alex regarded him coldly, staring down at him as Ellis remained motionless in the chair, and his voice, when he spoke was quiet but brooked no argument.

"I could send you all the way back to Chicago if I wanted to, Ellis. Now get out here. I don't want to see your face."

Ellis hesitated for only a moment, then pushed back from the table roughly. "Mountain out of a molehill, if you ask me," he muttered as he walked away.

Such a lovely day with such an abrupt end to it, Trudy thought to herself as she dabbed at the blood under Finn's nose.

"Coco, Asher," Alex said after a pause. "I must apologize for my cousin's delinquent behavior. Since he stole your chance at winning the grand price, please allow me to provide the $12.50 that you each would have received, had your team won fair and square. Finn, I'll make sure Uncle Vernon pays you the same amount."

"That's not necessary, Alex," Trudy responded immediately. "They probably wouldn't have won regardless.

"Hey, now, sis. Don't be so hasty," Asher interjected, his sudden smile decidedly lopsided due to that fat lip. "I took one in the kisser when I didn't deserve it. I think that's worth some financial compensation, don't you?"

fourteen

"How's the soup, Ash?" Finn teased as they sat at a table in the corner of the hotel dining room having lunch.

Trudy's brother looked up as potato chowder dribbled down his chin. He was having a bit of trouble navigating a spoon around his still-swollen lip, but tried to grin, nonetheless.

"It's delicious," he answered brashly. "And it smells divine, which you would know if your nose wasn't the size of a donkey's."

"Better to look like a donkey than a largemouth b ...ass," Finn replied casually, slurping soup from his own spoon.

"Boys," Trudy admonished quietly, although she was glad they were both in good humor.

It had been two days since the scavenger hunt ended in debacle, with Ellis leaving in a huff and the younger boys both leaving with bloodstains on their shirts. Trudy had tended to their wounds and spent the rest of the day handing dry handkerchiefs to a distraught Coco.

Although Trudy's patience for her sister's tears was usually low, on this occasion, she felt sincerely sorry for her. Not in a patronizing or pitying way, but rather in a loving, sisterly way.

The humiliation of being disqualified from the race by Mr. Plank was obviously weighing heavily on her, especially since Coco had played no part in the cheating but was considered guilty simply by association.

Trudy felt a little guilty, too. She was supposed to be watching out for her siblings until their parents arrived, after all, and thus far, she'd done a spectacularly abysmal job of it.

Dear Mother and Father,

In a valiant attempt to maintain the moral high ground, Asher's lip met with an unexpected fist while Coco received a second dose of humiliation. I'm certain her subdued demeanor will be a temporary phase.

Meanwhile, Lucy's prowess with a bow and arrow remains stellar. While she is hunting hay bales, I am preoccupied with hunting ghosts...

"A good day to you, Dr. Hart."

Trudy looked up from her lunch plate to see a smiling Mrs. Hobbs and her stout-bodied husband strolling past their table.

"Good day to you, Mrs. Hobbs, Mr. Hobbs," she replied, recalling their chaotic and haphazard introduction during the scavenger hunt as their team and Trudy's briefly formed an alliance to solve a particularly difficult clue which ultimately led them to a spittoon in the cigar lounge.

"Craic of a time the other day," Mr. Hobbs remarked. "Tippett outdid himself with that diversion, wouldn't you say?"

"I would, indeed," Trudy replied.

As the couple moved on, she sent up a silent prayer of gratitude. Thanks to Mr. Plank's generous and seemingly iron-clad discretion, not to mention Alex's harshly worded warning that no one was to speak of the incident in public, Ellis's poor judgment remained a private Bostwick family matter. They certainly didn't need the added scandal, nor did Trudy want her own family linked to the incident, even when they'd been on the side of honesty and integrity. Stories such as these often led to added speculation from which no one benefited, but thus far, it seemed nary a whisper of Ellis's cheating had reached the ears of any hotel guests.

That included Aunt Breezy for which Trudy was doubly grateful. Asher's split lip and Finn's broken nose, along with his accompanying black eyes, had been explained away as an incident of overzealous, boyish rough housing—which no one had trouble believing—so it seemed the entire episode could be placed firmly in the past.

"Miss Hart," Mr. Plank said enthusiastically as he arrived at their table minutes later. "I have some news I think will please you."

Trudy, Lucy, Coco, and Poppy all looked at him expectantly, and he chuckled.

"Miss Lucy Hart," he clarified.

Lucy dabbed her mouth with a linen napkin. "News for me, Mr. Plank?"

"Yes, indeed. Do you recall the other day when you asked if there were any telescopes at the hotel and I regrettably informed you that there were not?"

"Yes, of course, Mr. Plank, but please don't trouble yourself about it. I can manage without one for a few months."

He shook his head. "I cannot hear of it. At my Imperial Hotel, Miss Hart, no one should ever have to *manage without* anything. I sent Mr. Tippett to the mainland yesterday and he was able to procure not one, but five telescopes!" Mr. Plank held up a hand with his fingers splayed as if to emphasize the quantity.

"Five, sir?" Lucy asked, looking momentarily confused. "Your gesture is so very kind, but... I only have one set of eyes. I'm sure I don't need so many telescopes."

Hugo laughed at her response. "One set of eyes! You're a delight, Miss Hart. Of course, I realize you can only gaze through one at a time, but it occurred to me that if you have an interest in the night sky, there are likely other guests at the hotel with a similar fascination. With five telescopes set up in a row on the lawn, we can make star gazing a social event. I've even taken the liberty of sending a letter to Mr. Edward Singleton Holden at the University of California asking if he knows of any impending astronomical events so we might plan a celestial soiree, as it were. I've not heard back yet but I'll be sure to keep you informed."

"A celestial soiree?" Daisy said, clapping her hands together. "How adorable."

"What's a celestial soiree?" Poppy asked.

"It's a party to look at the stars," Coco responded.

Poppy appeared dubious. "A party to look at the stars? Is that something Sir Chester might attend?"

"Sir Chester may not attend," Trudy answered immediately. "If he got lost in the dark we would never find him."

Poppy's smile was prim, her voice polite as she replied, "Well, in that case, please accept my regrets, Mr. Plank. If Sir Chester VonWhiskerton is not allowed to attend this celestial soiree, I shall not attend either."

He gazed at her with much the same practiced expression of disappointment that he used with Aunt Breezy.

"You and Sir Chester will be sorely missed, Miss Hart," he responded with a perfunctory bow. "But I trust this idea meets with your approval, Miss Hart?" His gaze returned to Lucy, his smile returning.

"Gracious me, Mr. Plank. Of course. You are entirely too generous," Lucy responded, her eyes bright with excitement. "I certainly didn't intend for you to put forth such effort."

"It was entirely my pleasure."

"Might the telescopes be ready to use by this evening?" she asked tentatively.

"Not by this evening. We had to order them from Chicago so it may be a week or so, but as soon as they arrive and are set up, you'll be the first one I notify."

"Thank you, Mr. Plank," Trudy added. "You are, indeed, too

kind. In every way." Her glanced flickered over to her brother and Finn, then back to Mr. Plank who nodded in comprehension.

"Think nothing of it, Dr. Hart. I aim to keep all my guests happy and blissfully... content."

She smiled at his innuendo. Blissfully content or blissfully ignorant? Either way, she appreciated his dedication to keeping the whole ugly situation under wraps.

"And might I add, I spoke with Mr. Dunlap yesterday," Mr. Plank continued. "He was singing your praises, Dr. Hart. Apparently you provided medical care when he was in desperate need?"

Trudy offered a single nod. "It was a very minor issue and easily remedied."

"Well, nonetheless, he was most grateful,"

"I'm glad to hear that, Mister Plank."

"In fact, I wonder if I might speak with you privately when you have a moment," Mr. Plank continued. "About another medical matter that has recently come to my attention."

"Of course," she replied, wondering if she was about to learn that the hotel owner needed to eat more apples and figs.

"It's nothing urgent," he added. "But perhaps you could stop by my office after lunch? The conversation should not take long."

"I'd be happy to, Mr. Plank."

"Excellent. In that case, please do carry on with your meal. And if you're in the mood for dessert, I highly recommend Mrs. Culpepper's tipsy cake, or perhaps the lemon tart. You cannot go wrong with either."

With another slight bow, Mr. Plank departed, and Lucy turned to Trudy excitedly. "Five telescopes? Can you imagine?"

"It doesn't surprise me in the slightest," Daisy responded with humor. "Mr. Plank never does anything halfway. He is the master of excess, but I am very much looking forward to a celestial soiree. What does one wear to such an event, I wonder?"

As the younger girls began to talk of fashion, and Finn and Asher began plotting an afternoon of fishing near the boat docks,

Trudy's thoughts turned to what Mr. Plank might want to discuss with her.

An hour later, she was rapping lightly on the half-open door of his office to satisfy her curiosity.

He was sitting at a desk littered with papers, along with stacks of architectural journals, rolled up documents, newspapers, and various and sundry office items. Like many men of vision, Mr. Plank appeared to have no sense of organization.

"Ah, Dr. Hart," he said, looking up from his desk. "Please, do come in." He gestured for her to take a seat in the chair opposite him, which she did after stepping around several stacks of books, papers, and journals.

"You don't ever smoke in your office, do you, Mr. Plank?" she asked, settling into the chair.

He looked confused by the question, then laughed aloud as he caught her meaning.

"I do not, Dr. Hart. I don't smoke anywhere. I never caught the taste for it." He rose and crossed the room to shut the door.

"What might I be able to do for you?" Trudy asked as soon as he regained his chair.

"I am interested in your opinion," he responded.

"My opinion, sir? On what matter?"

"Mrs. Bostwick came to me recently. Mrs. Jo Bostwick, with complaints pertaining to Dr. Prescott. She informed me that many of my employees, especially my female employees, are uncomfortable with him. She says they find him dismissive, rude, intransigent, and even uncaring, and I wondered your thoughts on that."

She pondered his question for a moment. Even though her immediate thought was to simply agree with Jo and tell Mr. Plank that Dr. Prescott was all of those unpleasant things, she took the time to choose her words carefully.

"I've only encountered Dr. Prescott once, after the bicycle race," she finally said. "I did feel he was rude to me personally, but I assumed his attitude had more to do with the fact that I am a woman doctor. However, I was disheartened to learn from Mrs. Bostwick that he treated his patients with equal disdain. And while I confess it's not uncommon for physicians such as Dr. Prescott to be patronizing to their female patients, it is my frank opinion that a physician must *listen* to what a patient is telling them instead of making assumptions or dismissing their concerns out of hand."

"I see," Mr. Plank said, his brows furrowing.

"And since you have asked my opinion, I must inquire, did Mr. Dunlap tell you he'd consulted with Dr. Prescott before coming to me?"

His head tilted slightly. "He did not."

"According to Mrs. Dunlap, Dr. Prescott advised her husband to take a dose of castor oil even though Mr. Dunlap had informed the doctor that castor oil made it difficult for him to breathe. That isn't simply disdain or dismissiveness, and although I hesitate to use the term since it sounds rather dramatic, one might potentially consider that to be medical malpractice."

Mr. Plank's brows rose considerably, and he leaned back in his chair. "Good heavens. He's as bad as all that?"

"Perhaps Mr. Dunlap wasn't clear with his concerns. You should probably speak with him on the matter, but my impression is that Dr. Prescott is, as you say, intransigent. However, I must add I have not seen him interact with any patients. All of this is based on what others have told me, although I certainly trust Mrs. Bostwick's opinion."

"As do I," he said. "But this does leave me in a bit of a conundrum. Prescott's contract ensures him two years of employment at the Imperial Hotel."

"I see," Trudy responded. "Does that contract guarantee him a salary is based on the amount of time spent here or is it based on the number of patients he is able to treat?"

Mr. Plank considered this. "I'd have to check to be certain, but I believe he's paid the same for his time whether he treats anyone or not."

"In that case, it seems he's taking advantage of you," Trudy said. "He's here as stipulated, but if half your employees refuse to see him, and he's providing shoddy care to your guests, then you are paying him more than he's worth."

Mr. Plank looked both disappointed by what she said yet also impressed by her grasp of the situation.

"That is a very interesting insight, Dr. Hart. I would not have looked at the matter from that angle. How fortuitous that I asked you."

"I'm always happy to share my opinion. Although I'm seldom asked for it," she said, smiling.

He smiled back, but added, "I only wish someone had brought the matter to me sooner. I knew Prescott was gruff, of course, but I had no idea he was this bad. I was rather proud of myself for providing free health care to my employees, but it seems I've missed the mark."

"Your gesture is commendable, Mr. Plank," she said earnestly. "I don't know of many employers who give a single thought to the health and welfare of their staff. In fact, I suspect a number of your Imperial guests are wealthy businessmen who are not nearly as conscientious as you are."

Trudy knew from working in her father's clinic that most business owners focused on their financial ledgers while ignoring the working conditions their employees faced on a daily basis. Industrial accidents, lung conditions, exhausted children forced to work for hours at a time provided her with a steady stream of patients. She could alleviate some of their suffering but could only treat their symptoms while the disease of greed and neglect ran rampant.

"I can't speak for other business owners," Mr. Plank said. "But here at the Imperial Hotel, we are a family. An odd sort of family, but a family, nonetheless."

"I'm glad to hear you feel that way, Mr. Plank," she said. "I'm just not sure Dr. Prescott espouses the same philosophy of respect toward people that you do."

"I'm beginning to suspect he does not." He leaned forward and tapped his fingers against the desk for a moment as if deep in thought.

"I wonder, Dr. Hart..." He paused, regarding her carefully. Her curiosity piqued at his lengthy pause.

"Yes, Mr. Plank?" she finally promoted.

"I wonder if I might impose upon you... No, never mind. This is your summer holiday."

She sensed he was toying with her. Luring her in by building suspense. She'd seen what a showman he was. He wanted her to ask. And so, she did. Reluctantly.

"Impose upon me in what way?"

He spoke slowly, as if the words were hard to say. "If, by chance, there are hotel employees or guests not in favor of seeing Dr. Prescott, might they come to you? Only in cases requiring immediate attention, of course. For milder ailments they can wait until Dr. Hargrove is available, or they can take their chances and see Dr. Prescott."

Take their chances? That was not a method by which to choose one's physician. Medicine was a *science*, not a *casino*.

At her hesitation, he added, "I'm not suggesting you take on the role of Doctor Prescott, of course. As I said, I'm referring to matters of an urgent nature where he might not provide appropriate care. Naturally, I'd compensate you accordingly, and this would only be until I can make arrangements to secure another physician."

His suggestion seemed a slippery slope. This *was* her summer holiday, after all, and she'd already treated no less than three Bostwick's, her own brother, and a constipated Mr. Dunlap. If she hung out a shingle at this hotel, even a subtle one, people would be pestering her every day.

Then again... she couldn't help but consider how kindly and strategically Mr. Plank had handled the situation with Ellis's cheating, not to mention the five (*five!*) telescopes he'd just purchased for the sake of her sister's enjoyment, or the indulgent, endearing way he interacted with Poppy. And Sir Chester VonWhiskerton!

All things considered, Trudy could hardly say no.

"Of course, Mr. Plank. I'd be happy to lend a hand."

He placed his palms flat on the desk. "Thank you, Dr. Hart. I appreciate your willingness to help me look after my staff. We can work out the details later but please give some thought to what compensation you think would be appropriate. In the meantime, if anyone else shares concerns with you regarding Dr. Prescott's care, please send them to me."

He stood up and Trudy realized this conversation had ended. That was just as well, she supposed. She had a dozen questions but some time alone to reflect on them would be advantageous. She could come back to him with a written list when she'd gathered her thoughts. And caught her breath!

fifteen

"That sounds very much like Hugo," Jo said as she playfully linked arms with Trudy.

It was a rainy afternoon outside as they strolled from the main floor art studio where Jo had just concluded a painting class, and while she excelled as an instructor, Trudy was a mediocre student. When it came to art, Trudy appreciated its beauty, and the discipline required to create it—but rendering anything lovely or intriguing or peaceful was beyond her grasp. With a pencil and paper, she could easily depict an anatomically accurate heart and expound in lyrical detail how essential it was to the human body but ask her to paint something which evoked the emotions purportedly held within one's figurative heart and she was woefully out of her element.

"I do hope he's not expecting me to see people every day," Trudy said. "I'm rather enjoying this life of leisure and not ready to return to work. Not to mention how news of this will cause likely cause Aunt Breezy to have an apoplectic fit."

"Well, in that case, she can be your first hotel patient," Jo teased.

"Actually, my first hotel patient was you," Trudy responded.

"And as such, forgive the inquiry, but have you sent a note to your midwife yet?"

"I have," Jo replied. "I dispatched it the very same day you and I discussed it. She sent a note back straightaway and intends to see me next week. I'm quite relieved, although I know with you by my side, I'll be in good hands when this impertinent baby decides to arrive."

As if on cue, Jo burped, triggering giggles from them both.

"Do you think I might meet the midwife," Trudy asked when their mirth had subsided. "I'd like to hear her philosophy on the birthing process and think it would be beneficial to you if she and I were to get acquainted before your time comes."

"Of course. She's coming to see me on Wednesday afternoon. You may meet her then, if you'd like."

Trudy and Jo continued their sojourn through the lobby, stopping to exchange pleasantries with Mrs. Palmer who was adorned in an excess of rubies and diamonds despite the mid-day hour. Next, they encountered the vivacious Mahoney sisters, Iris and Dalhia, who regaled them with an excruciatingly detailed account of their recent trip to Bath, until they were set upon by none other than Miss Greta Watson and pet clairvoyant, Mrs. Delilah Lamb.

Mrs. Lamb was stocky, robust woman in a lime-green dress whose demeanor bore no resemblance to a timid little lamb in any way, shape, or form.

"At last, we meet," Mrs. Lamb said to Jo without the benefit of actually being introduced. "It's imperative I speak to your mother-in-law."

"My mother-in-law?" Jo replied. "You mean Constance Bostwick?"

"Yes, that's the one. I encountered her dogs the other day and one of them is suffering a great malaise."

Jo tried to disguise her chuff of laughter behind a cough. "And which dog might that be?"

"The one with the pale blue collar," Mrs. Lamb stated as if

surely that was obvious. "The poor creature carries a painful memory leftover from puppyhood, and I wish to alleviate it of this burden with all due haste. Would you kindly pass this news along to the other Mrs. Bostwick?"

"Uh... I will do my best, Mrs. Lamb, but I wonder... Would it not be more expedient for you to deliver this message to her directly? I imagine she'll have questions for you and I'm not sure when I'll see her next."

"I sent a note to her hotel room the very same afternoon that I crossed path with her dogs, but she has yet to reply," Mrs. Lamb said with an air of both exasperation and bewilderment, as if this lack of response was the most peculiar thing in the world. Even more peculiar than... a pet psychic.

"My mother-in-law keeps a busy schedule, Mrs. Lamb. I'm sure it's only her social obligations that have delayed her response. Perhaps you might wait a few more days?"

"A few more days? The tender beast is smothering beneath the weight of its discontent, but very well," she said with sigh so dramatic Coco would be envious. "I'll wait to hear from Mrs. Bostwick until tomorrow but then I shall send a second missive."

Without so much as a *by your leave*, Mrs. Lamb turned and strode away followed by an apologetic-looking Miss Watson.

At their departure, Jo looked at Trudy in amused disbelief. She opened her mouth as if to speak, then shut it again and shook her head at the absurdity.

"One might suspect you don't believe Mrs. Lamb's assessment," Trudy said wryly.

"The only thing I find more amusing than the suggestion that Flossie is troubled by a puppyhood memory is Mrs. Lamb's belief that I'd be willing to deliver such a message to my mother-in-law," Jo responded as they began walking once more. "I'll tell Chase, and he can pass the message along. In fact, he's playing billiards with Alex. Let's go tell him now. I'm eager to see his reaction."

Trudy and Jo arrived at the billiards room still giggling and as they paused at the entrance, a memory from the scavenger hunt flooded Trudy's senses. The one of Alex leaning over the table and expertly executing the perfect shot. It sent a rush of heat tingling through her body.

A curious rush of heat that made no sense.

Perhaps she could attribute her sudden warmth to their walk from the lobby—although they'd kept a rather sedate pace what with Jo being in a delicate condition. They'd hardly sprinted. And if a patient had come to Trudy with a similar symptom, she might have thought it was caused by a fever or heatstroke or wearing too many layers on a warm day. But none of those things were true just now. And so, in Trudy's expert medical opinion she could conclude only one thing.

It was... attraction.

Basic biological attraction.

Just because she'd chosen to remain unmarried, that didn't mean she was immune to the sensation of it. She even recognized its essential value to society. Sexual attraction—and its accompanying *urges*—was required for the propagation of the species. It was just *science*.

And yet, experiencing it at this moment was also damnably inconvenient. Because even though a sexual desire for Alexander Bostwick might benefit her *species*, it certainly did not benefit her *personally*.

"Hello, darling," Jo said, crossing the room to her husband's side.

Chase was standing next to the billiards table, a cue stick in one hand, an ale in the other. His countenance brightened upon seeing his wife, and Trudy felt the tremble of something else. Something more than just the meaningless pang of biological need.

It was the echo of longing.

An echo she'd buried down deep because her ambition to become a physician like her father and her brother had taken precedence. Years ago, she'd made a sound, sensible choice knowing that marriage and medicine were not compatible. Not for a woman. She accepted that. But occasionally, in the deepest recesses of her heart, she wondered what it might feel like to have a man look at her the way Chase looked at Jo.

With besotted admiration.

With recognition of exactly who she was.

With unconditional love.

But no man had ever looked at Trudy in that way, and none ever would. That was not her path.

"Hello, my love," Chase responded to his wife, placing a tender kiss on Jo's temple. "How was your class?"

"Exhilarating, as always. Trudy was my most exceptional student," Jo replied, gesturing to where she lingered in the doorway.

At her name, Alex turned and smiled, but the intensity of it paled in comparison to the adoration Jo received from Chase, and Trudy stuffed her longings back down deep where they belonged. She ignored those inconvenient flutters of desire. She was grateful for his friendship, and it was enough.

"I was exceptional in all the worst ways," Trudy replied cheekily, disguising any hint of yearning. She crossed the room to join them, asking, "I assume you're all familiar with Claude Monet?"

"Yes," Chase replied curiously.

"I am nothing like him."

"Oh, come now," Jo argued as the brothers laughed. "You are not as dreadful as that. The bowl of fruit you painted showed some lovely strokes."

"It was a cow in a meadow."

It wasn't really.

It was a bowl of fruit, but their laughter enveloped her like an embrace, and she welcomed it. It wasn't true love or even adoration, but it was genuine affection, and she was happy to accept it.

However, the two other gentlemen in the billiards room did not. They scowled and huffed at the boisterous disturbance.

"Ah, I think our interruption has violated the inner sanctum," Jo whispered. "I've a message to deliver, and then we girls will be on our way. I need to take this impertinent baby upstairs for a nap."

"You've interrupted nothing, my dear," Chase said. "Except a game of billiards that I'm sure to win, but what's your message?"

Jo's face was serious as she replied, "Mrs. Lamb, the clairvoyant who speaks to pets, wants your mother to know a painful memory from puppyhood is causing Flossie to suffer from malaise."

Chase stared down at her, his expression turning droll. "Flossie is suffering from malaise?"

Jo nodded.

"Flossie, the dog my mother dotes upon and feeds by hand who sleeps all day on a satin pillow. That Flossie?"

She nodded again as he smiled.

"And how much, pray tell, is it going to cost us to rid dear Flossie of said malaise?" he asked.

"Oh, we didn't get into that," Jo said, finally grinning back at him. "But surely Flossie is worth every penny."

"Flossie is hardly worth a single penny," he teased. "And anyway, I know why the poor thing is glum. She spends her entire day listening to my mother complain. I've done the same and trust me, it's demoralizing."

∽

The last time Alex had seen Trudy, she'd been leading a bloodied Asher from the ballroom with her sisters in tow while he escorted a similarly bloodied Finn into a back hallway so he might get him to the Bostwick suites without being seen. *What a fiasco!*

But today she'd appeared in the billiards room with his sister-in-law, smiling, making jokes, and suggesting that she'd painted a bowl of fruit that looked like a cow.

He highly doubted that was the case. She was likely a fine artist. In fact, he had a hard time imagining there was anything at which Trudy Hart didn't excel—a fact she seemed intent upon proving right this very moment.

After Chase and Jo had left the billiards room and gone upstairs, Alex and Trudy made their way to Jo's studio so they might converse about his haunting in private and not be disturbed. Once there, she gathered several sheets of paper and a sharp pencil, and they sat down at a small table near the window, while outside, grey clouds hung low in the sky and for once, the lawn was absent of hotel guests.

"I've formed two hypotheses," Trudy said without preamble, and he chuckled at her efficient manner.

"You are very scientifically minded, aren't you, Dr. Hart."

She smiled. "It is both a gift and a burden."

"Let's hope your meticulous system of investigation yields results. Am I safe to assume one hypothesis is that Izzy's things are being left by a living person and the other being it's her ghost?"

"A ghost or some other form of supernatural being, yes, but first, let's make note of all the irrefutable facts. First, you are finding your wife's belongings in unexpected places. Second, someone or some*thing* is leaving them for you to find. And third, all the items are physical in nature, meaning you can touch them. They aren't images or reflections of things that appear and then disappear. Would you say all of this is accurate?"

He nodded. "Yes, that's accurate except..." He hesitated to share this but perhaps it was relevant.

"Except?"

"Sometimes I smell her perfume. She always wore the same fragrance."

"And where has that occurred?" she asked, poising the pencil over the paper.

He felt his face heat inexplicably. There was no reason for him to feel awkward... and yet it seemed as if what he was about to say was overtly intimate even though he knew for a fact, it was not.

"I've smelled her perfume on my bedsheets," he finally answered.

"Ah, I see." Her expression remained neutral as she looked down and jotted a note. "I suppose since perfume is kept in a bottle, we should still consider it a physical item."

Damn.

He wished he'd thought of that or had simply said *in his room* because for some reason, causing Trudy to think of his wife in his bed bothered him. Which was nonsensical, of course. He and Isabella had been married for months. Naturally, people would assume they'd shared a bed.

Of course, the greatest irony of all was that *they hadn't*.

Izzy had *never* been in his bed.

And she'd *never allowed* him into hers.

Alex and his wife had never been intimate anywhere. They'd never consummated their marriage—but that was a fact he was not willing to share with anyone regardless of how irrefutable it was.

"And you're certain all the items were hers?" Trudy asked. "Not someone else's?"

"Most of her things were either embroidered or etched with an image of a gardenia, so yes, I'm sure the items belonged to her."

"A gardenia?"

"Her signature flower."

She paused, and he noted a tiny smirk playing at her lips. "I was not aware people laid claim to such a thing," she said.

He placed a hand against his chest in faux dismay. "Are you suggesting you don't have a signature flower? I thought every lady of fine breeding had a signature flower."

Her smile grew as she cast a glance his way. "Ah, well, there's your answer, then. I cannot claim fine breeding and therefore cannot claim a signature flower."

He leaned back in his chair and regarded her carefully. "I think your signature flower should be... an amaryllis."

"Why an amaryllis?" she said, setting down the pencil. "Because its stems are long and plain?"

He laughed her dry humor, responding, "They are tall, I will grant you that, but surely you know they symbolize confidence and determination. And while you say their stems are plain, I would say they are free from distracting adornment while their petals are richly hued and lovely. Exotic even."

Now it was her turn to laugh as she gestured toward her person. "Exotic?"

"Unique, then," he said.

She tilted her head as if considering it. "I'll allow that."

"And..." he could not resist adding, "An amaryllis requires patience and attentive care in order to bloom."

Her gaze met his at the innuendo, and the atmosphere around them shifted from humorously playful to something altogether different. He realized suddenly that he was flirting with her again—while they discussed his dead wife's perfume on his bed sheets. Perhaps it was that last bit that made her smile slowly fade.

She turned back to the paper and picked up the pencil once more. He cleared his throat and sat up in his chair as the rain outside began in earnest.

"Perhaps we should get back to work," she said, shuffling the papers, then finally asking, "What happened with Isabella's things after she passed? Are they still at your house in Chicago?"

He didn't really want to talk about this anymore but there seemed no way around it. He gave a single shake of the head. "No. A few weeks after the funeral our housekeeper packed up all her belongings and we had them delivered back to her parents."

"Did you keep anything?"

"No."

A flicker of surprise passed over her features, and no wonder. Certainly, a grieving bridegroom would want to keep a few trinkets or mementos of his beloved wife, wouldn't he? It was a fair—if inaccurate—assumption.

She jotted another note and asked, "What do you do with the items once they've appeared to you?"

"I give them to Daisy, but I don't know what she does with them. We've never discussed it."

"Have you ever witnessed anything moving of its own accord, or is it simply there?"

"I've never seen anything move. I just find it where it wasn't before."

"Has anything ever appeared a second time?"

He shook his head, she jotted another note, and a robust gust of wind sent raindrops pelting against the window. It was storming more intensely now, and Alex wondered how many more details he'd have to reveal about a time in his life he'd rather not recall. Still, he appreciated the deftly clinical manner in which she was handling this peculiar interrogation. As they proceeded, he made no more innuendos, and she received his answers without any visible sign of emotions or obvious judgment. Just straightforward questions and factual answers, as if she were evaluating him for an upset stomach or an aching back.

"Well," she said at last, "This is helpful information, but it supports both hypotheses equally."

"And neither suggests a reason why it's happening."

"True, but at this stage the reason behind it is irrelevant."

"Not to me, it isn't. I'm far more interested in why than how."

Thunder rumbled outside and her gaze turned sympathetic. "Yes, of course you are. What I mean to say is, if we focus too much attention on why this is happening, it might blind us to clues pointing to who—or what—is responsible. Unfortunately, motivation isn't... documentable."

He shook his head slowly. "I trust your analytical judgment, Trudy, but as you can imagine, these facts and my feelings are closely intertwined."

"I understand. Please know I am sorry for your troubles. What's happening to you is cruel and you don't deserve it."

Lightning flashed, as if an omen, and he chuckled at his own expense. "Isn't that an assumption on your part, Dr. Hart? Nothing on that list of irrefutable facts proves nor disproves if I deserve this or not."

"Far be it for me to rely on something as unscientific as a gut feeling, sir, but I am certain you don't deserve it."

"I appreciate your confidence," he said, as another rumble of thunder rattled the windowpanes. "But what do you suggest we do next?"

She looked down at the papers once more, her forehead momentarily creasing in concentration.

"I suppose if we focus on the hypothesis that it's a person, we must make a list of who has had access to your wife's belongings, as well as your room back in Chicago and your room here at the hotel."

"That's a short list," he said. "There's me but I assure you I am not doing this to myself. Then there's my mother, Daisy, Ellis, Finn, Lorna, Adele who is my mother's maid. Mother's seamstress has free reign of our house and came with us to the hotel with her husband, but Esther is seventy years old and not spry enough to hide items in the places I've found them."

"What about her husband?"

"Gerard helps tend our gardens and never comes inside the house."

"What about your brother or Jo?"

He shook his head and even laughed at the notion. "Jo hasn't been to Chicago since my wedding, and Chase only came home for a few days at the time of the funeral."

"Jo didn't attend the funeral?"

"She wasn't feeling well enough to travel, so neither she nor Chase have been around to have any involvement in this, not that I would have any doubts even if they had. In fact, I still haven't told either of them anything about it."

She pondered this for a moment, then, as if this had just now occurred to her, asked, "Do Ellis and Finn live with you?"

Alex nodded and stood up to stretch his legs. He'd been sitting too long, and all these questions and memories were making him restless.

"Yes, Ellis, Finn, and my Uncle Vernon moved in with us late last summer soon after my father had his heart attack. My uncle and Ellis have been lending a hand at our investment company."

Actually, Uncle Vernon was lending a hand while Ellis seemed more interested in a *handout*. If the lad could learn to apply half as much effort to getting the job done as he did to looking for a shortcut, he'd be well on his way to success. He was capable, he just wasn't motivated.

"Your investment company in Chicago? Bostwick & Sons?" Trudy asked.

"Yes."

He walked around behind her chair and leaned forward, perusing her notes and the short list of names, but then he caught sight of the most endearing little freckle right behind her ear. He stared at that instead of the lists although exactly *why* he found a freckle so captivating he could not say. After a brief moment, he stood upright once more and began to pace.

"I know we're not supposed to be contemplating motives, but I must say, the only two people on that list clever enough to pull off such a scheme are my mother and my sister, but I know neither of them would do such a thing. I'd stake my life on it. As for the others, Adele adores me, Esther is too old, Lorna too timid, Finn too foolhardy, and quite frankly, Ellis is too lazy. The only thing he's truly interested in is finding himself a wealthy heiress so he doesn't have to work for a living. Believe me. I have given this a great deal of thought and none of these people would have any reason to taunt me."

He paused in place and looked over at her. "That's why I keep coming back to there being supernatural forces at play, as much as I hate to say it out loud. I can't explain it with any facts, but I feel it, somehow. And... I've started having dreams."

"Dreams?"

"Yes, but it's the same dream every time, and so vivid. I see... I see Izzy falling down those stairs and I'm reaching out, trying to catch hold of her hand but I just keep getting farther and farther away. And then I see her standing off to the side, as if there are two of her. She's lying at the bottom of the steps but also staring up at me from the doorway of the front parlor. It's terribly disconcerting."

He shook his head vigorously as if to dispel the vision. He hadn't intended to mention the dreams to Trudy. They were only *dreams*, after all. Not ghostly visitations but rather a distorted memory playing itself over and over in his mind, but making the admission was almost a relief.

She nodded slowly. "That does sound disconcerting. Perhaps we should discuss the second hypothesis. The same irrefutable facts apply, and yet if the items are being manipulated by some spectral being, what other questions should we be asking?"

They gazed at one another, each equally befuddled.

"Since it seems neither of us possesses any useful knowledge regarding the occult," she said tentatively. "I suppose we must learn."

"How?"

She gave a quick, short sigh. "By consulting the... *experts* and asking them if spirits can manipulate objects on their own. And why they might choose to do so."

Once again he appreciated her pragmatic nature. She wasn't shaking her head with a *tsk, tsk, tsk*, or looking at him as if he'd lost his senses, as anyone else surely would. He ran a hand through his hair, wondering how his life had come to this strangeness.

"Experts. Are you referring to the spiritualists at the hotel?"

"It's a place to start."

"But how can we be certain anything they tell us is true?"

"Ah, I see my skepticism is contagious," she said with a sudden smile.

"I've been skeptical all along, but the fact remains someone, or some*thing*, is taunting me. And making a fool of me. I'd rather not add insult to injury by letting some fraudulent clairvoyants lead me further astray from reality... but I don't see that we have any choice but to consult them."

Trudy rose from her chair and crossed over to the window,

tapping her fingers against her chin as she gazed out at the rain. He smiled at the gesture. She'd done it numerous times during the scavenger hunt, and he recognized it now as an unconscious habit she performed while mulling over information. Like the little secret freckle behind her ear, he found her subtle motion oddly appealing.

Maybe he had lost his senses...

After a moment, she turned back to face him.

"An unconventional dilemma calls for an unconventional solution, and since the hotel is currently run amuck with occultists, we may as well take advantage of that."

"Run amuck? I only know of three. Well, four if you count Mrs. Lamb, but haven't you ruled out Mr. Gibson?"

"I'm willing to give the trance speaker another chance but more importantly, Mr. Tippet informed me earlier today that five more spiritualists arrive this week. Apparently he's planning some sort of event where all the psychics, mediums, mentalists, and clairvoyants gather in the ballroom to give readings. I believe he's calling it a Mystic Mylee." She arched her brow at the name and continued. "That seems a fortuitous opportunity for us to question several of them in a short amount of time."

"I cannot think of anything I'd enjoy less," he responded dryly. "And yet... as they say, nothing ventured, nothing gained. Perhaps we'll hear some common threads that are useful. If not, we'll be no worse off than we are now."

"Exactly. Didn't Mr. Edison once say he'd learned ten thousand ways to not make a light bulb before he succeeded?"

"Good Lord, I hope you're not suggesting we see ten thousand clairvoyants."

She smiled patiently. "I was thinking we'd start with four or five."

sixteen

A motionless Ambrose Gibson sat on a simple wooden chair in the center of the stage as Trudy entered the Imperial Hotel theater. The gasoliers burned brightly but with no patrons to occupy the crimson velvet seats and no enthusiastic chatter to dispel the hushed silence, the room felt shrouded in shadows and mystery. Especially with Mr. Gibson perched motionless like a hawk on a rooftop.

"Mr. Gibson?" she called out tentatively.

His head turned languidly toward the sound of her voice. Almost as if he'd been expecting her... but of course, that wasn't possible.

"Hello? Who's there, now?" he replied, his own voice a mellower version of the one he'd used during his performance.

Trudy strode purposefully forward, reaching the edge of the stage and smiling up at him. She thought to put him at ease and present herself as a devotee so he'd be free with his information.

Although she and Alex planned to attend Mr. Tippett's spiritualist event, they'd also agreed to meet with a few mediums in advance. While she was here to question Mr. Ambrose Gibson, Alex was on his way to meet with Miss Greta Watson.

"Good morning, Mr. Gibson," she said. "Please allow me to

introduce myself. I'm Dr. Trudy Hart. I wondered if I might speak with you for a moment. If you aren't too busy." She stole another glance around the vacant theater as if to suggest he couldn't be *too* busy given that he was alone in an empty room.

He wore a light brown suit and with his long hair pulled back into a queue, he looked exceedingly average, except for his dark eyes that seemed to bore into hers. A flutter of nerves rippled through her, but she ignored it. There was nothing to be unsettled about. She was here to gather information, nothing more.

"A pleasure to make your acquaintance, Dr. Hart," he said, rising slowing from the chair. He strolled to the edge of the stage and then jumped with apparent ease, but his leap surprised her, and she squeaked awkwardly as he landed just feet from where she stood. Was he trying to catch her off guard, or was he merely eccentric?

Perhaps both.

"What brings you to seek my council?" he asked, gesturing to the front row. She took a seat, and he sat down beside her smiling benignly and expectantly.

"First, may I say I found your demonstration a few weeks ago mesmerizing. I could not take my eyes from the stage."

"Thank, Dr. Hart. It brings me great joy to facilitate communication between the dearly departed and their loved ones. Just as you are a practitioner of healing, so too am I. These exhibitions I perform provide an invaluable form of spiritual healing which I'm sure you can appreciate."

"Of course, sir. Such a noble calling," she agreed with an exaggerated nod even while silently acknowledging he'd just equated his hypnotic *parlor tricks* to her medical degree. "I was wondering, though, if you might enlighten me about other methods the departed might use to communicate."

"There are several ways in which they might do so. Just as each of us has personal preferences while we are sentient beings here on earth, spiritual beings have their own preferences, too."

"And what might some of those preferences be?" she asked.

She strove to look pensive and demure, certain Mr. Gibson's false humility cloaked a pompous personality. A person could not stand upon a stage and manipulate an entire theater full of patrons the way he had without an overabundance of confidence, whether earned or not. He leaned back and steepled his fingers as if pondering her question before answering.

"If the spirits are powerful enough, they might appear as visible apparitions. They might whisper to us, or sing. They often visit us in our dreams when our level of consciousness is the most fluid."

She tried not to react to that last bit. It wasn't a surprise to hear, of course. People often spoke of seeing loved ones during slumber, but Alex's recent dreams of Isabella gave her pause.

"How might one discern between a visitation and a typical dream?"

"With practice."

She considered that a rather sly and convenient response. One that hinted more at a person's desire to believe a dream was something more rather than it being indicative of supernatural means.

"And what of knocking? Or moving objects? Can the departed do that?" She noted a glint in Mr. Gibson's eye at the question as he, no doubt, found her gullible and therefore malleable.

"Oh, yes. Spirits move things all the time. They seem to love nothing more than to knock items onto the floor or make draperies shimmy around a closed window. Some might flicker lights if they are able. These are mostly harmless bids for attention, but occasionally they'll move furniture and that can be a bit alarming to witness."

"I should imagine. But can they make solid objects appear where they weren't before? For instance, could a spirit place a token in a person's pocket?"

He pondered this for a moment. "I suppose some spirits may possess the capability to manipulate objects in such a manner, but it would take a great deal of psychic energy to do so. And intense emotions would be necessary from both sides of the veil. So now I must ask you a question, Dr. Hart. Have you been experiencing visitations?"

She'd anticipated such a question. In fact, she and Alex had devised a story for just such a prompt so that the information they shared with any of the spiritualists would be identical. It was the only way to accurately compare the responses.

"My grandmother passed recently, and I cannot shake the sensation that she's trying to tell me something. She's been leaving treasures for me to find."

"Leaving treasures?" A single dark brow arched.

"Yes," she nodded, trying to look bereaved when in truth, all of her grandparents had passed before she was born and she had no relationship with them whatsoever, other than what her own parents had shared. "I found one of her brooches pinned inside a coat of mine, one of her gloves appeared on the floor of my room, and just last month I found an old letter from her tucked inside a book I'd been reading."

"That's most peculiar, Dr. Hart. The act of pinning a brooch requires a great deal of dexterity. Was this an especially meaningful item between the two of you?"

She seemed to have captured his attention now, and she nodded.

"Very meaningful. The pin was shaped like an amaryllis, her favorite flower. My grandfather gave it to her as a wedding gift."

"And you discovered this inside your coat? Most peculiar," he said, tapping his still steepled fingers together. His brow creased in thought, but then he gave a tiny shake of his head.

"I confess I've never heard of physical objects just appearing in such a manner. As I've said, phantoms may reposition items inside a room, but to manipulate a brooch is extraordinary." He paused, still frowning, and turned to face her.

"Dr. Hart, as much as it may disappoint you to hear, I wonder if perhaps your grandmother placed the pin inside your coat before she passed on, perhaps even hoping that when you encountered it, you might think of her. Perhaps she did the same with the letter."

His response surprised her. She'd thought for certain he'd go along and say she was receiving messages, and that ghostly fingers could move things with ease. *That's what she would've said if she were a fraudulent psychic...* and yet his words supported her preferred hypothesis—that this was a human prank, not a phantom.

"So... you don't think she's visiting me?"

He patted her hand in a comforting gesture. "Don't fret, my dear. While I don't think it's possible she's moving those particular items, I am certain she visits you often because the link between you is obviously strong. When you think of her, when you sense her energy near you, you may be certain she is in your presence. I do hope that brings you comfort."

"Uh... it does. Thank you." She nearly rose to leave but had a sudden thought. One that she should likely ignore, but that was not her way.

"I wonder if I might ask you about something else, Mr. Gibson."

She sensed a moment of exasperation from him, but he disguised it quickly.

"Of course, Dr. Hart. I am at your disposal."

"The participants you brought to the stage at your exhibition a few weeks ago— what exactly transpired with Miss Albright, the last girl who tried to deliver a message but couldn't?"

"Miss Albright?" He said the name as if he were tasting it on his tongue. "Ah, yes, Miss Albright. That was a most unfortunate occurrence, and highly unusual. She is well, is she not?"

"As far as I'm aware, she's suffered no ill effects from the encounter, but I'm curious. Why wasn't she able to reveal the message she'd received? And why did it distress her so?"

His gaze flickered momentarily, as if he sought to peer through the veil of memory.

"As a fellow practitioner of healing, you're aware of how we apply our unique skills and God-given gifts and hope for a particular outcome, but as I'm sure you've experienced, occasionally things go awry. Such was the case with Miss Albright."

"Have you any notion as to why things went awry?" she asked, choosing to maintain a façade of agreeable acceptance—in spite of him comparing himself to a physician again. "All the other participants did so well under your guidance."

He nodded at her thoughtfully. "Yes, all the other voyagers traveled through the veil with ease. Unfortunately, when Miss Albright joined me that night, she was burdened by a number of hindrances that impeded her ability to reveal the message as intended, as well as blocking my ability to guide her through it. She was, to put it simply, too delicate to reveal a message that would cause her strife."

"But how could it cause her strife? Wasn't she merely the conduit?"

"In most cases, those compelled by the spirit guides to join me on stage are merely conduits. They are able to clear their minds completely so messages from beyond don't get muddled with their own thoughts."

"But Miss Albright wasn't able to clear her mind?"

"I don't believe she was, no. In fact, as soon as she reached the stage, I sensed the young woman was being influenced by forces beyond her control."

"Forces, Mr. Gibson? What kind of forces?"

"Powerful ones. I fear Miss Albright may be entangled in a web not of her own design. The more she struggles against it, the more intricate and binding it becomes."

"Bound in a web? You make it sound as if she's in some kind of danger. Is she?"

"She may be. I suspect these forces are playing upon her fears and vulnerabilities, making promises but also threats. She came to me filled with secrets and I believe it is those very same secrets which prevented her from delivering her message that evening."

"Fascinating," Trudy said with all sincerity. Whether honest or deceitful, Mr. Gibson was himself a skilled weaver of webs. "Could you sense what her secrets were?"

He smiled benignly at her question.

"If I could, I would not divulge them to you, just as I won't reveal your secrets to anyone else, should they come to ask."

"My secrets?" she laughed at his ploy of redirection. "What secrets have I?"

He gazed at her, his dark eyes boring into hers. It was most disconcerting, as if he could hypnotize her with just his stare.

"Your secrets are the most treacherous kind, I'm afraid. They are the ones you keep hidden from yourself, and until you confront them, you'll remain locked in an invisible prison of your own making. The world is full of magic, Dr. Hart, as well as love, if only you dare to open your mind and your heart to it."

Then he smiled, and she blinked.

His answer had been ambiguous, nearly obtuse. He knew nothing of Trudy's secrets, but he was as clever as Greta Watson with his ability to spin common human nature into metaphysical predictions. Surely everyone had fears they didn't want to confront. She was no different. He didn't *know* her.

"But regarding Miss Albright," she said, performing a bit of redirection of her own. "What should she do about this web you speak of?"

"Are you friends with Miss Albright?"

"We are acquainted, and I'm concerned for her."

"As you should be, but the choice is up to her. She may choose to fight with all her strength and pull herself free from this web... or she may choose to become the spider."

Trudy shivered with unease at his ominous phrasing and wondered if she'd underestimated Mr. Gibson after all. He *was* as much of a showman as Hugo Plank.

"Become a spider? That sounds dreadful."

But Mr. Gibson's smile had turned enigmatic again. "Not if you like spiders, Dr. Hart. It all depends on which you'd rather be. The predator or the prey."

seventeen

"You must tell me everything," Daisy demanded.

His sister was all but bouncing on the leather seat as he guided the sleek cabriolet away from the hotel and toward the lakeshore. Their plan was to enjoy a quiet picnic and visit the Bostwick cottage site to see the construction progress, but he'd carelessly let slip he'd gone to visit Miss Greta Watson earlier that morning and now his sister was—not surprisingly—peppering him with questions.

"There is not much to tell," he said, giving a gentle shake to the reins so old Henry might step livelier.

Alex was grateful Trudy had reduced his bandage to a mere finger splint allowing him more use of his hand, even if that had required him to be dishonest regarding how much it still ached. Apparently his threshold for discomfort was greater than his threshold for the embarrassment of having a wounded *pinky*.

"Not much to tell?" Daisy asked. "How could that be possible given all you've experienced lately? Especially with Isabella's ghost. I think you're just not telling me the truth."

He scoffed good-naturedly at her scolding, which only served to aggravate her more—so she punched him in the arm.

"Ow," he said although it didn't hurt. "Striking me isn't very ladylike of you."

"And it isn't very gentlemanly of you to tease me with dribbles of information when you know my curiosity is an unquenchable thirst."

He looked at her askance. "Well, at least you're not being melodramatic about it."

She punched him again. Harder this time making the chiffon ruffles of her cuff ripple in the breeze.

"Behave yourself. Stop hitting me and perhaps I will tell you exactly what occurred with Miss Watson."

Daisy crossed her arms and gazed at him expectantly.

They were taking a long, circuitous route that led them around the perimeter of the island. The wind was gusty, causing miniscule white caps to form over the lake and waves to splash along the shore more noisily than usual. Overhead, cottony white clouds occasionally blocked out the sun, but the day remained pleasantly warm.

He handed Daisy the reins so he could shrug out of his jacket —which was another ungentlemanly thing but perhaps they would not come upon anyone else on their ride. And besides, both he and his sister had already been caught without hats, an offense his mother was likely to hear about since they'd encountered Breezy VonMeisterburger on their way through the lobby.

A few of the more overbearing gossipmongers were still giving him the cold shoulder, but he'd decided the best way to defeat them was to meet their disdain with such impeccable manners and affability they'd have nothing else to judge him for. Hopefully the absence of a hat today didn't knock him down another peg with anyone other than Breezy.

"Well? I'm waiting," Daisy said with a huff as he took back the reins.

"Patience is a virtue, little sister," he teased.

"So is persistence. Tell me every detail."

Unable to resist, he said, "Very well. I walked into the parlor adjacent to her room. The rug was burgundy. Miss Watson's assistant greeted me at the door. She was wearing a blue dress and a white pinafore. Miss Watson herself invited me to sit down with her at a small table and offered me a cup of tea which I declined. She offered me coffee instead and I said yes. Then she asked if I'd like milk or sugar, and I said—"

"Hang it all, Alex!" His sister punched him a third time. "Must you be so tiresome?"

His laughter startled the birds overhead, but teasing Daisy was still a favorite pastime. "You told me to tell you every detail and now you punish me for it. Make up your mind."

She shook her head and scowled like an angry kitten, and at last he relented.

"All right. I'm sorry. I will tell you the pertinent details only. Miss Watson and I conversed for only a short while. She informed me that I have, and I'm quoting here, *built an impenetrable spiritual fortress which makes my aura too murky to read.* I don't actually understand what that last part means but the gist I got from her was that I'm guarded and not giving off any clues as to what I may be thinking or feeling which allegedly makes it difficult for her to, and I'm quoting here again, *have a chitty chat with my angels and foretell my destiny.*"

Daisy gave a little chuff of laughter. "So, you're telling *me* that the only thing she told *you* is that you're guarded? I could've told you that much," Daisy said.

"I warned you there wasn't much to share. You didn't believe me. Although she did mention something about me needing to put forth an effort to try new things, and you'll be pleased to know that I assured her I would do so."

There. Perhaps that would satisfy his sister. Daisy was still worried about him, and he was determined to make her stop. Which was precisely why he did *not* admit to her that Miss Watson had also informed him he'd allegedly built a secondary fortress around his *dear tender heart* (her words, not his) which made it nigh on impossible for him to trust anyone. This was not a revelation to him. Nor would it be to Daisy if he were to confess it to her.

He gave another gentle slap of the reins to Henry's backside to pick up the pace.

"Miss Watson did say I could go back when I was ready," he added.

"When will you be ready?" His sister sounded more exasperated than supportive.

"I have no idea. I thought I was ready this morning."

Truthfully, that was another lie. While he may have been ready to ask Miss Watson about ghostly capabilities and whether or not a phantom could leave calling cards, he was neither ready nor interested in taking down his *spiritual defenses*. He quite liked them where they were.

"However," he continued, "you may also be pleased to know I asked her about mysteriously appearing items."

Daisy turned to him once more, her eyes brightening with renewed interest.

"You did? What did she say to that?"

He and Daisy waved to a carriage passing by in the opposite direction containing Mr. Thomas Pendergrass and his family. They were a plump, smiling bunch and waved back enthusiastically which pleased him. There were still several guests at the hotel Alex felt were avoiding him, but just as many seemed to have put aside their concerns over the manner of his wife's death. Of course, if they knew she was haunting him, those concerns would likely reignite.

"Miss Watson said spirits could move any variety of items but that it was difficult for them to pinpoint their energies. In other words, if they want to move something heavy, say, a brick, they could do it, but everything around that brick would feel the force. I asked her about leaving a letter inside of a closed book and she said the energy necessary to open the book would likely damage the pages, and that it would be nearly impossible for a spirit to tear up a letter like the one I found in my boot. I didn't mention anything about Isabella, though. I told her I had a beloved grandmother leaving me trinkets."

Daisy snorted at that since both of their grandmothers were shrewish old women who hadn't liked them as children and didn't much care for them as adults, either.

"Why a grandmother?" she asked, humor lacing her tone.

He might regret telling her this next part, but his sister always seemed to find her way to the truth anyway so he may as well admit it now.

"Because Dr. Hart and I have come up with plan."

"You have?" Her humor shifted toward surprise.

"Yes. We're meeting with a few of the spiritualists, telling each of them an identical story about a dear old granny who is leaving us trinkets, and then afterwards we intend to compare the information we have gathered."

"For what purpose, exactly?"

"For the purpose of proving either the plausibility or the implausibility that it's Izzy who is haunting me."

"You think it could be some other spirit haunting you?"

He smiled over at her patiently. "Not some other spirit, Daisy, but perhaps a human being."

At her frown he added, "Surely the possibility of it being an actual person has crossed your mind."

"I suppose, but who would do that? And why? And how?"

"Those are all the question we aim to answer."

She was quiet for a moment, seeming contemplative, until she said rather forlornly, "Why didn't you include me in this plan. I've been trying to help you since the beginning."

Her disappointment was palpable, and he felt it.

"I'm sorry, Daisy," he said with all sincerity. "I didn't want to worry you. You've been fretting over me for months and I didn't want to add to that. You should be spending your days laughing with your friends, not stewing over how to repair my ill-fated history and damaged reputation."

She blinked back tears and Alex wondered just how many girls he was going to make cry this summer.

"I just want to be useful," she said tremulously.

"My goodness, what a thing to say! You're always useful, Daisy. You always have been, and since Izzy died you've aided me in more ways than you will ever know. Even on those darkest days, you could always make me smile when no one else could."

"I'm glad for that. But you must let me do more. Bring me in on this plan you have."

Her expression was pleading and placed him in an unexpected quandary, although he probably should have anticipated it. Of course, Daisy would want to help. She always wanted to help everyone—all the time. But she was not the most discreet when it came to secrets and her close relationship with Lorna created a unique predicament.

In fact, he realized with a wave of remorse, perhaps he shouldn't have admitted any of what he'd just said. He knew she would never deliberately do anything to cause him more difficulty, but she might do so inadvertently by sharing too much. Then again, perhaps if she knew everything, she'd understand the need for secrecy. Regardless, he'd said so much there was nothing to do but inform her of the rest.

"I will bring you into our plans, if your heart is set on helping, but Daisy there's something you must promise me."

"Of course. Anything."

"Promise me that nothing, and I mean nothing, that pertains to this situation or what we're doing about it can be shared with anyone. Not mother, not your most trusted friends, not your cousins, not Adele or Lorna."

"But I think Lorna could be useful, too."

"No, Lorna cannot be a part of this. You may trust her, but I don't know her. Promise me you will keep this between you, me, and Trudy."

She nodded, her expression serious. "Very well. You have my word."

Alex guided the buggy to a small clearing just off the road and pulled up the reins. Henry shook his head with a horsey snort as they eased to a stop, and Daisy pulled the picnic basket up from the floorboards. As they enjoyed the view of the lake and ate a delicious meal packed for them by Mrs. Culpepper, Alex told Daisy of his conversation with Trudy. He shared the questions she'd asked and the lists she'd made. And when he told his sister who'd they listed as potential human culprits, her eyes went round with surprise—but then she doubled over and laughed with abandon.

"Do you honestly think Mother or I would do such a thing?"

"Of course not. It's simply a list of who would have the means to carry out such a prank."

"We may all have the means, but Mother would never lower herself to engage in a prank. She might hire someone, but she would not do it herself," Daisy said with a giggle. "As for me, you know I'm not mean-spirited like that, and quite frankly, neither is Lorna. She's the tenderest soul I've ever met. Adele thinks you're a prince, Esther is nearly one hundred years old, and Ellis and Finn are both as dull-witted as spittoons. They would have certainly been caught by now. Surely there must be someone else for that list who you just haven't thought of yet."

"I am open to suggestions if you have any and agree with you wholeheartedly. The potential involvement of any of these individuals, including you, defies rational thought, but then again, so does thinking it might be Isabella. That's why I've resorted to meeting with a psychic. Regardless, not a word of this to anyone. Anyone at all. Agreed?"

"Yes. Yes, agreed," she said as she wiped her hands on a red-checked napkin. "Except..."

"Daisy," he warned, already regretting what he'd shared.

"I know. I promised and I will not breathe a word of this to anyone but why haven't you told Chase?"

"It hasn't come up in conversation."

Although the topic had been on the tip of Alex's tongue a

dozen times when he'd been with his brother, each time, something held him back.

"I think you should tell him," Daisy said, her expression turning somber. "He'll be confused if he finds out about this once it's all resolved and hurt that you didn't trust him."

"It's not a matter of trust."

"What is it, then?"

Alex turned in the buggy to face his sister. "How do you think Chase will react when I tell him I'm being *haunted*?"

She considered this only for a moment before responding, "Ah, yes. I see. He may struggle to take you seriously."

"For which I would not blame him."

"I understand. Now... might I ask you another question on a different topic?"

He sighed. "If you must."

She gazed at him for a moment, and then asked quietly, "Are you... fond of Trudy?"

"Good heavens, Daisy. Don't."

"Don't what?"

The girl was all guileless innocence, but she knew what she was about.

"Don't try to fabricate an association out of nothing just to amuse yourself," he said.

"I'm not asking just to amuse myself, and it didn't seem like nothing during the scavenger hunt. You two were thick as thieves and you hardly said a word to me or Lucy."

"That's not true." *Was it?*

"I don't mean you ignored us. The day was pure delight. I've seldom had such fun, but whenever we walked from one location to the next, you and Trudy were side by side, whispering and laughing."

"We were not whispering. You're imagining things and it's not helpful. Dr. Hart and I are friends. That is all."

"Hm," his sister murmured with a toss of her head. "I've heard that song before."

"Meaning?"

"Meaning you sound just like Chase. He spent all last summer insisting he and Jo were only friends and yet look at them now. Married with a child on the way."

"That's different. Chase wasn't in mourning."

Daisy scoffed. "Neither are you. I mean… I know you're sad about what happened to Izzy. We all are because her death was a tragedy, but lamenting her passing is not the same as recovering from a broken heart. It's not as if you two were happily in love. You were miserable, but now, you're smiling again. In spite of this haunting business, I've seen you laugh more with Trudy in the past few weeks than I saw you laugh the entire time you were with Isabella. Trudy's good for you and I like you two together."

Alex felt his jaw clench as he turned to look out over the water. Not because he disagreed with Daisy, but rather because his sister was right. Trudy was good for him. Being around her made him feel lighter and brighter and—dare he admit it? Optimistic. And he *was* fond of her, but that didn't mean what Daisy hoped it might mean. It couldn't.

Could it?

He gave a single nod without looking at her. "Yes, Trudy's friendship is probably good for me. In fact, yes, I'm sure it is, and I enjoy her company but that's all there is to that, Daisy. Let's not complicate things."

"How would being fond of her complicate things?"

"How would it *not* complicate things?"

His voice had risen to an embarrassingly unmanly octave, and he cleared his throat, bringing it back to his typical, robust, masculine register.

"Until I figure out how to stop Izzy's stockings from appearing next to my shaving kit, I have neither the time nor the inclination to think about anything else. I'm certainly not free to court anyone. I'm not even free to *contemplate* courting anyone."

Daisy sighed. "That's exactly why we need to get Isabella's spirit untethered from you," she said. "As soon as possible."

"Her spirit untethered? What are you talking about?" He felt weary just from asking the question.

His sister's eyes were suddenly alight with emotion, as if whatever she was about to impart to him was very exciting—and also terrible.

"I think the reason Izzy keeps leaving you all those trinkets and sundries is because her spirit is tethered to yours. Quite frankly, I'm surprised Miss Watson didn't say anything to you about it this morning because it seems rather obvious to me. Anyway, she explained it to me in great detail the other day. Isabella's spirit is clinging to you for some reason."

"Clinging to me?" he said dryly

"Yes. Clinging or tethered. It means the same thing," she said impatiently. She even had the audacity to roll her eyes as if she could not understand how he could possibly not understand. "You're going to need a powerful medium to free you from Isabella," she said, matter-of-factly. Then added with a casual wave of her hand, "And we might need to schedule a séance."

She included that last bit flippantly as if it were a simple, almost insignificant detail. As if she'd said, *"Go to the butchers for a pound of ham hocks, a large brisket, and oh, don't forget to schedule a séance."*

"A séance, Daisy?" Good Lord. He should not have brought her into any of this. He felt like a locomotive careening off the rails.

"Perhaps a séance," she said. "Or perhaps not. It's possible Madame Moyen can free you with just a few sessions between the two of you, but you won't know until you meet with her."

"Madame Moyen? Why Madame Moyen?" Not that it mattered. He was not going to participate in a séance no matter what this medium might say. Where did his sister even come up with such notions?

Land sakes! All this time he'd been worried he wasn't quite right in the head. But perhaps it was Daisy who had cracked.

eighteen

"Pawn to E4," Jo called out from a raised platform as she overlooked the life-size chess board Mr. Tippett had created with painted wooden squares laid upon the grass.

Trudy bent with laughter as Patrick Fitzpatrick moved forward, a felt hat upon his head with a sphere at the top designed to look like a chess pawn. All around her, other players were bedecked in similar hats representing their positions. Crenelated turrets for the rooks, pointy-tipped domes for the bishops, crowns for the kings and queens. And on either side of her, knights Harlan Callaghan and his brother Clancy, with knit, stuffed horse heads above their own, attempted to prance yet remain within the confines of their designated squares.

"An interesting first move, my love," Chase said sitting in the chair next to his wife on the platform. "I call pawn to C5."

"Also interesting," she responded, leaning forward in her seat as much as her rounded belly would allow. Next to her on a tiny, tufted stool, Poppy watched half-heartedly while trying to entice Sir Chester VonWhiskerton to chase a goose feather she'd found on the ground.

As the two opponents surveyed the board and called out their moves, Trudy stood next to Alex, him in a paper mâché crown and her wearing a rather lovely—and authentic—tiara provided by Mrs. Roebuck, the cost of which could have funded a medical clinic for a year.

"I feel rather regal," Alex said, smiling over at her. "I think I might wear this all the time."

"It's quite majestic," Trudy replied, "Although, unlike mine, I suspect the jewels on your crown may be paste and the gold is most certainly gilded."

"A shame." He shook his head, making the crown wobble. "And here I was so certain it was worth a mint."

"I think this tiara is. Perhaps I'll forget to return it."

"There you are, my boy," Mr. Plank called out as he approached. "I have some new designs for you to consider when you have the time. I think you'll be impressed."

Alex nodded at him. "Excellent. I look forward to seeing them. I have some thoughts for you as well. Perhaps I can stop by your office later this afternoon? Before dinner?" He gestured to his surroundings. "As you can see, I'm somewhat occupied at the moment, ruling my fiefdom."

"With a lovely queen by your side, I see," Mr. Plank said, bowing to Trudy.

"Don't let him dupe you, Mr. Plank. 'Tis I who rules this queendom."

The men's humor was evident as Mr. Plank responded, "I don't doubt that for a moment, Dr. Hart. And thank you for seeing to Mrs. Culpepper's issue. Without her in the kitchen there'd be no fanciful accoutrements to the evening meal."

"My pleasure, Mr. Plank."

"Rook to C5," Chase called out.

"I'll leave you to it, then," Hugo said, turning to leave. "But Alex, when you come to my office, be sure to bring your brother."

Alex tipped his crown at Mr. Plank as the long-legged gentleman strode away.

"Designs?" Trudy couldn't resist asking. "Is Mr. Plank adding to the hotel?"

"Something like that but I fear I am currently sworn to secrecy. As soon as I'm able, I'll tell you all about his latest endeavor."

"Intriguing," she said. "But before you meet with Mr. Plank, do you suppose we could take a moment once this game is finished and exchange our findings?" She lowered her voice for him alone and said, "My interaction with Mr. Gibson was most interesting."

He nodded, and whispered back, "As was my encounter with Miss Watson, not to mention the subsequent conversation I had with Daisy."

"Oh?" she said at his arched brow before glancing over at his sister. Daisy was queen for the opposing team and waved as she caught Trudy's eye.

Trudy waved back as Alex added, "She has the most interesting notion about me requiring a séance to relieve me of a tethered spirit."

"Oh, dear." Her gaze moved from Daisy to Alex.

"Were you aware of this?" he asked.

"I was aware of her opinions. I didn't bother to mention anything to you because that's all it was. Her notions, not something suggested by anyone else."

He nodded. "Nonetheless, I was compelled to bring her into my confidence. She knows our plans and would like to help."

"You don't seem eager for it."

"Her intentions are good, but as you may have noticed she's a bit excitable. I expressed our need for confidentiality and prudence but her association with a certain individual gives me pause."

"Lorna?" Trudy mouthed her name, and he nodded.

"That same individual came up during my discussion with Mr. Gibson, but I'll tell you more later."

"Knight to B3," Jo said causing Harlan to give a whoop of excitement.

He trotted to his new square, then turned back to grin at Lucy with merriment, causing her inevitable blush.

"Yonder knight seems on a quest," Alex murmured.

"Yes, he does, doesn't he."

It did seem Mr. Callaghan had been appearing with some increasing regularity lately, but whether or not Lucy was pleased about it was yet to be revealed. Trudy had questioned her sister about this a few days ago, and while Lucy had remained evasive, there was a sparkle in her eye.

Of course, if there was a romance brewing, Breezy would not approve. Harlan Callaghan was a hotel employee, apparently born on this island with little interest in leaving it. Hardly a society match, but as Trudy observed Lucy's slow smile at Harlan, she wondered if Breezy's opinion would matter much, and she hoped it wouldn't.

Meanwhile, Coco, in true Coco fashion, had recovered unscathed from her heartbreak over Alex's rejection, as well as Ellis's scavenger hunt chicanery. At present, she was wearing a bishop's hat, and a making doe eyes at both Patrick Fitzpatrick as well as rook Andrew Bentley, a young engineer working for the Edison Illuminating Company in Detroit. Trudy wasn't sure whether she should be concerned or relived by this current turn of events, and oh, how she wished her parents would arrive.

Dear Mother and Father,

For better or worse, Coco is once again on the hunt for a husband while Lucy is not so much on the hunt as she is the willing quarry. Poppy continues to enchant everyone with her precociousness, and Asher has formed an odd sort of kinship with Aunt Breezy. Possibly because nothing she says offends him, while nothing he does fails to offend her.

As for me? I'm standing next to a king and trying ever so

hard not to notice how damnably handsome he is—even while wearing a paper mâché crown.

⁓

"Shall we adjourn to the gazebo?" Alex asked Trudy once the chess match had ended in victory for Jo and all the players began to wander off for tea or other activities. Daisy was quick to join them as they walked the garden path leading to the wisteria-covered pavilion.

"I have some theories," his sister said excitedly before they'd even sat down on the delicate benches.

"Perhaps we should review what transpired with Mr. Gibson and Miss Watson first," Trudy said. "It may impact your views."

Daisy nodded. "Very well, but they are excellent theories."

"I'm sure they are," Alex said, sitting down next to Trudy. "But let's hear about Mr. Gibson first."

Trudy glanced at Daisy and said, "Perhaps you should go first, Alex. What did you learn from Miss Watson?"

He shook his head in disappointment. "Unfortunately, not much that was useful. She did say a powerful spirit could move objects but that everything around it would likely show signs of the attempt, and that to pin a brooch inside a coat would potentially rend the fabric. She didn't find it inconceivable, just unlikely. Of course, she also said anything is possible if a spirit's will and emotions are strong enough."

"Speaking of emotions," Daisy added with a dramatic whisper, "she also said Alex had built a fortress around his."

"Daisy," Alex said tersely. "Must you be so exasperating?"

"I'm just trying to move things along," she said. "It's nearly teatime."

"If you've someplace to be, please don't let us keep you," he said.

"Did you learn anything else, Alex?" Trudy interjected in an obvious attempt to keep things harmonious between him and his bothersome little sister.

"Miss Watson said I was free to visit her with more questions if I so chose."

"After he's lowered his defenses," Daisy whispered with a grin.

He ignored her and spoke to Trudy instead. "So, then? Mr. Gibson?"

Trudy hesitated and stole another glance at his sister making Alex even more curious about what the clairvoyant had said.

"Daisy, come sit down, please," Trudy said, patting the spot beside her on the bench. His sister complied and he wondered why she could be so agreeable with everyone *except* him.

"I know you're close with Lorna," Trudy said quietly. "And I know your brother has shared with you how imperative it is we keep this between the three of us, but I want to make sure you understand just how essential that is."

"I do," Daisy said, all hint of amusement gone from her expression. "Honestly, I do. I only want to help."

"Very well." Trudy looked over at Alex. "Mr. Gibson is of the opinion that phantoms can move any number of things within the confines of a space but doubts they could make physical items appear in new locations. But more importantly, I think, is what he said about Lorna."

"Lorna?" Daisy said with surprise and Alex felt a strange twist in his gut, which grew more extreme as Trudy shared Mr. Gibson's concern about powerful forces trapping Lorna in a complex web.

"Amazing," Daisy said, eyes round with both fascination and concern as Trudy finished speaking. "That goes along perfectly with my theory."

Alex felt certain he did not want to ask, and yet he did. "What theory is that?"

Daisy leaned toward them. "I told Trudy weeks ago I thought Isabella was the angry spirit trying to communicate through Lorna at Mr. Gibson's demonstration but now I feel more confident than ever ... I think Isabella is influencing Lorna's actions, too."

"Influencing her actions?" That twist in his gut did a full spin.

"Yes. If what Mr. Gibson says is true, it's possible Lorna is placing those things for you to find, Alex, but she doesn't even realize she's doing it because it's Izzy pulling her puppet strings."

"That can't be, Daisy," Trudy said somberly. "Are you suggesting that Isabella is... possessing Lorna?"

"No, not possessing, exactly. Isabella isn't with her all the time. She's just making Lorna do things occasionally without her being aware. It's as if Lorna is sleepwalking."

"Sleepwalking," Trudy said, looking back at Alex. "Or hypnotized."

nineteen

"These plans look good, Hugo," Chase said as he and Alex sipped Kentucky bourbon in Mr. Plank's study and reviewed his updated designs. "I see you've made some important improvements."

"Important enough to charm some money from your pockets?" Hugo responded, pouring another splash of amber liquid into Chase's glass.

He offered some to Alex, but he declined. His head was already cloudy enough from the conversation he'd just shared with Trudy and his sister. He needed something to clarify his thoughts, not muddle them further.

"Possibly," Chase replied to Hugo. "Although I'm not sure I want to spend another winter on the island. Are you still angling for a partner or is it really the cash you're after?"

"I'm after both, but if we form a partnership you'll have more input over what your investment is used for. I know you've got an excellent head for numbers, Chase, and your financial acumen would surely help put my mind at ease when it comes to tabulating those ledgers. And what about you, Alex?" Hugo said, shifting in his chair to look at him. "What do you think of these new designs?"

Alex looked down at the drawings in his lap. Drawings he had all but ignored.

"I'm afraid I find myself a little distracted this evening, Hugo. My apologies but I'm not ready to make a decision on this one way or another."

"Fair enough. I don't want to rush you. You can let me know tomorrow."

Chase and Hugo laughed at the joke, and Alex smiled.

"I'm sure you've heard my last investment didn't pan out," Alex said. "I'd like to make sure my next one is successful." *Didn't pan out was an understatement.*

"Of course you would, son, and you can be certain I'll respect your decision regardless of what it is. I do feel confident about the success of this venture, though, or I wouldn't have shared it with the two of you. I don't deal in alchemy or fantasy. This is pure strategy. The railroads are bringing more summer visitors north every day and they have to spend their money somewhere. I want to make sure it's at my hotel or at any one of the new businesses I'm about to establish. But to be clear, I'm not just thinking about my ledgers. I'm thinking about my legacy. As much as I want to be considered a successful businessman, I'd rather be known as a visionary."

"You do have humble aspirations," Chase said, smiling at Hugo.

"Don't we all? Why do you suppose your father named his investment company Bostwick & Sons? Why does any man name his business after himself? It's so people remember his name long after he's gone. They remember who he was and what he created. That's what I'm trying to do."

"So will you be renaming the town Plankville?" Chase asked in jest.

Hugo chuckled along with them. "I think Trillium Bay has a far more pleasing sound to it, but you can bet your last dollar that a few businesses will incorporate my name somehow."

"And isn't that exactly what you're asking us to do?" Alex said, also in jest. "Bet our last dollar?"

"Not your last dollar. Just all the ones before it."

Alex and Chase left Hugo's office soon after, and as they reached the stairs to go up to their respective rooms, Chase asked quietly, "Is something on your mind tonight? Is Hugo's persistence putting you off?"

"No, not at all," Alex responded. "In fact, I'm genuinely interested but think it's best to play my cards close to the vest."

"You always do." Chase's tone was laced with affectionate sarcasm because, yes, Alex always did keep his cards close.

But ... wasn't that what Miss Watson had warned him about? Being too guarded? Not being able to trust people? Hadn't she prodded him to try new things? And hadn't he promised Daisy he would?

None of this meant it was time to go into business with Hugo Plank necessarily. At least not until he'd looked over the latest plans with some due diligence but given the exchange he'd just had with Trudy and Daisy out in the gazebo, perhaps it was at least time to trust his own brother.

"Are you and Jo having dinner in the dining room this evening?"

"Not this evening, no," Chase responded. "My lovely wife is embarrassed that every time she eats a meal of any size she starts to burp."

Alex joined in with Chase's quiet laughter.

"It is rather like seeing a beautiful goldfinch squawk at you like a crow," Alex agreed. "Although please assure her, I still consider her to be the most ladylike of ladies."

"I've gotten used to it. I hardly notice it anymore," Chase replied. "Nonetheless, she's having a casual dinner with the Mahoney sisters this evening at their home. They're sweet old biddies, those sisters, and they talk so much, her burping goes completely unnoticed."

"And you weren't invited?"

"Invited to dine with sweet old biddies who never stop talking? Yes, I was invited but Jo graciously made my excuses for me. I was planning to get a tray in my room and look at these plans from Hugo, but I'll happily join you in the dining room, if you'd like."

"Actually, I'd prefer to have trays in your room, if you don't mind. There's something I've been wanting to discuss with you and privacy is necessary."

"Of course. May I ask if it's something pleasant? Or unpleasant?"

Alex shook his head. "Neither. Both. Let's just say it's something... peculiar."

～

"Let me see if I've got this straight," Chase said, staring back at Alex as their dinner trays remained untouched.

"Your dead wife...

Is somehow manipulating our sister's maid...

To place personal items where you will find them...

Because she's angry at you...

And the only way to make her stop...

Is to hold a séance?"

"When you say it in that manner, it sounds insane," Alex replied with banality.

"It is insane," Chase all but shouted, rising up from his chair. He strode over to a side table and poured himself a hearty glass of whiskey.

Alex had miscalculated.

He'd forgotten that he'd had time to ease into this situation. First he'd found a few items. And then a few more. Then Lorna had acted peculiarly at the trance speaker's show. Then there'd been talk of spiritual mediums. Then came the suggestion of a séance. It wasn't until today they'd considered the possibility of

Isabella influencing Lorna. But to hear this all at once was, understandably, too much for his brother to comprehend.

"It's possible that it's not Isabella at all," Alex added. "It's possible someone has hypnotized someone else to do this to me. In which case, no séance would be necessary."

Chase glared at him, then splashed more whiskey into his glass. "Oh, well, that's a relief."

"I understand this is a lot to take in and that it doesn't make sense to you. It doesn't make sense to me either, but I've been living with this since the day of Isabella's funeral. And you'd be justified in thinking that I'd lost my senses, but Daisy has seen every item I've found."

"Daisy, our sister who still believes in pixies and fairies?"

"She doesn't, actually. She's been humoring us."

"Adorable." Chase took a gulp from his glass.

"If it brings you any comfort, Trudy is determined to prove there are no supernatural elements at play here and that someone is taunting me for some other reason."

Chase sighed from deep within his chest and walked back to the table, sinking down into the chair.

"And how is it that Trudy got involved?"

"You didn't attend the trance lecturer's show, but she was sitting next to me when Lorna became agitated on the stage. I left at that point and Trudy followed me out of concern. I'm grateful she did. She's been a steadying force these last few weeks."

A wave of remorse passed across Chase's features. "I'm sorry you didn't feel you could come to me. All this time I've thought you were struggling with grief at the loss of Isabella. I thought what you needed was a distracting business project ...not an exorcist."

"I don't need an exorcist. No one is possessed. That would be absurd."

Chase's laughter held little humor in it. "I fail to see the distinction at this point."

"Fair enough."

His brother took another swig from the glass while Alex continued to sip from his.

"Who else knows?" Chase asked.

"Just the four of us," Alex replied. "You, me, Daisy, and Trudy. If you feel compelled to share this with Jo I'd understand. I would have told you both together but with the baby, I thought it might be best to keep her far removed."

"I'd appreciate that. She and I have promised to never keep secrets from one another, but I think this one can wait. I'll tell her when the time is right for her own peace of mind."

Alex nodded. And pondered. If he was going to trust his brother, he may as well trust him with everything. "There is something else I'd like to tell you that I haven't told Daisy or Trudy. Or anyone."

Chase's expression turned wary. Again. "All right."

"Do you remember Katharine Lawrence?"

"Katharine Lawrence from Chicago who jilted you for an Italian baron?"

"The same."

"Yes, of course. I remember her well. She was your first kiss, was she not?"

"She was my first of many things."

"And what has she to do with this?"

"She's a wealthy widow, now, and still stunningly beautiful."

Chase eyed him impatiently, but asked, "Are you thinking of renewing your acquaintance?"

"No. I suspect there's a rather long line of wealthy suitors and vigorous paramours keeping her content these days."

"Ah." Chase nodded. "Then might you get to the crux of the issue, Alex? I'm not in the mood for riddles and have no notion of where this is headed."

"My apologies. I'm trying not to bludgeon with you too much at once."

"I can take it, but please make haste."

"Very well. The week before my wedding, I attended a house

party at Jackson Winslow's country estate. It was a small, intimate gathering, but I encountered Katharine there."

"And by encountered, you mean ... what, exactly?"

Alex sighed, his remorse taking hold. "Isabella and I were struggling. It was obvious to me her feelings had changed but she refused to discuss our future. I felt that, like me, she'd got caught up in the idea of love, but in our hearts, we knew our affection wasn't strong enough to sustain a marriage. I was prepared to call the whole thing off."

"Alex, I had no idea. I'm sorry."

Alex took a sip from his glass. And then another. "Unfortunately, Isabella was more concerned about the humiliation of a cancelled engagement than she was about an ill-suited marriage. I could have retracted my proposal but felt the gentlemanly thing to do was to go ahead with the wedding."

"I see. And what role does Katharine Lawrence play in all of this?"

"At the house party, I confided my troubles and doubts to her. She was offering me advice on how to best navigate my upcoming marriage, but we'd been drinking all day, emotions were running high... and she kissed me."

"She kissed you? Did you... kiss her back?"

"I did. Only for a moment and I regretted it instantly, but that's no excuse. And of course, someone saw us."

"Who?"

"I have no idea, but Isabella confronted me about it on our wedding night and I chose to be honest. I didn't want to start our marriage off with a lie, especially since she wouldn't have believed me if I'd denied it. I assured her that such a thing would never happen again, and I meant it. Years of watching Father cheat on Mother has given me a rather puritanical view of fidelity, and I've always promised myself I'd be a faithful husband. I promised Izzy the same."

"Did she believe you?"

"No, and no matter how hard I tried to make amends and

prove my sincere devotion to her, she couldn't see past my mistake."

Chase shook his head slowly. "That's a rocky start to a marriage."

"In truth, there was no marriage. We were wed on paper only. It was never ... physical. We agreed to keep the disastrous state of our...non-union a secret. I thought she might forgive me in time, but after a few months, I asked for an annulment. She was adamantly opposed. She didn't want one. That's what we were fighting about right before she fell."

Chase's expression was full of sympathy. "And now you think she haunting you? Out of malice?"

"*Heaven hath no rage like love turned to hatred, nor hell a fury like a woman scorned.* She thought I'd been unfaithful. And for a brief moment, I had been."

"In the strictest sense, perhaps, but Alex, half the men we know continue such encounters well after the wedding day."

"That doesn't make it right. Would you ever cheat on Jo?"

"No, I would not, but we're a love match and you and Isabella were... less so."

"You're trying to absolve me, and I do appreciate it, but I cannot shake the sense that all of this, the ill-fated marriage, her terrible accident, these hauntings, all of it is my fault. I was the one who wanted to rush us down the aisle, I was the one dallying with Katharine Lawrence, and I was the one Isabella was arguing with when she fell down those stairs."

Chase leaned back in his chair and actually chuckled.

"Do you really think you wield such power over the universe, big brother? That your single error, your momentary lapse in restraint, created all these ripples of mayhem?"

"It's possible."

"Lots of things are possible. That doesn't make them probable. You've done this since we were children, you know," Chase said quietly, his tone growing thoughtful. "You have always taken on the burden of responsibility for things over which you held no sway. Catering to Mother's whims and trying to make her happy even while knowing that nothing would. Agonizing over a failed business venture yet refusing to acknowledge that Father and I have made plenty of investment mistakes. Just as every financier has. And now you seem intent upon wiping the slate clean of all of Isabella's flaws, as if she played no part in the demise of your relationship. Is it true she didn't want Jo and I at your wedding because she considered our marriage improper?"

Alex hesitated. "Yes. Did Daisy tell you that? She shouldn't have."

"That's beside the point," Chase replied. "The point is that Isabella was unkind, judgmental, and spoiled. She never would have been satisfied no matter how hard you'd tried to please her. Even without Katharine Lawrence in the picture, Izzy would have made your life a hellscape."

"She didn't deserve to fall down that staircase."

"No, of course she didn't. That was tragic, and it's wretched that you two were arguing when it occurred, but you didn't push her. Stop punishing yourself as if you did. Stop ruminating over things from the past that you cannot change, especially things that weren't your fault to begin with." Chase shook his head and sighed. "I'm no spiritualist, Alex. Not by a long shot. But even I understand that some occurrences are driven by fate. Some things are beyond our control. Just because you were born first, that doesn't mean you're in charge of everything."

twenty

Asher lay across the patchwork quilt, his gangly limbs seeming to sprawl in every direction like a drunken octopus.

"Must you occupy so much space," Coco admonished, tugging her skirt out from under his shoe and adjusting her parasol in an ever-persistent pursuit of keeping the sun from her nose.

Trudy and her family had gathered on the shore near the cottages to celebrate the arrival of her Uncle Albert, although few events could inspire less revelry. For every ninety-nine words uttered by Aunt Breezy, he uttered one, and it was usually more of a grunt than an actual word. Perhaps this was because she'd worn him down over the years and he'd simply ceased to contribute to conversations where he clearly wasn't needed.

His input was especially unnecessary today since the Bostwick family had joined them for the picnic and therefore Breezy's typical monologue was predictably dominating. She had no intention of letting Constance Bostwick get in the final word on any topic, regardless of how arbitrary.

"Miss Hart, there's room over here by me," Ellis said quietly to Coco as Asher rolled to his side in feigned slumber and flopped his arm across her ankle.

Alex's cousin seemed determined to make amends for cheating at the scavenger hunt, and although Trudy knew Coco had not forgiven him for humiliating her in front of Mr. Plank, Ellis was the only single man within a mile-wide radius—besides her brother—and of course Alex whom she had not spoken a single word to since that night at the dance weeks prior. Ellis was Coco's only option if she was of a mind to flirt—and she was always of a mind to flirt.

She scooched a few inches closer to him, and he responded by handing her a strawberry from the basket of delectable food Mrs. Culpepper had provided for their meal.

"Have I mentioned that you look *berry* pretty today, Miss Hart?" he murmured, and Trudy turned her face away to hide her chuckle.

"Perhaps he's redeemable, after all," she whispered to Alex who was sitting on the blanket behind her. He scoffed good-naturedly in response.

"Perhaps. But doubtful."

A few days after the cheating incident, Ellis had gone to Mr. Plank of his own accord and apologized profusely, even asking if he might spend some time as a porter to demonstrate his profound regret *(according to Alex who had heard it directly from Hugo.)* True to his good nature, Mr. Plank graciously accepted the olive branch while Alex had shared with Trudy he was less inclined to do so, at least until he was certain his cousin's remorse was genuine.

"Get up, lazy slug," Finn said a few minutes later, nudging Asher with his foot. "Let's go wading."

Asher let out a false snore.

"I'll go with you," Daisy said, hopping up.

"How do you intend to wade?" her mother asked. "You'll get your shoes and stockings wet."

"Not if I remove them," Daisy answered cheekily. "We'll be moving into the cottage soon so it's as if I'm in my own yard."

Trudy sensed the original Mrs. Bostwick wanted to argue but thought better of it. If Daisy was determined to go into the lake, she would go into the lake, no matter that showing off her bare feet would shock her mother.

"Mm, how I'd love to dip my toes into that cool water," Jo said quietly to Chase. "But I don't think I can manage it."

"I think you might if I put a chair at the water's edge. Would you like that?"

She smiled at him with gratitude. "You're my hero. My brilliant hero."

"You are easy to please, my love."

Chase made short work of moving a chair, and as Jo and Daisy went into the Bostwick cottage, ostensibly to remove their stockings, Aunt Breezy commented off-handedly, "Yours is such a quaint little abode, Constance. When do you intend to move in?"

Glances darted among the rest of them as they wondered what the slur might lead to, especially since there was nothing subtle about it. *Quaint little abode?* Breezy may as well have called it a ramshackle hut. Or a bawdy house.

"Soon. Very soon," Constance said, and Trudy heard Alex's quiet chuckle near her ear.

The sound sent a shiver through her limbs. She might have considered it enticing, pleasurable even, had it not been so bloody inconvenient. Her attraction to Alexander Bostwick seemed to be growing exponentially...like bacteria. And she needed to find some way to make it stop.

"Well, I suppose that's the advantage of filling it with mass produced furniture from Grand Rapids," Breezy said. "Fast, convenient delivery. I myself am expecting a custom vitrine from Francois Linke to arrive from Paris any day now,"

Constance sniffed with superior disdain. "What a shame they didn't make you a priority. My custom Linke buffet arrived weeks ago. It's already in the dining room, and I must say, the gold ormolu handles positively gleam in the sunlight."

Uncle Albert grunted something that Trudy couldn't quite make out while her aunt's peevish expression left no room for misinterpretation. She was vexed that Constance had bested her.

"Trudy, are there any more biscuits?" Poppy asked as she meandered past the quilt with the cat draped over her arm.

"More biscuits, Pop? Didn't you already have three?" Trudy replied.

Poppy hesitated. "It's not for me. It's for Chester."

"Chester shouldn't have biscuits. They're bad for his tummy."

Trudy watched as Poppy's little mind went to work.

"Did I say Chester? I meant Asher," she replied innocently.

Asher chuckled at her response without bothering to open his eyes, and although Trudy knew she should not reward her sister for telling a fib, the day was supposed to be a celebration of sorts, so she dug a biscuit from the basket and handed it to Poppy.

"Here you go, you scamp. But this is your last one or it's you who'll end up with a tummy ache," Trudy warned.

"You spoil that tot, Gertrude," an annoyed Aunt Breezy scolded tersely from her chair. "She'll be round as a piglet and self-indulgent to boot. Thank goodness you'll never have children of your own."

The mood could not have taken a frostier turn. It felt as if a tidal wave had risen from Lake Huron and doused them all with frigid waters. Even the birds seemed to hush in their singing as Trudy let out a tiny gasp of wounded surprise at her aunt's harsh comment. But that chill was immediately overpowered by a scalding wave of embarrassment, and somehow, shame.

Lucy offered up a false chuff of laughter, as if of course Aunt Breezy was only joking.

"How funny you are, Aunt Breezy. We all know Trudy would make a wonderful mother. If she wanted to be one. It's just her choice not to be. But if she did want to be, well, then she'd be a wonderful one." Lucy's stammering and repetition only made matters worse.

Trudy stared down at her lap and felt the eyes of each of them upon her.

Even Coco took pity, adding, "Yes, she would. Trudy could be a wonderful mother, but as a doctor, she takes care of far more children than she ever would if she had a family of her own to love and cherish. In fact, I don't find it all unnatural that she'd rather be a physician instead of just a normal wife and mother. I think she's...*progressive*."

Coco said it defiantly, as if the word *progressive* was about the most broad-minded, intellectual thing she could have possibly uttered.

But for her sister to defend her in such a manner without a hint of her usual facetiousness made Trudy feel more pitiful than she ever had before. Both of her sisters' comments were well intentioned and should have been a balm to Trudy's pride, and yet every word they'd spoken had felt like a slap to her face.

Because, for all their protestations, and all their outward support, she could tell they *did* find her choices unnatural. And abnormal. And suddenly she was aware of just how much of an outsider she was, even to the people who loved her the most. She knew the medical community could not fully accept her because she was a woman, and yet, she realized in that moment, her own family could not fully accept her because she wasn't *woman enough*.

twenty-one

"There you are. Where did you disappear to yesterday?" Trudy heard Alex ask as he approached.

She was sitting in a wicker chair that she'd dragged to the farthest recesses of the front porch, away from every other chair and every conversation area, in the foolhardy hope that this remote corner might provide her with some much-desired privacy to read in peace. Yet somehow, even in this remote corner, she'd been discovered. Repeatedly. As if there was some sort of marquee over her head that stated in big, bold letters *please bother this woman who is clearly seeking solitude.*

Surely there must be some sort of sign because over the past hour, no less than a dozen guests had sought her out seeking free medical advice *(an issue she intended to discuss with Mr. Plank)*, and a dozen others had wandered over just to say hello because they were certain she must be lonely down here on the far end of the porch all by herself.

No amount of staring intently at her medical journal or limiting her discourse to monosyllabic responses seemed to give them the impression that she was, in fact, fine down here on the far end of the porch all by herself. In fact, it did not seem to occur to a single, solitary person that she was sitting down here on the

far end of the porch all by herself specifically because she *wanted* to be sitting down here on the far end of the porch *all by herself.*
And now.
Here was Alex.
The last person she wanted to see.

She'd left the picnic early yesterday, slinking away and telling no one but Lucy that she was leaving. And today, she knew she had no justifiable reason for being irritable with him. It wasn't his fault he'd borne witness to her humiliation at Breezy's mean-spirited words. It wasn't his fault he'd been next to her on the picnic blanket when her sisters had inadvertently made matters infinitely worse with their clumsy, shallow defense. And it wasn't his fault that—apparently—his opinion of her had become the one she cared about the most.

But she was irritable with him. She was irritable with all of them. Sitting on that blanket, surrounded by her family and his, she'd become that awkward scrawny scarecrow all over again. The too-tall girl who meant well but just wasn't like the others. Not in the ways that mattered to proper society. Not in the ways that allegedly gave her *real* value. Matrimony and motherhood.

Being around Chase and Jo hadn't helped matters either. They were kind and wonderful, of course, but they were *so much in love* it only served to remind Trudy of the price she was paying for the choice she'd made. It was the right choice for her, of course, and she didn't regret it, but still, the cost hadn't seemed so high to her before.

"I... had some reading I wanted to finish," Trudy responded curtly. "Still do." She didn't look at him. Just lifted her periodical and then lowered it back to her lap so she could continue (pretending) to read.

"Is that a medical journal?" he asked amiably in spite of her rudeness.

"Yes it's a medical journal. I'm a doctor."

He laughed at her jest but quieted quickly as he realized she hadn't.

Gah! Shame on you, Gertrude.

Even Poppy wouldn't pout this way, but Trudy was just now discovering an unfortunate truth about herself. *Knowing* that she was behaving childishly and being able to *stop* herself from behaving childishly were two very different things. So, she continued fake reading and said nothing.

After a moment, Alex turned and walked away.

Her remorse was instantaneous, and she even thought to call him back to apologize for her lack of civility, but the vulture of irascibility had her in its talons. As Alex disappeared through the lobby doors, she looked back down at her medical journal only to have the letters blur as a tear splashed upon the page.

She toyed idly for a moment with the idea of silently admonishing him. *He certainly hadn't tried very hard to cajole her into a better humor just now!* But even in her peevish state, she knew she could not fault him.

From the corner of her eye, she saw someone else approach but kept her head dipped lest they see her silly tears. Then the figure pulled a chair up perpendicular to hers and sat down so they were facing her profile. And she recognized his shoes.

Alex's shoes.

"Hello," she murmured quietly.

"Hello. You seem rather cross this morning. Do you need a tonic or an elixir of some sort?"

"No. Thank you. I just need to finish reading this article."

"Mm. What's it about?"

She paused. "Enemas."

"Ah. How moving."

She pressed her lips together. *Damn him.* He was cajoling her, and it was working. He was going to make her laugh.

He'd brought a newspaper with him and proceeded to open and adjust it in the loudest manner possible, unfolding, refolding, rattling and fluffing it. He could have *sung* the news stories and made less of a racket.

"Are you being deliberately distracting with that newspaper, Mr. Bostwick?"

"Not especially. I can't help that it's windy out here on the porch." He shook the paper wildly as if he was caught in a gale, and she could not prevent the chuff of laughter from escaping.

"What is wrong with you?" she murmured.

"So very many things, Dr. Hart. I would not know how to list it all. But you excel at lists. Shall we make one together?"

He shook the newspaper again, and when she finally smiled he remarked quietly, "Your aunt once suggested, to my face, no less, that she wasn't safe standing next to me upon a staircase. The implication, of course, being—"

"Yes. I understand the implication. You needn't say it. I suppose accusing you of mariticide is more offensive than her saying I'd be a terrible mother." She nodded in agreement. "But at least your family believes in you. Mine seems to think I'm unnatural."

Alex laughed. "I don't believe that's accurate. If there's anything *unusual* about you, it's simply that you're so capable and unflappable. Your drive and ambition do make you different, but in the most amazing ways."

Her melancholy began to dissipate. Actually, it had begun to dissipate the moment he'd arrived on the porch. She just hadn't been ready to let it go.

"And anyway," Alex continued, "We all knew your aunt was just ornery because my mother outshone her with that business about the furniture."

"Those women do seem to thrive on their discord."

"That they do, but may I share a secret?' He lowered his voice as he spoke.

"I should think the answer to that goes without saying."

He smiled at her and looked around as if to impart the details of a great scandal.

"That custom designed Linke buffet my mother was crowing about? It was designed for someone else. The original buyer decided they wanted something less ostentatious so my mother accepted that buffet sight unseen simply because it could be shipped immediately. And," he leaned closer to whisper in her ear, "my mother hates it."

Trudy's throat filled with laughter, and her mind filled with the recognition that his sense of humor was one of her favorite things about him. It was silly and irreverent, bordering on juvenile, but there were not many people in her life who could make her laugh, and even fewer who bothered to try.

"Is it awful that your mother disliking it amuses me so?"

"Not at all. I'd prefer you not divulge that story to your aunt, but at least you may smile every time you see that buffet."

She closed her periodical. "I don't imagine I'll see it often."

He shrugged and set his newspaper aside. "You may. When my mother moves into the cottage in a few weeks, Daisy will be going with her."

"Oh. That... is rather disheartening. I rather like us all being neighbors on the third floor."

Then a more disheartening thought occurred.

"Will you be moving to the cottage as well?"

"Not at first," he answered.

Her relief was notable—which was probably something she should reflect upon later.

"Sometime this summer, perhaps?" she asked, wondering if her interest in where he slept boarded on inappropriate. *Also, something to reflect upon later.*

"Perhaps. I suppose it would be nice to see if moving to the cottage puts an end to Isabella's sundries showing up in my pockets, but I don't relish all those hours with just my mother and Daisy for company. Chase and Jo are determined to stay at the hotel for the foreseeable future."

"What about after the baby is born?"

"I suppose they'll decide that when the time comes. Jo and my mother are not overly fond of each other. Although you probably already knew that."

"I had my suspicions."

"Next summer though, your aunt will be in her cottage, and we'll all be neighbors once more on the West Bluff."

"I don't know that I'll ever come here again," she said, more wistfully than she'd intended.

"Not to the Imperial Hotel?"

"Not to the island at all. Breezy invited us here this summer with the sole purpose of finding us husbands. A scheme I was not made aware of in advance, mind you, and one I do not endorse, in case that wasn't made abundantly clear yesterday."

"I did hear something to that effect," Alex replied casually, stretching his arms over his head. "I just wasn't sure if it was true or rather something Breezy spun from her own imagination."

She paused before saying, "It's true."

Trudy had lost count of how many times over the years she'd explained to relatives, friends, even patients, *why a nice gal such as herself* remained unmarried, but this was the first time it left her feeling hollow instead of righteous.

Meanwhile, Alex frowned. Not in a condescending manner but he appeared perplexed, as if he was mulling this over in his head. Perhaps she was about to get the *nice gal* question from him.

"So, you're saying you prefer scalpels over men?"

"You could say I prefer a sharp blade to a dull one, but yes," she replied.

He took her jest in stride. Probably because there was nothing dull about Alexander Bostwick and well he knew it.

"The truth is," Trudy continued, "I've worked incredibly hard to become a skilled physician. Practicing medicine is not just something I do to occupy my time. It's an intrinsic part of who I am, and to give it up would be to lose a major part of myself."

"Why would you have to give it up?"

"Because trying to be both a physician and a wife would mean I could not excel at either. And it's not in my nature to be mediocre at something. I am competitive. Not just with my brother or with the Dr. Prescott's of the world. I'm competitive with myself. I know if I cannot dedicate myself fully to something, then I'm left unsatisfied. Not to mention society's view on the matter. I'd be seen as a negligent wife and mother. Even if I could accept that for myself, no man would want a wife whose attention was so often focused elsewhere."

"I should think that would depend a great deal upon the man," Alex replied. "Look at my brother. He fully supports Jo's artistic endeavors."

"And that's commendable. However, they're able to spend time together because she's an artist and they share a workspace. My vocation has me seeing patients at all hours of the day, either at the clinic or their homes. It's grueling and time consuming and it's not something I could set aside just because my husband expects me to make sure dinner is on the table each evening."

He contemplated this for a moment, then said, "The choice is yours, of course. If you decide not to marry because it's your preference, then so be it. But given how progressive you are in the field of medicine, perhaps you could find a way to cast off those shackles of convention when it comes to being a wife as well. Who's to say you cannot create a marriage where your medical aspirations don't prevent you from also enjoying the benefits of matrimony?" He chuckled, almost as if to himself adding, "Although, I suppose if you are a truly modern woman, you might enjoy some of the especially pleasurable aspects matrimony... without the matrimony."

Was he... referring to what she thought he was referring to? She was fairly certain he was. Her bemusement must have shown in her expression.

"My apologies. Have I offended you?" he asked while not appearing to be the least bit sorry.

"Of course not," she replied too quickly, hoping to seem cosmopolitan rather than aghast. "I am well aware that some people engage in... sexual congress... outside the confines of a marriage."

He chuckled at her choice of words, then said, "But... do you?"

She did gasp at this. Now she was aghast. "I beg your pardon?"

Once again, he did not seem the least bit sorry. "Do you partake in such activities?"

She blinked at him, momentarily rendered speechless.

His smile grew. "My apologies, once again. We've spoken in such frank detail about my life, it's made me curious about yours."

"And that was the first question you thought to ask?" she managed to reply. "Not, what's your favorite color or ... do you enjoy canoeing?"

"Well, I think the answer to my first question might make many of my other questions irrelevant. I thought you'd appreciate my expediency but if it makes you uncomfortable, don't answer it." He crossed his arms and leaned back farther in his chair, making himself more comfortable—and her less comfortable. Then he asked, "What's your favorite color?"

"Blue," she said warily.

"Do you enjoy canoeing?"

"Not especially," she said cautiously.

"Would you like to partake in sexual congress with me?"

"Uh..."

His question hit her like an arrow to the chest, and the query seemed a trick, but his gaze locked with hers and held fast. All Trudy wanted was to look away, to calm the sudden raggedness of her heart's rhythm, but she was paralyzed by his blunt words, his sapphire blue eyes, his illogical magnetism—and by her own overwhelming desire to say yes.

Yes, she would like that very much.

So much.

But she couldn't.

Of course, she couldn't.

And anyway, how dare he ask her such a thing! At ten o'clock on a Tuesday morning on the front porch of the Imperial Hotel. How dare he!

And... why did he?

She finally broke free of his gaze and looked down at her medical journal, although now all the words were darting to and fro like protozoa under a microscope. And she just might be a little light-headed. Where was that elixir he'd offered her earlier?

"I've heard you say it's important to get your pulses racing at least once a day. For your health," he said, the good-natured sarcasm evident in his tone.

She nearly smiled. Not so much because she was amused but rather because she was, quite possibly, on the verge of hysteria. Breathing was a chore. Her palms were moist, her mouth dry. She was quite taken aback.

And yet... oddly captivated.

Nonetheless, she tried to muster her sternest face as she looked at him once more.

"I meant that one should strive to get their pulses racing with a brisk walk or a swim in cool water," she said. "Not..."

"Sexual congress?" he quipped, not modulating his voice in the least.

"Stop saying that," she rasped, but the amusement in her own voice betrayed her. "You are shameful. Shame on you. Why would you even ask me such a thing?"

He quirked his brow. "I should think that much is obvious from the question itself. Although, I suppose it was unfair of me to ask."

"You suppose?" *He supposed?*

"Yes, I should not have placed the onus on you to answer without first stating my opinion on the matter. Please note, I would very much like to engage in sexual congress with you. Without marriage."

She paused for the space of a much-needed breath.

"How suave you are," she said at last, mimicking his sarcasm.

"What did you have for breakfast this morning, sir? A bottle of whiskey? Because surely you must be drunk."

He laughed and shook his head. "No, not drunk. Just lowering my defenses as Miss Watson instructed me to do."

"Now you're taking advice from the spiritualists?"

"That and I recently had an earnest conversation with my brother which prompted me to reflect upon some things. I am attempting to view my world with a fresh perspective. And to...try new things."

"I see," she said with a nod, realizing she was one of those *new things*. "And was it your brother's advice to accost me on the front porch and, without any illusion of seduction, ask me if I'd like to fornicate with you?"

Once again, she was trying to sound stern and bold, and yet her mouth very much wanted to smile.

And...

Her mouth very much wanted to kiss him.

Oh, my. How she wanted to kiss him.

She'd wanted to kiss him for days and days. *Cursed biology.* She'd wanted to run her hands over his physique and to touch him in all sorts of inappropriate ways. And she'd wondered how it would feel to have him do the same to her. *(She'd wondered about this a great deal, in fact.)*

She had scant knowledge of such things, of course. Her experience was limited to few clumsy pecks with a neighbor boy behind a barn when she was seventeen, some uninspired fondling with a classmate during medical school, and an awkward, sloppy encounter with a distant cousin under the mistletoe one Christmas that neither of them wanted to remember. That was the extent of it, and yet even in her naïveté she knew that Alexander Bostwick would not be clumsy or uninspiring or sloppy with his kisses.

But... he might be all of those things with her heart.

What in the devil's name was he doing?

Alex had come looking for Trudy knowing how her aunt's words had cut her to the quick. He'd been with her yesterday on that picnic blanket. He'd heard her quiet gasp at the insult and watched her posture change as she'd slowly hunched her shoulders as if to make herself smaller. He had felt her humiliation, and so had every person at that picnic.

Except for Breezy, of course. That woman just went on about her day as if she'd done nothing amiss. Alex had nearly confronted her for her abuse but knew it would only embarrass Trudy further.

Not long after the incident, Trudy had gone down to the water to sit with Jo. He'd thought to give her a moment to get her bearings, but the next time he looked for her, she was gone. He hadn't seen her at dinner last evening, nor had she been in any of the places he thought he might find her.

He knew because he'd looked.

So, this morning, he'd begun the search again knowing he couldn't rest until he'd made certain she was all right. He'd finally found her here on the porch, prickly as a porcupine and set about to cheer her spirits with his commiseration and foolish antics.

But he had *absolutely*...

Unequivocally...

Indisputably...

Not... intended to proposition her for intimacies as if she were some common doxie from a disreputable saloon. It was ungentlemanly behavior in the extreme to have even asked if *that* was something she indulged in, much less requesting she indulge in it *with him!*

And yet...

Trudy did not seem to be nearly as offended as she ought to be. In fact, he might go so far as to say there was a bit of mischievous sparkle in her eyes, and those dimples she got when she was trying not to smile were as deep as he'd ever seen. And suddenly Alex realized just how badly he wanted her to say yes.

Please say yes...

After his conversation with Chase, not to mention the prodding by Daisy and Miss Watson, Alex had done some introspection, and while he wasn't yet ready to excuse his involvement in some of the unpleasant things that had happened, he was...tentatively...thinking it may be time to step out from behind the shadow of his guilt and back into the light of the living. Isabella might still be, somehow, tethering him to the past, but he was ready to turn his eyes toward the future. It was time.

And, he'd realized during his self-reflection, that none had been more instrumental in nudging him in that direction than Trudy. Everything about her inspired him to face whatever needed to be faced, and to do whatever needed to be done to move forward with his life with fearlessness and courage.

Even so, he hadn't admitted to himself until just this very moment how much he wanted her to be a part of his future. He craved more from her than friendship. He wanted more than conversation and innuendo. He wanted... her.

But he hadn't meant to be so... obvious.

What a cad!

At least she hadn't rejected him outright.

Not yet anyway.

What had she said, exactly?

...without any illusion of seduction...

Was it possible she might consider him if only he would woo her a bit?

No, that couldn't be right.

He was being far too optimistic.

Any moment now she'd launch from that chair, throw her cup of leftover tea in his face, and never speak to him again. It's what he deserved. But she remained in place, gazing at him expectantly to respond to her volley.

And so, he did, in the same spirit in which he'd started.

"This was not my brother's suggestion. The request is entirely of my own volition. And I did not say fornicate. That would have been impolite. As for seduction, I can do that."

At his response, the sparkle in her eyes dimmed. As if a new thought had just now occurred to her.

"You're teasing me, aren't you? You're making sport of my inexperience."

Her sudden vulnerability pulled at his heart like a bell rope. He hated that the world made her feel odd compared to others when it was she who was remarkable. And he hated knowing he'd once made her doubt her beauty. He'd like to kick his ten-year-old self right in the ass because Trudy Hart was an extraordinary woman. He was blessed to call her a friend, and to call her something more would be a miracle.

He leaned forward in his chair. Reaching out, he touched her hand under the cover of her journal because a boisterous family was walking past in one direction, and a cluster of nannies was strolling by in the other, but the simple contact was electric. Her fingers wrapped around his and it could have been an embrace for the way it flooded his senses.

"The only one I'm teasing here is myself, Trudy, by allowing myself to hope you might want the same thing."

She paused, and then said quietly, almost sadly, "To indulge in intimacy without affection?"

He squeezed her hand. "No, that's not what I meant at all. I said without marriage, not without affection. Surely you know how fond of you I am."

"No, I don't know that." At last, her irritation flared. "How would I know that?"

"If you don't, then I must do my best to show you."

twenty-two

"A secret admirer?" Coco exclaimed as she plucked the card from the pot before Trudy could reach it. "Who, pray tell, is your secret admirer?" Then she frowned, adding disdainfully, "And who sends an amaryllis in July? It isn't even blooming. Someone sent you a pot of dirt."

"Do not open that note, Coco. It's for me." Trudy tried to grab it, but Coco twisted, tucking the paper against her bodice.

"Is it that odd little man who asked you about his gouty toe? Or perhaps it's that tall fellow from the chess match. The bishop who kept asking you about germs." Coco's eyes lit up. "Oh, I know who it is. It's Arthur Dugan, who sat with us at dinner a few evenings ago. I thought he seemed rather smitten with Pearl Mahoney. Oh, dear. Perhaps he's sent this bleak little pot to the wrong room."

"Oh, for heaven's sake, Coco," Lucy scolded as she walked from the bedroom into the sitting area of their suite. "How is Trudy supposed to know who it's from if she hasn't read the note?"

"Well, then, let's read the note," Coco replied holding it aloft as if to open it.

"Coco Hart, if you don't hand that note over to me right this instant I will tell everyone at this hotel you have an infectious rash and some disease that's going to make all your hair fall out."

Coco paused. "You wouldn't dare."

"Try me," Trudy retorted, glaring at her sister. She'd once successfully stared down the chief of surgery, demanding she be allowed to sit in the operating theater during a hysterectomy. She could handle Coco.

At last, her sister relented, tossing the note at her. "Very well. It's not as if you get flowers that often. I suppose I should let you open the card."

Trudy caught it and breathed a sigh of relief. Surely the pot was from Alex, and keeping Coco ignorant of that fact was essential. Keeping it from Breezy was equally essential. In fact, no one, inside her family, nor outside of it, needed to know that Alexander Bostwick had made her a most indecent proposal on the front porch of the Imperial Hotel at ten o'clock on a Tuesday morning.

> *Dear Mother and Father,*
>
> *You sent us here for proposals.*
> *I have news,,, but it's not the news you're hoping for...*

"Well, are you going to open it?" Coco demanded.

There was really no avoiding it. Hopefully the note would be something vague and anonymous. With a quick glance at Lucy for moral support, Trudy gently slid her finger under the wax seal.

> *Dr. Hart,*
>
> *My pulse is alarmingly slow. How might I get it racing?*

Trudy bit back a smile.
"Well?" Coco demanded.
"It's a medical question," Trudy replied.

"Let me see that," Coco scoffed, grabbing the note. "It is a medical question. Who sends a nearly dead flower bulb with a note that says... Oh, my goodness. I think someone might be dying."

Trudy chuckled and plucked the note back. "No one is dying, you silly goose. I just now recalled that when Mr. Tippett was showing me around the greenhouse the other day he mentioned that the amaryllis was his favorite flower but that he gets so bored waiting for them to bloom his pulse nearly stops. I said I might know of a way to speed the process. This must be from him."

Coco frowned suspiciously, and Trudy held her breath.

"That seems very odd," Coco replied.

"Oh, you know how Mr. Tippett and Mr. Plank pay attention to every little detail," Lucy interjected. "This seems just like something he'd do."

"Hm," Coco said, turning toward the door, "It still seems odd but enjoy your dirt. I'm off to Daisy's room. Lorna is styling my hair for the Mystic Melee with all the spiritualists. You are going, aren't you? Everyone will be in attendance. I'm sure of it. Trudy, I've heard even the skeptics are welcome."

"I am going," Trudy replied. "In fact, I intend to have a few readings."

Coco halted in her tracks and turned back to face her sisters. "You are?"

"I am. Someone recently suggested to me it's important to try new things. So, that's what I intend to do."

A smile eased across Coco's face. "Pip, pip for you. It's about time you let yourself have some fun."

Coco spun back around and flounced from the room, and Trudy chuckled, relieved that her quick thinking and sublime acting skills had prevented an unpleasant interaction. Coco was none the wiser.

Lucy, however, was not so easily duped.

Trudy turned to find her other sister staring at her, arms crossed, with a dubious expression on her face.

"Mr. Tippett told me that flowers of every sort make him sneeze and itch something fierce, so I suspect a trip to the greenhouse would have caused him a great deal of discomfort," Lucy said.

"Did I say Mr. Tippett? I meant... John. The gardener."

"Land sakes, Trudy. You're worse at fibbing than Poppy. That amaryllis is from Alex, isn't it?"

Trudy shrugged while silently acknowledging her acting skills were not so sublime after all. "How should I know. The note is unsigned."

"Oh, why won't you just admit it? It's one thing to try to keep the others in the dark, but you should at least confide in me."

Trudy was in a quandary. She wanted to bring Lucy into her confidence, but what Alex had suggested was scandalous. More scandalous still was the fact that Trudy was considering it. How could she explain to her younger, impressionable sister that she was on the precipice of something so immense? Something most would consider sinful, although Trudy herself felt fairly certain that the Good Lord was occupied with much bigger issues and not terribly concerned with what people did in the dark. Adultery wasn't acceptable, of course, but neither she nor Alex had pledged vows to other people—*Isabella's ghost notwithstanding*.

It would be a relief to share at least some of this with Lucy.

"You mustn't tell anyone," Trudy said at last. "Alex has expressed a fondness for me, but he knows my opinion on marriage, and we haven't discussed our expectations. It's all very... new."

"Did you express a fondness for him in return?"

"Not in so many words."

"But you are fond of him, are you not? Honestly, you needn't even answer that. I know you are."

"What makes you think so?"

Lucy's expression suggested the question was ridiculous. "He makes you blush, and nothing makes you blush. He makes you laugh at things you never would have found humorous before.

Every time I see you two talking, you're in such deep conversation I wonder if you realize there is anyone else around." Lucy reached out and clasped Trudy's hands and gave them a little squeeze. "I'm happy for you. I know being a doctor is important and your dedication to taking care of others is a virtuous attribute, but it won't make you less worthy if you allow someone else to take care of you once in a while."

Trudy smiled at her sister and nearly laughed at the irony of her words.

Ah yes. Trudy's *dedication* was virtuous.

But was she?

∾

"I feel like Daniel walking into the lion's den," Alex murmured to Chase as they entered the ballroom. "But you really needn't humor me. I can do this on my own."

"Nonsense. Jo wanted to attend as well. See? There she is over there with Daisy and... her maid? Isn't that Daisy's lady's maid?"

Alex's breath hitched, and his annoyance flared. What was Daisy thinking to bring Lorna today?

"It was the logical thing to do," Daisy whispered to Alex sometime later. "If Lorna is being influenced by Isabella then surely one of these spiritualists will sense it. And I intend to stay by her side for every single minute of the day so I can hear what they say to her. I've done you a favor so stop scowling at me."

"I wish you would've consulted me first but... I do believe you're right," he said.

"I'm sorry. Might you repeat that?" She put a hand to her ear.

"You heard me, you pest. I see your logic and it's sound. Having Lorna among all these alleged psychics makes sense."

"Alleged?" Now it was Daisy's turn to scowl, but Alex was unfazed.

"I'm trying to keep a level head today and not assume anyone is telling me the truth," Alex replied. "I've had two readings thus far and both were ambiguous at best."

"What did they say?" Daisy's eyes sparkled with interest.

"That I'm on the threshold of something new and mustn't be ruled by old fears."

"That sounds accurate to me."

He scoffed. "It's likely accurate for half the people in this room."

"But that doesn't make it less accurate for you. And if you go into a reading determined to disbelieve, it makes your aura murky. Miss Watson told you so." His sister all but stomped her foot.

"I am being as open and as vulnerable as I dare to be, Daisy, but the fact remains that between the two clairvoyants I've seen today, and Miss Watson, none have suggested anything about a tethered spirit or in fact anything about Isabella haunting me at all."

And wasn't that a good thing? He didn't really want to find out he was being haunted by his wife, after all. If nothing useful was heard today, at least he could return to the other slightly less distressing hypothesis that he was being manipulated by some living person.

Better taunted than haunted, he supposed. And he brightened at the realization that if he wasn't truly being visited by Izzy's ghost, then there was nothing to hinder his pursuit of a certain lady doctor he'd set his sights upon. Since their conversation on the porch, he'd thought of little else.

"But you haven't yet seen Madame Moyen, have you?" Daisy asked, not relenting.

Alex shook his head. "Not yet. There's a queue of people waiting and I don't fancy standing in line. None of these others have lines."

He gestured to the ballroom which Hugo and Tippett had transformed into a makeshift country fairground complete with booths of vendors selling rustic baked goods, colorful tents where the mystics were weaving their magic, games of skill and chance, and even a small corral full of goats for children to pet. Alex would never have imagined he'd see barnyard animals inside the Imperial Hotel ballroom, but that was Hugo. The man was a *visionary,* or so he said.

"I'll stand in line for Madame Moyen with Lorna," Daisy said, "and when we get close, you can come and join us."

Alex looked back at his sister and wondered how to reply.

While her poor maid was surely innocent in all of this, Alex didn't want to be anywhere near her. He'd encountered her a few times when visiting his mother's suite, or in the hall near their rooms, and once he'd even walked past her in a servant's corridor near some storage rooms, and each time they crossed paths, she'd smiled shyly but politely. Nothing in her expression or demeanor seemed in any way untoward. There was absolutely nothing suspicious about her behavior but when he'd remarked upon that to Daisy a few days ago, she'd reminded him that if Lorna was indeed involved in anything nefarious, she was likely unaware of her participation. The very notion of that was unnerving.

"Where is Lorna now?" he asked.

"She is over there, talking to Lucy. I've vowed to keep my eye on her all day. I won't fail you."

"I know," he said with a sigh. "I'll join you in line in a bit. Right now, I'm looking for Trudy."

Daisy chuckled. "Of course you are."

twenty-three

Perched on the edge of a velvet chair, nerves taut, fists clenched in her lap to still their trembling, Trudy faced the renowned Madame Moyen—a surprisingly petite woman with a magnetic presence. With dark hair cascading loosely down her back and a widow's veil worn over her luminous face, the medium presented a theatrical yet compelling mystique as she revealed, in a slightly French accent, a litany of things about Trudy she should not have known.

Things she simply could not have known—without some source from beyond.

Lights from the ballroom shone though the red silk of the tent lending everything within the tiny space an otherworldly crimson hue as Trudy's trepidation grew. The protective layers of her certainty in science were being slowly stripped away even as the messages she was receiving convinced her to remain dedicated to it.

"My dear mademoiselle," Madame Moyen continued in her melodious lilting accent, "If you come to me with questions, you must be prepared to receive the answers. But do not worry. All will be well. You are a woman out of step with time, but do not alter your path because of this. It is the world that must catch up to you. Trust yourself and your skills. You'll be called upon to use them soon enough."

"I will?"

Madame Moyen nodded. "A woman nears her time, and she will need you."

Thoughts of Jo filled Trudy's mind, but she realized Madame Moyen watched her reactions like a maestro and tried to keep her face devoid of emotion. She merely dipped her head in understanding and realized she'd seen at least a dozen expectant mothers staying at the hotel. It was a safe assumption on the psychic's part. Although how the woman had known, almost instantaneously, that Trudy was a healer still had her senses reeling.

Off to the side of the tent was a table filled with an eclectic array of curiosities fit for a spiritualist's trade, a cloudy crystal ball, tarot cards tattered from years of use, a few feathers and rocks, a brass pendulum, and a bundle of lavender. Madame Moyen plucked a strand from the bundle and rubbed it between her hands letting its scent fill the space.

"Others will need you, too, so do not let your own doubts discourage you. And do not be led astray by the whims of others. Make up your own mind about everything. Do you understand this?"

Trudy nodded hesitantly, wondering if it was the whims of Alexander Bostwick the psychic was referring to. But was he truly attempting to lead her astray, or rather guide her to a place she was eager to go? Definitely the latter. Whatever might occur between them, Trudy would be equally responsible. She was a progressive woman, after all, and she made her own decisions.

"And now, will you ask me about love?" Madame Moyen said with a languid smile.

"Love?" Trudy replied, startled that the mystic had mentioned the word at the exact same moment Trudy's thoughts had turned to Alex.

"Yes, you are as yet unmarried, and I sense it is on your mind."

Perhaps it was a coincidence. A fortuitous guess or the simple assumption that every single woman must long for a husband.

"Love is not on my mind."

Madame Moyen tilted her head, her smile enigmatic. "Ah, so you say, but I will tell you anyway, it is on the horizon. Just remember, some love rolls in like thunder, sometimes it is a gentle rain encouraging the bud of friendship to bloom into something more, and occasionally, it lies dormant for a bit before blossoming... like an amaryllis."

～

Alex felt like a child standing in line for a carnival game, but like the scavenger hunt, he was surround by sophisticated adult men who on any other day would have been commanding a boardroom. Potter Palmer was, at this moment, buying a meat pie from a vendor although not so much a vender as it was Harlan Callaghan dressed like a farmer in overalls and a large straw hat. Philip Armour, looking somewhat dazed and amazed, was leaving the tent of a clairvoyant named Lenora Piper. And Senator Gould was trying his luck at a ring toss. Like most politicians, he frequently missed the mark.

"You should go ahead of us," Daisy prompted when they'd reached the front of the queue to Madame Moyen's tent. "We don't mind, do we, Lorna?"

Lorna shook her head and smiled easily. "I don't mind. It's just nice to be out. I haven't seen much of the hotel. Oh, but please do tell your mother how much I appreciate her allowing me to come. It was so gracious of her."

Alex and Daisy exchanged smiles. He'd never heard anyone refer to Constance as gracious before and judging from his sister's wide smile, neither had she.

A moment later, the red silk curtain of Madame Moyen's tent opened, and a turbaned assistant guided Alex to a velvet seat. His heart was already thrumming inside his chest as if he'd run here from afar, and every muscle in his body was tense with unease, but he'd sat through four other readings today and none had alarmed him, nor satisfied him, and it was likely this Moyen woman would be no different, in spite of her reputation.

As he sat down, he took note of the woman before him. She wore mourning garb, and he wondered what she was hiding under that veil, although from the bit he could see of her face, she appeared pretty—in an eerie sort of way. Truthfully, he'd expected someone more flamboyant. And bigger. The woman was very tiny.

He knew that Trudy had seen her earlier and wondered about the exchange, but the two of them had agreed not to converse at this event so no spiritualists might see them together. They'd also agreed that while Trudy would ask about a spirit's ability to move objects, he would not, the purpose being to distance himself from Isabella's supposed antics as much as possible.

"Good afternoon," Madame Moyen said quietly. He heard traces of an accent. French, perhaps.

"Good afternoon," he said pleasantly, although his voice sounded strained, even to his own ears.

She instantly pressed back against her chair as he spoke, her posture stiffening. She rose up immediately and walked to a wooden chest not far from the table where they sat. Opening it, she took out a bundle of herbs and handed them to her assistant, whispering into his ear.

The assistant cast a wary glance at Alex, then set about lighting the tip of the herb bundle and gently waving it around the edges of the tent.

"Forgive me, sir," Madame Moyen said calmly as she sat back down. "What brings you here?"

"My destiny, I suppose."

"Not your past?" she asked cautiously.

"I beg your pardon?"

"Your past is draped around you like a shroud. Perhaps we should talk about that."

"Very well," he replied, a trickle of fear running down his spine. "What about my past do you think I should know?"

"You already know." Her voice deepened as she curled forward in her chair, causing him to lean back abruptly in his. Her response was most unnerving.

"Tell me anyway," he replied, uncertain if he believed her, and yet more certain that he did. His heart seemed to skip a beat and then race to catch up.

"You are troubled by an angry spirit. Someone once very close to you. Recently departed, although still too close."

Her words were like a physical blow and his breath went shallow in his chest. He suddenly longed for the vague ambiguities delivered with a comforting smile from the other clairvoyants.

"I am troubled," he admitted carefully. "What can I do about it?"

"Give me your hands."

He reluctantly reached across the table, and she flipped them over. She traced a single finger against one palm and then the next, saying nothing for what seemed an eternity. Meanwhile the assistant waved the smoking bundle of herbs all around them.

"This woman was... this is confusing," Madame Moyen finally muttered looking up at him.

"What's confusing?"

"She was... not a lover, and yet..."

He wished he could see her expression more clearly through the veil, not that it would change anything.

"Was this woman your wife?" she asked, her accent growing stronger.

Alex felt his jaw clench involuntarily and would have pulled his hands back except she grasped them tightly now.

"Yes," he said, his voice strangled.

"You wanted to be rid of her?"

"No."

Madame Moyen tilted her head and let go of his hands. He

pulled them back to his sides as she replied, "The spirits have no capacity for untruths. She believes you wanted to be rid of her."

He'd wanted to be rid of her *as his wife*, but not rid of her as in *rid of her*. He'd never wanted any harm to come to Isabella. He'd only wanted his freedom from the misery of their marriage.

"We had a misunderstanding right before she died," he replied.

"I see."

Madame Moyen reached over to a table beside them and picked up a small, purple velvet pouch. She shook it a few times, then offered it to him.

"Choose four and lay them on the table," she said.

Alex didn't relish the idea of reaching into a bag without knowing what was inside, but it seemed he had little choice. He did as instructed and placed four smooth stones with simple markings on the table between them.

Madame Moyen leaned over, humming as she examined his choices.

"Eihwaz, pertho, hagalaz, and algiz. You're fortunate you chose this one," she said, pushing one in his direction. "Algiz. This will shield you from negative spirits. Keep it. Put it in your pocket."

He accepted it gingerly as she shook her head at the others with a tsk, tsk, tsk.

"You are most certainly at risk from her energy. She is turbulent and chaotic. You will need a spiritual defense to protect you."

She looked up at him again. "Was she stubborn in life?"

"Very." He might have chuckled at the question if this whole encounter wasn't currently flooding him with dread.

"She will not go away without an apology."

"An... apology? You mean all I need to do is tell her I'm sorry?" Could it be so simple? Of course not.

Madame Moyen shook her head. "No, she's trapped in the void and cannot hear you. Once a spirit has moved on we can speak to them easily, but this woman is a tempest, and she's trapped."

"Then what am I to do?"

"We may attempt to pull her back to our side with a séance. Once she has your apology, with some good fortune, she'll move on. I can help you, but time is of the essence."

"Why?"

"The longer she remains in turmoil, the more difficult it may be to reach her. She'll become angrier, perhaps dangerous. She'll continue to trouble you until she's released."

"Released... by a séance?"

Madame Moyen nodded.

Her words spun in his mind like a cyclone, the notion of Isabella taunting him until the end of his days was more than he could fathom. And she didn't deserve to be trapped—wherever she was. He wanted Izzy to be free to move on just as much as he wanted that for himself.

And then there was Trudy. Beautiful, brilliant Trudy.

How could he hope to include her in his life in any way with an ever-angrier spirit tormenting him? He couldn't, and so, as outlandish as it was, it seemed there was only one solution.

"Then we must have a séance," he said.

∼

Alex had little recollection of leaving Madame Moyen's tent at the Mystic Melee. Nor did he recall walking back to his room afterward. He had a vague awareness of saying something to his sister and Lorna, and of seeing Trudy's face across the crowded ballroom, but now he was standing on the threshold of his room where he'd come seeking solace.

Only there was none to be found. Strewn haphazardly across the floor, on the bed, the desk, everywhere, were scattered gardenias. Not fresh, whole blossoms, but rather gardenias with their petals and stems torn asunder, ravaged by a vengeful force, shredded by wrath. Their cloying scent hung in the air like a foul stench.

He stepped inside, half expecting to see Isabella's ethereal form laughing at his dismay, but it was empty. At least, from what he could see it was empty. How was he to know if she lurked nearby, invisible and irate?

A gentle rap on the door behind him clanged like a warning bell and he whirled around in agitation.

But it was Trudy.

Thank heavens, it was Trudy, her hazel eyes full of concern for him alone then widening in surprise as she surveyed the chaos of his room.

She looked back at him, alarmed. "Are you all right?"

He hesitated, uncertain how to answer. Was he all right? Was he responsible for this mayhem? Was he doomed? In danger?

Was she?

As Trudy stepped closer, he raised a hand. She was already too enmeshed in this chaos. He could not, would not put her at greater risk.

"If this is what's to come, you should stay far away from me," he said, his voice sounding strange to his own ears.

"Has anything like this ever happened before?" she asked.

"No, but Madame Moyen says things may get... more turbulent until I rid myself of Isabella."

"Rid yourself?"

With a single nod, he answered. "With a séance. It's madness, I know, but so is this." He gestured to the disarray all around them, not quite believing his own eyes.

In spite of his warning, Trudy closed the distance between them, pressing gentle hands against his chest and gazing at him with a mix of concern and compassion.

"What can I do?" she whispered.

Alex stood motionless, his arms at his sides, torn between his need to pull her close, to take comfort in her tranquil strength, and his fear of putting her in harm's way. If he embraced her now, he might never be able to let her go, but this room was poisoned by gardenias and bad memories. And this was not what she'd agreed to all those weeks ago when she'd offered to help him solve a simple riddle. This was so much more than that.

His breath felt jagged in his lungs as he spoke.

"You should go. I couldn't bear it if you got hurt."

"It's just flowers," she murmured.

"You should still go. Let me clean up this mess and then I'll come find you."

She moved closer instead, molding her body against his and sliding her hands up to lightly rest her palms against his cheeks. She ran one thumb across his lips and whispered, "Or I could do this."

And then she kissed him.

Every nerve and muscle in his body felt the sensation of her mouth on his. It was exactly what he wanted, and what he needed. Her tender caress. Her concern. Her kiss.

A sense of calm washed over him, as if he'd just arrived home after an arduous journey and had found utter contentment, but that peace was quickly washed away, doused by a flood of pure desire. He wound his arms around her, pulling her tightly against him, as if he could not bear the thought of any space between them.

Every ounce of his being sank into that kiss and the thrill of her hands winding around to weave her fingers through his hair at the nape of his neck. The moment was sublime as somehow Trudy Hart turned the worst day of his life into the best day.

He wanted to go on like this for all eternity, but she pulled back after a moment, chuckling softly and looking at him as if surprised by her own boldness. Her eyes were luminous as she whispered, "We were all wondering if your hair is soft and it is." And then she smiled at the admission.

He smiled back, wishing he could pull the pins from hers. The thought of it cascading over a pillow nearly stole his breath away.

"We?" he asked, his voice husky.

"My sisters and I," she admitted sheepishly, and he laughed at her expression as he wondered how a woman so brave and self-assured could also be so adorable. It was a mystery he wanted to explore for days and days, but he sobered as the reality of the moment returned him to his senses.

"I do fear for your safety, Trudy," he said, grasping her gently by the shoulders and leaning his forehead against hers. "As much as I would love continue on this path, I think we have immediate matters that are more pressing."

"I know. Tell me what you need."

So many things. He needed so many things. He needed her. He needed answers. He needed Isabella out of his life for good.

But as he looked around his room at the shredded flowers he said, "I need a broom."

twenty-four

"Mother? Father?"

Trudy's voice rang out with joy as she walked into Breezy's suite and discovered her parents sitting, just as casually as you please, on the settee. Her heart leapt with emotion and she all but squeaked with excitement, her normally pragmatic manner discarded as she dashed across the room to fling herself against them.

"Good heavens, girl," her father said with laughter, standing up just in time for her to nearly knock him over. They managed to remain upright, and she reveled in his hug. "I missed you, too," he said.

She moved from his embrace into her mother's, forgetting for the moment her annoyance about the husband hunting. They could discuss that later. For now, the moment was all about a long-awaited reunion. Trudy breathed in deeply, absorbing the comforting and familiar scent of her mother's rose perfume.

"My goodness," Trudy said, dabbing an unexpected tear from her eye as she sat down between her parents. "I had no idea you were arriving today. I'm so happy you're here. I have so much to tell you."

But before she could share any of it, Jo and Daisy burst in, followed seconds later by Asher and Poppy, and soon the room was filled with voices as each of Trudy's siblings vied for their parents' attention.

"One at a time. One at a time," Samuel admonished tenderly. "You're like a flock of geese and I cannot hear for all the honking!"

Although Trudy longed to have her parents all to herself, she rose from the couch, letting her siblings take their turns. Basking in the sweet, warm glow of being together once again, she realized just how deeply she'd missed them both.

Her days were normally spent with her father at the clinic, and in the evenings, she'd be with her mother, sharing her thoughts and worries. But for the past several weeks, Trudy had been an island onto herself, with no one to confide in. She'd done her best to ensure her brother and sisters were managing well and staying out of trouble while at the hotel, but now she could— with immense gratitude—hand the reins back to her parents and focus on her own trials and tribulations.

Namely... Alexander Bostwick... whom she'd just boldly kissed without an ounce of hesitation.

She couldn't help it. He'd looked so despondent and forlorn, standing there in a hotel room full of shredded gardenias. She'd only meant to comfort him, but the moment her lips touched his, she'd forgotten everything else. Ghosts and psychics and pranks and riddles all flew from her mind as she'd melted into his strong embrace. His kiss left her breathless and desperately wanting more. She'd very nearly started pulling at his buttons, but some quiet voice of reason stopped her. She wished it hadn't ...

And then she'd said something silly about his hair, and wished she hadn't...

But perhaps it was for the best. They'd been surrounded by destruction and while Trudy still wanted to believe there were no spectral shenanigans at play, her encounters with the mystics this morning, especially Madame Moyen had left her with more questions than answers. Her skepticism had given way to a cautious willingness to consider the possibility of something supernatural involved in all of this. Especially since Lorna had been with Daisy all day and could not have put those gardenias in his room. So, if not Lorna, then who ... or what ...

But for now, Trudy would set aside all thoughts of Alex and ghosts and rejoice in her parents' arrival, instead.

"How is Calvin," Trudy finally asked, when the din of her siblings' excitement had quieted.

Poppy was now sitting on their father's lap (*with Chester in hers*), Coco was next to their mother, resting her head on Ada's shoulder, and Trudy's brother and Lucy were in the other settee while, for once, Asher was behaving himself. *She wondered how long that would last.*

"Calvin is fine," her father said quickly. "Just fine. He sends his love."

Trudy thought she saw a flicker of something in her mother's eyes, but it was gone as quickly as it came.

"Yes, Cal sends his love," Ada repeated. "And he wishes he could have come with us to see you all, but he looks forward to coming home for a visit as soon as he is able."

~

"My, oh, my! Mr. Plank, you have surpassed yourself yet again," Lucy's voice held a note of admiration as she surveyed the hotel's front lawn from the slope above.

"I will pass along your sentiments to Mr. Tippett," Mr. Plank replied. "He's the steward of tonight's Celestial Soiree. And we have Mrs. Bostwick to thank for the fine artwork, of course. She painted the constellations on canvases for those of us with less knowledge of the night sky." He gestured toward the edge of the lawn where five polished brass telescopes stood with Jo's handiwork resting on easels in between.

"Those will come in handy," Trudy agreed. She might know every bone inside the human body, but her knowledge of astronomy was as lacking as her ability to paint a fruit bowl.

"Your Imperial Hotel is quite the spectacle, Mr. Plank," Trudy's father commented as his gaze swept over the unfolding festivities. "My wife and I are captivated."

Trudy watched as her father exchanged a tender smile with her mother, a poignant reminder of their enduring love, and yet, something sad still lingered in her mother's eyes, and Trudy wondered at its meaning.

"It is a beautiful setting, indeed," Ada agreed. "Especially after dark. How long did it take to string up all those lanterns?"

"A bit," Hugo said with a broad smile. "Fortunately for me, the Callaghan brothers lost a bet and had to set this all up free of charge."

As he chuckled, Trudy stole a glance at Lucy who was tamping down a smile at the mention of Harlan's name. Trudy wondered how long it would be before their mother pulled that secret from Lucy. Then she shuddered inwardly, wondering how long she could face their intuitive mother herself before Alex became the focal point of a conversation. She hoped to put that off as long as possible and turned her focus to the soiree just getting underway.

Across the lawn, pierced metal lanterns hung from ropes strung between posts casting glowing mosaics onto a modestly sized dance floor. Off to the side of that was a small stage where an ensemble of musicians was currently tuning their instrument, as well as a collection of tables for guests wanting to sit down to enjoy a beverage or hors d'oeuvres. As usual, Mr. Plank and Mr. Tippett had thought of everything.

"Honestly, Mr. Plank," Coco chimed in, "If I didn't know better I'd think you'd arranged to have extra stars hung in the sky."

"No extra stars, Miss Hart," he replied good-naturedly. "But I did pray for clear weather, and it seems the Almighty favored us with this perfect evening."

"I believe He has," Lucy agreed, her excitement palpable. "Is there anything in particular we should know about the telescopes?"

"Only that they are there for your enjoyment."

With a quick questioning glance towards Samuel and Ada, and an encouraging nod from her father, Lucy dashed down the hill alongside Coco and Asher.

"Well done, sir," Trudy complimented Mr. Plank as she watched her siblings disappear into the crowd.

"You are most welcome, Dr. Hart. I hope your evening shines as brightly as the stars. And may I say to you, Dr. and Mrs. Hart, your daughter is both a delight and a blessing. I owe her an immense debt of gratitude since she willingly stepped in to be of service while the hotel seeks a new physician. I can only hope to find a replacement as capable as she is."

"Is that so, Mr. Plank?" Her father smiled. "I'm pleased to hear that and not at all surprised."

Trudy warmed at both Mr. Plank's compliment and her father's apparent pride. Neither was something she'd encountered very often, and both felt very pleasant.

As the evening progressed, and Trudy introduced her parents to other guests, she received even more compliments for her skillful care. She hadn't realized until then just how many people she'd assisted and having them share their gratitude in front of her parents filled her with professional gratification.

But all the while, she wondered when Alex would arrive. Since kissing him yesterday, she'd thought of almost nothing else. Even her parents' surprise arrival had not dimmed her memory of that brief moment in his arms, nor had it cooled her ardor. But she'd been so busy with her family, she hadn't seen him. In fact, none of the Bostwicks had been at dinner last evening and that worried her.

But at last, they arrived with a stoic, unapproachable Constance Bostwick leading the charge, her arm looped through Alex's. Daisy, Ellis, and Finn were behind them, with Chase and Jo trailing along at a much slower pace. All seemed well and she realized then just how worried she'd been about his safety given the state of his room yesterday.

She stood next to her parents, watching him as his gaze searched the crowd, and when he found her, his expression weakened her knees. He'd missed her, too, and she realized this was about to become the longest night of her life. Because all she wanted to do was kiss him again, and more, but they were surrounded by her parents and his mother, and by all their eagle-eyed siblings, not to mention every guest of the hotel. How was she to maintain her composure and be discreet when he was so damn handsome?

"There you are," Daisy said excitedly, bounding up to them with no regard for propriety. "You must be Dr. and Mrs. Hart. I've heard ever so much about you."

As greetings were exchanged and Constance sized up her parents, Trudy tried not to stare at Alex, but his proximity charged the atmosphere all around her. As their eyes met, a moment of understanding passed between them, along with an undercurrent of longing.

"It's a pleasure to meet you, sir," Alex said as he shook hands with Trudy's father. "I look forward to getting better acquainted."

Alex's mother looked at him askance, as if wondering why he'd want to form a friendship with a country doctor from Springfield, but Alex's demeanor remained as smooth as silk. As always. And when the musicians began to play, it took only a moment before he turned to Trudy.

"I do believe you owe me a dance, Dr. Hart," he said, his voice as velvety as nighttime sky as he held out his hand.

Trudy hesitated, taking note of her parents' surprise and Daisy's eager grin. And his mother's frown. The attention made her want to say no, but she could hardly turn him down without claiming a sprained ankle or a previous appointment—neither of which she had.

Reluctantly she accepted his hand, and as their eyes locked, a wave of reassurance flowed through her. She was with Alex and all would be well. But fast on its heels was a tremor of nervous excitement. To be in his arms again, even just for a dance was sure to set her ablaze.

Damn you, biology!

With a tentative smile, she followed him onto the makeshift dance floor where a few other couples were—thankfully—already in place. He pulled her toward him, resting a hand on her waist as she lifted hers to his shoulder. Their other hands were clasped, and he squeezed her fingers.

"Breathe, Trudy," Alex murmured, a hint of amusement in his voice. "It's just me."

"That's precisely the problem," she quipped, making him chuckle. "Suddenly you make me nervous."

"I'm the one who should be nervous," he whispered as the music started and they began to sway to the rhythm of a waltz.

"Why would you be nervous?" she asked.

"I've just encountered your father for the first time. What if he doesn't approve of me?"

"My father approves of everyone," she responded, before she had the chance to ponder his underlying implication. "Why are you concerned that he won't?"

His smile turned enigmatic. "No reason. Stop stepping on my toes."

"I am not stepping on your toes. You are putting your feet under mine," she responded with feigned annoyance.

He chuckled and pulled her closer than propriety allowed. As they moved in tandem, each graceful movement drawing them closer, Trudy lost her sense of time staring into his eyes and the rest of the world seemed to fade away.

She hadn't danced in far too long. And she had never danced with anyone as enticing as Alexander Bostwick. She was diving into depths far above her head. It wasn't sensible. It wasn't safe. But, oh, the water was fine.

When the last notes of Strauss' *Voices of Spring* faded into silence, she felt bereft. She wanted more. Then Alex leaned forward, his warm breath tickling her ear as he murmured, "You're not too tall, you know."

"I'm not?" she replied absently as they walked toward the grass.

"No," he answered softly, his voice full of mischief. "You're perfect. I could kiss you right now without straining my neck in the slightest."

She laughed at his playfulness, thankful she was not the only one longing for kisses. "In front of all these people? I think not."

"Then perhaps we should seek out somewhere more secluded."

She glanced his way, knowing as he said it, it wasn't a question. It was a challenge. A challenge that hung in the air between them, like an unspoken promise. But she stepped back from him with a smile full of regret. "The evening has only just begun, sir, and I'm here with my parents," she replied. "However, I think we might be able to slip away at some point."

His eyes lit up. "You do?"

"Perhaps," she replied, her voice laced with amusement. "I suppose you'll have to wait and see."

The next hour was a dance of its own as they navigated their way around each other—chatting with other guests, taking turns at the telescopes, their tentative fingers brushing against each other in passing. Trudy spent time with her parents, and siblings, and even complimented Aunt Breezy on her new gown. But throughout it all, Alex was never far from her thoughts. Then again, when was he?

Is this how it felt to be infatuated?

It was annoying.

But wonderful.

But also... annoying.

"Lucy," she whispered to her sister some time later, "Can you wait a while and then tell Mother and Father I went to bed with a mild headache?"

Lucy regarded her carefully, and then a smile spread across her face as she looked past her sister. "Of course. I do hope you find a cure for what ails you."

Trudy turned to see what Lucy had seen, and there, of course, was Alex. His gentleman's smile disguising some very ungentlemanly intentions. Trudy turned back to her sister.

"It's just a headache. I'll see you at breakfast," Trudy said, but her own smile betrayed her.

"Of course it is. I hope I have a headache like that one day."

There was no defending herself without telling a lie, and so she shrugged a self-satisfied shrug. She was progressive modern woman after all. She could do what she wanted. Then she turned again, caught Alex's eye, and walked away from the party, slipping around the corner of the greenhouse.

He was beside her in mere seconds, his rapid arrival making her laugh. Reaching out, he caught her by the waist and pulled her close. His other hand caressed her neck, his thumb tracing along her jaw as he leaned in close.

"I had no idea you were such a delightful tease, Dr. Hart. I've been chasing you all evening and yet you keep evading me."

His gaze was dark, his expression hidden in shadows created by the moonlight, but she knew what he wanted—because she wanted it too.

She wrapped her arms around his shoulders. "I am caught," she whispered.

"I'm the one who is caught," he whispered against her cheek. "You have me spellbound."

"Perhaps there's magic in the moonlight," she replied on a sigh. "For I am equally transfixed."

"No," he chuckled, nuzzling her neck. "The magic comes from you. I've felt it from the start. I tried to deny it, but this pull between us is stronger than I am. I need you, Trudy."

Her limbs went weak at his words, and the earnest way he said them, and she could not wait another moment. She tugged at his hair, and he lifted his face, gazing down at her with wonder.

"Kiss me," she murmured, her entreaty instantly silenced by

his compliance. As his lips captured her own, she melted into his embrace, reveling in the heat of his kiss. The textures and the taste of him, the scent of his cologne and his skin, and the sounds of their breath merging together.

He was careful with her but not gentle and she could not get enough of him. What little restraint she'd brought with her around the back of greenhouse was already gone as she gave way to the heady sensations he stirred within her.

This was more than infatuation. More than biology. More than lust. Everything about him intrigued her. Captivated her. Compelled her to be bold. His kiss was too much to bear and yet not enough. She wanted more. She wanted everything. She wanted all of him.

She pulled back a moment later, her breathing shallow.

"You know," she said quietly. "My parents have taken over my suite on the third floor, but Mr. Plank was kind enough to provide me with a smaller room on the first floor. All to myself."

Alex's paused, his eyes dark and mysterious. "Is that so?" he murmured, his hands now resting on her waist.

"Mmhmm," Trudy nodded, her fingers toying with the lapels of his jacket. "It is… private. We could… go there, if you'd like."

His paused was long and weighty.

"Trudy, I would like that more than anything in this world, but are you certain? What I said to you on the porch was too forward, and although I meant every word of it, I don't want you to think it's what I expect from you. We can take this slow. We can be… proper. The last thing I'd ever want to do is sully your reputation or make you think I don't hold your virtue in the highest regard."

"Are you finished?" she asked, her voice laced with sassy impatience. "Because I make my own decisions, Mr. Bostwick. I do what I want, and I was hoping we might… engage in some sexual congress."

His own laughter seemed to catch him off guard.

"By God, Trudy Hart. You are the most unusual, remarkable, wonderful woman I think I've ever met. Lead the way."

"I suspect we should traverse the lawn independently, but I'll meet you near Jo's studio. My room is near there. Don't dawdle." She kissed him quickly, then walked back around the greenhouse heading straight for the lobby, her heart pounding, her blood racing, and her soul full of joy.

Moments later, they stood just inside her room, and Trudy knew her life was on the verge of change. She and Alex were two souls converging, and whatever tomorrow might bring, tonight was theirs to cherish.

She crossed to the nightstand and lit the lamp. She wanted to see him, as well as touch and explore him. His face was enigmatic as he shrugged out of his jacket and tossed it on the nearby chair. Then his hand went to his tie, and Trudy crossed back over to him and started working the buttons on his shirt with unsteady fingers, her determination giving way to nervous energy.

He traced his fingertips over her bare shoulders, following his touch with tiny butterfly kisses that sent ripples of pleasure through her body.

"Have I mentioned how beautiful you are in this dress," he murmured huskily.

"A number of times," she whispered tilting her head to the left so he might continue those tender ministrations to that sensitive spot just beneath her ear while she fussed with his shirt.

"Have I mentioned yet how beautiful you are *out* of that dress?" he teased.

Her soft laughter sounded sensual even to her. It was interesting to realize she could still surprise herself, and yet this whole night had been full of revelations. And it had only just begun.

"You're making assumptions, Mr. Bostwick. You don't know what I look like out of this dress."

"Mm," he said, pressing a kiss to the upper curve of her breast. "I am entirely confident that you are beautiful out of this dress, but I know you do love your evidence so, therefore, we must remove this lovely garment so I may prove to you that you are, indeed, even more beautiful without it."

His words aroused her as much as his touch, and she kissed him, trying to put all of her feelings into the exchange, but it wasn't enough. A frantic sort of energy took hold as they divested one another of their layers, *so many layers,* stopping for a kiss every heated moment, until, at last, all of their garments were tossed about the room, a stocking here, a waistcoat there, and they were free from the constraints of clothing and pretense.

Now it was just them, with nowhere and nothing to hide, and Trudy realized Alex was right. She *was* beautiful without her dress. She'd never felt that way before, but she found assurance in the reverence of his gaze. But then he paused as a shadow of doubt crossed his features.

"Trudy," he whispered solemnly, staring at her as if trying to see into her soul. "You are perfection and too fine. I don't deserve you. I fear I haven't earned this privilege."

"No, you haven't," she answered with a throaty chuckle. "But I have."

And then she kissed him again, erasing all their doubts.

They were past the point of words now, but his touch and kiss spoke volumes. She marveled at each sensation, giving as she received, and savoring each whispered breath and heartfelt sigh. He pressed her down onto the bed and wove an invisible thread around them, linking them together irrevocably. Her heart beat in rhythm with his as he set her skin aflame and soothed it with more kisses. And when she thought she might die from the exquisite torment, he set her free and she soared.

twenty-five

"Oh, good heavens, Trudy," her mother said, a delicate hand covering her mouth as laughter overtook her. "Why would you ever take your Aunt Breezy's word for anything? You know her stories are full of falsehoods and obfuscations."

Trudy's brow furrowed. "Do you mean to say she made it up? You didn't send us here to find husbands?" Her posture straightened in annoyance—at herself. She should've known better. Her mother was right. Aunt Breezy considered accuracy tantamount to tedium and was forever embellishing. Trudy should have trusted that her mother would never betray her that way.

"No, of course I didn't." Her mother's gaze softened reassuringly, the smile still tugging at her lips.

"Then why did she think you did? Or did she just pluck the idea from thin air?" That was certainly possible.

Ada adjusted a modest ruffle on her skirt, her expression turning thoughtful. "I'm going to share something with you in confidence, dear, because I believe you should be aware. Your brother has been... struggling in Boston. Your father and I went to visit him to see if we could assist him in some way."

Trudy's heart filled with sympathy. "Struggling in what way?"

"We weren't entirely certain before our trip, but it seems the demands of working at Massachusetts General has left him feeling overwhelmed. I'm certain you understand that pressure better than anyone. I do think he's feeling better now. He's met a lovely girl, and I believe that's helped him think about life beyond the walls of the hospital."

"I had no idea," Trudy said sadly. "I wish I'd known. I would have sent him encouraging words."

Ada smiled as she patted Trudy's hand. "That's precisely why we couldn't tell you. We knew you'd want to help, too, but he would be embarrassed if he knew you were aware of his hardships. He wants you to believe he's infallible."

Trudy shook her head in mild disbelief. "No one is infallible. I would never judge him."

In fact, knowing he wasn't perfect might have made her more fond of him, and softened her need to complete.

"I know you wouldn't judge him," Ada agreed softly, "but try convincing a man his flaws are anything other than egregious. They don't realize it's their imperfections that are often the things we love about them the most."

Trudy understood that now in a way she might not have before. Alex was deeply concerned his past *scandals* and previous mistakes would impact the way she felt about him, and perhaps they did—they made her love him even more.

She startled herself with that sudden admission.

Did she love him?

Oh, dear.

Oh.

Dear.

She did. Of course, she did. She could ponder the idea, and look at all the evidence, and make lists of his attributes—and flaws—but she already knew the answer. It wasn't just biology or mere physical attraction that drew her to him. It was something so much more. Something intangible yet undeniable, so, although she could not quantify it with *facts,* in her heart of hearts, she knew. She did love him.

How terribly inconvenient.
And wonderful.
And yet... still inconvenient.

"But how did Calvin's struggles result in Breezy's invitation and her spinning of the truth?" Trudy asked, setting aside her silent and seismic revelation about Alex to inquire about her aunt.

Ada shook her head. "When your father and I realized we needed to visit Calvin without the rest of you, I didn't want to leave you in charge of the younger ones. It would've been too much of a burden and you would have felt you needed to keep working at the clinic if you'd stayed in Springfield. So, I asked Breezy to bring you all to Trillium Bay until Samuel and I could join you."

"And she arbitrarily decided that meant you wanted her to find us husbands?"

Ada chuckled with bewilderment. "She'd mentioned something in a letter saying she'd make the attempt. I didn't pay much attention to it, but I see she took my lack of dissent as an endorsement. She undoubtedly wants to find you all rich husbands so she can be smug and remind me of how I could have and should have given my daughters a better life by marrying money the way she did."

"Does she realize that if you hadn't married Father, you'd have completely different children?" Trudy inquired.

Ada patted her hand. "I don't think that's the part she cares about."

They laughed in unison and Trudy was struck once more by how very much she'd missed these conversations with her mother.

"Even so," Ada continued, "Breezy tells me that Coco and Lucy have captured the attention of many a suitor."

"That they have."

"And you? I couldn't help noticing a certain handsome gentleman who could not take his eyes off you last evening. Tell me about him." Ada's voice was full of warmth, but Trudy wasn't yet ready to share. Her feelings for Alex were too fresh and fragile.

"I don't know who you're referring to," Trudy said, even as the memory of his touch set her cheeks aflame.

"Then why are you blushing, Gertrude?" her mother teased, amusement twinkling in her eyes. "Can it be? Has someone captured my independent Trudy's attention?"

"You're imagining things, Mother. I've just been in the sun. I do believe Lucy may have a beau, though."

"Lucy can tell me about Lucy's beau. I want to hear about yours." Ada's words were gentle but insistent.

"I... I don't know what to say, exactly, Mother. It's very new and very... complicated."

"Love often is but I've never known you to shy away from a challenge."

"I don't want to give up being a doctor," Trudy replied, almost by habit.

"Then don't." Ada wrapped a maternal arm around Trudy's shoulders and leaned against her. "If this man is worthy of you, he'd never ask you to. I know you've always said that marriage and medicine don't mix if you're a woman, but perhaps that's a faulty assumption. Perhaps you need to reexamine your reasons and your goals."

Trudy nearly chuckled as her mother's wisdom resonated deep within her. Wasn't that the same advice Trudy had been giving herself but just didn't trust? Maybe she'd been on to something all along but refused to accept it. Maybe Alex was correct, as well. Perhaps a modern, progressive woman such as herself could defy society, cast off the shackles of propriety, and be both a doctor and a wife. *Was it possible?*

At the very least, it was worth gathering a little evidence.

"You know I'll support you no matter what you decide," Ada continued. "But if you've found someone who makes you blush like this, I think it's worth considering."

"Perhaps, but you should be aware that Aunt Breezy doesn't like him," Trudy said.

"I suspect that's something in his favor," her mother replied.

They shared a smile and as Trudy leaned into her mother's warm embrace, she felt safe from all of life's challenges. Eventually, she'd have to make some difficult choices about her future. She'd have to make decisions with no clear answers. But for now, she'd simply breathe in the familiar scent of her mother's perfume, listen to the soothing beat of her heart, and feel loved for exactly who she was.

∼

"Is there any day that is not some sort of special extravaganza?" Trudy's father asked as the Hart family walked down the hill and to the lawn.

"Nope," Asher responded, jogging backwards. "Ain't it great? Today is Mr. Plank's birthday so there is going to be a horse race later this afternoon and then fireworks this evening.

"It's excessive but you get used to it," Lucy replied. "In fact, that whole Celestial Soiree came about simply because I asked Mr. Plank if he had a telescope."

"That does seem excessive," Samuel agreed. "But it was a lovely party. I'm sorry you missed some of it, Trudy, darling. I trust you're feeling better today."

Lucy let out a chuff of laughter as Trudy replied, "I feel today, Father. Thank you."

"Anyone fancy a game of croquet?" Asher asked a moment later. "None of you will beat me but I dare you to try."

"Son, I accept your challenge," Samuel said. "Ladies, who is going to play with us and help me give this young man a lesson in humility?"

"I would be interested in that," Coco said.

"I'll join you," Lucy added.

"Me, too," Poppy added, skipping along merrily. "Chester loves croquet."

"I'd rather take a stroll around the grounds if it's all the same to you, dear," Ada said. "I've long since given up trying to teach humility to any of you."

"I'll walk with you, Mother," Trudy said.

As they meandered over the lawn, Ada remarked, "Oh, imagine that. There's that handsome gentleman I was referring to. What's his name again?"

"I'm sure I don't know who you mean, Mother," Trudy said but her heart raced, and her smile could not be contained as Alex and Chase approached.

"Good afternoon, Mrs. Hart. Dr. Hart," they said in unison causing laughter all around.

"Good afternoon, gentlemen," Trudy's mother replied. "How nice to see you both, but where's that lovely wife I recall one of you has?"

"That would be me," Chase said, raising his hand. "She's in our room, resting."

"Good for her. She should rest as much as she's able to before the baby comes. And what about you?" Ada turned her full attention to Alex and Trudy braced for what was sure to come next. "Do you have a wife somewhere?"

"Somewhere," he said slowly, causing a ripple of dark laughter between the three of them and leaving Trudy's mother bemused.

"He's teasing, Mother. He does that." Trudy said. "This Mr. Bostwick is... not married."

She'd explain that to her mother someday, but not today.

"We've actually come to ask a favor," Chase said to Trudy, blithely changing the subject.

"What favor is that?"

"We were considering going to the horse race this afternoon and spending a few hours in town with Hugo. He wants to discuss some business with us but I'm not comfortable leaving Jo without having someone on hand to assist her if she needs anything."

"Oh, of course. I'd be happy to visit with her," Trudy responded. "You don't mind, do you, Mother?"

"Not at all," she said, still looking curiously at Alex.

"Splendid," Chase replied. "Thank you. She just went up to rest so perhaps check on her in a few hours? She feels fine today. Just tired."

"Do the same rules apply as last time? Am I to pretend you didn't ask me to watch over her?" Trudy asked.

Chase shook his head and smiled. "No, she's on to me and knows full well what I'm up to."

"All right then. Carry on," she replied with a dismissive wave of her hand.

"Might I speak with you for a moment before we go?" Alex asked, causing her heart to offer up an extra beat.

He seemed more handsome than ever now that they'd... gotten more thoroughly acquainted. She nodded, and they stepped to the side while Chase chatted idly with her mother—and her mother stared at them surreptitiously.

"I don't know what made me say that about having a wife somewhere," Alex whispered, clearly chagrined, but Trudy smiled.

"My mother has a fine sense of humor. She would have laughed if she'd understood the joke."

"Are you certain? Should I apologize?"

"No," Trudy said laughing herself. "Think nothing of it."

His sigh was audible. "Very well. There is something else I wanted to discuss, though. Two things, actually."

"Yes?" Her unease rose at his hesitation.

"First, I very much wish I could kiss you right now. Last night was... perfection."

"Yes, it was." She was glad to know he thought so, too.

"On a second, on a far less pleasant note, I spoke with Madame Moyen this morning. She says she can lead a séance next week." Then he shook his head as if he could not believe it himself.

"That's good. I suppose."

"Have I lost my senses?" He gazed at her earnestly.

"No more so than the rest of us. Madame Moyen said things to me I cannot explain and if this séance works, then it will have been worth it. If it doesn't work…"

"We try something else," he finished for her.

"Exactly."

"Are you sure you don't want to step away from all of this, Trudy? I never dreamed it would become so macabre."

If her mother hadn't been observing them, she would have reached out a hand to touch him. "I'll be there, Alex. Whatever you need."

"I don't know how to thank you for this. But I should tell you, Madame Moyen says Lorna must participate as well."

"Lorna?"

He nodded. "They met at the Mystic Melee and Moyen says there's some connection between Lorna and Izzy. Perhaps all of Daisy's theories are correct after all."

"Then let's hope this séance provides some answers."

"Let's hope. In the meantime, I'll be reminiscing about last night. Trudy, I've never felt so… I really wish I could kiss you right now." He glanced at her mouth so intently she could almost feel it.

"I wish you could, too," she whispered. "But you cannot."

"Hm."

They stood silent for a moment while their eyes said all that could not be said. Then Alex chuckled. "I'm quite enamored of you, Dr. Hart. Have I convinced you of that yet?"

He had, and then some. But she replied, "No, it will take a great deal more convincing. Perhaps when you are back from town."

"I would like that, but we may be late. Hugo has a number of sites for us to tour… ah, that's a secret."

She laughed at his instant remorse. "Your secret is safe with me. I still don't know what you're talking about so I will certainly keep that private."

His eyes lingered on her with silent longing, and she smiled in response.

"I know," she whispered. "Me, too. Now go enjoy the horse race and whatever it is you may or may not be doing with Hugo."

He nodded, and murmured one more time, "Damn, I wish I could kiss you."

twenty-six

Trudy rapped gently on the door of Jo's room. "Jo? Are you sleeping?"

"Hello?"

Trudy heard her voice faintly through the door. She knocked again but something told her to open it immediately. She did and found Jo sitting on the edge of the bed with damp hair and a pale face.

"Jo," Trudy exclaimed, rushing to her side. "What's wrong? What happened?"

"I think this impertinent baby wants to be born. Now."

"Oh, my. Well, if that's what he wants then... that's what he wants. Are you having birth pangs?"

Jo nodded.

"For how long?"

"They started as soon as Chase left but he said you'd be coming to see me, so I've just been waiting."

"Oh, my goodness. I'm so sorry I didn't come sooner. He said you were sleeping."

"I thought I would be." She frowned and clutched the quilt beneath her as a labor pain took hold. "But this keeps happening."

Trudy felt a ripple of unease. She'd delivered her fair share of babies but none that arrived early, and it seemed as if Jo's progress might be farther along than she'd like. It didn't give either of them much time to prepare. A quick examination proved her right, and never before had she so wished to be wrong.

"I need to go and get a few supplies," Trudy said with false tranquility. "I'll send someone to town to find Chase, but I'll be back to you lickity split, all right? You stay right here."

"Where would I go?" Jo murmured, and Trudy was glad she still maintained her sense of humor. That wouldn't last.

Trudy quietly shut the hotel room door, then hoisted up her skirts and ran as fast as she could to the to the lobby—the nearly deserted lobby.

It seemed everyone had gone to the horse races, including her own family. It certainly would have been handy to have her mother or father here, but the only person Trudy could find was the scruffy-haired, freckle-faced porter who had been in the reading room on the day of the scavenger hunt. He was perched behind the registration desk reading a newspaper.

"Hey, I know you," he said, smiling brightly as she arrived at the desk breathless and in an obvious hurry. "Somethin' wrong?"

"Let's hope not," she said emphatically, slapping her hand against the desk. "I need you to do several things for me. Are there any other porters around?"

He shrugged casually. "Can't rightly say but I bet there's some folks in the kitchen. Are ya hungry?"

She shook her head. "No, I am not hungry. I'm delivering a baby."

He raised up on his toes to look at her belly, confusion adding to his already present squint.

"Not me," she said tersely. "Mrs. Jo Bostwick in room 201 is about to have her baby and I need to help her, but I also need some supplies, and I need to find her husband."

"She don't have no husband?" His eyes went round with shock.

"No," Trudy said impatiently. "I mean yes. She does have a

husband but he's in town with Mr. Plank and I need someone to fetch him."

"Fetch Mr. Plank?"

"No. Uh! Never mind. I'll check in the kitchen."

"Dr. Hart?"

Trudy spun at the sound of a feminine voice to find Lorna walking toward her, concerned etched on her pretty face.

"Is something wrong?"

Lorna was certainly not the first person Trudy would have solicited assistance from, but it was either her or this sweet but useless young man behind the desk.

"Mrs. Bostwick is about to have her baby, and I need several things. Can you help me?"

Lorna's eyes widened in surprise. "Yes, ma'am. Of course. What to you need?"

Trudy took a breath and exhaled slowly. "I need someone to go to town and find Mr. Bostwick. I need someone to track down the midwife, Mrs. Worthington. Someone needs to find Constance Bostwick and Daisy. And I need an assortment of medical supplies which we could probably get from Dr. Prescott's office if he's willing to share."

"There are a few employees in the lounge, ma'am. I was just there. I can run back to see if they might help, and if you give me a list of supplies, I know where Dr. Prescott's office is, too."

Relief flooded through her. "That's excellent, Lorna. Thank you. If you could go to the lounge now while I write a list, that might be the most expedient."

"Yes, ma'am. Certainly."

True to her word, Lorna was back in minutes with Mr. Tippett, Harlan Callaghan, Mrs. Culpepper and a handful of employees Trudy didn't recognize but who she very much appreciated.

She doled out the various tasks then sprinted to her room to find her copy of *The Principles and Practice of Obstetrics*. Coco had teased her for bringing medical textbooks along on their holiday but thank goodness Trudy had ignored her. She tucked the manual discreetly under a towel since it surely would not put anyone at ease to see her flipping through the pages while Jo was in the thick of childbirth, but in the event of a complication, she'd be glad to have it nearby.

Outside Jo's door once more, Trudy smoothed her hair and her skirts. Her nerves were jangled by adrenaline, but it was essential she present a calm and professional manner. She could panic on the inside if necessary, but Jo needed her to be confident and soothing. Everything was fine. It would all be fine.

"This baby is so rude," Jo whimpered as soon as she saw Trudy, but in spite of her teasing words, it was obvious she was in distress. Her hair had grown more damp and her cheeks were flushed. She'd rolled to her side and was curled into as much of a ball as her body would allow.

"Yes, very rude," Trudy agreed quietly, moving to the bed and rubbing her back. "But you'll forgive him and love him anyway. At least that's what my mother says. Now let's see if we can make you a bit more comfortable."

Mrs. Culpepper arrived minutes later with a tea made of black cohosh, yarrow, and red raspberry leaf, just as Trudy had instructed.

"Here, darling, drink this," Trudy encouraged she mopped Jo's brow and watched the clock. She was keeping track of the birth pangs as well as wondering if Chase would arrive in time. Things were progressing quickly.

Jo took a few sips then let out a stifled groan as another pang took hold.

"They're getting stronger," she said with a grimace, once it had passed.

"That's good. They're supposed to, and you're doing so well, Jo. But drink the tea. It will help," Trudy said soothingly. "And just remember that every breath you take brings you closer to welcoming your beautiful baby into the world. I'm sure the midwife will be along any minute."

Jo turned her eyes to Trudy, her expression filled with worry, even as she said, "You're here. I know you'll take good care of us."

Her trust filled Trudy with warmth and a renewed determination to provide the best care possible. She would have done that anyway, of course, but this was personal. Jo was dear to her. They were sisters of a sort. Two bold, unique women determined to leave their mark in a world that sought to keep them small and silent. But they would not be ignored. And neither would this baby.

"Focus on my voice, dear," Trudy murmured as another pain rolled over Jo. "You're getting there."

But when she examined Jo just a few moments later, Trudy realized she wasn't getting there.

She was there.

∽

"We need a proper racetrack," Hugo shouted above the chaos of the crowd lining Main Street. "It's no good missing half the race because the horses are out of sight."

"Add that to the list or our new businesses," Chase shouted back. "The Bostwick Derby."

"I was thinking Hugo Downs," he replied with a wink and a hearty gulp of ale.

They were standing outside the saloon, aptly named *The Saloon*. The racehorses had galloped past just moments before, starting at the south end of the street and heading north before disappearing behind buildings and it would be a moment or two at least before they reappeared. Alex was tempted to get himself another ale but spotted a lone rider galloping down Main Street.

Surely not one of the racers. No horse could run that fast.

Alex craned his neck as the crowd took note of the rider and he realized with a start that it was Mr. Tippett. He tugged on his brother's sleeve, nodding at the hotel's social director as the man he pulled up the reins in the center of the road.

"Chase Bostwick," Tippett bellowed. "You're about to become a father!"

Alex laughed as the crowd cheered, but his brother was not amused. He looked stricken and fearful.

"Give me that horse," he shouted to Tippett as the sidewalk crowd parted to let him pass.

"Take mine. He's fresh," another man called out, and somehow, within moments, Chase and Alex were each mounted on trusty steeds and in a race of their own back to the hotel.

Alex had never ridden so fast, nor seen his brother move with such alacrity and focus. Once they arrived at the Imperial, they took the stairs three at a time, rushing to Jo and Chase's room. They entered through the suite finding Constance sitting primly on the settee. The door to the bedroom was ajar and Chase rushed through it, causing their mother to gasp.

"He has no business being in there," she uttered tersely. "Childbirth is no place for a man."

Alex knew it wasn't a place for him, at least, but he found himself drawn to the opening between the door and the frame. He had to know what was happening in that other room.

A quick peek revealed Jo on the bed with Trudy sitting at the foot of it. He saw Mrs. Culpepper and Daisy and... Lorna? What on earth was she doing there? She was lingering at the edge of the room, but his attention was quickly drawn back to Trudy who offered a quick smile of relief as she saw Chase, and then returned her full attention to Jo.

Alex turned away, not wanting to impose on their privacy, but remained standing next to the door so he might listen. It was all right for him to listen, wasn't it? He hoped so because hearing Trudy offer clear, calm instructions and words of encouragement to his sister-in-law filled him with a sense of wonder. Something miraculous was occurring, and she was in the thick of it, using her hard-earned expertise and God-given talents to guide a new life into this world. He was mesmerized just from the sounds of it.

"Darling, I got here as fast as I could," Chase murmured to Jo. "I'm so sorry I wasn't here sooner."

"You're here now," she mumbled tiredly.

Time hung suspended as the women moved about the room, and Trudy continued soothing Jo with her words and her ministrations.

"You're almost there, Jo. Almost. One big push, push, push, push."

Then came a silence that seemed to last for an eternity, until a slap echoed throughout the room, followed by a hearty squall, and Alex sagged against the doorframe.

"It's a boy!" Trudy announced, her voice trembling with emotion. "He looks perfect. Now let's get that second one."

Alex's head snapped back up and he looked into the bedroom once more.

"The second one?" Chase croaked, appearing more dazed than elated.

"Twins," Constance muttered, shaking her head. "Of course, it's twins."

"Two impertinent babies," Daisy said with a smile. "Isn't it grand?"

Chase looked toward the doorway, caught Alex's eye, and then they both began to laugh.

"Hush, now," Trudy scolded gently. "Jo and I are still working."

Alex nodded at his brother, then turned away again to let Trudy do her job.

As he stood there, listening and in awe, he suddenly understood what she'd meant when she'd told him being a doctor wasn't just something she did. It was part of who she was. And she was wonderful at it. She should never give it up.

He would certainly never ask her to... if she were his wife...

The thought came to him like a thunderbolt, although he realized just as quickly it had been there all along. His destiny had been determined the moment Trudy had stepped outside into the rain to wait beside him, to care for him. To make sure he was all right. To offer him hope. He wanted to provide her with the same.

He wanted to *marry her.*

He was *going to* marry her.

He'd be patient this time, though. No rushed engagement or hasty trips down the aisle. She was meant to be his wife, just as soon as she was ready.

And just as soon as he'd set Isabella free, once and for all.

twenty-seven

"Must I be really here?" Lorna asked, fear etched across her features as they gathered around a table in a small, dimly lit room just minutes before midnight.

"I'm sorry, Lorna," Daisy said, reaching out to squeeze her wrist in reassurance. "Madame Moyen says this séance is the only way to free us from Isabella."

"But I don't remember anything about being on that stage," the maid said pensively. "I don't feel as if she's connected to me at all."

"I know it seems a great deal to ask, Lorna," Alex said quietly, "but it's possible you're in danger. We just want to get this settled once and for all."

Trudy heard the tension in his voice as she looked over at the apprehensive maid and wondered what to make of her. The girl had been a gem while Jo was delivering the twins, running to fetch things, keeping the room tidy, making sure everyone had cool drinks or hot tea, and yet Madame Moyen had been so insistent on her participating, she'd even declared a séance without Lorna would be pointless. So, whether wittingly or unwittingly, the maid was involved.

Moyen had also declared they needed at least eight people to create a strong enough pull to draw Isabella to them from wherever she may be so Trudy had brought along a very curious Lucy, while Alex had reluctantly enlisted the participation of a frowning, dubious Chase along with a glib and grinning Ellis. His cousin seemed to find the entire thing a lark.

"Yes, were all in grave danger, Lorna." Ellis snickered. "From the invisible ghost of Alex's itty bitty little wife. Mwah ahh ahh."

"Stop it, Ellis," Daisy admonished. "It's not funny. If you don't want to be here, then go. We can find someone else."

"I'm just trying to lighten the mood," he said. "You're all so damn serious. Or should I say I'm trying to *lift your spirits*?" He laughed again at his own jest until Chase leaned over and muttered, "Shut up or get out."

The door to the next room opened and Madame Moyen's turbaned assistant came in with a single taper. He wordlessly traversed the room lighting several other candles before turning off the lamp and departing. He didn't acknowledge them in any way, and without the lamplight, the walls began to dance with flickering shadows, aided by a dozen tiny mirrors hung from strings above the table.

Trudy silently acknowledged Madame Moyen's skill at setting a mood even though she didn't particularly care for this one. It was ominous and foreboding and did nothing to steady her jangling nerves. And if she was uneasy, she could only imagine the distress that Alex was feeling.

"Are you ready for this?" Chase asked his brother quietly.

"No, I'm not ready for this," Alex replied. "But I am more than ready to be rid of Isabella."

The door opened again, and Madame Moyen entered this time, dressed in the same mourning garb she'd worn inside the red tent, complete with the veil. She sat down in the only empty seat and looked around, seeming to take note of each of them.

"Have you brought the items?" she asked no one in particular.

"I have them." Daisy nodded and Trudy watched as Alex's sister set a jeweled hair comb, a lock of her hair, and a garnet ring in a row in front of the medium. Beneath the table, Alex reached for Trudy's hand, clasping it tightly.

Madame Moyen picked up the comb and whispered, *"Spiritus Isabelle Bostwick, obsecramus te ut praesentiam tuam manifestes."*

Trudy recognized it as Latin, but her translation skills were inadequate. Then Moyen continued in English. "Spirit of Isabelle Bostwick, we beseech you to make your presence known."

Swapping the comb for the lock of hair, Moyen repeated her entreaty, then did the same with the ring. Trudy looked over at Alex, noting the stern set of his jaw, and the tension emanating from him. His eyes, however, were glued to the medium, as were everyone else's. Even Ellis seemed oddly captivated now, although a strange smirk still hovered around his lips.

Suddenly, Daisy gasped as Lorna's eyelids began to flutter. Chase leaned forward in his chair.

"I feel strange. What's happening?" Lorna asked, her voice full of fright.

"Nothing can harm you," Madame Moyen said. "Relax and welcome her."

Trudy squeezed Alex's hand as Lorna slumped in the chair and then with a twitch, suddenly sat up, ramrod straight. She chuckled, a deep, throaty sound and her half-closed eyes surveyed the room, until her gaze landed on Alex.

Alex let out a huff of breath, and Trudy realized she was not the only one suddenly frightened. A tiny whimper came from Lucy, and Daisy looked near to tears.

"Hello, darling," Lorna drawled, her voice low, almost raspy as her eyes remained on Alex.

"Are you Isabella Carnegie Bostwick?" Moyen asked.

"I am."

"Welcome. We are all friends here and mean you no harm. But tell us, Isabella, why are you troubling Alexander and Lorna?"

Lorna—or Isabella—murmured, "He troubled me first. And the girl was... convenient." Her gaze moved around the room, not seeming to see any of them.

"How did he trouble you?" Moyen questioned as the rest of them watched, mesmerized and silent. Trudy could feel her heart pounding in her chest and couldn't look away from the maid's face.

Lorna's head twitched ever so slightly. "He made me fall in love with him, but he was false."

Alex shook his head. "I wasn't," he said quietly, staring back at her, and Trudy wondered yet again how distressing this must be for him. Her heart ached on his behalf.

Last night, in the dim light of the moon shining through her bedroom window, he'd told her about a woman named Katharine Lawrence, and about the discord in his marriage. He'd explained how he'd wanted to call off the engagement and that on the day Isabella had fallen down the stairs, they'd been arguing over his desire for an annulment. He'd shared all of this, he'd said, because he didn't want Trudy to learn these things about him in the midst of a séance. As he'd spoken, she'd sensed his deep regret, and she sensed it now, as well. The words were hard to hear, and yet she'd understood his choices. She believed in his faithfulness and his version of events. It seemed, however, that Isabella did not.

If this was, indeed, Isabella with them now. Trudy was determined to remain skeptical. Her analytical mind remained full of doubt and questions, but even so, she was captivated by this spectacle as it played out before them. It was strange and unreal, and yet sweet, timid Lorna could not be such a fine actress. Could she?

"Tell us more," Madame Moyen prompted.

Lorna's eyelids fluttered again, whispering, "I recall the day we met. I was so enamored."

"Speak not of your first day together," Moyen interjected. "Speak of the last day. How did you die?"

As the candles continued to dance, Trudy noticed the scent of gardenias beginning to permeate the air and stole another glance at Alex. His brow was furrowed, his lips pressed tightly together, and he pulled his hand from hers. She wasn't sure why.

Just then, a floorboard creaked overhead, the sound sharp and startling in the hushed room. Everyone jumped, and Chase muttered a curse under his breath. Daisy fanned her face as if to stem off those tears, and Lucy's mouth was agape. It was just a squeaky board. The hotel was full of them, but this felt like something more.

"What have you come here to say, Isabella Bostwick?" Madame Moyen urged as Lorna paused. The medium lifted the veil of her hat over her head, revealing a pale but beautiful face. Something about it tugged at Trudy's mind, but given all that was happening, her disquiet hardly seemed out of place.

"Tell us, Isabella." Moyen's tone was demanding, her eyes gleaming with intensity, and Trudy had the presence of mind to wonder if it was a wise idea to speak so harshly to an already troublesome spirit.

"Tell us how he was false. Tell us why your love faded," Moyen prompted, but Lorna's eyelids began to flutter once more. Suddenly, the candles flickered wildly, casting eerie shadows into every corner of the room, and Ellis chuckled nervously.

"Why won't you speak to us, Isabella Bostwick? You have much to say. I feel it in your energy. Do what I command," Moyen all but shouted.

"Forgive me. I cannot." Then Lorna slumped down in the chair and a collective gasp went round the room.

∽

Alex had never been so rattled in his life. His heart raced a staccato rhythm in his chest as he tried to calm his breathing. Finding Isabella's belongings in his pockets and under his pillow was nothing compared to this macabre agitation. The only thing keeping him remotely steady was Trudy's soothing presence next to him. Even so, he'd let go of her hand lest Isabella notice he was holding it.

And yet, his wife had said almost nothing of substance. Only that she'd loved him, and that he'd been false. If she was truly so angry, why not admonish him now? Why not explain why she was leaving her things in his path, or forcing Lorna to do it for her? She hadn't answered any of his questions and now it appeared she was already gone. What did that mean?

"Lorna," Daisy asked cautiously, placing a gentle hand on the maid's arm.

His mind still whirling, Alex's nerves stretched taut once more as he watched Lorna sit back up, a calm yet almost contrite expression on her face. She returned her clear-eyed gaze to his face.

"Isabella did love you" Lorna said quietly, "but she was selfish to a fault and jealous beyond all reason."

Madame Moyen's eyes narrowed. "Now, Isabella. We have no time for tricks. You cannot fool us. Tell us what we need to hear, and I can set you free. I will set you free," Moyen said again, an angry edge to her voice.

But Lorna tossed her head, looking directly at the medium, and Alex's unease ratcheted up another notch.

"No more lies," Lorna said defiantly. "I am finished with this madness."

Moyen's face contorted, her composure slipping. "You are done when I say you are done. I control your fate. Not you. Tell us how Alex pushed you down the stairs and I can set you free."

Alex flinched at both the words and the fact that it was Moyen who said them, as if she was forcing Lorna to utter a falsehood.

"I did not push Isabella down the stairs," he said tersely.

Lorna turned and nodded at him. "I know you didn't. I saw it all."

A dawning realization suddenly flooded his veins. This was truly Lorna sitting there before them. And she *had* been there the day Izzy fell.

"You were there," he said out loud. "I thought it was a twisted dream, but it's a memory. Lorna, you were standing in the parlor door the day Isabella fell. You saw what happened."

"Hush!" Madame Moyen snapped, her eyes never leaving Lorna's face. "Let Isabella speak."

But Lorna shook her head emphatically. "Enough with that. Isabella Bostwick is not here now and never has been. She has not been haunting anyone, either. You know that." She pointed at Madame Moyen.

"And so do you!" Lorna added scornfully, and then she pointed directly at Ellis.

"What?" Ellis exclaimed. "What have I to do with this? I know nothing of the sort."

Alex felt his breath go shallow and his head begin to spin, as pieces of this puzzle began to fall into place, although the image of it was far from clear.

"Ellis?" Daisy exclaimed. "What is she talking about. Lorna, what are you saying?"

"Friends, friends," Moyen said, her voice unnaturally melodic. "Fear not. Isabella is a trickster using Lorna to fool you all."

"It's over," Lorna snapped impatiently. "You're the trickster. The schemer, the defrauder, the blackmailer."

"Blackmailer?" Chase asked, glaring at first the medium and then his cousin. "What is she talking about?"

"I don't understand," Ellis murmured, staring at Lorna in disbelief. "Why are you doing this?"

"It's lies!" Moyen hissed, dropping all pretense of having control of this situation. Even her accent seemed to fade away as everyone at the table looked around at everyone else with varying levels of confusion and fascination and Alex felt Trudy take hold of his hand once more.

"Yes, lies," Lorna spat out, staring at Moyen. "Ellis lied when he said he loved me, and you have lied to me time and again, just as you have used me time and again."

Lorna turned to Alex now, her expression despondent and her eyes filling with tears.

"Mr. Bostwick, I am sorry, but Madame and Ellis have conspired against you, and I'm ashamed to admit I helped them.

They wanted you to believe that you'd gone mad, that you killed your wife but had blocked your involvement from your mind. But I was there that day, just as you remember. I know for a fact you were too far away to have pushed her. I saw Isabella fall of her own accord. It was Ellis who told the newspapers a servant heard her accuse you of pushing her before she died."

Alex felt those words like a sledgehammer to the gut, and his mind flooded with confusion, as if his world was suddenly submerged underwater. Sounds and sensations and pressure converged leaving him breathless and fighting for air.

"Why? For what purpose?" he managed to rasp out.

"Shut up, stupid girl," Moyen hissed, rising from her chair. "You've said enough. Everything we've done, you've done. You incriminate yourself."

But Lorna seemed determined to go on and tried to answer his question.

"Greed. Jealousy. Malice," the girl continued. "Moyen and Ellis sought to lure you into confessing to a murder you didn't commit in the hopes that, even if your family didn't turn you over to the authorities, you'd be ostracized and banished from society. And once you were no longer welcomed at Bostwick & Sons, Ellis would step in and take your place. Your Uncle Vernon is attempting to usurp your father, as well. He's the one who shared details of that affair with the opera singer."

Ellis erupted from his chair, tipping it over in his haste, his anger was a palpable thing as he lunged for Lorna.

"We were this close, you idiot!" he ground out as he sprinted around the table to reach her. "You've ruined everything."

Lorna ducked as Chase rose from his own chair, and with a single punch, knocked Ellis to the ground.

"Ellis?" Alex whispered, unable to formulate a precise question as he stared at his cousin currently writhing on the floor like a bug on its back. But even from there, Ellis sought to vent his spleen as he struggled to sit up.

"You have everything," Ellis shouted, pointing up at Alex.

"You're the first born, the golden child. You married a God damned Carnegie. All I ever wanted was my piece of the pie, but you and Chase claim everything for yourselves, and leave nothing for me but scraps."

"That's not true," Alex ground out, his own temper rising at what they'd done to him. His own cousin had been tormenting him for months. Playing him for a fool, playing upon his guilt and his sense of integrity. Twisting his few fond memories of Isabella into something that elicited nothing but fear and regret.

"How could you be a part of this," Daisy asked at last, her voice cracking as she directed the question at Lorna.

It was then that Lorna broke, tears now spilling out hot and fast.

"I'm so sorry, Daisy. I never wanted any of this. I swear. I couldn't see a way clear of it. I thought this was who I was doomed to be, but you've always been so kind to me. You've shown me I can be a better person, and I want to be."

"Then why?" Daisy asked again.

Lorna glanced at Ellis, who remained on the floor—with Chase looming over him. "Ellis convinced me. He said it was just a game, and that if I loved him I should go along, but when I realized what harm this was causing you and your brother, I told him I was done with it. But," she rubbed her wrist absently, "Ellis can get rough."

"You think he can get rough?" Moyen spat stalking toward her. "Just you wait until I get my hands on you, you ungrateful little wretch."

Trudy pushed her chair out into the woman's path, slowing her down just as Lorna cried out, "Stop. Just please stop. It's over now, Mother."

twenty-eight

"Do you mean to tell me this entire spectacle was unfolding right beneath my very nose, and I missed all of it?" Jo said, punctuating her disbelief with the rhythmic motion of rocking two identical cradles holding two identical and precious baby boys.

"In all fairness to you, my love," Chase responded, "Your vision was rather obscured by a burgeoning belly thanks to these two."

He nodded down at his sons, and Trudy could not help but notice the pride on his face and in his voice. Truthfully, Trudy felt a bit of pride in those two babies herself having helped to coax them into the world. Granted, Jo was the true hero, having done virtually all of the difficult work, but Trudy had done a bit, and neither had been aided by the absent midwife who, through no fault of her own, learned of the births hours after the fact.

It had been nearly a week since the séance, and Chase had invited Trudy and Alex to visit, under the guise of a social call, but with the real intention of having them help regale his wife with a tale so fantastical she never would have believed him without their assurance it was true.

"So, who then was responsible for placing Isabella's things where you would find them?" Jo inquired.

"All three of them," Trudy answered. "Lorna, Ellis, and Moyen. Apparently Lorna is a rather deft pickpocket, as well as a thief."

"A thief? She was a thief, a pickpocket, a lady's maid, a spy, and a liar?" Jo asked, arching a brow as if impressed.

"And she has a deft skill with styling my mother's hair," Alex added dryly.

Trudy smiled over at him, hoping he could sense how much she cared for him.

It had been a difficult few days as he contemplated all he'd been through—a debacle of deception fueled by treachery and envy turned upside down by a remorseful accomplice. The betrayal still loomed over him. Trudy could sense it, just as she could sense his lingering mistrust and confusion. He'd even admitted to her that he wondered if perhaps Isabella might be lingering nearby, somehow, and that he wondered what she might think of all this if she was. It was going to take time for him to work through it all, but Trudy intended to remain by his side and to help in any way she could.

"It seems our housekeeper instructed Lorna to pack up Isabella's things to be sent back to the Carnegies, but Lorna burgled most of it. That's where the items to haunt me with came from," Alex said.

"Lorna pilfered Isabella's diary, too," Trudy added, shaking her head the girl's brazenness.

In some ways she *almost* felt sorry for the spy turned maid. She had been trapped in an intricate web of deceit, woven by her own mother, no less, but Trudy could not forgive what the three of them had done to Alex. She never would. Trudy was quite capable of holding on to a grudge and this was one she had no intention of ever letting go of.

"The diary was a wealth of information, it seems," Alex agreed wistfully. "That's how they knew which items would disturb me the most. Isabella kept a rather detailed account of my every failure and transgression. Her every disappointment and unfulfilled wish was recorded upon the pages."

Trudy looped her arm through his and pressed against him as they sat side by side on the small sofa in Chase and Jo's suite. "That was Isabella's twisted perspective of events but even Lorna admitted she was spoiled and jealous. You cannot take to heart was she wrote in a journal. It wasn't about you. It was about her and her own meanness."

But Alex would take it to heart. Trudy knew he would, and she'd made it her mission to remind him of what type of man he truly was—caring, generous, patient—and damnably handsome. Oh, and skillful with regard to sexual congress...

"Trudy is right," Jo said, casting a warm gaze toward Alex. "Izzy had a cruel streak, but we all know you to be witty, and thoughtful, and considerate. You must trust us women on this. Trudy and I are both very wise."

"I shall endeavor to do so," he said, smiling back at her and pressing Trudy's arm tightly in response.

"Good," Jo said, then added, "Now explain to me how it was that Ellis got involved in this? How did he and Moyen come to work together?" Jo picked up a baby from one of the cradles and handed it to Trudy, as if something in her expression had revealed just how badly she wanted to hold one. She didn't even know which baby she had but it didn't matter. Either would do.

"Ellis and Lorna became... acquainted soon after he moved in with us," Alex said. "According to her, when he complained about how we *mistreated* him, she brought him to her mother, and a plan was hatched."

"So, she was certainly not an innocent victim. What do you suppose made her finally confess?" Jo continued, taking the other baby and handing it to Alex who accepted him with some hesitation.

"If she's to be believed now, it was Daisy's wonderful influence over her. Lorna said no one had ever treated her with respect before or treated her as if she had any intrinsic value, but Daisy's trust in her—misplaced though it was—showed Lorna a new path. She was afraid of Moyen and Ellis, though, and thought the only way to convince us of what they'd done was to bring everyone together and make her mother so angry it would all come spilling out. And she was right. It did."

"Lorna became the spider," Trudy murmured with a chuckle, suddenly recalling what Mr. Gibson had said.

"The spider?" Jo asked.

Trudy chuckled. "She was caught in a web and the only way to escape was to become the spider."

"A rather large web, apparently," Alex added. "It seems Moyen has an entire network of spies all over Chicago working as servants, shopkeepers, bartenders. All of them have been providing her with details about wealthy families that she uses to either convince them of her clairvoyance, or more often to blackmail them. I'm the only one she pretended to haunt, however. I suppose that should prove I am exceptional."

He looked down at the infant in his arms, and Trudy tried not to dwell on how vastly attractive that made him.

"What happens to them all now?" Jo asked, smiling at them as if she had some trick up her sleeve. As if it wasn't obvious she was playing Cupid by *forcing* them to snuggle with her babies.

"That is to be determined," Alex answered. "They all belong in jail, of course. But Hugo doesn't want the guests at the hotel to know he hired a charlatan. A felonious charlatan, no less. Our family isn't too keen on creating another scandal by having Vernon and Ellis arrested, and as for Lorna, she's young. There may be hope for her yet but she's certainly not welcome in any home of mine."

"And what of poor Finn," Jo added, her eyes getting suddenly misty. "He's a sweet boy. He shouldn't pay the price for misdeeds he had no part in."

"We won't let him fall to the wolves, my darling," Chase

responded. "We'll think of something. I don't necessarily want him in my home, either."

"I suppose," she said with a nod, then turned her gaze to Alex. "Speaking of homes, Alex, Chase tells me you're considering staying on the island for a few extra months after the summer season has concluded. Something about some new scheme of Hugo's?"

Alex stole a glance at Trudy. "I haven't quite decided yet, but Hugo has tapped both Chase and I to form a financial partnership with him."

"He has?" Trudy asked. She was surprised... but not necessarily disappointed by this news.

Alex nodded. "He wants to restructure the entire town of Trillium Bay and fill it with his own businesses, but that will require a great deal of time spent on the island. And suddenly I find myself not wanting to be that far from... Springfield."

"That's interesting," Trudy said with a smile. "Mr. Plank seems intent on forming all sorts of new partnerships."

"Meaning?"

Her smile broadened. "He told me yesterday that the Imperial Hotel is in desperate need of a qualified physician since Dr. Prescott has abandoned his post and returned to Detroit."

"Is that so?" Alex replied, his brow lifting. "And is that a permanent position?"

"I got the impression it was a flexible arrangement, but I did discuss the possibility of a leave of absence from the clinic with my father. Working on the island for a few months seems like just something a modern, progressive woman such as myself might want to try."

"Interesting," Alex said, his own smile growing. "So, you're saying that, in case I were to stay on the island for a few extra months as well and found myself with a broken finger, you'd be here to tend to it?"

"It appears so."

"Well," Jo said, smiling smugly. "I like the sound of that."

"Have I told you yet this evening how very beautiful you are in that dress?" Alex whispered to Trudy as they lingered on the periphery of the ballroom—because three dances in a row would have set the gossips to their mongering.

"Yes," she responded with feigned annoyance. "You have told me, but you mustn't stand so close. My father is watching."

"That doesn't concern me in the least. Your father likes me," Alex replied.

"My father likes everyone," she said, keeping her own voice low. "But if he finds out where you've been sleeping at night, he might change his mind."

Alex shrugged, the very picture of nonchalance. "Well, I can't sleep in my own room. I realize it's no longer haunted but it's unpleasant to be in alone," he teased. "Your room is ever so much more comfortable. And besides, I have another very logical reason for spending my nights with you."

She arched a quizzical brow.

"And what reason is that?" she asked, trying to sound stern.

But when she turned to look at him, his blue eyes were soft in the light of the gasoliers, and the orchestra music was sweet and romantic, and his smile had turned from teasing to tender as he whispered softly in her ear, "I spend my nights with you, Trudy Hart, because I am in love with you, as if you didn't know it."

"How would I know it if you haven't told me?" she replied breathlessly.

"I'm telling you now." He took ahold of her hand. "I love you, Trudy," he whispered again. "I'll never ask you to give up medicine for me because it's part of who you are and I love that about you, too. But I am asking you to be my wife. When you're ready. Even if that means I must find my own dinner or miss you for days on end because you're busy healing those who need you. Or when you're off delivering babies. Perhaps our marriage won't look like anyone else's but that's fine by me. We're progressive. We'll figure it out."

He paused then, and Trudy's breath hitched in her lungs, and her heart tumbled over itself inside her of chest—which she knew wasn't anatomically possible—but that's what it felt like because there it was in Alex's expression... Everything she'd ever wanted... Everything she'd ever needed... Everything she'd secretly longed for...

His besotted admiration...

His recognition and acceptance of exactly who she was...

And his true love given freely with no conditions...

Her eyes puddled with tears at his words, but a smile she had no intention of hiding spread across her face.

"I love you, too, Alex," she whispered tremulously. "But, I fear I don't deserve you. You're too perfect and too fine. I'm not sure I've earned this kind of happiness."

"Yes, you have," he whispered back. "And so have I."

And then defying all sense of good manners and decorum, he kissed her, right there in front of everyone in the Imperial Hotel ballroom.

The End

author's note

A rose by any other name...

In 1889, it would have been unusual for individuals to address one another by their first name except in the most familial circumstances. I chose, however, to use first names whenever possible for simplicity, clarification, and to help establish relationships between the characters. Imagine trying to keep things straight when there are multiple Mr. Bostwicks and multiple Miss Harts.

Good help is hard to find...

Wealthy gilded age society often traveled with an entire retinue of their own servants. Even to a hotel such as the Imperial, they would have brought their own lady's maids, valets, seamstresses, nannies, as well as their own horses, groomsmen, and carriages. I chose not to include most of their personal attendants since it would have cluttered up the story, not to mention messing with the plot.

It's a Love Shack, Baby...

It's no secret Trillium Bay is my re-imagined version of Michigan's Mackinac Island, and the Imperial Hotel was inspired by the island's Grand Hotel. However, I have taken a great deal of creative license. (I can do that. I'm a writer.) When the Grand Hotel opened its doors in July of 1887, it was not how I describe the Imperial Hotel in this series. Although it was deemed "luxurious" by the standards of the time, it wasn't what modern readers would consider opulent. Tourism was in its infancy and even the "fanciest" resorts would be considered rustic today.

However, many of the details I include about the actual construction of the hotel are based on my research, and the "cottages" of Mackinac Island are truly palatial and ornate. Many were built in the 1880's by wealthy titans of industry for use as their summer homes. Quite a few have been kept true to their original design. To see some fabulous images, I recommend the book *TIMELESS: Inside Mackinac Island's Historic Cottages.*

Back to the future...

The Bostwicks of Trillium Bay is actually my second series set in this location. My other series is contemporary and although you can read the series (or the individual books) in any order, I did use many of the same family surnames to hint at an ancestor/descendant link between characters.

other titles by tracy brogan

THE BOSTWICKS OF TRILLIUM BAY

ART OF THE CHASE

MAGIC OF MOONLIGHT

COMING SOON

A DAISY IN BLOOM

THE TRILLIUM BAY SERIES

(Contemporary)

MY KIND OF YOU

MY KIND OF FOREVER

MY KIND OF PERFECT

THE BELL HARBOR SERIES

(Contemporary)

CRAZY LITTLE THING

THE BEST MEDICINE

LOVE ME SWEET

JINGLE BELL HARBOR (A novella)

STAND ALONE TITLES

HOLD ON MY HEART (Contemporary)

THE NEW NORMAL (Contemporary)

WEATHER OR KNOT (Contemporary novella)

HIGHLAND SURRENDER (Historical romance)

about the author

USA Today, Wall Street Journal, and Amazon Publishing bestselling author Tracy Brogan writes happily ever after stories full laughter and love. A three-time recipient of the Amazon Publishing Diamond award for sales exceeding three-million copies, a three-time finalist of the RWA® RITA award for excellence in romantic fiction, and a three-time finalist of the Booksellers Best award, Brogan's books feature re-imagined versions of her favorite Michigan locations – including famed Mackinac Island - and have been translated into more than a dozen languages worldwide. Her debut novel, CRAZY LITTLE THING, hit #5 on Amazon Publishing's bestselling titles across all genres.

Brogan is currently at work on several projects including a gilded age series set in Trillium Bay, the long-awaited sequel to HIGHLAND SURRENDER, and a dual-timeline rom-com that just *may* include ghosts. (Psst... it totally has ghosts.)

Brogan loves to hear from readers so contact her at tracybrogan.com or tracybrogan1225@gmail.com.

Tracy Brogan Books. Witty. Whimsical. Wonderful.